TAYLOK

Allen Mabra

DEDICATION

To my wife, Joy and children, Linda Cole, Michael Mabra, David Mabra and Judy Born who helped edit and gave critical assistance in evaluating the final product. Special thanks to Michael who worked long and tirelessly on the setup for the paperback.

This is a fiction novel. Any resemblance to persons, living or dead, or events is purely coincidental.

ACKNOWLEDGMENTS

My thanks to Joy Mabra, Linda Cole, Michael Mabra, David Mabra and Judy Born for encouragement and editing the book

Cover and Frontispiece created by Allen Mabra with Poser Pro 2012 and Photoshop CS5

Table of Contents

Frontispiece

Taylok finds Xantopec and his priestesses in Eldar Temple

Foreword

Modern day discovery of the cavern, called Rockworld by its inhabitants, occurred more than twenty-five years ago. Hiking alone in the Wind River Mountains of Wyoming, Gregory François Delchant located the entrance by accident, painfully and abruptly. Delchant thus became the first contemporary man to explore the spectacular cavern in its awesome majesty. He found its fearsome beasts and met its human inhabitants. His story is chronicled in other works and the events described herein began eleven years prior to Delchant's momentous find.

In order to understand the environment of Rockworld as compared to other caves and the outside world, it is necessary to avail ourselves of Delchant's notes and observations, along with his deductions and some we have made on our own.

To be as accurate as possible in telling what befell Taylok, the heroine of our story, during this harrowing period of time, I relied extensively on historic chronicles, memoirs and interviews with one hundred and twenty two Nehwisna individuals who had direct or indirect contact with Taylok.

Rockworld children exhibit extremely rapid intelligence maturation, probably due to the brief, average life span (around twenty-five years) the tribe endured when they first entered the cavern. (Today their life span is similar to our own). Taylok, as you will discover, proved to be one of the most advanced intellects in her early years. While considerable latitude may be evident in formulating early conversations, the reader should be aware that all have some foundation in fact. The thoughts and utterances attributed to young Taylok and others by interviewees may also have been altered by the effect of time on memories. The interviewed witnesses, however, insist that the reported conversations are nearly correct and have been recorded correspondingly, herein. Regardless of these potential minor discrepancies, the main events of the story are well documented in New Rockhome Hall annals and supported by witness memoirs and interview articulations.

The humans inhabiting the cavern, who call themselves "Nehwisna," evolved devoid of sunlight over a period, believed to

i

be, around thirty thousand years, placing them well ahead of the generally accepted time line for early migrations into the Americas. Today, they are smaller than their counterparts on the surface, although they rarely exhibit dwarfish or gnomish characteristics. In fact, without some scale to compare height, at a distance, one might mistake a Nehwisna man or woman for an ordinary human. But the similarity ends when they are examined closely. There are three obvious evolutionary changes directly attributable to their cavern environment. These changes are most apparent in the (1) extreme increase in eye size, (2) attenuation of pigment in skin, hair and eyes and (3) the aforementioned diminution of stature. The evolution occurred so slowly, over thousands of years and more than six hundred generations, that the Nehwisna remained unaware of the changes.

It is no coincidence that most of the people's names have derived from cave features; Sander, Flint, Salton, Chalka – all have been taken from geological occurrences. (It is noted that the American Indians customarily chose to take many of their names from familiar surroundings; Black Elk, Crazy Horse, Red Cloud, Cornplanter, Rain-in-the-Face and many others.) Only a few of the Nehwisna's names seem random and those may have been taken from ancient words, as the language evolved as well as the people.

The original human inhabitants and discoverers of the cavern may have been nomads who came from, what is today, eastern Siberia. We speculate that they fought their way across frozen wastelands in Alaska and Canada until forced, by deadly cold and fortuitous coincidence, into the wondrous cavern. Another theory suggests they were cave dwellers by heritage and simply chose the cavern when fortune handed it to them. Regardless of the reason they went inside, glacial activity sealed them there by crushing, collapsing and depositing two hundred feet of frozen glacial moraine over the only entrance, forcibly making the cavern their permanent home. We are reasonably certain that modern technology has located that early entrance in recent exploration with seismic and age-dating equipment, as it fits the expressed hypothesis.

Food and water proved plentiful in Rockworld. Fish, a natural subsistence food to the natives, occur in great abundance throughout the river and lake systems. Ulok, a type of mushroom, is also widespread and highly nutritious to the human body. Absent sunlight, the natives learned to cultivate this life-sustaining nutrient early in their history. It is the main food staple of the Nehwisna people and is present in abundance.

Although mushrooms are not a subsistence level food outside the cavern, the varieties called ulok by the Nehwisna contain all the protein, vitamins and other nutrients necessary for sustaining life. We are still studying this unique occurrence in an attempt to understand the phenomenon.

Unexpected light and favorably oxygenated air occurs throughout the lower cavern. There seemed limitless room to expand and settle with many great halls and more than two hundred miles of connected tunnels. Lack of sunshine and confinement in the underground world, with its own variety of radioactive substances, brought the aforementioned strong, albeit slow, changes to the clan members.

In the first thousand years of confinement, having no written evidence or other form of durable archive documenting events prior to the cavern's discovery, the tribe forgot their existence outside and believed that Rockworld constituted the world in its entirety. Only in the last thousand years did any Nehwisna rediscover the outside world, but by then, such radical alterations had evolved into their makeup that they could not withstand the effects of sunlight on their skin and eyes. Thus, the Nehwisna relegated the outside world to the gods and the cavern once again became their human universe.

The wanderers who found the cavern thousands of years ago were probably not more than fifty or sixty in number. Procreation within the cavern led to a present day population of almost thirty thousand according to the Shotai. It probably would have been much larger if not for the natural hazards of the cavern, other lethal cave inhabitants and tendency on a part of all mankind toward civil war, unreasoning anger, hate and wanton human destruction instead of what should be our natural gifts of tolerance, mercy, love and protection of our fellow man.

* * * * *

Following are a few excerpts combining Delchant's notes, data from the Shotai's memoirs and several interviews that I undertook, to describe New Rockhome Hall.

Light from phosphorescent ulok'neh, a unique form of mushroom, casts slender stalagmite shadows on the alabaster walls of New Rockhome Hall. This form of ulok'neh glows with an intensity characteristic of such fungal growths throughout the lower part of Rockworld (note: some large, cultivated caps have the candlepower of a two watt electric globe and are present in profusion). The fungi transform an otherwise lightless expanse into an inviting hall of warmth, beauty and safety.

New Rockhome Hall displays a plentiful supply of speleothems, or secondary mineral deposits as are found in most large caverns. Expansive carbonate draperies and glowing alabaster stalactite spikes hang in majestic beauty from the sturdy cavern roof. The floor exhibits small and large stalagmites, some of which reach heights of thirty feet and possess shining coats of carbonaceous beauty. They sprout from the ground like limbless tree trunks. One area of New Rockhome Hall contains more than two hundred stalagmites in less than fifty acres and is referred to, by the Nehwisna, as 'the stalagmite field.'

Nine grottos are located along the walls of the hall. Seven are natural developments and two designed and carved out by the Nehwisna. Four grottos are used selectively as storage chamber, hospital, meeting place and entertainment. Five of the cave rooms are located across the wide river, Ohana, and rarely utilized because they lack easy access.

One grotto is of interest for its beauty. It is called Mystical Grotto and lies across from Megalith Rise within a three-hundred-foot, vertical, virtually unscalable cliff high above the river. A deep gorge (natives call it Snake Canyon) separates the grotto from viewers by a hundred feet, but its' beauty is clearly visible and known throughout Rockworld. Thousands of visitors come each annum, braving numerous rattlesnakes, very dangerous footing along the climb to the peak of Megalith Rise and, due to the mist from the falls, a treacherously slick, although flat, viewing pad, to gaze at the Mystical Grotto's astounding wonder. Wild ulok'neh glows from the interior like spotlights.

The grotto is coursed with hundreds of thin, travertine icicles, hanging in close-spaced lines resembling transparent curtains. Some reach the floor. Three modest pillars of alabaster limestone grace the entrance. Large amethyst crystals encrust both walls and roof, interspersed between the icicles. One of the crystals is said to be as long as a Nehwisna man is tall. Four travertine stalagmites, ranging from chair size to around eight feet high, are scattered randomly over the modestly pitted grotto floor. Six stalactites hang between the icicles and amethyst crystals like exclamation marks. Some believe Mystical Grotto is part of a tunnel network that extends for untold lengths, joining other tunnels in the cavern.

Seven visitors have lost their lives in falls while attempting to climb the steep path to Megalith Rise viewing site. Twelve others have died of snakebites. Another five have fallen from the viewing site itself into the gorge below. At least two of those are believed to have been suicides. But, still, they come by the thousands.

The waterfall, which formed the deep canyon, drops a spectacular, steady gush of water almost a thousand feet from its originating tunnel located high in the wall at the upper end of the hall. The watercourse extends two hundred miles throughout the cavern, contains numerous tributaries, fills many lakes and crosses through each of the inhabited halls yielding fresh water and abundant fish to the inhabitants.

The river, Ohana, life-giver and life-taker, shimmers in verdant translucent glow as it plods pleasantly down the broad, serpentine corridor carved into the main hall floor. Microscopic creatures called noctiluca gather by billions in a multitudinous array of glowing, rounded balls, some more than two feet in diameter, and bear responsibility for the light from the water. Somehow, the balls hold their shape fairly well against all but the swiftest of the river's current, maintaining relatively consistent light from that body of water. The ubiquitous noctiluca, with phosphorescence and characteristic globe-like congregation habits, create interesting light displays in the water, and above, causing stalactite shadows to move eerily counter to the currents.

A species of trout unique to the cavern occasionally leaps at play to splash in the wide stream, creating louder sounds than the soft ripples of the river itself. They feed on fish, river worms and the noctiluca. These trout are not phosphorescent, amazingly so in view of their diet. Fish, as previously noted, are also a food staple of the Nehwisna.

Women bend their backs near the river as they select wild or cultivated ulok for a future meal. It is not uncommon to see plates of steaming ulok and fish being hawked by vendors along the main village path.

The village, containing hundreds of houses, is concentrated near New Rockhome Hall's center along a main stoneway. The stoneway is a walk path, which originates at the hall main entrance and extends to Megalith rise. The larger housing structures often serve as trade loci as well as social gathering places. Some houses serve the dual purpose of business and family dwellings. Living quarters for village inhabitants range from modest mud huts to elaborate stone structures with many rooms. Most are the former.

Shops, located along the main stoneway, are generally single room affairs with space enough only for the wares and a proprietor.

The largest man-made structure in New Rockhome Hall is Eldar Temple. It is a huge pyramidal building with three large floors and many elaborate rooms. It ordinarily houses as many as two thousand acolytes, warriors and their families.

Eldar Temple holds an abbreviated fourth level, which contains a marble floor and a short stairway leading to a room that encompasses the pinnacle of the structure. The room is classed as taboo and warriors guard the single doorway to prevent access. The structure is enigmatic, for no one who enters is ever seen again. Many believe there is a vast treasure inside, but others think only death resides within. It is called, simply, level four.

A unique feature of New Rockhome Hall is Mordane Pit. It is thirty to forty steps in diameter, of considerable, but varying depth, signifying molten rock at the bottom. Lava rises and falls on some irregular pattern, not yet fully investigated, but to date, it has never flowed to the surface and conveniently remains at a depth of one hundred to five hundred feet. It is located in the wilderness area of the hall, far from occupied lands. Tourists and locals alike are prevented from approaching Mordane Pit by a circular wall of stone, erected hundreds of rings ago by the cautious natives. Recognizing the value of lava's heat, however, the ancients provided a gate, which allows refuse and the dead to be properly disposed. The pit's energy is also used for metal castings.

The Nehwisna estimate their world to contain more than two hundred halls, but it is only a guess since no one except Delchant has traversed the entire distance and he confesses to have lost track after many hours of wandering in the darkness. Twenty halls are actually known or explored, but only six are fully or partially occupied by the Nehwisna. Each developed hall houses between four and six thousand inhabitants.

Much of Upper Rockworld is without light and further avoided because one must pass through the enormous Hall of the Mohk'wa with its vicious, predaceous inhabitants, called collectively by the natives, the Mohk'wa, a Nehwisna god of terror and death. (Author's note: Delchant believes the Mohk'wa is a miniature descendant of the T-Rex and having seen his drawings of the creature, I tend to concur). Fortunately for the Nehwisna, the Mohk'was are contained, by natural narrow accesses, to the halls and rivers in and above the Hall of the Mohk'wa. I say 'fortunately' because no Nehwisna had ever killed a Mohk'wa before Delchant arrived.

It is interesting to note how the Nehwisna cope with ordinary details when faced with the loss of visible astronomical and meteorological events, such as sunrise, sunset, moon phases and weather changes. A water wheel, permanently fixed in the river of each inhabited hall, slowly turns toward the next marking, which denotes end of a turn (about an hour) or an isa (equivalent to our twenty-four hour day). Years are counted by marking the depositional rings on growing stalagmites or by tracking the number of isas that have passed. Since the cavern atmosphere rarely changes and the people lost knowledge of the outer world, the Nehwisna never needed nor developed a mechanism to mark seasonal events.

Only the most ancient songs hint at a human world beyond Rockworld. Their sky is the roof of the cavern. They have lived in

Rockworld since the beginning of their recorded time and know no other view of the universe.

The sole place in Rockworld where the sun may be observed is through a vertical shaft, thirty feet wide and almost a mile in length, which allows the sun to be visible in the cavern for a few isas (days) at the peak of summer and then for only minutes at a time as it passes over the surficial opening. The base of the shaft, located in the Hall of the T'sa'wa, has been encased with a pyramid–like structure. There, a cult of the Nehwisna bands together in pagan religious worship of the sun, called T'sa'wa or Sun God. Unfortunately, during the period of this story, the T'sa'wa priests still practiced human sacrifice. The T'sa'wa is said to be a vengeful god and no Nehwisna may look upon His face without suffering blindness. Modern man knows that the sun can cause blindness so we do not stare at it unprotected, although our eyes are considerably less vulnerable than Nehwisna eyes.

Xantopec is the supreme Crystal Master and high priest of the T'sa'wa. He is uniquely qualified, as his eyes have been replaced with crystals.

Currency of the Nehwisna consists of almost any crystal as well as fossil spirifer shells, moderately rare in cavern strata. The less damaged a shell, the more value placed upon it. Perfect crystals, called Prime Crystals (an extreme rarity even in the cavern), are prized above all else. Gold, silver, iron and copper ores are mined and refined, often cast into jewelry, weapons, etc. and then traded for food supplies and processed ulok'neh, which provides excellent clothing (when converted to thread), bedding, rope and string and other household goods. The Nehwisna are masters of conservation, utilizing every scrap of material available to them.

Only two classes of wild animals capable of human predation inhabit the Nehwisna universe. The aforementioned Mohk'was and flying predators called Fisher Bats, descendant of Pterodactyl-like animals. The Fisher Bats are found only in one hall and few Nehwisna have stumbled upon it. War, rock-fall, human sacrifice, snakebite or careless climbing causes most premature deaths.

(Note: while the rattlesnake is a poisonous creature and a predator of small animals in the outside world, it is not a human predator in either world. In Rockworld it subsists, primarily, on ulok and fish and only strikes humans defensively. The rattlesnake is unequipped to devour a human.)

Gods of the Nehwisna number many and include the Death God, Mohk'wa, the Bat God, Tadi'wa, the Giant God, Fronds'wa, the Sun God, T'sa'wa, the River God, Ohana and the Wind God, Blow.

Chapter 1 - New Life

A newborn's shrill cry penetrated the mildly pungent cavern air. Young women, gathering ulok nearby, looked up briefly from their task and shook silver-haired heads. They did not speak.

It is the ring of the Wind God but the wind feels, as usual, soft and warm.

The new mother, Windsong, and midwife, Chalka, temporarily occupy a well-worn grotto off the main hall, scene of most births in New Rockhome Hall. Windsong, almost four feet tall, stands average for a Nehwisna of either sex. Her well toned body and muscular legs result from many isas of walking the long corridors and halls of Rockworld, but ugly, livid bruises can be seen on both legs. Platinum colored hair would hang to her waist but is tied back in a long tail, meeting the current fashion.

The new mother's eyes are very large, almost the size of her fists, pale blue with long eyelashes that protect them from cavern dust. Windsong's features are plain, except that her ears are slightly larger than the ideal. She wears a thin, tan, ulok'neh fiber, toga-like birthing dress. In brief, except for the bruises, she is an average Nehwisna woman with a new child.

No man is present, not unusual here.

Chalka offers Windsong several medicinal ulok caps.

"These will take away some of your pain," said Chalka.

"I'm okay," responded Windsong, though her furrowed brow claimed otherwise.

Chalka nodded and placed the mushroom caps back into her woven bag.

"Have you considered a name?"

"Taylok," said Windsong, without hesitation.

Chalka looked up and stared at Windsong, then the newborn as a questioning thought slightly tilted her head.

"I do not know that name. Is it from the ancient songs?"

"Yes. The meaning is charm."

"Fitting," she nodded. "I understand that the father is not in New Rockhome Hall?"

1

"He is not."

Windsong's eyes trailed aside, not meeting Chalka's. A solitary tear streaked her face and her lips quivered, but she did not cry.

Fireseasoning rites are fully observed throughout Rockworld and the birth of a child generally strengthens the bond between the Fireseasoned man and woman. Now, Windsong regretted her decision, a ring ago, to join with Pebblic in the ancient rite. The man viciously beat her over mere trifles, yet the blame fell upon her when she stole away and, unobserved, left the Hall of the Tadi'wa and came to New Rockhome Hall. Either party, without repercussion or resentment, may normally end Fireseasoning, but Pebblic appealed to the Most High Priest of the Tadi'wa and received an edict condemning Windsong for leaving without Pebblic's consent and abandoning the Hall of the Tadi'wa. Such bending of the Bat God's laws is too common when it comes to women.

"He does not know that you are in New Rockhome Hall?" Chalka persisted.

"No."

Chalka straightened and a brief look of sympathy crossed her face.

Windsong cuddled her newborn daughter and hugged her close, hiding the fear that Chalka's questions had aroused. If authorities should trace her to New Rockhome Hall, she would have to flee or suffer the wrathful whims of the Tadi'wa priests. At the extreme, her capture might mean death in the jaws of the Mohk'wa, at the least, imprisonment for many rings. Windsong could not imagine what would happen to the baby, would not let her thoughts stray there.

"You will grow up strong and wise," Windsong whispered, her voice trembling.

As if reading Windsong's thoughts, Chalka said, "You should not stay in New Rockhome Hall. I must report the birth and you will put every woman in the hall in danger if warriors of the Tadi'wa priests search for you."

For the first time, Windsong realized that her secret was no longer secure.

"The warriors do not enter lower Rockworld," countered

Windsong. "Besides, no one in Tadi'wa Hall knows that I came here," she whispered.

"Many who live here do know. And you should not believe that all support you. Some would turn you in, even many of the women, if they thought it would not jeopardize this hall. And, though the warriors of the Tadi'wa priests will not enter lower Rockworld they have their spies who are deemed many. It is also rumored that they have an alliance with the Crystal Master."

Windsong shivered.

"But the man I escaped is malicious," she appealed. "He is a beater of women and, perhaps, one isa, a murderer. And, where would I go? Certainly not to the Hall of the T'sa'wa where Xantopec rules."

"Perhaps, the Shotai will protect you," suggested Chalka. "You could talk with him and ask."

"I don't know him."

"I'll take you to him when you feel strong enough. It's a full turn's walk to the temple."

"I've seen Eldar Temple."

Ten turns, almost half an isa, passed before Chalka pronounced Windsong ready to journey to the temple of the Shotai. They walked slowly and were met with many scowling faces as they passed the shops and open vendors of the village on the main stoneway to the temple. Windsong did not look to either side avoiding the stares. Chalka carried the baby Taylok carefully as some of the village children were prone to verbally harass or throw rocks when their parents expressed a dislike for someone. Fortunately, no one threw stones this isa and the women breathed sighs of relief as the acrimonious villagers receded into the distance behind them.

"They hate me," said Windsong.

"You bring discomfort to them," replied Chalka. "They fear the priests of the Tadi'wa almost as much as they fear the Crystal Master and his minions. Our lot in life is fraught with danger, much of it caused by our own people. Ah, there is the temple."

Windsong saw the shining pyramidal structure. Made of polished quartzite, Eldar Temple shimmered on the side where the river flowed, reflecting the noctiluca swarms and eddies that

3

exemplified the quiet stream. The shiny pyramid surface reflected a triangular luminescence to the high cavern roof illuminating a group of stalactites. The other three sloping walls, illuminated only by phosphorescent ulok'neh, were darker than the wall by the river. This caused the quartzite pyramid to acquire a somewhat sinister look in Windsong's frightened eyes.

Chalka hailed the warrior guarding the wide entrance to the temple.

"Peace and tranquility, Tektitus."

"Peace and tranquility, Chalka," responded the guard. "What brings you to Eldar Temple this isa?"

"We wish to meet with the Shotai."

"He is very busy at present, Chalka. What is the nature of your business?"

"This woman," Chalka gestured to Windsong, "and her baby are in critical need of sanctuary. She fears for her life as do I."

"I see," said the warrior, protruding his lips and frowning. "Perhaps I can get you in to see His Eminence Graystone."

A look of distaste crossed Chalka's face for an instant, but quickly disappeared.

"Is it not possible for us to see the Shotai?" Chalka implored.

"Not for two or three turns," said Tektitus, dismissively. "You may wait in the ulok garden beneath the pergola, if you wish."

He motioned toward a tall, open, four-legged structure, of which three of the legs were natural stalagmites and the fourth upright a cut stone from another part of the hall. A web of ropy ulok'neh fiber covered the structure. The ropes, attached to two long, hand-carved stalagmite poles lying atop the edifice at opposing ends, gave the garden weak luminescence and a bit of protection from roof debris. A pair of benches, crafted from onyx speleothem, adorned the garden and added a bit of magnificence, but the hardness of the seats discouraged long-term rest. The walk paths afforded better seating for lengthy stopovers as they were covered with a soft component of the fibers.

Chalka and Windsong, already tired from their long walk, dragged themselves to the garden and slumped wearily onto the path. Taylok cried and Chalka handed the newborn to Windsong for feeding. Chalka picked a few ulok caps from the garden and the women enjoyed a meal while they waited. Three turns later, a young man came to them.

"Peace and Tranquility," he said. "I'm Flint. Tektitus asked me to tell you that the Most Holy Shotai cannot see you this isa. Come back next isa if you still desire to meet with His Holiness."

"Did Tektitus say if a meeting with His Eminence Graystone is still possible?" Windsong asked.

Chalka glanced at Windsong and shook her head.

"Tektitus did not say," replied Flint, "but I happen to know that His Eminence is unburdened at the moment. He may be available to see you, but it is only a guess on my part. Tektitus would have to consult with His Eminence."

"I must see one of them," Windsong said to Chalka. "I have nowhere else to go and the baby needs a bed and shelter."

"His Eminence Graystone is a snaker," spat Chalka, bitterly.

"Surely, he would not . . . in the presence of the baby. Surely, not."

"Be on guard, always, with His Eminence Graystone."

Half a turn later, Flint ushered Windsong, Chalka and Taylok into Eldar Temple. The interior glowed with light from many ulok'neh baskets revealing a lengthy, curving hallway with ceilings higher than three tall Nehwisna men. Painted murals of brightly colored scenes decorated the hallway walls. The artists used yellow, red and white pigments extensively while adhering to the accepted style of people standing and looking into the distance. Windsong assumed that the bright yellow figure near the end of the hallway represented the Sun God, T'sa'wa. The gleaming yellow, half globe, jutted prominently from the wall.

"This image of the T'sa'wa is painted on the polished outer shell of an amethyst geode," said Flint. "Behind the wall you can see the magnificent crystals encrusting its interior. Some of the stones are larger than your baby's head."

Flint motioned for them to enter an arched, broad entryway that led to a magnificent, high chamber. The expanse boasted several statues and wall paintings, which artfully characterized rattlesnakes intertwined with human arms and legs. Flint did not enter with the women.

His High Lord Eminence Graystone, the official title, sat on a soft cushion of fibers atop a hewn stalagmite stump crafted into a chair with polished marble back and arms. The stalagmite had been moderately large and possessed a magnificent raised base of alabaster limestone that sloped to each side affording His High Lord Eminence Graystone physical elevation above any who approached, as a throne might have done. Two broad steps led to the seat.

The man owned a narrow face with angular cheekbones and hooked nose. His eyes, large, like all Nehwisna, were a slightly darker shade of blue than most and he wore dark makeup around them to emphasize the sinister look. Eminence Graystone's silvery eyebrows stood out from his forehead like curved beacons. Everything else about the High Lord seemed quite ordinary for a Nehwisna. He stood at an average height, was neither fat nor thin and walked with slightly slumped shoulders.

A triangular, pyramidal fiber hat woven with a symbol of the T'sa'wa on one side and the Tadi'wa on another rested on his head. A snake symbol filled the remaining side, positioned so that when the High lord looked at someone, the snake appeared dominant. He wore a colorful cloak of pale blue, trimmed in heavy, dark purple cords. In his hand rested a light green serpentine staff.

"Peace and tranquility," rasped His Eminence Graystone as Windsong and Chalka approached with the baby. "How may the benevolence of Eldar Temple serve you? Do you wish to offer the child as a sacrifice to the gods?"

Windsong desperately turned, pulling Taylok away from the strange man.

"Peace and tranquility, your Eminence," said Chalka, calmly. "Most assuredly not. Windsong and her child, Taylok, require succor until they are strong enough to travel to another hall."

"Have you shells to pay for your keep?" His Eminence addressed Windsong.

"I have no shells, Eminence," she replied.

"I see. Unfortunately, our accommodations do not allow for newborns. Their cries disturb the elders and the acolytes. No, I fear we may not assist you."

A coiled rattlesnake, somehow tethered to the base of His Eminence Graystone's alabaster seat, buzzed ominously. Both women recoiled at the sound as His Eminence smiled a toothy grin. He motioned for the women to leave.

"Peace and tranquility," barked His Eminence harshly. "Biter gets hungry at this mark of the isa," he continued, mildly.

The man looked down casually at the snake and tossed a fairly large ulok cap in front of the serpent. A quick, frightening strike and the chunk disappeared into the snake's mouth. It bulged grotesquely in the snake's gullet as the animal slowly swallowed. The triangular head then lifted and turned and the large, round, unblinking eyes rested on the women and baby.

Windsong and Chalka hurriedly departed the room where Flint met them.

"Did your meeting go well?" he asked.

"No," answered Chalka. "His Eminence said he could not help us."

"Too bad," said Flint. "Would you like to see the rest of Eldar Temple?"

"We are tired," said Windsong.

"It could be worth your time to see the temple," he persisted.

He gave a secretive nod and motioned for them to follow him. He passed several rooms without entering, and then turned back to the women.

"The Most Holy Shotai is inside the next room." He whispered. "He knows that you are here and has expressed a willingness to see you. He is not like His Eminence Graystone."

"The Most Holy Shotai?" said Windsong. "But, I thought His Eminence . . . Who has the final word here?"

"The Shotai is supreme," said Flint, "although sometimes the lines of power are blurred. His Eminence Graystone takes it upon himself to make some decisions not sanctioned by the Shotai. The snakes are a good example. Please enter. The Shotai awaits you."

The young man entered, briefly nodding to the man seated on the floor of the expansive room. The chamber, while large, had lower ceilings and fewer statues and wall paintings than His Eminence Graystone's room. The smell of the room seemed to fit the seated man, however, with whiffs of sweet ulok and talc permeating the air. The Shotai obviously liked gardening as many pots of ulok and ulok'neh adorned walls and filled niches.

A stunning display of crystals lined shelf-like indentions in one wall. Windsong thought she recognized large specimens of diamonds, rubies, sapphires, corundum, rose quartz and topaz among the excellent collection. Light emitted from the ulok'neh bestowed warm colors, illuminating the crystals favorably in a manner that Windsong had never before seen.

The Shotai smiled broadly as they entered and stood from where he had been sitting on a floor cushion. The Shotai's skin had faded to a grayish color and other marks of age had obviously overtaken him. The pale cheeks sagged and the skin around his eyes wrinkled. Once silvery hair had lost its luster and teeth and nails begun to yellow. The wrinkled hands trembled slightly as he extended them to the women. The Shotai's pleasantly rotund body reflected the success and prosperity of Eldar Temple and he must have recently bathed with pumice soap because he smelled clean and fresh. His fine, ulok'neh fiber raiment also exuded a pleasant, though unidentifiable odor.

"Peace and tranquility," nodded the Shotai in a voice that had lost little of its deep, youthful quality. "Ah, Chalka. It's good to see you, again. And, who have you brought with you?"

"Peace and tranquility, Shotai," said Chalka, also nodding. "This is Windsong and her daughter. Taylok is but a few turns old."

"I can see that," laughed the Shotai. "Bring the baby to me, Windsong."

Windsong hesitated but a moment before allowing the Shotai to hold her newborn.

"Taylok, is it?" said the Shotai, patting the baby's back as he held her against his shoulder. "An ancient name meaning charm, is it not? I can see that she is well characterized by the name."

His eyes lit up as he held Taylok and she lay contentedly still, breathing the sweet, aromatic fragrance of his garment.

"She is a bundle of happiness," he laughed. "But," he handed Taylok back to Windsong, "you have come for another purpose than to make an old man smile. What can I do for you?"

"Peace and tranquility, Shotai," said Windsong with a nod. "We need a place to stay until Taylok and I are strong enough to travel."

"Why must you travel, my child?"

Windsong hesitated.

"I will allow no harm to come to you," said the Shotai. "Speak freely."

"My Fireseasoned mate has sworn to have me executed under the laws of the Tadi'wa. He is an evil man who beat me mercilessly and refused to release me willingly."

Windsong paused and lifted her tunic slightly to show ugly bruises on her legs.

"I escaped him," continued Windsong, "but the new law says that if a woman leaves a man without his consent, she may be punished by death."

"I have heard that abominable law is in effect in the Hall of the Tadi'wa," said the Shotai, sadly. "I disagree with it in its entirety and promise you that as long as you are in Eldar Temple, I will do my utmost to protect you from that ridiculous punishment. There is considerable disagreement about the change in general. For uncountable rings, either party to a Fireseasoning could depart without consequence. This is such a drastic deviation that all, save the High Priests of the Tadi'wa and a few misogynistic men, have rejected it. The warriors of the Tadi'wa will not enter lower Rockworld and even if they did, they would not enter this temple. You are safe here, Windsong."

"But, His Eminence Graystone told us that there is no place here for a newborn."

"Hm. He must have forgotten the garden room on the side of Eldar Temple by the river, Ohana. It is spacious, almost soundproof, and very comfortable. And, it is yours and your baby's for as long as you need it."

"You are most generous, Shotai," said Chalka.

"Thank you, Shotai," said Windsong.

"You may," he continued, "while respecting the privacy of others, explore the three lower levels of the temple as you will. You must not, however, under any circumstances venture to the fourth level. Only death waits inside that highest room and I forbid all to enter.

"Flint will show you to the garden room, Windsong and Chalka . . . oh, and Taylok," said the Shotai. "Peace and tranquility."

The women nodded to the Shotai and Flint appeared. Only then

9

did Windsong notice how handsome Flint really appeared. His strong jaw line and even features harbored a modest nose and smooth, sensitive lips. Flint's eyes were large and soft blue revealing empathy and resolve at once. His silver hair had been cut moderately short, hanging to mid-neck. Flint's open-front tunic revealed a muscular, hairless chest and hinted at well-toned abdominals. The man's legs looked like he must be constantly moving with the well-defined musculature of his calves.

He motioned for them to follow and made several turns ending at a wide stone stairway. He climbed the stairs and turned again into a lengthy hallway. Ulok'neh baskets lighted the walls with a pale green glow revealing colorful paintings. The artwork depicted a similar scene as the lower hall, but ended with a relief of the Bat God instead of the Sun God. The Tadi'wa looked ferocious yet wise. They passed a few darkened areas, which Windsong assumed to be storage niches. At the end of the hallway, Flint stopped and motioned for them to enter a modest, arched entryway.

"This is your new home," he said.

"You have helped us immensely, Flint," said Chalka.

"It is nothing," said Flint. "His Eminence Graystone often dismisses those who bring him no shells. The Shotai never asks for payment. Try to stay out of sight of His Eminence for a few isas. He is less likely to make things difficult for you after you are established and settled here. You will find the garden room well supplied with ulok and fresh water. Our best fisherman, Marlbrek, catches fresh fish each isa and someone will bring you a portion. The cooking area is here. If you need anything else, I am always available."

The room brought cheer to Windsong's heart. Even Taylok's eyes opened wide as if to capture the essence of the space. Ulok'neh blazed in each corner and a large light basket sat atop the modest, one-legged onyx table. The table and two chairs, made of alabaster stalagmite cores topped with ulok'neh fiber cushions, defined the eating area. Colorful paintings, depicting soothing scenes of the river with white, sandy beaches and children playing, covered most of the walls. A carved stone bed covered with three layers of fiber padding completed the furnishings of the room.

A spectacular view, through the large opening that led to an exquisite garden balcony, enthralled Windsong. Ulok and ulok'neh grew from beds of fresh river soil lavishly spread in wide trenches built into the edge of the terrace. Windsong stood briefly on the balcony and watched nearby Ohana flow leisurely down its meandering course. Below, a light fountain, constructed to be visible only from this side of the pyramid, sparkled with pulsating cascades of gleaming rivulets. The changing density of light-producing noctiluca caused different flow rates and the result brought thrills of delight to viewers.

Having explored the room, garden and views, Windsong and Chalka wearily sat down at the table.

"Will you be staying, also, Chalka?" asked Flint.

Chalka turned to Windsong.

"Have you further need?"

"No, Chalka. You have done me a great service, not the least of which is directing me here. I feel my strength returning and this will be a wonderful place to enjoy for a few isas with Taylok."

"Then, I will return to my home in the village."

"I will repay you as I can," said Windsong.

Chalka and Flint departed and the new mother moved to the comfortable bed with Taylok.

"Don't cry, little one," said Windsong, and she sang a soothing lullaby, one she learned from her mother.

Chapter 2 - The Sling

The rings passed slowly for Windsong, quickly for Taylok who became a veritable sponge for learning new words and information. She babbled her first words before she reached the age of one ring and spoke in sentences before her second ring. Her vocabulary almost matched that of her well-educated mother by her third ring, an incredible accomplishment even for the quick learning Nehwisna. And with the words came an intellect far beyond her age. Windsong shook her head in wonder when Taylok offered a well-reasoned intellectual leap that many grownups could not fathom.

The young girl grew strong and sturdy and her bright demeanor earned praise from Windsong's friends. Taylok laughed easily and made friends quickly with the temple youngsters. Her hair, platinum blonde, as all Nehwisna's, fell below the middle of her back and she usually wore it in a long tail. Sometimes before bedtime, Windsong brushed it with an ulok'neh fiber brush that made the hair shine as the brush fibers themselves contained light oil. Friends did not describe Taylok as beautiful at her youthful age, but her facial features pleased and her large, pale-blue eyes sparkled with good humor. She possessed no outstanding faults and her friends often sought her out to play or talk because of her athleticism and wit. Thin and wiry, Taylok seemed tireless to her mother. In truth, the child stayed on the go almost all the time and built excellent stamina.

Windsong avoided confrontation with His Eminence Graystone by remaining mainly on the second and third levels of Eldar Temple. When it became necessary to venture to the lower level, Windsong made certain, with the help of Flint that His Eminence ventured away or slept. The Shotai remained their mainstay, insisting they linger until danger from the warriors of the Tadi'wa and the equally dangerous T'sa'wa no longer threatened. Rumors of incursions into Lower Rockworld by those warriors grew. Stories of assassinations, abductions, beatings and other frightening atrocities reached the ears of Windsong. Taylok, almost three, could read fear in her mother's face when such a murmur circulated. But Taylok never heard the entire story from her mother. She only knew that, somehow, her father hated her mother and her mother lived in almost constant fear of the consequence of that hatred. Taylok felt that, somehow, the blame fell on her for the dangerous separation.

Taylok grew strong on the steady diet of ulok and fish provided by the garden and members of the Shotai's staff. The youngster's leg strength and athleticism made her the fastest child on levels two or three, surpassing even some eight and ten-ring-old youths. She, therefore, excelled at the semi-ring races and played a serious game of Stones. She did not excel at crystals although she tried endlessly. She almost gave up on producing a significant spark from her tourmaline crystal, alternately throwing it into her "treasure" bag or leaving it on the floor.

Occasionally, Taylok and some of her friends would sneak to the stairwell leading to fourth level. They never reached higher than about half way up fourth stairwell before guards stopped them. The children laughed and considered it a good prank, but the warrior guards admonished them forcefully enough to frighten even the older children.

And then, between the second and third anniversary of her birth, Flint gave her a sling. Taylok squealed in ecstasy until her mother intervened.

"Please take it back, Flint," said Windsong. "Taylok is much too young to possess such a weapon. She'll hurt herself or one of her friends."

"Ah, my dear Windsong, while there is an extremely remote possibility that Taylok might injure herself or a friend, there is an even greater possibility that she will save same from one of the snakes that seem to find their way into many hallways and rooms of Eldar Temple. I, myself, will teach her the fundamentals and if she should be unable to grasp them or fail to become reasonably adept with the instrument, I will make certain it becomes lost."

Taylok's smile spread across her face like a crimson bow when her mother nodded approval.

Flint taught the sling use carefully and completely to Taylok. The child took to the instrument like a fish to water. Her athletic form came naturally and she delivered the missile with great accuracy and force. Flint carried a perpetual look of awe on his face at Taylok's aptitude for the ulok'neh fiber sling. He taught her little more than basics regarding form because every time he watched with the intention to instruct, her form and graceful movements were so nearly perfect that he stood flabbergasted with nothing to say. Her ability extended to accuracy as well and Taylok picked off pebbles at a distance Flint had trouble believing. He could not understand how a child under three rings could be so accomplished in a field that many adults, thoroughly trained, could never attain. The phrase 'sling virtuoso' kept nudging Flint's mind as he watched Taylok practice. And, when Taylok encountered a temporary barrier to perfection, she practiced endlessly until reaching her goal.

The most difficult training involved learning a position other than standing upright. Flint chose various physical positions for Taylok such as leaning against a stalagmite, sitting and lying down. He instructed her how to use the sling while in those positions and she responded with amazing aptitude. The most difficult position for Taylok, and most other sling students, involved lying on her back, swinging the sling horizontally, and then releasing toward a target. She tried over and over but seldom came close to the target.

"That has always been the hardest for me, as well," confided Flint. "I have found a way, however, to practice while lying in bed."

Flint gathered several round, moderately firm ulok'neh caps. He demonstrated the horizontal throwing technique by tossing one of the caps toward a nearby stone. The cap smashed against the stone, leaving a colorful, lighted smear.

"You can use ulok'neh that doesn't produce light, but when the light baskets are put away for sleep period, the lighted caps are easy to trace and your hits easier to find when they leave a stain on the target. Now, if you miss the target and hit the wall . . . come to think of it, you'd better check with your mother before doing this in your bed. She may object to her walls being stained."

After many turns of practice, Taylok became proficient in all positions. Then, Flint introduced her to the curving throw.

Although Taylok had trouble controlling the accuracy of the curve at first, to Flint's delight, she quickly mastered a technique that worked for her.

"Remember that the rougher the stone, within limits, the greater the curve," lectured Flint.

Taylok practiced the curve until she excelled at it.

"You are now ready for the final exercise. Give me your sling and stones," said Flint, holding out his hands.

A young acolyte with a water drip timer joined them. Flint did not introduce him.

Although Taylok complied with Flint's request without complaint, she did question the act of giving up her sling.

"How can I practice?" she asked.

"One of the most difficult times occurs when you are attacked without your sling. To test your ability to retrieve your weapons and deliver a stone quickly at a target, we will time you. The sling will be placed there, and the stone here. As you can see, they are only a couple of steps apart. The target is that stalagmite covered with a fiber sheet. It is not far away. You will stand here," he said, positioning Taylok almost four steps from either piece of equipment.

"When I say, 'attack,' you will collect your weapons and try to hit the target. The acolyte will time you from my command to the striking of the target. Do you understand?"

"I think so," Taylok nodded.

"Are you ready?"

"Yes."

"Attack."

Taylok ran to the sling, positioned it in her hand, ran to the stone, placed the stone in the sling and threw at the stalagmite target.

"Eight drops," announced the acolyte.

"Not bad for the first try," Flint conceded.

By the third isa of practice, Taylok had cut her time in half.

After Taylok had trained for twenty grueling isas, Flint approached Taylok's mother.

"Come with me, Windsong. I want you to watch your daughter use the sling."

Windsong went to the balcony entrance and saw Taylok on the far right side, idly swinging her sling. A pile of pebbles lay near Taylok's feet and a pouch filled with smooth stones hung by a strap at her side. Flint walked to the left side of the balcony and set up three items. The first, a soft ulok cap the size of Flint's fist, he placed at the farthest distance. The second, a stone equal in size to the ulok cap, he placed a little nearer. The third, a pebble the size of Flint's thumb, he placed closer to Taylok and in line with the first two.

"Those are too far from her," complained Windsong. "She won't even be able to get her stone that far, much less hit them."

Flint smiled.

"Not only will she hit them, but it will be in a way that you cannot expect. Are you ready, Taylok?"

The youngster nodded enthusiastically.

"Okay," said Flint. "I want you to hit the pebble and the ulok cap, but not the larger stone, with one throw from your sling. Do you understand?"

Taylok nodded, more slowly this time. She deftly removed a pebble from the pouch, rolled it in her hand and rejected it, tossing it into the pile at her feet. She chose another and, after rolling it for a moment between her fingers, dropped it into the sling. A single whirl and the missile sped toward the closest target. It struck the thumb-sized pebble and stopped, spinning wildly. The target pebble flew over the larger stone and struck the ulok cap behind it, shattering the soft fungus.

Windsong laughed.

"That was a good shot, Taylok," she said, softly.

"Your daughter is quite masterful with the sling, Windsong," Flint said. "You must let me enter her in the contest to be held in three isas."

"Three isas? That is her third birthring. Do they have age groupings?" Windsong questioned. "I can't believe there would be any other children of three competing."

"Not exactly age groupings," said Flint. "The groups are derived from pre-contest trials. Taylok would be placed according to her accomplishments in the trials. I think that she will do well."

"Don't the contestants have to pay a fee to enter?"

"True. But, I can arrange for an anonymous patron to pay the fee."

"Flint, you can't afford to do that."

"No. But I know someone who can and will. I have already spoken to them and it is set if you agree."

"Who would do such a thing?"

"He would remain anonymous, Windsong, even to you."

"I will always think it was you."

"I promise that it is not me. He will remain anonymous."

Taylok smiled broadly as Flint countered her mother's arguments. But Windsong had not given up, yet.

"Will the contest be held near the fountain, again?" she asked.

"The target courses will be set up between the fountain and Ohana. Everyone in New Rockhome Hall will be there along with many others from nearby halls who will be here to compete and join in the festivities."

"Yes, I'm certain. Everyone will be there including His Eminence Graystone. If he saw Taylok or me, he would be angry that we have deceived him for so long. That's why we never attended this contest before."

"The crowd will be large, at least several hundred people, maybe a thousand. I doubt that His Eminence would recognize you and I'm certain that he wouldn't recognize Taylok. He only glimpsed her as a newborn and even His Eminence could not now imagine Taylok from that introduction."

"But, the people of New Rockhome Hall would remember me. Many of them hated me."

Taylok fidgeted as the adults discussed her entering the contest and finally burst into the conversation.

"Stay here, Mom," she cried. "People won't see you, and you can watch me. I want to do it. Please, Mom."

"That's actually a good idea, Windsong," said Flint. "I'll stay with Taylok as her second during the contest. That way, no one will question her regarding parents."

Taylok held her breath as her mother contemplated the idea. The youngster squealed recklessly when her mother nodded assent. People walking below glanced upward when they heard the sound. Taylok clapped hand over mouth, but could not suppress a broad smile. In all of her three rings, she had never been so happy.

The isas before the contest brought a rush of activity to Eldar Temple and the contest venue. The Shotai shouted orders and people scurried about as if their lives depended upon reaching their goals. His Eminence Graystone walked faster than usual between the fountain and the temple as he tried, in vain and almost comically, to order the people setting up the grounds.

On the final isa before the event, Taylok sat with Flint on a wide temple stairway ending at the sandy path that led, in serpentine fashion, to the river Ohana. The walkway bordered the left side of the contest venue. Taylok had finished a lengthy practice session, but her youthful mind strayed elsewhere.

"Flint, did you know my father? His name is Pebblic."

Flint pulled back slightly and his face twisted in a quick grimace.

"No, I did not know him," he answered. "But, there are rumors that he has become a very powerful man in the Hall of the Tadi'wa. You never asked about him before. Why now?"

"He hates mother and me," she said matter of factly. "I don't know why he hates me, though. I never saw him."

"What makes you think he hates you?"

"Because, Mother says he hates her and if he hates her, he must hate me, too."

"Not necessarily, Taylok. The relationship between adults is different than between parents and children. You must not believe that your father hates you just because he is at odds with your mother."

"But, Mother believes he would have us sacrificed if he found us."

"Sacrifice of human life of any age is evil in its worst form. As long as the Shotai is around, and you and your mother are in Eldar Temple, you're safe from this corruption."

"The Shotai doesn't have many warriors, though, does he?"

"No. The Shotai doesn't believe in making war."

"What if he has to defend Eldar Temple?"

"He depends on the acolytes and people like me to ward aggression against Eldar Temple."

"Are you a warrior, Flint?"

"Not exactly, Taylok. But, I can handle myself in combat and I stay in good condition."

"Could you protect Mother and me if someone tried to sacrifice us?"

"Do you know what 'sacrifice' means?"

"Not exactly. I think it means to trade something you treasure for something else that somebody else treasures."

"Well, that's close. For the followers of the Bat God and Sun God, it means to offer a valuable gift to the gods in hopes of gaining a gift from them in return. Often that valuable gift is a human life in hope of gaining favor with that god."

"Does it work?"

"No, it rarely works, in that sense. Life, to me, is more precious than anything else you might gain from the gods. A human sacrifice to the Mohk'wa doesn't keep the Mohk'wa from killing the next human it sees."

"I don't want to be sacrificed. I'm only three."

"I promise that if anyone tried to sacrifice you, I would do my best to defend you and your mother. Now, that's enough of this talk. You've had plenty of rest. Let's go back to your room. Windsong will be worried."

"Mother doesn't worry when I'm with you."

"Mothers always worry when they can't see their children."

Taylok placed her hand, calloused from many turns of sling practice, in Flint's as they walked up the steps toward the temple entrance. He looked down at her in mild surprise since she had never done this before. Flint smiled benevolently and then leaned over and whispered to her.

"If I ever have a daughter I hope that she is just like you."

Taylok beamed a broad smile all the way back to her room.

Chapter 3 - Sling Trials

On the isa of the trials, Taylok arose with the morning cry from the wheel. She roused her mother and quickly downed a hearty portion of ulok that her mother cooked. When she finished, Taylok dressed in her best pale tan tunic and shorts.

"How do I look, mom?" she asked, pirouetting.

"You look beautiful, Taylok," Windsong answered, smiling. "Happy birthring. How is your vision this isa?"

"I can see the smallest pebble on the far side of Ohana," Taylok laughed.

It constituted a standing joke between them. Taylok's vision had always been exceptional and the child would point out tiny, distant objects to her mother or Flint that neither adult could perceive without approaching. Taylok rarely misjudged distance, either. These factors aided her use of the sling.

Flint arrived at the door shortly after Taylok had eaten and called out to her.

"Taylok. Happy Birth isa. Are you ready to show the hall your sling skill?"

"Ready, Flint," Taylok responded, bouncing out the door with her sling over her shoulder.

Windsong followed to the door, but did not come outside.

"Take care of her, Flint," Windsong admonished.

"Always," Flint replied, seriously.

"Do your best, Taylok," Windsong said.

"Always," Taylok said in a voice that imitated Flint's tone.

Windsong and Flint both did a double take and laughed at Taylok's antic. As they walked away, Taylok nervously tugged at the sling cord.

"There's no need to be afraid," said Flint as they walked down the stairway to the lower level. "Remember, these are just trials. They are designed to place you within the groupings. There will be ten courses with nine targets ranging from a large stalagmite with a simple fiber target, to a fish eye set in the center of a ground target. The tenth course is for distance and the scoring will be based on your position in the group: longest throw gets ten points, next longest nine, then eight and so on. Everyone below the top ten will receive a score of zero. You can score up to ten points on each target-bearing course depending on how close you come to the center of that target. Naturally, if you miss the target altogether you will get zero points. The first group will consist of those who score more than eighty points, second group sixty to eighty and third group below sixty."

"Don't worry, Flint. I'll be in the first group."

"I believe you will, Taylok. But, there is some disadvantage to being in the first group. You will be competing against the best Slingmen in New Rockhome Hall and I have heard there is a man from Banestone Hall who will enter. He is reputed to be the best snaker in Banestone Hall and may be hard to beat. There will also be several contestants from the Hall of the T'sa'wa. I don't know much about them."

"I'll do my best, Flint."

"Your skills are unknown to them now. But, next isa, if you qualify for the first group, everyone will know how good you are. They will all try to outshoot you simply because you are so young. None will want to say they were beaten by a three-ring-old girl."

"Or maybe they'll overlook me for the same reason."

Flint gave her a serious look.

He said, "Are you sure you are just three?"

They found a short line at the registration tablet. A temple elder, Shaleman, looked up from his writing when they reached him.

"Ah, Flint. Ready to try your hand in the contest?" Shaleman asked.

"No," Flint laughed, "I am seconding for this young lady, Taylok."

"Oh, I see. Well. We have very few young ladies who choose to enter. Taylok, eh? And in what hall do you reside?"

"This one, New Rockhome Hall," Taylok answered.

"I thought I knew everyone in New Rockhome Hall," said Shaleman. "These young people always surprise me. So, Flint, you are seconding this fine lady."

Flint nodded as Shaleman wrote furiously on his fiber tablet.

"All right. That will be fifty shells."

Flint produced the shells and Shaleman counted them slowly, methodically, before dropping the pieces into a large container. Finished counting, Shaleman handed Flint a thin fiber sheet attached to a lightweight slate writing board.

"This is Taylok's registration and score pad. Have the judge at each court fill out and sign the pad after Taylok's try. The judge will record the score for that court. Court number one is just there. Don't break the slate. Good luck, Taylok," said Shaleman. "Next."

Flint and Taylok looked over the venue. It glowed with a festive atmosphere. The fountain pulsed colored water high into the air. Placards announcing the contestant's names and halls represented hung on many stalagmites. One sign hung from a stalactite high above the contest venue. Taylok never knew how they had placed the large sheet there. Three or four acrobatic youths wandered through the crowd doing cartwheels and flips for entertainment. One teenage boy climbed a tall, thick stalagmite and stood precariously atop the monolith calling to friends below.

Almost a thousand people filled the venue to watch the contestants ply their skills in the trials. They crowded in clumps around favorites and cheered wildly when a fine throw occurred. Taylok carefully observed each contestant but did not recognize anyone. She saw Tektitus inspecting the crowd and Chalka milling with a cluster of people.

"Do you know any of these contestants, Flint?" she asked.

"Oh, yes," he replied. "I know them all. The one getting ready to throw on the large stalagmite court is Marlic. Sander is the man standing closest to the fountain. Silton is the one who just made the throw near Ohana."

"Are those three the best in New Rockhome Hall?"

"Yes. They've proved it ring after ring. One of the three usually wins the contest. I haven't seen the man from Banestone Hall, though. He may be in the running."

"Who's that man with glasses?" she asked.

"He's Driggett Ventaya, a political activist. He's not a sling contestant."

Taylok said nothing but her jaw muscle tightened.

Few in the crowd paid any attention to Taylok as she strolled with Flint to the first court, a narrow, chalk-lined range ending with a large fiber fish eye target twenty steps away from the stop marks in the shooters box. Each contestant received a fresh target set up by an attendant. The soft surface of the target retains a mark where the stones strike, thereby leaving a permanent record to be examined if a contestant questions his score.

"Good isa, Flint," said the court judge, a pleasant faced, heavy-set woman of indeterminate age. "Glad to see that you entered. Let me have your score sheet."

"Good isa, Meta. This is Taylok's sheet. I will second, this isa."

"Oh. I see. Very well, but I hoped you would enter this ring. I've seen you use the sling and think you would do well."

"Thank you, Meta. Taylok may surprise you."

"Well, you can't expect a . . ." she looked at the score sheet . . ."three-ring-old to be serious competition for the adults."

"As I said, Taylok may surprise you."

"Do you know the rules, Taylok?" Meta asked.

Taylok nodded and stepped onto the hard, clay, shooter's-circle.

"Quiet," shouted Meta, unnecessarily, for only a handful of people stood nearby and those already silent.

Taylok stared for a moment at the target before selecting a medium, round stone and loading her sling. A quick whirl and the missile sped to the target, making a solid thump when it hit. Meta walked to the target to record the score. She looked close and then looked again.

"By the tail of the bat," said Meta, loudly, "the youth, Taylok, scores a perfect hit on the first trial course."

Taylok blushed in time for a few bystanders to see her as she exited the shooter's ring. Most voiced polite congratulations. Taylok looked toward their balcony and waved to her mother who blew a kiss in return.

But, a teenage boy shouted, "Lucky shot. Wait until you get to the fourth course."

Flint gave him a look and the youth scurried away, laughing. Windsong frowned and Taylok looked up.

"Pay no attention to him," said Flint.

Taylok glanced at Flint, but said nothing. Instead, she stretched out her sling and smoothed the straps and cradle.

"I'm ready for course two," she announced, brightly.

Course two presented a simple 'between the stalagmites' shot that required the stone to pass between two guard stalagmites, stationed halfway between shooter and target. Taylok took only a few moments to study the shot. She stepped gracefully into the shooter's ring and positioned herself carefully to give the maximum chance for success. The throw whirred slightly as it left her sling and passed almost exactly between the guard stalagmites.

Taylok registered a perfect score on course two.

Course three combined greater distance with a leaning position for the contestant. Taylok smiled as she placed her shoes in the fixed box and leaned far to her left to place her shoulder against the stalagmite. The foot box and stalagmite had obviously been prepared for an adult and Taylok appeared awkward as she set up to throw. Indeed, her shoulder rested against a low part of the rock mass that had not been smoothed as well as the higher zones, normally reached by taller contestants. The target looked insignificant and distant, but free of encumbrance and Taylok remained confident. She spun her sling at the odd angle and released the stone as the crowd of spectators cheered.

"Taylok has delivered another perfect score," announced the judge after careful examination of the target.

By the time Taylok reached the very difficult course four, a modest crowd had gathered to watch the "three-ring-old girl" fall from the perfect trial ranks. The youth who had heckled Taylok stood near the front of the crowd.

Course four looked almost impossible. The distance measured more than forty paces and the target concealed from the shooter's box by a tall stalagmite, thick as a man's arm span. The defending stalagmite stood five steps in front of the target, requiring the stone to curve around the monolith in order to score a strike. To hit anywhere near the center of the target required a very strong curve, indeed.

Taylok walked the course and looked over the target when Flint insisted that she do so. The blocking stalagmite showed numerous chip marks where contestants had misjudged the angle. The target, slightly smaller than the others, provided increased difficulty. As she walked back, she noticed a paltry but consistent, left to right breath of wind, common throughout the hall. Returning to the shooter's circle, she saw Flint with his hand out.

"Use this, Taylok," he said, holding a blocky stone with strongly rounded corners. "It's lighter in weight and will curve more than a more rounded stone so start it well right of the stalagmite."

"Oh," said Taylok, rubbing the stone with her fingers. "Now, I see why you made me practice with this so much."

She stood in the clay-surfaced box, placed the stone into her sling and swung it gently, getting a feel for the weight.

"You'll miss the whole target, including the floor," yelled the youthful heckler. "Ow!"

Everyone turned to see Tektitus towing the youth away by his ear.

"Ow! Ow!" cried the boy to no avail. His cries faded into the distance and the crowd became extra quiet when they turned back to watch Taylok shoot course four.

Taylok knew that she had to twist her wrist just so, keep the speed of the whirl slow but not too slow and aim far enough to the right to barely miss the stalagmite. A slight adjustment for the light breath of air would then be necessary to make the stone curve in and strike the target. She stood near the right edge of the shooter's ring and stared at the faintly visible outer arc of the target. She visualized the remainder of the target behind the stalagmite. Satisfied that she knew the location of the center, she stepped sideways to the middle of the ring, visualizing her target all the way. She whirled the sling once, too fast. She stopped and began again, slower. The stone sped away with a different sound than the others. It made a strong whirring noise and for a moment she thought she had started it too far right. The stone broke sharply toward the stalagmite just over halfway down the course. As Taylok's missile whistled past the stalagmite, the crowd cried out as one.

"Oooh!"

A thump signified that the stone had completed its journey and the crowd grew quiet while the judge, a temple elder, walked to the target and examined it carefully.

"Incredible," he announced. "Taylok scores a fish eye on course number four. I should add," he continued, "that it is the first perfect score made on course four in sixteen rings."

The crowd cheered wildly.

Flint clasped Taylok on the shoulder.

"I knew you could do it, Taylok, well done."

Taylok glanced toward the balcony where her mother had been standing, but couldn't see her there.

"I hope Mother saw that shot," she confided in Flint.

Flint looked at the balcony.

"Hmm. That's not like your mother, but I'm sure everything's all right. She probably stepped away after your shot to get water or some ulok."

"There is plenty of ulok on the balcony. Maybe she did need water, though."

Course number five proved complex and almost as difficult as four. The target nestled closer than four, and there were no obstructions, but the contestant had to lie on his or her back to make the shot.

Flint anticipated the complication and required Taylok to practice many turns while lying on her back. Once Taylok mastered the position, Flint presented harder targets for her to hit, increasing the difficulty. As Taylok lay quietly, waiting for the judge to silence the crowd, Flint looked down at her.

"This target is much too large," he said.

"It is bigger than anything you let me shoot," Taylok replied, laughing.

"Okay. I just don't want you to think this is too easy because you practiced harder shots. Relax and remember your practice."

Taylok served up a perfect score, again.

After trial five, the contestants were allowed a brief break to eat and drink, if they so desired. Flint brought a warm plate of ulok, which they shared.

"You are doing even better than I hoped, Taylok," Flint beamed.

"These are easy," Taylok replied. "I was afraid I would have to stand on my head to shoot some of the shots."

Flint started to reply, but the crowd swarmed around them, congratulating Taylok on her current standing. Most were people she had never met before, but a few of her friends also joined in

26

the throng of people attending the contest trials. She never got to speak directly to any of them, however, because of the crowd's press. The ground master retrieved Taylok and Flint and informed them that they must appear at the next venue.

Course six increased the complexity by adding a guard stalagmite and requiring the contestant to shoot while lying on his or her side. Taylok also practiced this shot so did not find it to be an insurmountable obstacle.

After Taylok took her shot, the judge walked to the target and took it down to examine the hit.

"Amazing!" the judge announced. "The young shooter, Taylok, has registered another perfect ten on trial six."

The crowd registered its appreciation in typical fashion.

Trial seven presented only moderate difficulty and Taylok easily scored ten. The growing audience burst into cheers when the judge made his announcement.

Taylok kept looking toward the balcony, however, beginning to feel considerable unease since her mother had not reappeared.

"Something's happened to Mother, Flint," Taylok said during a moment between course seven and eight. "Maybe she's fallen or become sick."

"I'll get Tektitus to check on her."

Flint motioned to Tektitus and the two whispered for a moment. Tektitus walked toward Eldar Temple as Taylok prepared to try the next course.

Course eight looked very difficult as the target stood behind six, irregularly spaced stalagmites of different widths and heights. A narrow opening could be seen from only one angle in the shooter's circle and that presented only the upper part of the target. A precise shot must conclude by dropping over the last few steps to avoid a short stalagmite standing directly in the path between shooter and target. To complicate the task, the contestant had to lie on his or her side when making the shot. The needed throw calculated to be a soft, straight shot. Taylok nailed it with uncanny precision.

The crowd screamed when the judge announced another perfect ten. Taylok beamed and looked up toward the temple. She saw Tektitus walking around the balcony, but did not see her mother. Taylok turned and walked to course nine, concern wrinkling her youthful forehead.

The target at course nine, flat on the ground some thirty steps away, presented the contestant with but one option to score a ten. The shot must be a perfect combination of height, speed and direction so that the stone falls onto the target at the exact center. A lone stalagmite offered some guidance as to the distance of the fish eye in the center of the target as it stood exactly parallel to that spot and two steps to the left.

Taylok stepped into the shooter's ring and weighed a moderate sized rock in her sling. She let the stone sway gently with the straps and made a single loop before releasing. The missile soared high narrowly missing the sign hung on the stalactite and then arced and dropped to the center of the target. The stunned crowd fell breathlessly silent as the judge examined the hit.

"Contestant Taylok has scored yet another perfect score," cried the judge, sending the crowd into loud paroxysms of praise.

"Wonderful."

"Great."

"Fantastic."

"Eeeeeee . . . yes."

"Incredible."

It went on and on.

Taylok glanced at Flint, but Flint looked toward the balcony. Taylok followed his gaze in time to see four or five men wearing dark trappings with hoods scurrying about.

"What is it, Flint?" Taylok asked.

"I . . . don't know," Flint replied, his voice almost inaudible.

"Taylok," called the judge, "you are up at trial course ten."

Taylok ran to the clay ring, swung her sling twice with great speed and flung the stone far down the course. She left before the judge called out the distance.

The crowd mumbled in surprise about Taylok's sudden departure, but silenced when the judge raised his hand to announce the distance.

"One-hundred-four and one-half steps," came the judge's pronouncement. "Taylok places third in distance, thus far in the trials."

An audible, "Ahhhh," could be heard from the bystanders as

they registered a tinge of disappointment. Taylok scarcely heard the announcement as she raced to Flint. He talked with Tektitus who held a sheet in his hand. She heard the end of their conversation.

" . . . Are more than twenty of them and they control the second floor," said Tektitus. "There is no point in resisting. They're all well-armed and have this warrant from Xantopec."

"Xantopec? What does he have to do with this?" retorted Flint, glancing at the sheet.

"The high priest of the Bat God signed the warrant as well. It authorizes Xantopec and his warriors to carry out the capture and punishment. Flint, Taylok is included in the warrant and there is a fifty shell reward for her capture."

"What? That must not happen, Tektitus. She is innocent of any wrongdoing."

Flint turned to see Taylok standing behind him.

"Taylok," he said, "I have bad news. Xantopec's warriors have taken your mother prisoner and are looking for you. We have to get you out of the hall."

"What will happen to Mother, Flint?" Taylok cried.

"She'll be taken to the Hall of the T'sa'wa for trial, Taylok, but now your safety is my main concern."

"I don't want to leave Mother, Flint. Can't we do something?"

"We can talk to the Shotai, but they have a legal warrant, signed by Xantopec and the high priest of the Tadi'wa. I doubt that he can do anything. He could already be in trouble just for harboring you and your mother. Legally, he is supposed to turn you over to the warriors, not that he would do so, unless forced.

"I have a few loyal friends who would willingly help us escape," Flint continued, "but we are only half the number of Xantopec's warriors even if all my friends joined against them. And my friends are not warriors. They would be slaughtered."

"I will help you," said Tektitus. "I can fight if needed."

"Good," said Flint. "If we escape, I'll take her to Banestone Hall. I have a few friends there who would welcome her."

Taylok saw the Shotai approaching, holding a sheet similar to that held by Tektitus. He smiled at her briefly but as he approached Flint and Tektitus his expression became serious.

"Our sovereignty has been challenged," he began. "I now see the futility of our passive stance against the war makers. But, it is too late."

"Do you wish us to gather and fight?" said Flint.

"No. There are too many of them. What of Taylok?"

"I will try to get her out of the hall."

"Flint, you understand that you will be banished forever if it becomes known by Xantopec's warriors that you assisted her?" he said, quietly.

"Yes, Shotai."

"And that Xantopec's warriors would have the legal right to kill you on the spot if you were caught in an attempt to prevent them from exercising the warrant?"

"I willingly take that risk, Shotai."

"Then, go with the gods and may good fortune be with you. If I can help, I will. Stay out of it, Tektitus. Flint and Taylok will be harder to find with just the two of them and I need you here. Get her out of the hall, Flint," said the Shotai, softly. "You will only have a short time before they realize she is not in Eldar Temple and come looking for her here. I will delay them as long as possible. Move quickly."

He waggled a finger at the two men.

"This conversation never occurred."

Flint and Tektitus nodded in understanding. Taylok looked up at the men with tear-filled eyes.

"Don't let them take Mother, Flint," she sobbed.

The three men shook their heads, sadly.

"Come with me, Taylok," said Flint. "We must leave. If we get the chance to help your mother later, we will. For now, all we can do is protect you by leaving the hall. Your mother is in the custody of the warriors."

"Where will they take her?"

"To the temple of the T'sa'wa."

"Can we go there, too?"

"That would be far too dangerous at the moment. These warriors come from the temple of the T'sa'wa and are already looking for you."

"But, what about my clothes and stuff?"

"Leave them. You couldn't get them anyway with all those men searching for you. Those idiot priests have placed a reward on your head as well as your mother's for your capture. We're lucky that you weren't in your room when the warriors came. Let's take advantage of our luck."

Taylok barely held back tears as she took Flint's hand. She glimpsed the palace and the Sling venue as they hurried away. The large crowd evaporated quickly as news of an invasion of Eldar Temple by Xantopec's warriors spread. Taylok regarded Flint as they briskly walked along the path to the village.

"I am coming back here, Flint," she announced.

Flint smiled at her, but did not reply. They skirted the edge of the village on their way to the hall entrance.

"Why are we going this way?" Taylok asked. "The road is better through the village."

"It's just a precaution, Taylok. If someone saw you they might be tempted to turn you in for the reward."

"Who would do such a thing?"

"You'd be surprised, Taylok. People do strange things for even a little reward and Tektitus says this one is for fifty shells. Now remember, if we are separated for any reason, turn to the right at the main tunnel and go to Banestone Hall. Find Leana. Tell her that I sent you to be safe from Xantopec and also the priests of the Bat God."

Taylok looked back at the only home she had ever known. Her life had been undone in a few moments and it seemed things could get no worse. She held back a sob.

On the far side of the village, Flint steered them back to the main road, making the walk easier.

Later, as they approached the entrance tunnel, Flint stopped abruptly.

"There are six warriors ahead, guarding the entrance," he whispered. "I'll talk to them. We must pretend that we are someone else, uh, I'll be Marlon, and you'll be my daughter, Whitewave. Understand?"

Taylok nodded fearfully.

"What have we here?" said one of the warriors as Flint and Taylok approached. "Stop and identify yourselves."

"I am Marlon and this is my daughter, Whitewave," said Flint, easily. "Who are you, and why are you standing at the entrance to New Rockhome Hall?"

"Marlon and Whitewave? I am Berylon, squad leader for Xantopec's force." The warrior ignored the latter part of Flint's question and checked a scroll. He looked up suspiciously.

"Are you certain her name isn't Taylok?"

The five warriors standing behind Berylon shifted restlessly, fingering swords and knives. Flint pretended not to notice the movement.

"Taylok?" said Flint, dryly. "Who would name a child Taylok?"

Taylok frowned slightly, but caught herself before Berylon noticed. The man closed his scroll.

"We are looking for a child, about the age of Whitewave, named Taylok. We have her mother in custody and our warrant calls for the daughter as well. What is your name, girl?"

"Whitewave," said Taylok, immediately.

"How old are you?"

Taylok dutifully held up three fingers.

Berylon scrutinized Taylok, intensely.

"Unfortunately," he said to Flint, "we have no recent description of Taylok and all children of this age look alike to me. It will, therefore, be necessary to take you and Whitewave into the village where our informant will identify you to our satisfaction. If the girl is not Taylok, then you may go on your way."

"This is going to mean an unnecessary delay in our departure," complained Flint. "We are meeting people in Stonehaven Hall in less than an isa and the walk is at least that long."

"Unfortunate," said Berylon, "but necessary. Please give me your sword."

Flint removed his sword from its scabbard and approached Berylon with the handle first. As Berylon reached to take the sword, Flint's sudden move stunned Taylok. He flipped the sword and struck Berylon on the head with the handle, felling the warrior. The other warriors looked on incredulously for a moment before hastily drawing weapons.

"Get out of here," Flint directed Taylok. "I'll try to catch up later."

Flint moved toward the five warriors and a loud clang of clashing swords spurred Taylok's gait. She did not look back as she sped through the poorly lighted, unguarded entrance tunnel, but felt in her heart that she might never see Flint again.

Chapter 4 - Run

When Taylok reached the main tunnel, she followed Flint's instructions and turned to the right toward Banestone Hall. Running as fast as she could, she encountered no one in the tunnel, but never having been there before didn't know whether or not that was unusual. She suddenly realized how sheltered her life had been in New Rockhome Hall. She knew no one outside the hall and would have to rely entirely on strangers for support. The clothes on her back and the sling she used in the contest constituted her sole possessions. The two people she knew best, her mother and Flint, were either incarcerated or dead. She didn't want to think about Flint being dead, but it had to be a possibility considering that he threw himself into a sword fight with five warriors. She couldn't believe that Flint sacrificed himself for her. She really cared about Flint and thought he liked her. He's like a big brother or uncle or maybe even the father she never met but, being neither in reality, he shouldn't have to give up his life for her. But then, no one should have to do that.

Breathing hard and with a stitch developing in her side, Taylok slowed and finally stopped to rest. She had run for quite some distance and now looked around at her surroundings. The tunnel's ulok'neh, growing on both sides near the walls, brightened it with a welcome greenish glow. She looked carefully, but found no edible ulok among the cheerful, but poisonous mushrooms. Disappointed, she walked slowly up the tunnel. It made sense, though, if this were a well-traveled path, that passers-by would rapidly consume any new, edible growth as soon as it matured.

"I'm going back," she said aloud.

" . . . I'm going back," voiced an echo

Slightly startled, Taylok realized that going back would undo Flint's sacrifice, which allowed her to escape.

"I can't go back," she argued with the echo.

" . . . Can't go back," agreed the echo.

Taylok giggled and the echo responded in kind.

Movement in the dense Ulok'neh stems along the cave wall

froze Taylok in her tracks. A rattler emerged from the growth ten steps away and she heard the ominous sandy rasp as it slithered toward her. Taylok loaded her sling with a rough stone and held her breath. At five steps away, the deadly snake saw her and hesitated, lifting its triangular head to better view the young girl. And then, it moved across the tunnel to the far side, avoiding Taylok. When it continued down the tunnel, Taylok ran toward Banestone Hall.

The youngster didn't know how long it took her but she eventually reached, what she believed to be, the entrance tunnel leading to Banestone Hall. Nothing marked the dark adit, but the distance seemed right based on what she had learned from Flint. To walk alone in this unknown place frightened her. She took a deep breath and looked once more up and down the main tunnel. She saw no one and fretted over what to do.

Thirst and hunger made up her mind and Taylok plunged into the darkness of the unknown tunnel. She had only gone twenty steps when she heard it, the angry buzz of a rattlesnake. It lay, undoubtedly coiled, less than five steps ahead. In the darkness of the narrow corridor she could not safely pass. She concentrated on the sound and thought she located the poison-fanged snake. Taylok loaded a stone into her sling and made a quick motion, releasing the missile toward the sound. A satisfying thump, as opposed to the clack of stone against stone, told her that she had hit the snake. The buzz of the rattle abruptly stopped.

Taylok made a wry face in the darkness for now she must pass the snake without knowing if it died or slithered away down the tunnel. Or, maybe, it lay in wait for her where she had heard it before. The answer struck her quickly and she retraced her footsteps to the main tunnel. She constructed a light basket of six ulok'neh caps, which she carried by the stems. Arriving back at the point where she had heard the snake, she found the rattler, dead. The stone had hit the reptile just below the head, nearly severing it, and killed the viper almost instantly.

Taylok now faced a different problem. Flint had taught her that she should dispose of the body, at least the head, so that no one would step on the fangs in the darkness and receive a poisonous injection from the dead snake. Trouble wass, she didn't want to touch the rattlesnake and didn't have a knife to finish severing the head. She settled for dumping sand over it until it had been completely covered by a thick mound. Satisfied that she had done all she could, Taylok moved deeper into the tunnel only to find that it abruptly ended a few steps farther along. A thin crevice served as a passageway fit only for a snake. Taylok's shoulder's slumped in disappointment and she trudged back to the main tunnel, taking the light basket to the cultivated bed that illuminated the path. She wanted to give the fungus a chance to produce new ulok'neh so she lightly tapped the caps over the fertile soil to dislodge the tiny spores.

Taylok became so involved with the trivial matter at hand, that she didn't hear the warriors until they were only a few steps away. And then, escape became impossible.

"This is her," said a warrior, running up to Taylok and grabbing her roughly by the arm.

"You've led us on a long chase," said another warrior, taking her other arm.

"Yes," complained a third warrior, "and now, we have twice as far to go to get back to the Hall of the T'sa'wa."

"Maybe so," said the first warrior, "but, I want to see Berylon's expression when we bring her back. He thought we didn't have a chance to find her."

"His expression will just be angry with that black eye."

"Did they ever find out for certain if this is the one we're looking for? I'd hate to think we came so far and this kid turns out to be someone from New Rockhome village who doesn't even know Taylok."

"I'm pretty sure she's Taylok, but it really doesn't matter because neither the warriors nor Xantopec have ever seen Taylok, so this one will do. Besides, they said she ran off when the man with her started that fight with Berylon's team. That's incriminating in itself."

Taylok could not stop herself from asking, "What happened to that man?"

One of the warriors guffawed and the two men holding her tightened their grip, but they did not answer.

"Let's move it," said the first warrior who had grabbed her, jerking her arm painfully. "We have a long way to go."

"I'm thirsty . . . and hungry," said Taylok.

"Tough," replied the warrior.

"Here," said a fourth warrior, handing her an ulok'neh fiber, water jug and ordering the warriors holding her to release one arm.

When Taylok finished drinking, the warrior, Salton, retrieved his jug and handed her a few crumbs of ulok, which she hastily devoured. Meanwhile, another warrior tied a strong fiber cord around her neck. He tied it so tight that Taylok coughed and strangled enough that Salton made him loosen it.

Taylok had no doubt that Salton led these warriors. His muscular arms bulged when he simply moved them to hand her water. His silver hair looked neatly trimmed and his large eyes exuded intelligence. His nose had been broken sometime in the past but it did little to mar his handsome features. Taylok thought that in a fight Salton could defeat every one of his men, maybe all together. Besides, when he barked an order, the other warriors jumped to obey.

"We want her alive when we get back, Clayman," said Salton. "If you kill her, you'll get no part of the reward and you'll carry the body back."

Some of the warriors laughed but the one called Clayman muttered under his breath just loud enough for Taylok to hear.

"Don't see what difference it makes since she's going to be sacrificed, anyway."

Salton heard Clayman, too.

"Fool," he rasped, " the reward says she must be alive and virginal. What part of that do you not understand?"

Clayman snorted in disgust, but said nothing.

The trip back took the party a long time and Taylok felt exhausted by the time they reached the New Rockhome Hall entrance. The warriors, too, complained about the tiring trek and Clayman, holding the cord around her neck, jerked it savagely, causing Taylok to fall.

Salton said quietly, "Clayman, if we lose that fifty-shell reward because of you, I swear I'll kill you. Besides, I want to see if she runs to her mother when we reach the encampment. I'm still not sure if she's Taylok."

Salton did not smile and Clayman rolled his eyes, but backed down.

Taylok felt sure Salton had not intended for her to hear, but his unintended prompt had caused her to think about seeing her mother again and what it meant for their safety.

They entered New Rockhome Hall and found the warrior encampment along the main village stoneway. Taylok glimpsed her mother lying on the ground, guarded by several warriors. She wanted to run to her mom but understood that if any doubt remained in the warrior's collective minds about her identity, such a move would erase them. Besides, with the cord around her neck, going anywhere would be difficult.

Many warriors milled about, talking or eating, while some sat on the ground and some lay prone. Taylok searched for Flint among them, but couldn't find him. Most of the prone men wore warrior's attire. Some could have been asleep, but two of them looked dead, and a medicine man tended to one. Taylok tried to count the standing warriors, but as they moved toward her, she became confused about which had been counted already. There were at least twenty-five, maybe thirty.

They quickly pressed in around Salton and his men and stared at Taylok. Berylon approached the youngster.

"Found her did you?" said Berylon to Salton. "I'm surprised, fast as she ran out of here."

Berylon's face looked a mess with a black eye, swollen nose and forehead and bloodstains in his hair. Taylok could not refrain from smiling. It earned her a cuff from Berylon that sent her sprawling.

"Careful, Berylon," said Salton. "She's worth fifty shells alive. Maybe even a couple of crystals."

"We're ready to move ahead to the Hall of the Sun God."

"No," said Salton, mildly. "We have just returned from a long trek to Banestone Hall and my men and I need a rest before we leave here. Six turns, at least . . . and a good meal. We have our quarry, let's not kill ourselves getting back."

"The first sacrifice takes place in three isas," Berylon reminded. "Xantopec says that the T'sa'wa will look in on us only four times this ring, and the first ceremony is the most important next to the final one."

"That still gives us plenty of time," said Salton.

"I say we leave at once," growled Berylon. "You can stay here and rest before you start but I will present Xantopec with the sacrificial prisoners next isa."

"Take the woman if you have to go at once, but the child stays with us. She's not fit for walking farther, now, any more than we are."

Taylok saw an evil spark in Berylon's eyes, as she lay crumpled on the ground in front of him. It died quickly, however, when Salton glanced up. Berylon turned and walked away, muttering to himself. Taylok thought that Berylon might be a coward.

As they moved Taylok into the midst of the warriors, a space cleared and Salton instructed her to lie down on a thin ulok'neh pad. He did not remove the cord from her neck, but gave her food and water. Taylok caught a glimpse of her mother looking back at her. Neither acknowledged the other, though Taylok felt sorely tempted to call out to her. But Mother shook her head, sadly, and Taylok could tell she had been crying. Her mom's long white tresses were dirty and wet and her face swollen. Taylok stifled a sob, but could not keep tears from streaking her cheeks. She had never felt more miserable and intuition told her that it could get even worse. Happy Birth isa.

When the warriors settled for sleep, Taylok quickly dozed off. She did not know how long she had slept when someone shook her awake and clapped a hand over her mouth to keep her from crying out. Taylok looked into the face of a warrior she did not recognize.

"Be quiet, you little brat, or I'll strangle you," the warrior whispered into her ear.

He lifted Taylok and began, stealthily, to walk away with her under one arm, still holding his hand roughly over her mouth.

Taylok observed movement at the hall entrance. She noticed a group of warriors departing through the spacious tunnel. It startled her to see her mother struggling between two warriors who held her rigidly by the arms. Her mouth had been covered to muffle her cries. Berylon stood at the entryway quietly urging his men to haste.

The warrior carrying Taylok abruptly stopped and from her

awkward position under his arm, the young girl saw the tip of a sword blade slip past her and stop at her abductor's breast.

"Put the girl down, Goldic, or I will cut you into ribbons."

Taylok recognized Salton's voice.

"Berylon ordered me . . ." began the warrior.

"I don't care what Berylon ordered," retorted Salton. "She's my prisoner, not his. Put her down, now."

Goldic reluctantly placed Taylok on her feet in front of him. He looked over to Berylon, but the cowardly man had hastily exited into the tunnel. Goldic turned to Salton and shrugged, exaggeratedly.

"I was only following orders," he said, lamely.

"Get out and find your team, Goldic, and tell Berylon to send some warriors back here to take your dead. We're not carrying them back and if you don't take them, they'll end up in that lava pit. You'll find no friends in my camp after trying to steal our reward."

Goldic raced to the entrance and soon returned with three warriors.

The reprieve did not particularly work for Taylok. She wanted to go with her mother and now they would be separated again. Her life seemed to constantly spiral downward. Now, she felt a lump in her throat as Berylon's warriors carried the dead men from the hall.

On the brighter side, Salton allowed her enough rest to regain her strength while his warriors slept. But, following a meal of raw fish pieces and ulok crumbs, Salton ordered her taken from the hall. Taylok again felt the cord tighten around her neck as the men shoved her into the entrance shaft.

The tunnel to the Hall of the T'sa'wa seemed somehow familiar even though she had never been in it before. The ulok'neh grew the same and the tunnel width and height remained fairly constant. Only once did she notice a major change. She stepped from a carbonaceous floor to a siliceous one and the erosional chamber looked different. Large slabs of thin sandstone beds had fallen over the eons and created a conglomerate of stone fragments between some medium-sized stalagmites. Taylok glanced upward and saw long fractures and several dangerous-looking slabs that seemed ready to fall. She shuddered.

"Don't worry, little girl," said Clayman glancing upward as he temporarily held the cord around her neck. "Those things rarely fall and if they did, it would kill you so fast that you'd never know what hit you."

"Shut up, Clayman," said Salton. "You want her to try to escape even more than now?"

"What did I do?" Clayman grinned a toothy smile.

As they walked down the tunnel into safer bedding, Taylok's thoughts turned to Flint. What could have happened to him? No one would tell her about the fight with Berylon and his men. Maybe he had beaten them and escaped, but he was just one man against five. No, no way could he have won that fight. But, where had he gone? Come to think of it, who were the dead warriors? Who had killed them?

Those thoughts kept coming back to her but she found no answers.

Chapter 5 - The Hall of the T'sa'wa

"This is it," said Salton as they walked into an enormous, well-lighted hall. "Follow me with the girl into the temple. Xantopec will reward us there."

Taylok felt insignificant and awed at the size of the Temple of the T'sa'wa. The shape resembled the pyramid in New Rockhome Hall except the top point seemed to have been shoved up into the roof, cutting off a fourth of the structure. The roof, where it met the temple's upper layer of stone, seemed to Taylok to be a hundred-men-high and the sides of the temple two-hundred-men-long. At least, the men standing around the temple looked insgnificant. The blocks of the sloping stone sides had been carved from thick beds of black obsidian and left unpolished so that little reflection could be seen. It appeared ominous to Taylok and the large number of warriors milling about the outer grounds did little to comfort her.

She searched in vain for a sign of her mother. Aside from the warriors standing beside her, she recognized no one in the crowded hall. She glimpsed a woman being dragged along the stoneway by several warriors and yet another girl, who looked to be ten or twelve rings, pushed into one of the temple's entrances near a large stalagmite. She recognized neither woman.

"How long do we have to keep her on this leash?" asked Clayman. "I'm tired of holding onto this thing."

"Do you want to let her go?" asked Salton. "You can certainly do so, if you're willing to chase her when she runs away. Or, maybe you'd rather just hold her arm."

"I don't want to touch her, she might bite me" grumbled Clayman. "I just want to get rid of her."

"Xantopec will present the reward when we get her to the amphitheater in the center of the temple. We'll be rid of her, then, and not before."

"What should I do with her sling?" Clayman asked, holding the weapon up for Salton to see.

"Do you want it?" Salton asked, seriously.

"No. Look how short it is. I'd look like a fool using it."

"I'll take it," chirped Taylok.

Clayman ignored her.

"Give it to me," said Salton. "I'll dispose of it later."

Clayman handed Taylok's sling to Salton and the warrior draped it on his shoulder. Neither warrior looked at Taylok, but Clayman smiled broadly as Salton had to adjust Taylok's short sling around his muscular shoulder. The smile vanished when Salton glanced up at him.

"There you are," shouted Berylon as he approached them from the temple entrance. "Xantopec is waiting for the girl. Better get her inside or suffer the consequences. Xantopec gets angry when he is made to wait."

"Did you collect the reward for the woman?" asked Salton.

"Of course," said Berylon, smiling grotesquely through his swollen face. "Xantopec placed me in charge of the sacrificial prisoners as well. My men are in the dining area of the temple with the prisoners. This girl is the seventh and final sacrifice of the four-isa festival."

"I can see why you are so anxious to get them all together," said Salton, sarcastically.

"You are bat guano, Salton," growled Berylon. "Do your duty and get the girl inside."

Salton slowed his pace after that, to the frustration of Berylon, stopping to talk with every warrior he knew. It became almost comical and Taylok couldn't help from giggling after a time. Salton looked sternly at her, but softened with a secret smile before turning away to talk with another warrior.

Eventually, the party came to the main palace door. Before they entered they received good-natured ribbing from the other warriors.

"I'm surprised that it only took six of you to bring this one to justice," laughed one.

"Are you joking?" said Salton. "We lost twelve good men before we subdued her."

The warriors laughed.

"How far can you throw a stone with your sling, Salton?" said another, referring to Taylok's short sling hanging over his shoulder.

"Farther than you are standing from me," quipped Salton, making a feint as though to ready the sling.

Everyone laughed again and Salton walked into the structure followed by Taylok, her tether held by Clayton. The other four warriors followed.

Some areas along the corridors were dark but Salton obviously knew the way. The long, wide hallway floor felt smooth and well trodden to the young girl. As they passed many open rooms on the way to the amphitheater, Taylok glimpsed more warriors and some ordinary citizens of the hall dressed in festive attire. Large circles of yellow representing the Sun God, with many varying lengths of pointed rays emanating from them, could be seen in almost every room and several places along the corridor. The caricatures, inlaid in obsidian and carved from transparent quartz crystals, had been backlit with bright, yellow ulok'neh, giving the illusion of molten lava.

Taylok shivered when they came upon a wall panorama depicting the sacrificial ceremony. The scene showed a woman lying on a narrow altar with a knife in her chest and bright red blood flowing from the wound. Many people stood watching the heinous event. A priest with strange eyes stood beside the woman. His raised arms glistened from white light that poured in from a golden orb hanging above. Taylok realized the orb must be another depiction of the Sun God, T'sa'wa. She felt a pang of revulsion that gripped her stomach as they passed the painting.

After a long walk, the party entered a huge amphitheater. The sides of the great bowl sloped gradually toward the central flat floor and contained long, curved benches so that all the spectators had a good view of activities on the floor. The benches circled the bowl and were interrupted by six evenly spaced ramps leading from the top to the floor. At the center of the venue, a flat, sandy floor covered a circular area almost thirty steps across. Glowing ulok'neh had been planted at strategic places so that the entire room exuded a brilliance Taylok had seldom witnessed.

A solid marble bench graced the center of the floor. It contained numerous, sometimes overlapping, ominous, dark stains. It stood about waist high to an average warrior and Taylok didn't want to think about its use. Next to the bench rose a structure like none

Taylok had ever seen. The warriors called it "spawn of the T'sa'wa."

It sprang from the earth like a stalagmite but the resemblance stopped there. The magnificent structure sprouted thin, green, hair (?) growing from long brown filaments. The sparse green things all looked alike; shiny verdant side above and a duller yellowish side beneath and all had similar shapes. The imperfectly rounded base of the main structure spanned a width of almost three steps. Taylok thought she could easily hide behind it. The skin of the "spawn" looked fractured in irregular patterns, yet the body as a whole seemed strong and solid. Its long arms tapered gradually to points and sported moderate numbers of the green sheets. It stood higher than the roof but the top seemed thin and vulnerable as it stretched into a huge hole. Although said to be alive, the "spawn" never moved, that Taylok saw, except for an occasional flicker of the thin sheets.

High above the floor, an enormous expression of the T'sa'wa, which blazed with light that resembled flowing molten rock, partially concealed something totally unique to Rockworld. While Taylok watched, the magnificent structure rumbled opened, fully revealing the huge hole in the center of the amphitheatre's roof. Taylok saw a circle of bright blue light gleaming from the top of the vertical tunnel. The warriors said that the T'sa'wa would look in upon them and its "spawn" from atop the hole and bestowed his blessings . . . or curses. It definitely looked brighter than an ordinary tunnel planted with ulok'neh. Taylok feared that the Sun God might be up inside the huge tube at that very moment, but no one else seemed to notice so she guessed that the Sun God had not yet arrived.

She did not believe that harm would come to her, even though a procession of priests and priestesses dressed in abbreviated finery had started down the ramp to the left of them and they would almost certainly be deposited near Taylok and the warriors when they arrived at the floor. The priests had heavy metallic ornaments that represented the T'sa'wa draped from their necks. They wore long, open robes and skirt-like garments that touched the ground.

The priestesses wore golden symbols of the T'sa'wa hung from chains around their necks, with wavering rays of yellow and gold.

Elaborately worked, heavy, gold-colored headpiece's made of bright yellow material and shaped to resemble the round Sun God, adorned their heads. They wore golden bracelets and gold trimmed fabric clothing to complete the effect.

The High Priestess walked behind Xantopec adjacent to her male counterpart, the High Priest. He wore warrior decorations as well as emblems of the T'sa'wa.

Taylok's indomitable resolve began to crumble when Xantopec appeared.

Xantopec, Crystal Master, Supreme Priest and promulgator of the cult, led the procession to meet Salton, Salton's men and Taylok. The warriors said that Xantopec could communicate with the Sun God face to face. As the parties converged on their descent to the floor of the amphitheater, Taylok saw the reason. It was his eyes . . . his eyes.

Taylok's stomach churned when she saw, beneath the multiple golden rays extending from a large, jewel-encrusted crown, a face with eyes of crystal. She had been told, of course, about the wild Crystal Master of the T'sa'wa and how he would come and get you if you weren't good. She had believed the tales were made up by the adults to frighten children, like the mythical Balka in the river. But, seeing the Crystal Master in person and staring at those crystals, which replaced his eyes, changed her opinion dramatically.

Xantopec stood slightly taller than other Nehwisna men and his height amplified by the towering headwear. He sported narrow shoulders, slender arms and legs and a slight paunch that smoothed his otherwise wrinkled body. His gaunt face seemed to effuse cruelty and the thin, hooked nose squarely separated the crystal eyes. But Taylok saw immutable determination in the thin, tight lips and cold, fearsome evil in the crystals that were his eyes.

An inadvertent, "Oh," escaped Taylok's lips, loud enough for Salton to look down and for Xantopec to turn his head ever so slightly toward her. She could not take her eyes off the malignant Xantopec and for the first time in her short life, a feeling of raw fear coursed through her body. When the Crystal Master's face turned toward Taylok, the crystals in his eye sockets glittered as though they contained lights of their own. Her heart thumped wildly and she stopped moving, transfixed, only to be shoved back into motion by Clayman.

"Keep moving," he growled.

Taylok could not do otherwise as the determined warriors pushed her along at a pace that almost made her run to keep up. In a short time, she stood before the Crystal Master, quaking as he stared at her with those awful crystals.

"This is the one?" he rasped.

"Yes," responded Salton. "This is Taylok, daughter of the one called Windsong."

"And, you are sure of this?"

Salton hesitated. "My Lord, Crystal Master, this girl ran away from Berylon when he and his men approached them in New Rockhome Hall. The man she was with fought Berylon's men and allowed her to escape. My men and I captured her near Banestone Hall and brought her back to you."

"Your eloquent speech did not answer my question, Salton. Are you sure this is Windsong's daughter? We strive to keep our sacrifices to those who are properly accused and deserve death."

Salton hung his head. "I cannot prove that she is the daughter. But, I believe that she is."

"Hm. Interesting. Young lady, is your mother Windsong?"

"M . . . My name is Whitewater," said Taylok, weakly, immediately realizing her mistake.

"She told Berylon that her name was Whitewave, Crystal Master," said Clayman.

The Crystal Master's lips tightened in a frightening smile. A man standing next to Xantopec looked carefully at Taylok.

"Let the T'sa'wa blind her, Crystal Master," he said. "We can prepare her for the final sacrifice. Think of it. A blind virgin sacrificed on the final isa of the T'sa'wa's appearance."

"An excellent suggestion, Potaxl," said Xantopec. "But, can you force her to look into the face of the T'sa'wa?"

"I can arrange it, Greatness," said Potaxl.

"Before the blinding, bring her to watch the initial sacrifice next isa," he said. "We will see if she reacts to Windsong's death."

Taylok's vision blurred and she almost fainted from the impact of the heartless words. She could hardly believe they were going to sacrifice her mother at the altar of the Sun God much less make her watch their sadistic ceremony. Her knees grew weak and threatened to collapse, but she refused to give up and let them see her fall.

"My men have, um, done their duty, Crystal Master," said Salton, hesitantly.

"Yes," said Xantopec.

He reached into a deep pocket of his robe, withdrew a bulging sack and handed it to Salton.

"Perhaps you have done well, Salton. We shall see. Take the girl to Berylon and confine her with the rest of those to be sacrificed."

"At once, Crystal Master."

Salton took the cord tied to Taylok's neck from Clayman and led her away up the ramp, followed by his men. When Taylok glanced at Clayman, the big warrior's face carried a smile of satisfaction.

"I told you that she would suffice, Salton," he said. "When do we divide the shells?"

"As soon as we give her to Berylon."

"He'll hit me again," complained Taylok.

"I'll help him," said Clayman.

"Shut up," growled Salton.

He looked down at his charge.

"Do you have a final request before we turn you over to Berylon?" said Salton.

"Could I have my sling back?" Taylok asked.

"This? Why do you want your sling?"

"It was a gift."

"Well, I don't see any stones around so I guess it would be all right. Here." Salton took the youth's sling from his arm and handed it to Taylok.

Taylok gratefully lifted it to her shoulder as they walked from the amphitheater.

Soon they arrived at a holding room. Except for the opening to the hallway, the room's walls were solid rock. One wall sloped at the same angle as the outer wall, identifying it as an edge room. Two warriors guarded the slender opening. Berylon stood to one side conferring with another warrior. When he saw Salton approaching with Taylok he broke into a toothy smile.

"I am turning the child, Taylok, over to you, Berylon," said Salton. "Such were the instructions of the Crystal Master."

"So," replied Berylon, "you finally agree that she is Taylok?"

"I have no idea, Berylon. Everything fits, however, and we have been paid for the capture and return of this child."

"Xantopec has a special treat for her in any event. The first sacrifice to the Sun God will take place next isa and Taylok will witness the event. That sacrifice," Berylon turned to Taylok, "will be Windsong, your mother."

"How did you learn this?" asked Salton. "Xantopec just made that decision."

"This type of news travels faster than a man can walk, Salton. You should know that."

"Ah. The man you were talking to is a temple runner."

"Yes. He also tells me that Xantopec and Potaxl have planned two special events around the child."

"Two?"

"Yes. The first will follow the sacrifice of Windsong."

"But, even the Crystal Master cannot sacrifice the child twice."

"Ah, but he can if the first is not fatal."

"In any event," quipped Salton, "the child is now officially in your custody."

"Why does she have her sling?" said Berylon, fingering the strap around Taylok's shoulder.

"She wanted it. Said it was a gift. If you're afraid, take it away from her."

"Afraid? Me? Nothing frightens me, Salton. Least of all a three-ring-old girl."

Salton handed the cord to Berylon and the warrior jerked Taylok and pushed her into the room, leaving the tether around her neck and the sling strap around her shoulder. Taylok immediately saw her mother sitting on the floor along with several other women. She feared to rush to Windsong so she pretended not to recognize her at once. Instead, she sat beside a girl age ten or twelve, seated slightly away from the rest.

The girl looked beautiful to Taylok with long white eyelashes fluttering over large orbs of pale blue. Her waist-length platinum blonde hair had been brushed and parted behind thick silver bangs, which almost touched her lashes. Her nose turned up slightly and her lips were pink as rose quartz. The heart-shaped face balanced perfectly over her long, thin neck. Her tunic fit gracefully around the curve of her shoulders and her hands seemed well cared for with long, pink-tinted nails. Taylok felt a pang of jealousy.

The young girl raised her head and spoke.

"Here, sit," she said, patting the floor next to her. "Make yourself miserable."

Taylok sat.

"What's your name?" Taylok asked.

"Shalea," said the girl. "What's yours?"

"Whitewave," replied Taylok, still reluctant to reveal her name and chagrined about the 'Whitewater' answer she had given the Crystal Master.

Taylok stole a glance at her mother and was rewarded with a sly smile. Taylok looked at the door and saw no one. She chanced a tiny wave of her hand and her mother responded in kind.

"They've been watching us almost constantly," said Shalea. "Be careful."

"Why are you here?" Taylok asked.

"My mother sold me as a sacrifice."

"Your mother? Why?"

"They gave her a sizeable reward for me since I am still a virgin."

"Are all these women virgins?"

"No. Some are here for crimes and some have been sold to the Crystal Master as sacrificial fodder. I am told that the Sun God's face is the most brilliant light ever seen and that the ceremony is stunningly beautiful."

"Not for us."

"True. Why are you here?"

"Because my father hates my mother and me," Taylok whispered.

"I don't understand."

"Mother left him and took me with her before I was born."

"So?"

"There's a new law of the Bat God that says mother can't leave father without his consent, under penalty of death," Taylok continued in hushed tones.

"That's a stupid law. Anyway, the Tadi'wa law doesn't rule here."

"They have a letter signed by both the Bat God priest and Xantopec."

"Xantopec and the Bat God priests have a pact?"

Taylok shrugged.

"You're less lucky than me," said Shalea. "At least I have only one person to blame for my being here. You have your father, the Tadi'wa Priest and Xantopec. Where is your mother?"

"I must not say. The warriors are still uncertain about who I am, although the way it's going I'm not sure it matters. It seems I'll be sacrificed anyway . . . twice."

"Twice? How is that possible?"

"I don't know."

Taylok turned when her mother spoke.

"Did you say they were going to sacrifice you?"

Tears flowed down Windsong's face as she realized that Taylok would not survive the ceremonies of the Sun God.

"Come here, Taylok," said her mother, holding out her arms. "There's no further need for pretense."

Taylok ran to her mother and collapsed in her arms.

"I tried to escape, "whispered Taylok, sobbing," but they found me. I think they killed Flint."

"Flint? Dead?" Windsong whispered.

"The last I saw of him he fought five warriors with swords and knives. He gave me a chance to escape into the main tunnel, but he must have given his life doing it."

"Flint is resourceful," said Windsong. "Still, it doesn't seem he could walk away from a hostile encounter with five armed men. Don't count him out just yet, though. Wait until you know for sure."

"We'll never know for sure if they sacrifice us next isa."

"I am so sorry that I dragged you into this, my daughter. I do love you so much. It seems so unfair that you should be victimized for something that I did."

She hugged Taylok, again.

"I love you, too, Mother. Can we escape?" Taylok whispered.

"You see the way we are guarded. I don't see how we could get away from them. Besides, I don't want to spend the rest of my life running from the warriors of the Sun God as well as those of the Bat God. I had grown weary of the constant anxiety."

Taylok sighed, deeply. In her heart, she did not believe that they would die at the hands of Xantopec. Somehow, they would escape. Somehow. Nestling close to her mother, Taylok fell asleep and dreamed about the beautiful grotto high above Ohana in New Rockhome Hall. She rested on her back, next to her mother, her eyes on the grotto roof with its translucent icicles and alabaster stalactites. Near the end of her dream, a gleaming, bright stalactite shard broke away and fell directly toward them. She cried out and jerked involuntarily as the silvery image jarred her awake in her mother's arms.

"It's just a bad dream, Taylok," whispered Windsong, holding her close, rocking back and forth.

But, Taylok knew they were living that nightmare and she sobbed quietly.

"How long did I sleep, Mother?" she asked, between sobs.

"A long time," her mother replied.

Taylok heard activity in the hallway and quickly, Berylon appeared in the entrance with two warriors behind him.

"Didn't think we had forgotten you, did you?" Berylon rasped as he starred at Windsong and Taylok. "You two will come with us."

He held the cord, still tied to Taylok's neck, grasped Taylok around the shoulders and lifted the child from her mother's arms. He set her on her feet, still holding the tether.

"Get up," he ordered as the warriors with him brushed past and thrust Windsong to her feet.

They moved across the room and Taylok glanced at Shalea as they passed.

"Be brave, Whitewave," said Shalea.

That was the last time Taylok ever saw Shalea.

When they arrived at the amphitheater, a huge crowd filled the bench-like seats that circled the floor. Warriors and citizens alike had come to witness the sacrifice of the first appearance, their faces painted into grotesque caricatures with dark, sometimes black, clay paint. It made the entire venue seem surreal since almost everyone exhibited the paint in some fashion.

Taylok could see that the floor around the grotesque structure growing from the ground had been rearranged. Side by side altar tables stood near the weird growth and a large bowl had been set adjacent to the further altar. As they drew closer Taylok could see grooved channels leading from the altar to the side where the bowl waited.

Taylok suddenly understood and again her knees felt weak and almost buckled.

"Windsong will be here," said Berylon," indicating the altar with the bowl adjoining, "and Taylok here. The priests and priestesses will prepare both sacrifices."

Four robed priests along with four scantily clothed priestesses approached and ceremoniously took charge of Windsong and Taylok. Berylon and his men bowed and retreated into the amphitheater.

Potaxl and the priests laid Windsong onto the far table. They tied her hands at her sides with cords and removed her shoes. They bound her legs with stout fibers and placed another tightly over her neck. Potaxl cut her tunic around the waist and lifted the upper segment to her breasts, laying her mid section bare. He poured an oily substance over Windsong's midriff, moving quickly, occasionally glancing upward into the brightening window to the world of the gods.

Taylok watched the proceedings with growing horror and a sick feeling in the pit of her stomach. Potaxl and the priestesses next approached Taylok. They bound her legs with strong, thin cords and tied her hands behind her back. Then, Potaxl attached a kind of sticky tape to her upper and lower eyelids so that she could neither blink nor close her eyes. He fitted her head into a carved stone block that permitted no movement and placed her face at such an angle that she had a clear view of the bright blue circle above and her mother lying next to her. The opening above grew steadily brighter. They left the cord attached to her neck as well as the sling around her shoulder. The sling would be of no use without stones and free arms.

Windsong gazed at her daughter.

"Be strong, Taylok," she said. "I love you. There will be an end to this insanity whether in death or freedom."

Chapter 6 - Of Death and Blindness

The incredible brightness silently smashed into the floor on the side farthest from Taylok bringing a gasp from everyone in the crowded amphitheater. The Sun God with its omnipotent power had arrived. Taylok could still see some of the audience beyond her mother. The acolytes shielded their eyes as the maddening brilliance expanded toward the sacrificial altars. Potaxl, the priests and priestesses hurriedly departed the floor and Xantopec appeared behind the enveloping brilliance. He wore a golden hooded robe that covered him head to toe leaving only his face exposed with those ghastly crystal eyes. His face bore the clay paint Taylok had seen on most of the audience, except that a large yellow circle extended from forehead to chin and rays emanated from the circular depiction of the T'sa'wa. He stepped into the radiance and looked upward into the face of the Sun God bringing another exclamation from the frenzied onlookers.

"Hear me, O great T'sa'wa," his voice boomed across the amphitheater. "You come to us in our time of need. You give us this mighty sign of your magnificent presence."

His robed arm swept across the encroaching brightness.

"Your light outshines all others and your power is of a billion ulok'neh. Give to us an abundance of fish and ulok. Let us be fertile in all things. In return, we first offer the lifeblood of this woman, Windsong. We will present even more when you return next isa. We are your most loyal servants. Show us your power over the virgin girl we believe is Taylok. Take from her what you will."

The crystals in his eye sockets sparkled brilliantly and continued to glow after he stepped ahead of the brightness and walked to the table where Windsong lay. Taylok fully believed the ancient priest to be evil personified. Therefore, the T'sa'wa must also be evil.

The maddening effulgence crept steadily but mutely toward Windsong and Xantopec. When it enveloped the first altar, Taylok's mother screamed in pain and held her eyes tightly closed.

With Taylok's eyes taped open and head locked in place, she could not avoid watching Xantopec withdraw a long silver blade from the folds of his robe. With both hands, the strange priest held the blade high over her mother's chest as she continued screaming. The T'sa'wa's destructive power seemed insatiable to Taylok.

The ceremony continued to envelop Taylok's sight and mind. Xantopec plunged the knife into her mother's chest and Taylok's mind's eye saw the falling shard of her dream. Taylok screamed shrilly when the evil Crystal Master, hands dripping blood, lifted the heart from her now silent mother.

Almost mercifully, the agonizing glow reached Taylok. Powerless to avoid it, she watched the circle of the powerful, evil god creep through the opening above until she could see nothing else. The intense, burning rays seemed to penetrate straight into her brain. It seared her eyes relentlessly and she screamed again and again in pain greater than any she had ever known. Her mind attempted to block the deadly rays from her eyes and within a brief, miserable time her vision went blank. Still awake, Taylok fell into darkness as black as the lightless regions of Rockworld. Even that merciless light, with which the T'sa'wa had so painfully tortured her, vanished.

The Sun God had blinded her.

An eternity passed and then, after the blistering heat of the Sun God crept away, from somewhere nearby, she heard the voice of Xantopec addressing the audience.

"Look. The Sun God has taken Taylok's vision. That is the strength of our god. Now, He will see all that we do for Him. In three isas, this virgin will again, as final tribute, be sacrificed to the T'sa'wa by taking her life blood."

The crowd roared and Taylok heard an unfamiliar chant begin.

"Blood to the T'sa'wa, blood to the T'sa'wa."

It filled the amphitheater and Taylok's head. She tried to close her mind to the chant and the ceremony but it helped not at all as strong hands untied her and lifted her off the altar. They forced her to stand on uncertain legs as the nascent blindness temporarily stole all sense of direction and balance. If not for the hands holding her upright, she would have fallen immediately. When they released her, she balanced precariously for a moment but quickly fell, using her hands and arms to break the fall. Laughter from those nearby stung her worse than falling. The rattle of a snake caused Taylok to jump back, quickly, amid laughter from the warriors. The rattles buzzed again and Taylok reacted as before. Raucous laughter filled the amphitheater and Taylok realized she had been the butt of a joke. Someone probably held a snake's rattle and shook it to scare her into a reaction. She tried to steel herself against jumping when she heard it again, but failed. The reaction had been too ingrained and the danger too great to ignore.

"Here, Berylon," said someone's voice, after no less than seven rattles, "she's back in your custody until the final ceremony. Surely, you can watch after a blind child, who can scarcely stand, for three isas."

More laughter ensued from those gathered, but Taylok could not distinguish individuals among them. Berylon, or one of his warriors took the cord tied around her neck and led her away. She almost fell again before she recognized the ramp when they came to it. The warriors laughed at her unease and awkward, stumbling gait with her arms outstretched to avoid running headlong into major obstacles. Whoever held her tether led her, perhaps deliberately, into a column of stone from which she barely caught herself in time to keep from suffering a blow to the face or head. The walk back to the holding room took much longer than the trip down because Taylok fell several times. When they arrived, someone shoved her into the room and she stumbled over one of the women as she sought an open spot to sit.

Taylok had heard of people becoming blind for various reasons and they seldom survived many rings because of the abundant, literal pitfalls of Rockworld. Flint said that some of the domepits dropped to the center of the universe. People who fell into them were never seen again. The shallow ones usually had acid that would eat your skin away if you didn't get pulled out quickly.

Selecting edible ulok as opposed to deadly ulok'neh also required vision or an excellent sense of smell. A few of the mushroom varieties killed with the first bite and most people could only distinguish a lot of species with spore patterns. Maybe you could learn to pick the right ones by feel or smell, but it would take a lot of practice. You might not survive your first mistake.

The few blind survivors that she could think of had constant guides to lead them past potentially deadly encounters. Rarely did one endure blindness alone in her world so how could she go on? Death had probably taken Flint and, now, Mother from her. Who would help her?

She didn't stop worrying about surviving blindness even though she understood that she would be sacrificed in three isas.

"There has to be a way out of here," she said aloud.

"None of us will escape our destiny," said the voice of Shalea from across the room. "We will be sacrificed to the Sun God. Some say it is an honor."

"Maybe that's not our destiny," argued Taylok. "How much blood does one god need? Besides, I'm little. I don't have much blood."

"What happened to you, down there?"

"Xantopec sacrificed my mother and then the T'sa'wa stabbed me in my eyes until I couldn't see."

"I thought you were having trouble walking. You're blind? Can you see anything?"

"No. Nothing. Everything's black."

"You poor child," said the woman next to her, hugging Taylok.

"I'm still alive, though," Taylok said in a high-pitched voice.

"Not for long," said a warrior's voice from the door, followed by laughter from several outside voices.

Taylok buried her face in her hands and sobbed as the unknown woman tried to console her.

"It's unfair, what the Sun God has done to you," whispered the woman. "Your mother told me her story. You are innocent. I will help you get proper food and water until they take me."

"Take you?" sobbed Taylok.

"I will be sacrificed next isa. The Sun God is a cruel master."

"Who are you?"

"I am Marla."

"Marla, it's Xantopec and those stupid priests and priestesses who are cruel. The Sun God is slow and ugly. He is just a horrible brightness that comes into Rockworld once in a while and lets His followers think He can do good things for them."

Marla gasped at Taylok's words.

58

"Don't speak that way, child. The T'sa'wa knows everything we do."

"He can't do more than kill us, can He?"

"Xantopec has some horrible ways to torture non-believers. You'd be shocked to know how long a person can live as they cut pieces of you away."

"Why do the people stand for it?"

"They know it could happen to them if they aren't careful."

"I want to get out of here."

"We all do."

"Aren't there enough of us to overpower the guards?"

"They have weapons. We have none."

Taylok felt the strap over her shoulder.

"I still have my sling," she whispered, confidentially.

"You are blind and three-rings-old," reminded the woman.

"So, we are going to just sit here until Xantopec comes to cut our hearts out?"

Marla fell silent for a moment.

"There is nothing we can do," she said, miserably.

Taylok heard quiet footsteps as someone entered the room.

"Who is it?" she asked Marla.

"Two serving girls with our meal," Marla replied.

Taylok heard the girls as they delivered their plates of ulok to the other women. They eventually arrived where she and Marla sat and handed Marla a plate. Taylok didn't know what to do so she did nothing.

"She's blind," said Marla. "Give me her plate and I'll help her eat."

The girls said nothing and quickly departed.

Marla handed Taylok some crumbs of ulok and the youngster ate sparingly, not hungry.

When Taylok slept, she dreamed that she could see. Mother stood in a garden of ulok'neh and familiar brightness lit her face. She smiled and beckoned to Taylok. Next to Mother stood Flint, tall and muscular, holding his sword as she had last seen him. Taylok wanted to run to both of them, but her feet mired in mud and she could hardly move no matter how hard she tried.

Flint made a hand gesture. It meant to wait. She had seen him make the same gesture many times when she wanted to use the sling, but something or someone stood in the way. What did it mean, now? How could she do anything but wait?

"Wake up, child," said Marla, shaking her gently. "You were dreaming and kicking your feet."

"Sorry," said Taylok. "I saw Mother and tried to go to her."

"You can see?"

Taylok turned to Marla and opened her sleepy eyes to blackness.

"No," she said, "but my dreams can see."

"Go back to sleep, then, and dream of your mother."

Taylok returned to a dreamless sleep.

The next isa, someone came for Marla. Taylok listened as the woman resisted the people trying to take her away, but in the end, her sobbing voice trailed off down the corridor.

"Goodbye, Marla," whispered Taylok.

A few moments later a different group came and took another woman away. Taylok did not recognize her voice and the woman did not resist her escorts.

Someone came to Taylok and sat beside her.

"Are you thirsty?" said the voice of Shalea.

"Yes," admitted Taylok, holding her hands out.

She felt the cup, brought it to her lips and sipped the water.

"You are too easy," said Shalea. "I could have poisoned you just now."

"You didn't, did you?"

"No, but I could have."

"For what? They're going to sacrifice both of us soon."

"You are just too trusting."

"I'm only three."

"Wait until you're older."

"Unless there's a miracle, I won't get much older. Neither will you."

Taylok heard Shalea crying softly.

"I don't want to die," Shalea sobbed. "I'm too young."

"You're older than me."

Shalea wailed louder.

Taylok could count only four people in the room, including her.

She knew Shalea, but the other two kept to themselves, talking quietly. Taylok caught a few words and a sentence or two, but little else. Next isa, she learned what the women had planned.

When the guards entered the room with the escorts, one of the women started a conversation with them.

"You're making a mistake," she said. "I am Taylok and this is my mother, Windsong. We are to be sacrificed next isa."

Taylok stood, baffled. Why would someone want to claim that they were . . . of course.

Taylok said, "She's lying. They sacrificed Windsong first and she's not Taylok. If you don't believe me, bring Berylon in here. He knows Windsong and Taylok."

"Shut up," screamed the woman. "Shut up."

"What is your name?" asked some man's close voice."

"Whitewave," answered Taylok.

"No, she's not," said Shalea. "She's Taylok. You can tell because the T'sa'wa blinded her during the first ceremony."

Someone grabbed Taylok by the face and she felt his breath on her skin.

"This one is Taylok," said the man's voice. "She's blind."

"Take those two," said another voice.

"No, no," cried the two women in unison.

They left the room after a scuffle. Their screams took a long time to fade away, but eventually the room became quiet, again. Taylok's heart still raced from the women's attempt to send her to her doom ahead of schedule. Without sight and exhausted from the excitement, Taylok slept several turns, waking only when the serving trays arrived.

"Don't tarry," said the guard at the door, speaking to the girls with the trays.

"How long did I sleep?" Taylok asked.

"Seven or eight turns," said Shalea.

"No," Taylok protested, "I can't have slept that long. You should have wakened me."

"We don't have long to live, Taylok. I thought you should do as you pleased."

"I didn't mean to sleep the rest of my life away."

"Here. Have some ulok."

For the first time since being blinded, Taylok felt hungry. She took the morsels from Shalea as listened to the serving girls shuffling out of the room. The ulok had been cooked just the way she liked them and she ate heartily.

"They brought enough for four people," said Shalea, "and, I'm not even hungry."

"Well, I am," said Taylok. "Try some of this. It's really good."

"How can you eat when we are going to die in a few turns?"

"Things can happen. I want to be ready for any break we get."

Shalea sighed, deeply.

"Never give up, do you, Taylok?"

"What's the point? Giving up won't help. Flint always said, 'You can do whatever you want as long as you want whatever you do.'"

"You can . . . what does that even mean? And, who is Flint?"

"Flint was a friend of mine. He died helping me escape from Berylon in New Rockhome Hall. I believe it means that if you think you can't get what you want and give up, you have a lot less chance of getting it."

"Okay, I can see where your friend's saying works in some cases, but how will it help us escape from Xantopec with all these guards watching?"

"I don't know. What I do know is, we can't give up. If we do, our chance to escape may pass us by."

"Taylok, you're crazy. Let me remind you that you're blind as one of those bats living in that huge hole, and I'm giving up because I can't see a way out of this. Only an insane person would have any hope."

"We're not dead, yet."

"As good as."

"Not yet."

"Are."

"Are not."

"I'm not going to argue with you, Taylok. If you find a way out, let me know and I'll go with you. If not, we won't waste our time arguing. I'm going to sleep."

Chapter 7 - Friend and Foe

Several turns, Taylok couldn't tell how many, passed as Shalea slept. Taylok heard someone walking up the hallway to the door.

"What are you doing here?" said the guard. "The ceremony won't start for two turns and it will be in the amphitheater."

"Right," said a voice. "We came to take the sacrifices to the white robes to get them ready for the ceremony."

"Just wait," said the guard. "I don't know you and you're too early. I have to check this out with Berylon."

"By all means," said the voice.

"I'll be back in a momen . . ."

A heavy "thunk," followed by another, with the sound of falling bodies and accompanying moans, made Taylok jump to her feet.

"Wake up, Shalea. Something is happening."

"What?" Shalea came fully awake. "What is it? Who are these men?"

"Be very quiet," said a voice. "We have little time to get you out of here before the other guards find out what's happening. Taylok, you'll have to ride in the sling I have around my neck. You must ride in front of me. I'll cover you with this large robe so that together we'll look like a fat man. You'll have to hold tight and not bounce around too much, understand?"

Taylok nodded and allowed the man to lift her into the sling facing him. She felt his warm tunic against her cheek and grabbed hold of the sides for steadiness. He donned a robe and covered her back, tying the garment loosely around them both.

"You must pretend you are my daughter," whispered a different voice, obviously to Shalea.

The voice sounded somewhat muffled by the robe around her, but Taylok could hear the quiet conversation.

"What is your name?"

"Shalea."

"Okay, Shalea. You should realize that if we were caught they would kill us all. Put this robe over your tunic."

"Who are you?" Shalea asked. "What's the stuff on your face?"

"This. Hold still while I paint your face," said the man.

After a brief pause, he said, "There. Done. Now, we must hurry or they will find us before we can get out."

Taylok thought she recognized the second voice, but couldn't be sure because of the whispering. Besides, it couldn't be him. He died in the fight with Berylon's men. Didn't he?

Her heart leaped. Flint. It is Flint. She could tell his voice even when he whispered. She couldn't identify the man holding her, though. She didn't recognize his voice. It wasn't Tektitus or the Shotai, of that she felt sure. Flint said he had a lot of friends in New Rockhome Hall. It must be one of them. Taylok felt grateful to whoever it might be

She bounced as the man walked and he held her gently by the sides to keep her steady. Quickly, they walked into a noisy crowd of people.

"You're going the wrong direction," said one. "The amphitheater is this way."

"My daughter's ill," said Flint's voice. "We have to go back to Banestone Hall."

"Too bad. You'll miss the final appearance of the T'sa'wa this ring."

"Isn't that the way it always goes?"

"Long reign the T'sa'wa," said the man, his voice fading as he walked away.

"Long reign the T'sa'wa," echoed Flint, unenthusiastically.

The man carrying Taylok moved at a leisurely pace and she assumed that Flint and Shalea were walking along with them although the crowd made so much noise that she couldn't tell for sure. Confirmation came when Flint spoke confidentially to her transport.

"The warriors at the gate are checking everyone as they leave. Shalea, I'll have to carry you because you are 'sick.' Are you all right, Your Eminence?"

"I'm fine," said Taylok's host.

Flint had called the man "Your Eminence." Taylok's mother called His Eminence Graystone a "Snaker" and inferred that he only acted for profit. Taylok never met him that she remembered.

Without realizing it, Taylok had pulled her head away from the man.

He gently pushed her head back down, saying, "We're almost to the entrance. You must be still."

"What's this?" said someone in front of them. "Leaving so soon?"

Taylok recognized the voice of Clayman.

"My daughter's sick," said Flint. "Weak stomach, I think."

"Yes," said Clayman. "Some are affected that way from the ceremonies. Why are you leaving?"

He must have been addressing His Eminence because he spoke.

"We came together and we leave together," he said, simply.

"Salton," called Clayman. "Come over here."

Taylok heard footsteps.

"What's wrong, now, Clayman?"

"Doesn't anything look suspicious to you?"

A moment of quiet as Salton looked over the men and Shalea. Taylok jumped involuntarily as she suddenly felt a hand moving on her back. Salton had discovered her and their attempted deceit.

Another moment of silence ensued as Salton stepped back.

"A man cannot help it if his stomach encroaches on his beltline, Clayman," said Salton.

"Well, sorry," said Clayman. "It just looked . . ." his voice trailed off.

Taylok heard footsteps departing as Clayman walked away.

"There is trouble afoot," whispered Salton, easily. "It will take the guards only a turn to search the temple and then another to search the grounds. After that, they will take the main tunnel traveling at high speed. They will not be easily fooled. May the gods protect you. Goodbye, Whitewave or Taylok. You're a courageous girl."

Flint responded, "Make certain that you are well back from point when the search reaches mid tunnel. There will be surprises."

Salton patted Taylok on the back before ushering His Eminence and Flint, carrying Shalea, out the hall entrance. When they reached the main tunnel, His Eminence broke into a run and Taylok could hear Flint's rapid footsteps nearby. It seemed to Taylok that they ran for a turn before they stopped.

"This is the grotto," said His Eminence. "The impediments are inside."

He removed the outer robe and took Taylok from the sling where she had been sitting, placing her on her feet. Sightless, Taylok reeled, but strong hands took her by the shoulders, holding her upright.

"I am so sorry that we couldn't arrive before they did this to you, Taylok," said Flint, near her ear.

"I knew you would save me," said Taylok, reaching out into her darkness to take his hand.

Taylok heard His Eminence's footsteps fading in the direction from which they had come.

"Where is he going?" she asked.

"To set a deterrent," answered Flint.

"What kind of deterrent?" asked Shalea, standing nearby. "What was in the bag he took?"

"It's better you don't know," said Flint.

"Well, can you at least tell me who you are?"

"I am Flint of New Rockhome Hall," he said. "Now, we must make haste. His Eminence will catch up with us shortly. By the way, in which hall do you live?"

"Stonehaven," said Shalea. "But, I can't go back there. My mother sold me to Xantopec for sacrifice. I won't let her do that again."

"Do you have relatives or friends in another hall?"

"No. Everyone I know lives in Stonehaven."

"I'll ask His Eminence if you can stay at Eldar Temple in New Rockhome Hall. If not that, then someone will take you in at the village."

Taylok squeezed Flint's hand as the trio set out at a brisk clip. Taylok's confidence soared with Flint leading her by the hand and she walked without faltering. He skillfully guided her around all impediments on the tunnel floor until she felt like running, although Flint held her back from achieving too much speed. They had not gone far when she heard His Eminence catching up to them.

"It's done," said His Eminence, breathing hard.

"Good. We'll need the extra time," replied Flint.

They fled up the tunnel without slowing until Shalea pleaded for a rest. Almost as soon as they sat down, Taylok heard remote cries echoing from far down tunnel. Whatever deterrent His Eminence had arranged seemed to be working.

"Are you ready to move?" Flint asked. "It seems our pursuers have found the impediment."

Both girls answered affirmatively.

"They will not be held up for long," said His Eminence.

"Perhaps not," said Flint, "but they'll be more cautious after the encounter. It will buy us time."

"Yes," said His Eminence Graystone. "We should, nonetheless move on."

The girls alternated between running with the men and being carried by them. The foursome made infrequent rest stops as a result. His Eminence Graystone called for one of the stops.

"I'm not as young as I used to be," he admitted. "There was a time when I could run for an isa without stopping. Now I can barely keep going for a turn."

"Are we there, yet?" asked Taylok.

"We are about a turn away from New Rockhome Hall," said Flint.

"Won't the warriors follow us inside like they did before?"

"They came inside your hall?" interrupted Shalea.

"Yes. That's how they captured my mother. Flint got me out of the hall, but they still caught me in the main tunnel."

"They won't enter the hall this time," said Flint. "Another deterrent is waiting for them at the New Rockhome entrance."

"What changed?" asked Taylok.

"The Shotai was upset that the warriors took Windsong and you from Eldar Temple without advising him. He organized and armed the acolytes and young men from the village into protectors. There are sentries at the main tunnel and armed men encamped at the hall entrance. No warrior from another hall will be admitted. If we get inside, we will be safe from Xantopec, at least for a while."

"But, Xantopec's men are trained warriors," said Shalea.

"We have a few strong swordsmen," replied Flint. "Xantopec's warriors will have our best to fight if they try to invade again. The entrance to New Rockhome Hall is narrow and easily defended by a few good men. The rest of our men are in training. Some will be fighters sooner, but all will eventually be competent swordsmen."

"That reminds me," said Taylok, "what happened when you fought Berylon's men to get me out of the hall?"

"Ah, Berylon's warriors were clumsy and slow. I hardly worked up a sweat."

"Did you kill all of them?"

"What a question. No. You must have seen Berylon since the fight. He was unconscious but alive when I left him. I did not kill them all. I only wounded two, including Berylon. I had to kill two of them, but the other two ran away."

"So, that's why they were laughing at Berylon when Salton brought me back. No one would tell me what happened to you."

Flint laughed. "I suspect that Berylon did not enjoy his little group being beaten by a lone warrior. I have no doubt that he'll want revenge if he can get it. To me, I would enjoy fighting him again for taking your mother. I think he would not survive next time."

"I am rested," said His Eminence. "We must press on."

True to Flint's word, within a turn, the four fugitives arrived at the entrance to New Rockhome Hall.

"Stop," shouted a guard. "Oh. Your Eminence. Flint. All may enter."

"A squad of Xantopec's warriors is less than a turn behind us," said Flint. "Prepare your men and I will return to help defend the entrance after His Eminence and I take the girls to safety."

Taylok heard the guard touch his chest in salute, acknowledging the imminent danger. He assigned another warrior to take the warning to the village and to the Shotai's temple.

Flint lifted Taylok and carried her through the entrance tunnel. Shalea followed them as His Eminence trailed close behind. They passed a long row of warrior guards waiting for signs of hostility or invading forces. Flint spoke to many of the warriors, as did His Eminence. The guards, in return, returned greetings and exchanged comments.

"Peace and tranquil . . . er . . . This may not be the appropriate occasion for that greeting," said His Eminence, laughing. "It will not be peaceful or tranquil for a while."

The men cautiously joined in the laughter.

"Isn't that Taylok?" said someone as Flint walked by.

"Yes," replied Flint.

"Glad you found her. Is she all right?" said another.

"Not completely," said Flint. "But, she's alive."

"I saw her at the Sling Contest. Most amazing exhibition of sling control I ever saw," a different voice said.

"I saw that, too," said another. "You're terrific, Taylok."

"Thanks," she mumbled, without raising her head from Flint's shoulder.

Many of the warriors made comments about Taylok's sling expertise as they walked the long entrance tunnel. Soon, there were shouts of, "Taylok, Taylok," resonating through the tunnel. A tear slid down her cheek as they walked on. She held Flint in a death's grip, never wanting to let him leave her.

Word of Xantopec's warriors approach carried quickly through the ranks and the men began shouting as if they had waited all their lives for this moment.

Flint said to His Eminence, "I wouldn't want to be Xantopec's warriors meeting these men. They want blood."

"I have no doubt that they will serve the hall well."

The four travelers walked into the village and were met by a group of angry citizens, armed with knives and slings. The hostile villagers surrounded the four refugees.

"You have no right," said their spokesman, "to subject us to potential abuse by Xantopec's cult of T'sa'wa worshippers. We demand that you leave the hall at once and return these legally obtained girls to Xantopec."

"Faulton, isn't it?" said His Eminence. "So, is it your opinion that sacrificing a life or two is good for the hall?"

"If it protects the majority, yes," said Faulton.

"Fine. Xantopec doesn't care who the victim is to be. He only wants blood. Will you, then, offer yourself as the sacrifice?"

Faulton hesitated.

"No," he cried. "I have done nothing wrong."

"Then, how about you, Whiterock?" His Eminence pointed to another man. "Or you, Gabbro?" he pointed again.

"No."

"No, we are innocent. We have done no wrong," said

69

Whiterock.

"Neither have these girls. Therefore, you are all equally innocent but just as guilty. Perhaps, you would have the Shotai randomly choose the next victim for Xantopec, and the next? Or would you prefer a lottery drawing for the sacrificial pawns? Either way, your names would eventually be called."

Twenty-two warriors-in-training arrived at the scene and surrounded the angry crowd as well as the four travelers. The hostiles' weapons disappeared.

"Your Eminence," said Chert, one of the warriors. "Are these people bothering you?"

"No, no," said His Eminence. "We are merely discussing the best way to give Xantopec the blood he needs for his sacrifices to the T'sa'wa. Faulton, here, was about to tell us how he prefers that we select those victims."

"I . . . I never thought of it that way, Your Eminence," said Faulton.

"How do you think of it, Faulton? Xantopec will get his blood, somehow. We can either pick victims for him from our citizens, let his warriors into our hall to kidnap the victims or fight to defend the hall and our people and keep his warriors out. Which do you prefer?"

"Xantopec doesn't send his warriors into our hall, often," whined Faulton.

"Then, if you are the victim of one of his soirees, that is just your fate?"

"I can defend myself."

"Against twenty warriors like he sent last time? You'll pardon me if I doubt that. So, you think it's okay to defend yourself but not the most vulnerable and defenseless of our citizens?"

"You're twisting my words," cried Faulton.

"I'm trying to uncoil your twisted mind, Faulton. The children we just saved from the sacrificial knife of Xantopec are pure and innocent. Both are virginal, which made them targets for Xantopec's convoluted sacrifices. If you are willing to allow these girls to die, who are you willing to save? Surely not Gabbro, there, or Whiterock?"

"I . . ."

"I'm interested in your answer, Faulton," proclaimed Whiterock.

"So am I," growled Gabbro.

Taylok heard the fading crunch of sand as Whiterock and Gabbro backed away from the dwindling group of hostiles. She imagined Faulton's darting, frightened eyes as the warriors moved closer.

"Your Eminence," said Chert, "will you allow us to escort these 'welcoming' citizens back to their homes? I'm certain that you are weary from your long walk."

"Yes," said His Eminence, "a bit of rest would be welcome. Come along, Flint. Children."

Flint walked slowly, one hand around Taylok, the other on his sword hilt. Taylok continued to hold Flint tightly around the neck. At last, Flint took his hand away from his sword.

"You can relax, Taylok," said Flint. "The mob has gone away. Would you like to walk for awhile?"

Taylok nodded vigorously and Flint set her on her feet.

"Don't let go of my hand," said Taylok, grabbing Flint's hand with both of hers.

Flint laughed. "Don't worry, Taylok. I'll be your eyes for a while."

"I can tell that we are through the village, now," said Taylok.

"Really?" chimed Shalea. "We are, but how did you know?"

"The sound of the path when we walk is different here than in the village. Also the village noises have gone away."

"You are very intuitive, Taylok," said His Eminence. "And, your hearing is extremely acute."

The small party trudged onward until the walking sound again changed.

"Is this the front entrance to Eldar Temple?" asked Taylok.

"Does it sound like that?" asked Flint.

"Yes," said Taylok.

"Peace and tranquility," said a man. Taylok recognized Tektitus' voice.

"Peace and tranquility," said His Eminence.

"Please come inside," said Tektitus. "The girls' room is prepared."

The group, with Tektitus leading, walked until they reached a room unfamiliar to Taylok. They went inside. The room smelled of fresh ulok.

"Flint," said His Eminence, "please contact the medicine man Ganaga on your way to the entrance and send him to the girls' room."

"Is somebody hurt?" asked Taylok, in all sincerity.

"No," said Flint. "We just want him to look at your eyes and see if anything can be done to restore your sight."

He placed Taylok on a firm bed that smelled of sweet ulok fiber.

"He's not going to operate me, is he?" asked Taylok, squirming.

"Well, he certainly won't 'operate' you this isa, Taylok. You do want to see again, don't you?"

"I would like to see again, but I'm afraid to be operated."

"Ganaga wouldn't do anything to hurt you," said Flint. "I have to go, now, but I'll be back as soon as I talk to Ganaga and contact the entrance guards."

"You're leaving me here?"

"I'll return soon, Taylok. Just rest until Ganaga gets here and let him check your eyes while I'm gone."

Taylok wanted to say something to Flint, but he left before she could form the words. She lay on the bed and fidgeted, rolling onto first one side then the other, laying on her back and flipping to her stomach. Shalea had been quiet for a while and Taylok assumed she slept. She heard her regular breathing. His Eminence and Tektitus talked in low tones, but Taylok caught a few of the words.

They talked about a new law that the Shotai and Ventaya wrote. Taylok couldn't understand it all, but they droned on until Taylok fell asleep.

Someone arrived within a turn. The man spoke to His Eminence when he walked into the room.

"Is she in pain?" said the new voice.

"I think not, Ganaga," said His Eminence. "But she has no visual perception."

"I'm blind, too," said Taylok.

That brought a chuckle from both men.

"Do you know how long she was subjected to the T'sa'wa's

rays?"

"Not exactly. The most it could have been is a quarter turn. I never heard of the Sun God tarrying longer."

Taylok felt someone sit on the side of her bed. His soft hands touched her face and he raised her eyelids with his thumbs.

"I am Ganaga," said the man's voice. "I do not think you have been my patient before. I need to look at your eyes to see if we can repair the damage done by the T'sa'wa."

Taylok lay very still during the examination and soon, Ganaga arose.

"Taylok, tell me if you can see this," Ganaga said.

"I can't see anything."

"You don't see the light change?"

"No. I don't see anything at all. But, I smell ulok'neh."

"Yes. That's not surprising. Sometimes our other senses are heightened when we lose a sense."

"Have I lost my sense?" Taylok grinned into the darkness.

"Only your sense of sight. Certainly not your sense of humor."

"Can you do anything for her?" asked His Eminence Graystone.

"Eventually," replied Ganaga. "But, it will be many rings before the best crystal treatment can be used successfully. The retina has been burned. An extremely slow process has already begun to heal the burn with scar tissue. Eventually, we can cross crystals and, perhaps, remove the scarring. I think it will take ten to twelve rings before she will reach the stage necessary for the operation. Attempt it too soon and the damage could be permanent."

"Wait. Flint said you wouldn't operate me."

"Oh, no. I will not. It will be a very long time before anyone can successfully perform crystal surgery to restore your sight. But, perhaps, some isa."

Ganaga and His Eminence stepped outside the room and spoke in muffled tones.

"How are you doing, Taylok?" asked Shalea.

"I'm okay. How long have you been awake?"

"Long enough to hear Ganaga tell you that a crystal cure might be available to you in ten or twelve rings."

"That's a long time," said Taylok.

She fell asleep almost immediately. She waked only when Flint returned. She heard him enter and speak to someone.

"Peace and tranquility, Shotai," said Flint's voice.

"Peace and tranquility," said the Shotai's voice. "Excellent work by you and Graystone. The only problem, Xantopec is furious and there are some very angry warriors, including Berylon, because Taylok escaped their clutches. Xantopec will get over his anger. He has larger problems. Berylon? I'm not so sure. I cannot protect you from his wrath and sooner or later, he will try to get revenge."

"I'm not afraid of Berylon," said Flint. "I do not want his revenge to disrupt New Rockhome Hall, however. Do you think that Xantopec will back Berylon against me?"

"I doubt he would actively back him on such a trivial matter, although you did kill two of Berylon's men. The problem is that we have become a focal point for both Xantopec and the Tadi'wa priests. We must not encourage them to join forces against us. They already signed a pact that allowed them to invade our hall."

"Our defenses are getting stronger. Xantopec discovered that this isa."

"Taylok, Shalea," said the Shotai, "you will both be joining me next isa for schooling. I'll see you then."

The Shotai departed leaving Flint and the girls alone.

"I want to ask something, Flint," said Taylok.

"I'll answer if I can," Flint replied.

"His Eminence and Tektitus talked about a new law."

"I've heard of it."

"I thought they said that New Rockhome Hall would defend itself against barber's laws. That didn't make much sense."

"They must have said, 'against barbaric laws.'"

"Oh. Also, nobody could serve Warren's without the Shotai and Venture's sign."

"They were talking about a warrant, like the paper they had when they arrested your mom. Under the new law, serving a warrant in New Rockhome Hall requires the Shotai's and Driggett Ventaya's signature."

"Okay. Anyway, they said, warriors entering New Rockhome Hall without our consent constipates an active wart."

"They said . . . What?"

" . . . Constipates an active wart. That's what they said. I couldn't understand why they talked so seriously about the thing. I thought it was funny."

"Oh, oh, I see. If a warrior enters New Rockhome Hall without our consent, it 'constitutes an act of war.' It means that we'll fight warriors who illegally invades our hall."

"Oh. I must have been sleepy."

Chapter 8 - Learning to Cope

"We have some clothing to attend to," said Flint. "First, we'll find things for Taylok and then, we'll shop for you, Shalea."

The girls squealed eagerly and Shalea jumped out of bed to join the shopping spree.

Flint lifted Taylok and carried her on a convoluted path, ending in the room that Taylok and her mother had occupied for three rings. Shalea followed close behind.

"I know where we are," cried Taylok. "We're back home."

"You'll be staying in the new room, though," said Flint. "If someone should get through our defenses, they would probably come here to see if you had returned to your old room. No need to give them an advantage, right? We're just looking to see if anything of yours is still here. Where would you keep any spare clothes?"

"Over in the cubby hole, near the garden wall."

"Oh, yes. I see. Can you wait here while I look for your clothes?"

"Yes."

Taylok listened as Flint walked to the far wall and rummaged around in the stone opening,

"Did you find anything, Flint?"

"A couple of items," he replied. "It seems that Xantopec's warriors went through all of it."

A cold chill ran down Taylok's spine as she thought of the warriors inside her room. She suddenly felt alone in an alien place. This room that she should know better than any other felt foreign and bare, exposed to the world and without refuge. Nor, would it ever again be a sanctuary for her. She turned her head, but found no light. She could hear Shalea and sounds of Flint rummaging through the clothing, but bound by blindness, she felt trapped and alone. She teetered on the brink of tears when Flint called to her.

"Come over here, Taylok, and tell me which of these you want to take with you."

"But, I can't see," whined Taylok, not moving.

"You can hear my voice, can't you?"

"Yes, but . . ."

"And you can walk, can't you?"

"Yes, but . . ."

"There are no obstacles between us. Just walk toward the sound of my voice."

"I can't, Flint . . . I can't."

"Taylok, there is nothing that you can't do."

"No. I would fall."

"And then? You would get up again. Right?"

"I . . . would fall again."

"What are you doing, now?"

" . . . Just standing here."

"Why don't you fall?"

"I might."

"Taylok, you will eventually get enough confidence to balance yourself, without seeing, when you walk. It may take a few tumbles to learn the new way to stand upright without being able to see the floor, but you will quickly get the hang of it."

"Easy for you to say. You don't have to walk with your eyes closed."

"Neither do you, unless that's easier for you. I know that you have walked short distances before with your eyes closed."

"Well, yes, but then I could open my eyes when I felt like I might fall. Now, it doesn't matter whether my eyes are open or closed. I still see the same thing. Nothing."

"You don't have to see to walk. You know that."

"It's a lot easier, though."

"Now is the time to try it. Close your eyes, if it helps, but walk toward the sound of my voice."

Suddenly, the room grew very quiet as Taylok tried to visualize Flint's location.

"You can do it, Taylok," said Shalea from behind her.

It threw her off for a moment.

"I won't move," said Flint's voice. "Walk toward me. It's very pleasant here and the gardens are filled with succulent ulok. Ohana is flowing and . . . a little to your left. All right. You did it."

Taylok felt exhilarated as Flint lifted her to his shoulder. He hugged her gently and then set her back on her feet.

"Now," he said. "You must select the clothes you want to take."

"How can I?" Taylok asked.

"Feel."

"Feel what?"

"This. Is it yours?"

Flint handed here some cloth. It felt soft and smooth, but large and unfamiliar.

"No. This is Mother's tunic."

"Not yours?"

"No. It's too big, see."

"I see. But, what do you see?"

"I see . . . nothing. But, I can feel how big it is. Lots more material than there is in my tunic."

"Okay. Try this one."

"Yes. This one is mine."

"How about this one?"

"No." Taylok laughed. "This is your shirt. I can smell it."

"Oh, really?"

"Okay, I get it," said Taylok. "I can tell what some things are without seeing them. But, I can't go around feeling and smelling everything."

"You can feel everything that you need to feel, though."

"I can't walk three steps without help."

"That will come later. You will regain your confidence and balance, Taylok. But, it's like everything else that you are just beginning to learn. It takes time. And, you're only three, so you have lots of time."

"That's a pretty one," said Shalea.

"Yes, it is," responded Flint. "Taylok, how would you feel about Shalea having some of your mother's clothes?"

"Mother would give them to her if she were here, so I think it would be good for Shalea to have them."

"Come here, Shalea," said Flint. "Take this one and try it on in the alcove. Let's see how it fits."

"Where can I change my clothes?" asked Taylok.

"You can go with Shalea," said Flint. "Do you remember where the alcove is located?"

"Yes, I think so."

Flint handed Taylok her garment. Taylok touched the edge of the cubbyhole and turned to her right. She took three steps.

"Am I going right?" she asked.

"So far," said Flint. "But, you're still here."

Taylok took three more steps and stopped.

"Am I still okay?"

"What do you think?" asked Flint.

"I think I can't see."

"Keep going as straight as you can until you touch something. I won't let you hurt yourself."

Taylok held out her empty hand and walked slowly toward the far wall where the alcove waited.

"This is scary," said Taylok as her legs wobbled.

"I'm still here for you, Taylok," said Flint. "I'll tell you if you head toward trouble. Shalea, say something to Taylok to guide her."

"You're doing good, Taylok," said Shalea. "Keep coming this way."

"You're getting close," said Flint. "I'd tell you to slow down, but then you'd be going backwards."

"Ouch," said Taylok. "Don't pick on the girl who can't see."

"You're almost here," said Shalea.

"Your voice sounds close," answered Taylok.

"It should," said Shalea. "You're at the alcove. Come inside."

"It's hard to trust someone telling you where to go when you can't see," confided Taylok. "Even with Flint it feels like I'm about to step into a hole all the time."

"I heard that," called Flint, laughing from across the room.

Chapter 9 - School

Following the sleep period, Taylok waked to the smell of freshly cooked ulok and the sound of someone entering the room.

"Hello," said Shalea.

"Who is it?" Taylok inquired.

"Hi," said a youthful sounding girl's voice. "I'm Pumice. I'll take you to the Shotai's school. I also brought you some breakfast."

"That looks good," said Shalea.

"Smells good to me," Taylok offered.

After they finished eating, Pumice escorted them, with Shalea leading Taylok by the hand, outside Eldar Temple to an ulok'neh garden where the girls found cushioned seats. Taylok heard others chatting quietly, close by.

"Tell me what the place looks like," Taylok asked Shalea.

"It . . . Wait. The Shotai just walked into the garden."

"Good isa, children," rang the Shotai's voice. "Peace and tranquility."

"Peace and tranquility," replied the children in quasi unison.

Taylok's face registered surprise to hear so many voices.

"Before we get started," said the Shotai, "I have a couple of items to bring to your attention regarding your safety and security in Eldar Temple and Snake Canyon. First and foremost, you must never attempt to enter the room accessed from fourth level. No one has ever returned from that room. Guards are posted there to remind you not to go inside, but occasionally someone lets curiosity overcome their sense of self-protection and tries to enter the forbidden room. Few succeed, but those who do are never seen again.

"The second item is the upper canyon. It is extremely dangerous to enter Snake Canyon. It is aptly named and the danger is the snakes. There are many hiding places along the banks of Ohana and plenty of snakes to fill those hiding places. Are there any questions? No? Now, we can get on with your schooling.

"We have some new faces this isa. Pumice has brought two

students with her. Shalea. Will you please stand?"

Taylok felt Shalea move beside her.

"Everyone, say hello to Shalea."

The children replied, again in unison, "Hello, Shalea."

"Taylok. Will you stand, please?"

Taylok shakily stood.

"Students, say hello to Taylok."

"Hello Taylok," rang the voices.

"Taylok is a special young woman," said the Shotai. "She is unable to see you in the normal way. We are going to conduct an exercise so that each of you will understand Taylok a little better. First, choose a partner. Everyone must have a partner."

Pumice chose Taylok.

"Now, close your eyes," continued the Shotai. "That's it. You too, Gneissa. Okay. Everyone touch your partner's face, gently. Keep your eyes closed, Gneissa. That's it. Feel the contour of the face and the nose. Do the eyes seem large or small? How about the ears? Does your partner have long hair or short; thick or thin; curly or straight? Is the chin round or pointed or flat? Are the lips thin or thick? Are there any indentations, like dimples or cleft chin?"

Taylok began to get an idea of how Pumice's features appeared through the process. She held Pumice's rounded face and chin. Taylok's fingers detected large eyes and medium ears. Pumice's lips were thin and dry and her hair short and thick. She seemed older to Taylok, maybe teenage. She wore long bangs over her forehead and had something that felt different on her right cheek.

"Is this a scar?" asked Taylok.

"Yes," replied Pumice. "I fell and hit a rock when I was seven rings. Mother says I'm lucky to be alive because it bled so much."

"Sorry," said Taylok.

"It was a long time ago."

"The Sun God blinded me just a few isas ago," whispered Taylok.

"The Shotai told us what happened to you. We all hate Xantopec."

"All right," said the Shotai, "Now, everyone will wash your hands and switch to another girl."

Several bowls of fresh water and soap circulated through the students.

"That's it," chimed the Shotai. "Playa, you take Taylok and Pumice, Shalea. Good. Now, close your eyes and use the same technique with the new partner."

They continued the exercise, changing partners until Taylok had touched the face of each girl in the group. Then, the Shotai called for a break. Bits of fish and ulok arrived in onyx platters and the girls ate the mid-isa meal.

"All right, students. What have we learned, here?"

"Some people have bad breath."

"Thank you, Gneissa. What else?"

"You can determine facial features by touching them?"

"Very good, Alaba. Anything else?"

"Sometimes you get a different picture of someone by touching them than by looking at them."

"Very true, Pumice. What about you, Taylok? What did you get from the exercise?"

"I feel like I know some of the girls, now. It was interesting touching Shalea's face. I know what she looks like because I saw her in the T'sa'wa's Hall, so touching her face helped me know what the other girls look like when I compared the way they felt. Does that make sense?"

"Perfect sense, Taylok. Perfect sense. How old are you?"

"I'm three."

"Amazing."

The next exercise required assistance from six acolytes. Each brought a tray with twelve ulok/ulok'neh caps aligned in two rows. The varieties of ulok and ulok'neh had been randomly placed and were different on each tray.

"This exercise is one we will repeat once each session for the next ten rings," lectured the Shotai. "It is that important to you. It could mean the difference between life and death for each of you on a given occasion. It is the proper selection of our primary food supply, ulok. What do we know about ulok that makes it different from ulok'neh?"

"That's easy," said Gneissa. "Ulok'neh makes light and ulok doesn't."

"That's one factor, Gneissa. What else is different?"

"Ulok is nourishing and ulok'neh is poisonous," offered Alaba.

"That is true for most ulok and ulok'neh, although some varieties of both genus's are not poisonous, yet have little nutrition. Anything else?"

"The caps of different genera are shaped different."

"Good, Playa. Do you know how many different shapes there are?"

"At least twelve."

"That is correct. There are more if we get into the details, but there are twelve basic shapes. What else do we know?"

"Some of them smell better than others."

"The odor of the fungus is an important factor, Gneissa. Well done. Anything else?"

"The different species all have unique spore patterns," Pumice said.

"Very good, Pumice. They do all have different spore patterns. Now, who knows how to find the spore patterns? Shalea?"

"You tap the cap onto a white surface and lift it carefully so you don't disturb the spores. Then you observe the spore pattern."

"Excellent," said the Shotai. "And that's what we will do for this exercise. But, wait a moment. Taylok cannot see the pattern nor ascertain whether the fungus provides light. As long as she cannot see, she will be unable to tell which fungus is phosphorescent so she must rely on the feel, smell and spore pattern. Does anyone know what Taylok must do to identify the spore pattern?"

The garden became still as the students mulled the problem.

"I'll give you a hint," continued the Shotai. "Taylok has to feel the pattern with her fingers, so how can she do this without disturbing the tiny spores?"

"She has to tap the spores onto a sticky surface."

"Correct, Playa. Who knows how to make a sticky surface?"

Everyone laughed.

"Everyone knows that ulok and ulok'neh caps are both a little sticky until they are too old."

"Right, Ula. What a bright group we have this ring," said the Shotai. "Before you, are trays of the most common ulok and ulok'neh caps with the spore patterns cemented beside each cap.

The name of the fungus is written above the cap, along with a notation about its edibility. Observe or feel the cap for its shape, roughness or smoothness, stickiness or dryness. Take very careful mental note of the ones marked 'poisonous.' They are identified with a large black dot under the picture of the cap. Learn them first. Many are quite deadly so you must be able to avoid them at all cost. Also, remember the ones marked 'succulent.' They're my favorites."

"My father likes halulok," said Playa.

"Yes. Well, we'll study those later. Each pair will have an acolyte working with you for this lesson. The acolyte will go over your tray with you until you have memorized the contents. I will come around and test each of you on those contents at the end of the lesson."

The class moaned.

"Our next session will introduce an acolyte who has been studying the ancient language. Her name is Jade. She will teach you to read and understand the ancient language as well as modern Nehwisna. Also, bring a proper swim suit nest isa," said the Shotai. "We will have swimming lessons one turn per isa until each of you knows how to swim."

"Or drown," said Ula.

* * * * *

Taylok's studies took most of her free time for the next ring. Students were taught much of the cavern geology, concentrating on crystals and shells, which were used in monetary circles. When she had time off from school, she sought Flint with Shalea's help.

"Ah," said Flint, "it's Shalea and that other girl . . . oh, yes, Taylok."

"I haven't been gone that long," protested Taylok.

"Your sense of humor is still gone."

They both laughed as Flint hugged first Taylok and then Shalea.

"What did you learn, this isa?" asked Flint.

"We spent half an isa discussing quartz crystals and all their varieties. Trying to find the colors always gets me. Then, we had to identify ulok and ulok'neh, again," groaned Taylok. "It's getting so that I can tell which one it is by smelling. When do they stop teaching us fungi?"

"I'm afraid you will have to put up with that all through school. The study of fungi is so basic to us that it is death to be ignorant on any part of the subject."

"Okay, okay. But, why can't they teach us . . . like . . . the sling, or something fun once in a while?"

"Did you sign up for the sling class?"

"Did I . . . what sling class?"

"I missed that one, too," lamented Shalea. "In fact, I didn't see where we could sign up for anything but basics and swimming."

Flint laughed.

"Well, if the Shotai won't teach you the sling, I guess that I'll have to do it. But, you can't tell anyone. And we'll have to go a fair distance from Eldar Temple to practice. I don't want any innocent bystanders to become victims of errant stones."

"When can we start?" cried Taylok.

"When do you have time off from school?"

"Now!" they yelled.

The first session frustrated both girls. Taylok couldn't orient herself well enough to hit a target and Shalea couldn't make her sling work properly due to poor coordination between her body and arm. Flint worked with her until she successfully launched a stone in the general direction of her target.

"I did it, Taylok," said Shalea. "I didn't hit my target, but I got close."

"Work on those exercises with your arm, Shalea. I'll come back to you, later. Okay, Taylok, you still have that perfect form you had when you scored so well at the trials. The problem is, of course, that you can no longer see your target. So, we'll have to substitute something for visualization of the target. What could it be?"

"Quit teasing me, Flint," croaked Taylok. "Nothing can substitute for my sight."

"Oh, really?"

"Really."

"What did I tell you when you were practicing for the trials? You can do what you want, if you want what you do. Remember?"

"That's what Taylok told me you said when we were waiting to die," recalled Shalea from behind them. "How about that, it worked . . . with some help from you and His Eminence."

"So, you remembered."

"I remember," sniffed Taylok.

"So, do you want to be able to use the sling, again, or not?"

"Yes, but I'm . . ."

"You can do what . . ." Flint began.

"I know, I know."

"Okay, on the blind using a sling with skill," said Flint, "you really have to want it to be successful at it. It will take time and a lot of practice to get it right."

"I don't know how to start."

"You need to keep working on your form, although it's almost perfect. I noticed that you're beginning to let your hand roll out a little on the down swing. It's not enough to throw you off, yet, but if you continue in that direction, your stone will tend to go right of where you aim. Also, when you reload your sling, your absent vision makes you slower. Practice will overcome that problem."

"Okay, I can do those, but what can I do about not being able to see the target?" lamented Taylok.

"I'll speak to the Shotai. He's the expert in that area. For now, keep practicing the release and reload."

"What about me?" asked Shalea.

"You, I can help. Come over here."

* * * * *

At the next school session, the Shotai dismissed them after swimming class and a difficult test on fungi classifications.

"See all of you, next isa," said the Shotai. "Taylok, will you and Shalea stay behind?"

The rest of the class departed, quickly; glad to escape the dreaded math lecture.

"We're here, Shotai," said Taylok.

"Ah, good. I want to give you a lesson in supplanting your blindness with other senses. Flint said that you needed some help in that area."

"Yes, Shotai. I can't hit targets with my sling."

"So, you are only interested in being able to hit a target with your sling?"

"If I can find a sling target, I can get around better, too."

"Quite so. Shalea, if you should find this boring, you may leave and come back after Taylok in one turn."

"I would like to stay and hear, Shotai."

"Good, good. Close your eyes, then, Shalea. Let's begin by determining how someone can locate a large object without being able to see it. 'Look' at me, girls. No, keep your eyes closed, Shalea."

Taylok and Shalea both turned toward the sound of the Shotai's voice.

"Very good. No, no, we won't be using the sling for a while, Taylok. Let's concentrate on what you both just did to 'look' at me."

"I heard your voice," piped Taylok.

"So did I," said Shalea.

"Yes. Good. Now, I will walk about and I want you to keep facing me as best you can."

The Shotai walked slowly around Taylok and Shalea, speaking occasionally. Both girls rotated to keep up with his movement.

"How did you follow me?" he asked.

"We heard your voice and steps."

"So, as long as you can hear your target, you can sense approximately where it is located."

"Yes," said Taylok, "but what if I wanted to hit a silent target?"

"There are no silent targets . . . because of the wind."

"Wind?"

"I'm certain you've noticed that Rockworld always has a light breeze blowing. You can open your eyes for this, Shalea. The wind blows from Ohana's headwater, through Snake Canyon to Ohana's exit from our hall. Air movement creates faint sounds all around as it is flows past irregularly shaped objects. I hear a very slight whistling sound coming from that stalagmite behind the garden. Can either of you hear it?"

"No," replied the girls almost in unison.

"Why not? It's constant."

"I still can't hear it," Shalea said.

"Neither can I," admitted Taylok.

"That's because those subtle sounds are present all the time and you are not trained to distinguish one from another. The pitch of the sound is critical. I will teach you how to listen for certain sound levels and pitch. Each person, stone, pit, snake and ground or water surface makes a sound that can be identified, if you know what to listen for."

"How long will it take?" asked Taylok.

"Unfortunately," answered the Shotai, "it is a very long journey and requires patience and much practice. You are honing a new skill and to be proficient, you must dedicate much of your time. Just remember, 'you can do . . ..'"

". . . what you want, if you want what you do," the girls finished together, laughing.

It would be a very long time before they would laugh at the subject again.

"To begin," said the Shotai, "let me tell you the story of Ripple, a young woman blinded by an accident when she was seven rings. She embarked on the program I will teach you and by the time she reached twelve rings, she could identify any object within ten steps just by listening.

"Beach, a young man of twelve, blind since early childhood, claimed he could, on rare occasions, visualize an entire scene by listening to the sounds emitted from living and inanimate objects within that scene. I confess that his claim is hard to believe and no one else has ever alleged such an extraordinarily perceptive feat. I tell you this only so that you will know what may be possible to achieve if you sincerely 'want what you do.'"

Taylok would experience many mistakes as she searched for the ultimate means to identify every object around her.

In her sixth ring, Taylok began to explore the brightening world of new Rockhome Hall. It brightened for her because she learned to listen, and identify, many sounds of the world around her. Imperfections remained in her repertoire of sounds, however and Shalea accompanied her on most lengthy excursions, helping Taylok verify her identification of objects with senses other than vision.

"There are three stalagmites . . . in that direction. Two are very tall and one is short," Taylok announced, emphatically pointing.

"That's close," said Shalea. "There are two stalagmites and a man, sitting on the ground with his back to us."

"A man?"

"Yes. Didn't the teacher say you could hear breathing if you listened for the correct pitch?"

"Okay, I did that too fast and missed an important factor," admitted Taylok.

"What else do you hear?" asked Shalea.

Taylok pivoted slowly, listening carefully as she turned.

"There is a building twenty steps away . . . there, and a pit fifteen steps away . . . there," she announced, pointing.

"Right," said Shalea. "This pit has a barrier of stones to keep children from accidentally falling into it."

"I can tell that. It also has water in it," said Taylok.

"How can you tell that?" asked Shalea. "I can't see any water from here."

"Flint told me two rings ago that they used that pit as a water well. I remembered."

"That's cheating," laughed Shalea. "But, I guess all's fair when you're blind."

"At least I know the pit is there and won't fall into it. Let's go into the village and get something to eat," said Taylok.

"Sorry, Taylok. I didn't bring any shells."

"I can get us a couple of ulok caps," said Taylok. "Take us to the main stoneway."

The two girls talked and laughed as they entered the busy village street. Vendors exhibited their wares on makeshift tables near the walkway where their customers could peruse the merchandise and make a purchase by calling to the merchant. Most of the merchants marked up their wares by a sharp margin to allow for spoilage.

"This one," said Taylok as they passed a table filled with ulok varieties.

"What's different about this one?" asked Shalea.

"There are some really good caps on the far side of that table. They are imported and the taste is excellent."

"How can you tell that just in passing by the table?"

"Smell. Besides, this is Halsha's stand and he carries the best ulok. That particular variety has an odor that is easily distinguished from the others. I'll grab a couple for us."

"No, Taylok, don't," admonished Shalea.

But Taylok had already slipped behind the table and taken two ulok caps. Taylok ran when the merchant stepped out of his storehouse.

"Thief!" he cried. "You are an ugly Mohk'wa thief."

He stamped the ground rapidly as if he were running after them, but never left his stand. Taylok and Shalea reached the outskirts of the village before they stopped running.

"Here," said Taylok, "try this ulok cap."

"How could you do that?" questioned Shalea. "It's stealing."

"That's merchant Halsha. He has the best ulok and the highest markup of any of the merchants. He can afford to let us take a couple of ulok caps."

"It's still stealing."

"Did he chase us?"

"No."

"Then, eat up."

They both took bites of the tasty fungus.

"Well, what do you think?" asked Taylok.

"It is delicious," said Shalea, "but it's still stealing."

"Okay, okay. I get it. Better to be hungry than a thief. But, remember, you said, 'All's fair if you're blind.'"

"You can't justify breaking the law by reminding me that you're handicapped."

The admonition stung Taylok and she learned a valuable lesson, but she still ate the succulent ulok cap.

The two girls continued along the main stoneway with Taylok honing her ability by pointing out stalagmites and other, less prominent, features of the area that she recognized. Her adaptation to blindness included an ability to balance herself while walking or running. She never seemed to falter and seldom stumbled due to the ability to recognize objects and irregularities in the path as she approached them. She also perceived people when they appeared within fifty steps or so if she listened for sounds of life.

"Someone's coming up the stoneway," Taylok said.

"Can you tell who?" asked Shalea, a smile in her voice.

"No," Taylok admitted.

"It's Flint."

"Hi, Flint," Taylok called.

"Do I know you?" he laughed.

"What are you doing out here?" Taylok asked.

"Actually, I came to find you two," he said. "Word has come from Stonehaven Hall that Pebblic initiated a new push to find you, Taylok, and deliver you to Xantopec for completion of the sentence imposed on you and your mother. We fear that Xantopec will try to invade and take over New Rockhome Hall and capture both you and Shalea in one raid. It is rumored that the Crystal Master has a new weapon to bring the halls in line but His Eminence still thinks he can resolve the major issues through negotiation."

"What difference does that make, Flint? Both of us are still under Xantopec's death edict," said Shalea.

"The difference is this; the next appearance of the Sun God is imminent and when you are alone, you are more vulnerable. Xantopec routinely sends parties of warriors to round up sacrifices during this part of the ring. Disguised, they can travel almost anywhere and if they find you alone, they would have little trouble abducting you and taking you back to the Hall of the T'sa'wa."

"I don't want to live my life a prisoner in the temple," said Taylok.

"Neither do I," Shalea agreed.

"The imminent problem will fade after the T'sa'wa appears this ring," offered Flint. "You just need to take a warrior guard along with you for a while when you go for these walks. Now, don't look that way. These won't be babysitters, they're protectors. And they have better things to do than walk around the hall every isa, so it's an honor that they are willing to do this for you."

"Xantopec's warriors won't come into New Rockhome Hall after us, will they?" asked Shalea.

"Don't count on it," said Flint. "They've done it before. It causes problems between the halls, but Xantopec is crazy with power."

"So, you want us to go back to the temple?" asked Taylok.

"You'd be safer there."

"But, you're here. Couldn't you protect us against a war party?"

"Well, if there weren't more than thirty or forty," he laughed, again.

Flint strode ahead of them so they could walk side by side on the narrow stoneway.

"When I grow up," said Taylok, "I want to join the family of a princess and a chieftain . . . or, maybe even a god, where I can get my sight back and eat good ulok whenever I want and not have to worry about Xantopec or anyone like him sending someone after me. They'll let me practice with my sling every isa and I won't have to run from the merchants, either. Wouldn't it be great to have someone who would help you and let you eat with them? What do you want to do when you're grown, Shalea?"

Shalea fell silent for a moment, clearly thinking.

"I want to meet a strong warrior," she said, "who falls in love with me and invites me to Fireseason with him. We'll have many fine children and be happy forever."

"I don't know about getting Fireseasoned. I don't think anybody would want to Fireseason with me," complained Taylok.

"Why not?"

"I'm blind and I'm too ugly. The merchant said so."

Shalea laughed and did something with her hands that Taylok didn't understand.

Chapter 10 - Betrayal

In the Ring of the Water God, Taylok reached the age of seven and had become proficient at recognizing objects by using wind sounds. Taylok also learned to read scrolls specially created for the blind. The scrolls contained many temple laws and rules plus a few paragraphs that Taylok did not understand. Several included short stories that seemed to be for pure enjoyment, although the Shotai pointed out that most had a moral to be learned.

In spite of all she had been taught, Taylok had not been able to visualize a scene as the boy, Beach, had reputedly done. She did not let that stop her from trying almost everything.

As they waited for Flint one isa, Taylok had an idea to vary their sling training.

"Let's have a sling contest when Flint gets here, Shalea," said Taylok.

"It's not fair," said Shalea, "you've always been better than me with the sling."

"Not fair?" retorted Taylok. "I'm still blind, Shal. How does that not level the field?"

"Just because I can see the target doesn't mean I can hit it."

"I thought you had become a lot better."

"I have improved, like a thousand percent over when I started, but, Flint says you're the best he ever saw. He called you a 'natural,' an artist with the sling."

"Flint deserves the credit for that. He gave me my first sling and taught me how to use it."

"Where is he? He should be here," queried Shalea, looking in the direction of the palace. "Oh. I think I see him coming," She finished.

"If that's Flint, it sounds like he's in a hurry," observed Taylok.

Moments later Flint arrived, breathless.

"Sorry, girls," he said. "No practice. The Shotai has been attacked and bitten by rattlesnakes. I called for Ganaga but I have to go back, now. You both should come with me and then check in at your room. There will be changes if he . . . until he recovers."

"The Shotai?" whispered Taylok.

"What will they do?" asked Shalea.

"I'm not sure, yet," said Flint. "Ganaga should be with him, now. Maybe he can tell us something."

The trio arrived at the temple to find it in turmoil. Taylok heard women wailing and men whispering comfort. His Eminence Graystone could be heard, trying to maintain order. Many people attended who rarely came to Eldar Temple; at least, Taylok did not recognize their voices. She stayed beside Flint as he strode through the main floor of the palace, along the hall to the Shotai's room. He walked inside with Taylok and Shalea beside him.

"What did you find, Ganaga?" asked Flint.

"It is dire, Flint," replied Ganaga. "His heart beats slowly, barely keeping him alive. I have administered the serum, but . . ."

"Where did the snakes bite him?"

"Do you see these dots on the swollen side of his leg? Those are the fang marks. The Shotai received multiple bites."

"Where is His Eminence?" said Flint, angrily.

"Don't be hasty, Flint. His Eminence Graystone may be entirely innocent in this. Tektitus heard the Shotai's cry for help just before I arrived, noticed the fang marks and immediately went to His Eminence. Woke him from a sound sleep. Even if the snakes do belong to Graystone, he does not appear to be involved."

"If the snakes are Graystone's, he's automatically implicated."

"This is a serious matter. We must hold a council meeting with elders in the hall. If His Eminence is involved in the attempt on the Shotai's life, we are faced with the most difficult time of our lives. You do know that His Eminence is next in line, do you not?"

"Of course, Ganaga. I fully understand the complications this presents. Taylok and Shalea, you must go to your room and remain there until after the council meets," ordered Flint. "You should also be on the lookout for the snakes that bit the Shotai, for they are dangerous."

The Shotai shivered uncontrollably and Ganaga covered him with a blanket. Then he ushered Flint and the girls from the room.

"I must go to the village," said Flint. "You should hurry straight to your room."

"When will you be back, Flint?" asked Taylok.

"As soon as the council meets. I may no longer have a place at the temple."

"But, if His Eminence . . ."

"If His Eminence is elevated, he will select a person to replace me as his assistant. There is no guarantee that I will be retained."

"But His Eminence helped you rescue us from Xantopec."

"He received a prime crystal in pay from the Shotai for that effort. His Eminence seldom does anything without some form of remuneration."

"I didn't know," said Taylok.

"Nor did I," admitted Shalea.

Flint departed as Taylok and Shalea made their way via the stairway to the second level and set out toward their room. The girls found the hallway curiously empty as inhabitants of the second level and visitors had evidently opted to remain outside.

"This is eerie," commented Shalea. "I can't believe there's nobody up here."

"This must be deserted as the fourth level. Stop for a moment," whispered Taylok. "I think I heard something."

"I know that your hearing is good, Tay, but there's nothing here. I can see all the way to the end of the hall."

"Okay. Maybe it was just our sling stones rattling in the pouches."

The girls arrived at their room and Shalea stepped inside.

She screamed, "Taylok, run. There are snakes . . . Ow! Ow!"

"What's happening, Shalea?" Taylok cried.

"Snakes. I . . . I've been bitten."

A familiar voice inside Taylok's head told her to isolate the sounds, as the Shotai had told her time and time again over the past rings. She readily identified Shalea from her footsteps and voice. A faint rasping sound described serpentine movement, one of which, she noted, approached her. A hissing sound located the mouth of a second snake, which seemed very close to Shalea. A strong buzz established the position of a third snake, beyond Shalea and under one of the beds, probably where the snakes had been hiding.

Taylok's heart stopped and her brain raced. Without forewarning, the entire scene flashed into view within her mind. Taylok let her instincts take over. It seemed as though her sight had been restored and she could virtually see what lay before her. She 'saw' Shalea, the snakes, the bed and the room.

Taylok's hand flashed to her pouch and came up with a stone. She loaded her sling and loosed it at the rattler slithering toward her. Before it hit, she had loaded another stone and let it fly at the snake making the hissing sound, near Shalea. She "saw" the coiled serpent under the bed and a third stone sped from Taylok's sling. The neck part nearest the head seemed the best place to strike each snake so that's where she aimed. A staccato thump, thump, thump echoed into the hallway as three stones struck targets in impossibly rapid succession.

It occurred in the time it takes to snap a finger and now, the only remaining sounds originated with Shalea. The virtual scene faded from Taylok's consciousness and her eyes connected only with darkness once again. She knew that she had hit the targets, but didn't know how much damage her stones had done.

"How many bites, Shal?"

"Two," moaned the suffering girl.

"Are the snakes still coming after us?"

"No. They're not moving. Any of them."

"Okay. I'll be back as soon as I can," cried Taylok as she raced blindly down the hallway. "Ganaga! Ganaga! Come quick."

Taylok found the stairway by counting her steps and listening for the change in wind tone at the top of the stairs as she approached. She took the flight carefully, not wanting to fall and delay help getting to Shalea. All the while she kept calling for Ganaga. When it seemed that she would never find him, she heard him respond from down the hall.

"Taylok. What's wrong?" cried the healer.

"It's Shalea. She's been bitten."

"Where is she?"

"Upstairs, in our room. Follow me."

Taylok traced her footsteps back to the stairs and started climbing them two at a time, counting each pair. When she reached the top, she turned back to Ganaga.

"Still with me?" she asked.

"I'm here."

Taylok raced ahead, again counting her steps. She stopped at the door of the room.

"Shal, you okay?"

"Not . . . really," croaked Shalea, "my leg hurts really bad."

"In here, Ganaga," called Taylok.

Ganaga brushed past Taylok and she heard him, still breathing hard, as he knelt beside Shalea.

"I see a pair of bites on your leg, Shalea. Were there more?" asked the healer.

Shalea did not respond.

"Taylok," called Ganaga, "did Shalea receive more than two bites?"

"That's all she told me about,' recalled Taylok.

"Were there just the three snakes?"

"I didn't see any . . . I . . . I mean, hear any more," stammered Taylok.

"These are young snakes which usually carry very potent venom. You weren't bitten were you, Taylok?"

"No. Shalea went into the room first and warned me about the snakes."

"I'll treat Shalea with serum. It's usually effective if given soon enough, but potency of the young snakes worries me. Shalea, luckily, killed them all before she received more bites."

"Uh . . . yes."

"Now, this is odd. Shalea still has her sling tied over her shoulder and her pebble pouch is full. Taylok, did you . . . how could . . . this is impossible. These snakes have each been struck with a single stone in a vital place that killed them instantly. Our best Snakers would have taken at least three stones per snake to accomplish this and you . . . you, Taylok . . . are blind and . . . no, this is crazy."

"I shouldn't have let her go in first," whispered Taylok.

"What's happening here?" said a voice Taylok recognized as His Eminence Graystone.

"Your Eminence," said Ganaga. "Misfortune follows us this isa. The Shotai is stricken and now, Shalea bitten and near death."

"My snakes," cried Graystone, ignoring Shalea. "What happened to my precious snakes? Who brought them here? Did that spiteful girl Shalea kill them? Three snakes with three stones is an accuracy level few attain. It serves her right that she was bitten."

"She didn't kill them," cried Taylok. "I did, after they bit Shalea."

"What kind of nonsense are you spouting?" growled His Eminence. "You could no more take out three snakes than you could fly like a bat. You're protecting Shalea."

"Your Eminence . . ." began Ganaga.

"Silence, healer. If your patient survives, she will no longer reside in the palace. It pains me to witness this carnage against the youthful snakes. Even now, their lifeblood lies spilt on the floor. And you, Taylok, are also banished from Eldar Temple. The Shotai was always too generous with the likes of you."

"Your Eminence," said Ganaga, "you cannot just dismiss these girls from the temple. Taylok is blind and Shalea is very ill with the snake bites."

"You forget your place, healer. The Shotai is no longer capable of countering my commands and soon, I will be in charge of Eldar Temple. You may be necessary to the site for the health of our acolytes, but these two are not. They benefit none and I will retain no one who does not contribute."

"But, you rescued us from Xantopec and we have been going to school," said Taylok.

"Yes, a significant mistake," replied His Eminence, dryly. "I argued against the rescue effort at the time, but Flint and the Shotai prevailed. I had no choice but to join in the rescue when the Shotai offered his only prime quartz crystal if I rendered my services. I lost nine valuable snakes in that delaying action. Since then, New Rockhome temple has been anathema to the hordes of the T'sa'wa. They would gladly destroy us if not for our warriors defending the hall entrance."

"You lost nine snakes? Couldn't you just recover them by catching some that breed in Snake Canyon?" asked Taylok.

"Little fool! My snakes obey my commands. I cannot simply take serpents from the wild and teach each to obey. I do not have the time."

"If your snakes obey you, why did they bite the Shotai and what were they doing in our room?" asked Taylok.

"I . . . I do not know," stammered His Eminence. Then, he roared, "But, I will find out . . . and, if I believed for one instant that you . . . you . . . could have . . . killed my pets . . . but, no, it cannot be. No blind person could possibly have caused this level of destruction with three stones. Wait! Ganaga. Look at Taylok's eyes. Has she regained her sight?"

Ganaga came to Taylok's side and tilted her head back, gently. He held her lids open with soft fingers as he examined the orbs.

"Well," demanded His Eminence, "Is she blind or not?"

"Her eyes remain unchanged, Your Eminence," revealed Ganaga. "She cannot see."

"Very well. Then, she could not have killed my pets. Will Shalea survive?"

"I do not know, Your Eminence. She is scarcely breathing, yet, otherwise young and healthy. I have given her the serum. She might live."

"If she survives and I take charge, I will mete out justice to her for destroying my pets."

"In truth, Your Eminence, I do not believe . . ." Ganaga paused.

"Yes, yes," prompted His Eminence. "You do not believe what?"

"Nothing, Your Eminence. Nothing at all."

"Get someone here to clean up this mess," growled His Eminence Graystone, as he departed.

Ganaga also hurried away while Taylok stood in the hallway listening to the sounds of fading footsteps.

"Are they gone?" Shalea said softly from her bed.

"Yes," answered Taylok. "Are you okay?"

"I've been better. Listen, Tay, I've been thinking. His Eminence is convinced that I killed his pet snakes and maybe that's a good thing. I can claim self-defense and show the proof. I know that they would have bitten you, too, if you hadn't killed them, but we can't prove that. I also think that Ganaga knows the truth, but I don't think he will tell His Eminence. Let His Eminence continue to believe that I killed the snakes. It won't help anyone if he knows that you did it and I think he would come after you to avenge the snakes, weird as that seems."

"I hear Ganaga coming back with two others."

"Okay. I'll go back to pretend sleep."

Ganaga arrived and the two acolytes proceeded to drop the dead snakes into bags and clean the polished stone floors with rags and water. They finished quickly and departed.

"Shalea," said Ganaga, "you may end your pretense, now. Why did you want His Eminence to believe you unconscious?"

Taylok heard Shalea sit up on the bed.

"I'm afraid of him, Ganaga," Shalea said. "He seems determined to have Taylok and me thrown out of the palace or worse."

"His Eminence has always had a penchant for building his fortune, often at the expense of the less fortunate. I would not wish that to be repeated to His Eminence as a quote from me, however," whispered Ganaga.

"What are we to do, Ganaga?" asked Taylok.

"The council will take several isas to discuss the events and select the Shotai's temporary replacement. Meanwhile, you may remain here. After the council selects the next leader, things will change rapidly, no matter who is chosen. If I were you, Taylok, I'd seek new dwellings. I can give you the name of a merchant who occasionally hires skilled but impaired youths for his business."

"What kind of business does he have?"

"He imports ulok from other halls and sells to locals. He's quite wealthy, I am told."

"What about Shalea?"

Ganaga turned to Shalea but did not speak.

"What should I do, Ganaga?" Shalea implored.

"If you survive the snakebites for the next two isas, I would advise leaving the hall. His Eminence will seek vengeance for the loss of his snakes and it could include lengthy incarceration plus repayment of a tidy sum as well. I further advise that you disregard the virtue of your case. While I, myself, would testify that you acted in self-defense, if Graystone rules, no argument, regardless of its validity, would secure your release. You are of an age, Shalea, for Fireseasoning, if you choose, so you can seek a young man in Banestone Hall or even Stonehaven Hall. You are certainly pretty enough to entice a proposal."

"I can't go back to Stonehaven Hall," lamented Shalea. "My

mother is still there."

"Things change, my child. Perhaps your mother regrets her actions."

"You don't know her, Ganaga. She's a lot like His Eminence when it comes to fortune building."

"Then go to Banestone Hall. It's big and colorful with a large population and I am told that there are many eligible men from whom to choose."

"Who will help Taylok if I leave?"

"It seems that Taylok gets along very well alone. After all, who annihilated His Eminence's pets? Who found me when you were in danger of dying from snakebites? I confess that I am amazed at her skills despite her blindness. Taylok is self-sufficient. I trust her ability to fend for herself anywhere within New Rockhome Hall. Am I right, Taylok?"

"Maybe," Taylok replied. "I'd miss you, Shalea. We've been together for a long time."

"I'd miss you, too, Tay," admitted Shalea. "His Eminence is as bad as Xantopec. And that's pretty bad."

"Well, I guess that Flint will still be here," speculated Taylok.

"Flint and His Eminence got along while the Shotai ruled," observed Ganaga. "But, the Shotai almost always sided with Flint against His Eminence. I don't know how much animosity that generated, but I would not count on Flint being able to remain in New Rockhome Hall if Graystone is given the honor of leadership."

"I hate politics," said Taylok.

* * * * *

Flint returned to Taylok's and Shalea's room three isas later with the news. He did not enter, but spoke from their second floor doorway.

"Graystone has been selected to rule, temporarily, while the Shotai recovers," he announced. "I believe that I will be replaced and moved out of the temple, maybe even New Rockhome Hall. Graystone wants to make an alliance with the T'sa'wa followers and Xantopec, which means that Berylon and his men will be allowed back in the hall. Graystone thinks that I would be too great a distraction to remain."

"Don't they know that Graystone was in on our escape?" asked Shalea.

"No," said Flint. "I do not believe they do."

"What if they find out?" asked Taylok.

"It might create some hostilities, but if it did, he will control about fifty warriors. He could simply close the hall, again, to Xantopec's men."

"Who controls the rest of the warriors?" asked Shalea.

"The council commands three hundred warriors.

"Where will you go?" asked Taylok.

"I have friends in Banestone Hall. I suppose I'll go there. I might even go to Stonehaven Hall."

"What happened in the council meeting?" asked Shalea. "How did they get around the Shotai's attack without blaming Graystone?"

"An entrance guard testified that he admitted a man from the Hall of the T'sa'wa. He said the man was unarmed but acted a little strangely. He could find no reason to refuse him the right to visit our village as he said he was meeting his brother there. After the attack, the man disappeared, however, and no one in the village claimed to have a brother in the Hall of the T'sa'wa. No evidence appeared that the man did anything wrong, but it took some of the onus away from His Eminence. Even so, only a six to five vote favored making His Eminence Graystone the new leader until the Shotai recovers."

"When do you have to leave, Flint?" asked Taylok.

"His Eminence will choose an assistant this isa. It will not be me. I'll need a couple of isas to put things in order for the next assistant. I haven't been fired officially as yet, but I think it won't be long. Ganaga thinks the Shotai will be incapacitated for at least a ring, possibly two."

"You should take Shalea with you," said Taylok. "Graystone said he would prosecute her for killing his snakes, even though she didn't do it and the snakes attacked her. Ganaga thinks Graystone might put her in prison and fine her as well."

"Can you travel?" Flint asked Shalea.

"My leg is still swollen and tender from the snakebites, but I think I can walk okay."

"What about you, Taylok?" Flint asked. "What will you do? Want to come with us?"

"Yes," Taylok answered. "When do we go?"

"I'll pick you up when I leave for Banestone Hall. I'm going, now, to begin getting the Shotai's papers in order."

Flint walked away and the girls gathered their possessions in readiness for a quick departure.

"I need to exercise my leg," said Shalea. "I think I'll walk to the village and back. Want to come with me?"

"You go ahead," said Taylok. "I'll hang around and learn what I can from the acolytes. This really seems strange."

"Okay. Be careful, though. His Eminence could be dangerous to us both. I'll see you in a couple of turns."

Taylok listened as Shalea walked out of the room, limping slightly by the irregular sound of her walk. Taylok waited a short time before making her way down the stairway to the main level. The hallways seethed with activity and Taylok had to keep to a wall to avoid an accidental collision with someone. She listened for bits of conversation as she proceeded up the main walkway.

" . . . Is moving into the Shotai's room," said someone passing by.

"I hope he restarts the school," someone else responded.

"Who will teach? I doubt that His Eminence . . ."

The sound faded as the speaker moved away.

"Please move aside," said a masculine voice that sounded strained.

"I don't know why he has to have this chair," said another man, also straining.

"He is definitely not going to be like the old . . ." the utterance faded into other sounds as a new group came down the hall.

"Find them," a male voice articulated. "They're in the palace."

"We'll check second and third levels," said another man.

Taylok heard sounds of metal scraping against material. These were warrior guards. She tried to count them but it proved impossible. She concluded there were more than a dozen but less than twenty.

"Try to take Flint without a fight," said the first warrior. "He's deadly in combat and it wouldn't look good if he died in the temple, anyway. The girls shouldn't be any trouble."

"Say, isn't that one of them?"

Taylok froze as someone grabbed her arm.

"Taylok, isn't it?"

"Yes."

"Have you seen Flint?"

"I'm blind."

"Cute. Have you heard from Flint?"

"He came by our room last isa."

"Did he say where he was going?"

"He mentioned Stonehaven Hall sometime in the conversation."

"Did he say he was going there?"

"He said he was thinking about it. He didn't say when, though."

"Do you have any idea where he is at this moment?"

"No."

"How about your friend, Shalea"

"She's out of the temple."

"When will she return?"

"I don't know."

"You stay here," said the warrior. He turned to his men. "She either doesn't know anything or she isn't telling us. And I don't have time to find out which. These seven-ring-old girls give me a headache. Let's search each room. Taylok's blindness won't let her get far alone and Flint's our main problem. We'll have to keep watch for Shalea."

He released Taylok's arm and strode rapidly down the hallway, leaving her standing against the wall.

Her thoughts raced. Those warriors were after Flint and it sounded like they would take him dead or alive. She had to warn him. He said, " . . . he had to put things in order for the next assistant." What did that mean? Where would he have to go to put things in order . . . the Shotai's room? She turned around and walked away, rapidly as she dared. Down the hall, she almost hit someone.

"Hey. Watch where you're going. This is heavy," said the man carrying the chair.

"Sorry," said Taylok. "Are you going to the Shotai's room?"

"What of it? Who are you, anyway?"

"I'm Taylok."

"Oh, the blind girl."

"Yes. I need to go into the Shotai's room for a moment."

"No one is supposed to go in there until His Eminence moves in."

"I'll only be a moment. Besides, you'll be in there won't you?"

"I don't know . . ."

"I'm blind," she reminded. "What harm can I do?"

"Well, okay, but don't touch anything."

Taylok walked ahead of the two men carrying Graystone's chair toward the Shotai's room. She felt her way along until she came to the opening and then walked inside. The sound of a slithering snake came from her right side as the men entered.

"Sand," cried the man in front. "One of the snakes is loose. Set the chair down. It's coming this way."

"Wait . . ." said the other, struggling with the weight.

Taylok automatically loosed her sling, loaded it and fired at the sound of the snake.

"Great boulders, did you see that?"

"I couldn't see nothing," said the second man. "I'm stuck behind this blasted chair."

"Well, she . . ."

Taylok shook her head and put a finger to her lips.

"Why?" he began.

"You would have had to kill it anyway, wouldn't you?" Taylok asked.

"Yes. It sure looked like it might attack," said the man. "You may've saved me a snakebite."

"Don't tell anyone that I did it, especially His Eminence, okay?"

"Well, okay, if that's the way you want it. Right Copperel?"

"I don't know what you're talking about, Coalus. I still can't see nothing. Let's set this thing down."

"We might as well take it on past the table where we're suppose to put it."

"Well, hurry up."

Taylok heard footsteps in the back of the room.

"Hello, Flint," said Coalus. "Did you know that warriors are looking for you?"

"Warriors? What do they want?" Flint sounded surprised.

"Didn't say," said Coalus.

"Can I talk to you, Flint?" asked Taylok.

"Sure. Hi, Taylok. Good throw, by the way. I hadn't seen that snake until you downed it. Come over here. Careful, there are some writing sheets spread to your left."

Taylok listened to the sounds and located the sheets before proceeding to his side.

"Flint," Taylok whispered, "those warriors are coming after you, Shalea and me and it sounded like they were going to take us in, even if they had to fight you to do it. They also said that it wouldn't look good if they killed you inside Eldar Temple."

"His Eminence is acting even quicker than I thought. Where is Shalea?"

"It's good luck. She's walking toward the village on the main road. You could catch her."

"Where are the warriors?"

"Some went upstairs and some stayed on this level, but headed toward the front entrance."

"How many are there?"

"I couldn't tell, exactly. Maybe fifteen or so in all."

"That many? Think I could avoid them by going out the back?"

"If you really hurry."

"Okay. Take my hand, or do you want me to carry you?"

"Carry me? No. You don't have time to take me, now, Flint. I'll try to leave the hall later, after you've escaped with Shalea."

"Taylok, are you sure? I don't want to leave you here by yourself. We might get through the warriors together."

"I'd like to, but I'd just slow you down. You'd better go."

"Okay, Taylok. Goodbye for now." He hugged the youngster. "I'll see you in Banestone Hall as soon as you can make it."

"I'll be there when things quiet down."

"Hope for sooner rather than later."

Flint hurried out the door, turned right, and the sound of his footsteps faded into the busy hallway. Taylok followed but turned to the left at the door and edged down the corridor, keeping to the wall for orientation and support. She heard the warriors shouting over abnormally loud hall noises, far ahead, still checking the rooms for Flint.

"Taylok," said a voice that she recognized. "It's Ula from school. How are you?"

"I'm good," Taylok answered. "You?"

"A little confused about what's going to happen to us. Do you think His Eminence will conduct a school?"

"Hard to say. He's a strange person."

"Yes. Oh, would you like to go to the ulok garden with us?"

"Sure. Who's with you?"

"Gneissa and Windess. We're meeting at the back entrance."

"Okay."

"Where's Shalea?"

"Oh, she won't be joining us. Since the snakebites, she's spent a lot of time exercising her leg. She's out for a walk, now." At that point something jarred Taylok into an unprovoked lie. "Said she was going toward the headwater, I think."

"Toward Snake Canyon? She should have better sense. Too bad. I liked Shalea. Will you wait here a moment for me? I forgot something. Be right back."

Ula raced down the hall and the soft pad of her steps quickly blended with other noises. Taylok waited for a moment, quietly listening to the scurry of people around her. Then, on a whim or a premonition, she stepped into the room across the hall. It housed the huge amethyst geode she remembered from a time when she could see. She stepped inside the room, now void of people, located the alcove in the wall beneath the geode, sat on the floor inside it, and waited. Only a few moments passed before she heard warriors outside in the hallway.

"Are you sure she was here?" said a warrior.

"I . . . I think this is the place." Ula's traitorous voice filtered into the room. "Maybe she went out back where we were going to meet our friends."

"You're certain that Flint or Shalea weren't with her?" asked the warrior.

"They definitely weren't with her," said Ula. "In fact, Taylok agreed to go to the ulok garden with us. I haven't seen Flint or Shalea for . . . for several isas."

"And she said that Shalea is out walking toward Snake Canyon?"

"Yes."

Another group joined them and Taylok assumed it was the other warriors who had been upstairs.

"Anything?" It sounded like the first warrior.

"No, Silver. The room's empty and no one recalls seeing Flint for a while." Taylok didn't recognize the voice. "We checked every room on level two and three. Both Flint and Shalea are gone."

"They've skipped, then. His Eminence will be furious," said Silver.

"How do you think they knew that we were coming after them?"

"Flint's no amateur when it comes to temple politics. But, I think he had help."

"You think Taylok . . .?"

"Wouldn't surprise me," said Silver. "You there . . . aren't you the ones who carried Graystone's chair to the Shotai's room?"

"Yes." Taylok recognized the voice of Coalus, the man she had saved from the snake.

"Have you seen Flint?"

"You asked me that before and I told you, no."

"How about you?"

"I been with him in back of the chair. I didn't see nothing."

"You've been in the Shotai's room?"

"Yes."

"Did you see Taylok or Shalea?"

"We saw Taylok earlier, while we took the chair down the hall," admitted Coalus. "I wouldn't know Shalea if I saw her."

"I didn't see nothing," repeated Copperel.

"Okay. Be on your way," said the warrior. "Check that room across the hall, Steel."

Taylok tried to make herself invisible in the alcove, but knew it would not save her. If they looked inside the room, she would be found. She heard the clop of heavy, warrior's shoes entering the room. The steps drew closer to her hiding place and Taylok held her breath. For a moment, Taylok could hear the person breathing right above her. He'd have to be blind to not see her.

"Don't worry, Taylok," a male voice whispered, "I won't give you away. Tell Flint that he still has friends in New Rockhome Hall. We're here for you and Shalea, too, if you need us. Just tell Ganaga."

"What's going on in there, Steel?" said Silver from the door. "Did you find anything?"

"No. Nothing here. I was just checking out the geode. It's a beauty."

"Quit fooling around. We have work to do."

Steel departed leaving Taylok alone. She waited a quarter of a turn before venturing out into the hallway again. Instinctively, she walked toward the main entrance, away from the direction in which the warriors had gone. Reaching the end of the hall, she heard Tektitus talking with someone.

"It is a pity that so many are being moved out of Eldar Temple," he said. "Without someone to occupy the rooms or care for the gardens, the temple will fall into disrepair."

"I don't know why they are moving me out," said a female voice that Taylok didn't recognize. "Anyway, I have an aunt and uncle in the village who have room for me. They told me to come stay with them until I found something permanent."

Taylok called, "Hi Tektitus. How are you?"

"Ah," he replied. "Did you know that some of the guards are looking for you and Shalea?"

"Yes. I'm trying to keep from getting caught."

"Caught? I thought they were just moving you out of the temple. Oh, this is Lithica. Lithica, Taylok."

"Hi, Lithica. Did I hear you say you were moving out of the temple, too?" asked Taylok.

"Yes. I received a notice early this isa."

"Would you let me walk into the village with you? I think the warriors will detain me if they catch up with me again.

"Sure," said Lithica. "Where's your stuff?"

"I'll come back for it later," said Taylok.

"Taylok," whispered Tektitus, "tell Flint to watch his back. His

Eminence has issued some strange and serious orders in regard to his status."

"I know. I hope he'll be safe."

"All right. Move along, you two," said Tektitus, loudly. He leaned over and whispered, "I see warriors coming this way in the hallway. You'd better hurry."

"Give me your hand, Taylok," said Lithica. "We'll run for a while. Okay?"

"Let's go," answered Taylok.

Taylok kept up with Lithica all the way to the village. The warriors searching for her in Eldar Temple had not pursued them. Undoubtedly, Tektitus had steered the warriors away from the main pathway long enough for Taylok and Lithica to reach the village.

"Where does Ganaga live?" asked Taylok.

"His is that large home with the view of Ohana," said Lithica. "Sorry . . . I pointed toward it. I'll walk you over. You get along so well walking that I forgot you can't see."

"That's okay. Sometimes, I can tell the size of a structure by its sounds, but I don't get into the village much and there's a lot of new stuff. Makes it hard to recognize anything."

"Do you need me to stay with you for a while?"

"Oh, no. I'll be okay if you'll take me to Ganaga's home. He said he knew a place where I could stay."

They walked to the front of a large building and Lithica called Ganaga's name.

"He's not here," answered a woman's voice. "Who are you?"

"I'm Taylok. Ganaga told me he knew a place where I could stay."

Taylok heard shuffling footsteps at the door.

"Where did you see him?'

"He was in Eldar Temple, treating the Shotai and my friend for snakebites."

"Too many of those dangerous snakes in the temple. Okay, you can come in and wait for him. Who's your friend?"

"I'm Lithica," answered the young woman. "I'm just helping Taylok. My relatives live near here."

"You can come in, too, if you like. I'm Cobalta, Ganaga's

Fireseasoned mate. Would you like some freshly cooked ulok?"

Both girls entered, Taylok trailing behind Lithica. Taylok counted the voices of five children playing in the room into which they were ushered. From the pitch of each voice, Taylok gathered they were stair-step in size.

"Out in the back," ordered Cobalta, and the children ran, walked and toddled out, laughing. "Please sit. I'll be back in a moment."

Cobalta returned after a short time with a sizzling platter of ulok. Taylok recognized the tangy smell as a particularly rare variety. She hadn't realized her hunger until she smelled the pleasing odor. Cobalta made each of them a plate of the delicacy and carefully handed one to Taylok.

"I'd guess you have not eaten much of this type of ulok," said Cobalta. "It's very rare."

"The only time I ever even smelled this species was at school," said Taylok, placing a morsel on her tongue and chewing thoughtfully.

"Do you remember its name?" asked Cobalta.

"Of course. It's a reddening lepiota."

"Excellent. You're right. Only a few people in New Rockhome Village have ever heard of it. How can you tell without seeing it?"

"The shape, size and smell, mostly. Our teachers pounded this kind of information into us, continually. I don't think I'll ever forget the ulok varieties."

"I took the same course a few rings earlier than you," said Lithica, "but I don't remember half of the species anymore."

The girls finished their ulok and Cobalta took the empty plates to the kitchen. Taylok heard footsteps walking up the path to the house.

"Good Isa," said Ganaga, who just entered. Taylok listened as he walked across the room and hugged Cobalta. "Taylok, Lithica, nice to see you. I trust this is not a call for my professional services."

"Right," replied Taylok. "You said that you knew someone with whom I could stay. The warriors are looking for me at the temple to throw me out. I'm just saving them the trouble."

Ganaga laughed.

"Yes. I have been apprised of your situation. It's worse than you

111

think."

"Worse? How?"

"His Eminence says that you owe Eldar Temple one hundred shells for the time you spent with them. It's ridiculous, of course, but His Eminence is trying to collect from all former students and free tenants. The temple warriors are incarcerating all debtors, which means they will never be able to pay because they are imprisoned and therefore unable to earn. Someone needs to wake and smell the fish. By the way, were you able to retrieve your belongings from the temple?"

"Just the clothes I have on my back and my sling."

"I'd forget the rest. It's too dangerous to go back."

"How is the Shotai?"

"Still alive, but barely. He keeps his heartbeat slow and, with the serum I gave him, it should enable him to survive the attack. He has a long way to go to recover, but he is a strong individual and, although elderly, always kept himself in shape. He has been moved to the Shaman's home, near Ohana, for extended treatment and the council has placed two warriors on rotating watch against further snake attacks."

"What about Flint and Shalea?"

"A much more serious matter. Flint is wanted 'dead or alive' by His Eminence. He is accused of treason against Eldar Temple and complicity in the injury of the Shotai even though the Shotai denies it. If the Shotai should die, the charge would be elevated to murder. Shalea is accused of killing three sacred snakes. Do you believe that she could conceivably be executed for her 'crime' under the new law?"

"But, Flint wouldn't harm the Shotai and Shalea is totally innocent of killing the snakes. You know she's innocent."

"To prove her innocence, it would be necessary to prove someone else's guilt. Not a path I wish to take. After all, someone killed those snakes and His Eminence is adamant that whoever did it will be punished. As for Flint, his whereabouts at the time of the Shotai's encounter with the snakes are unknown. Tektitus claims to have seen him running away from the temple soon after the attack. Of course, the same may be said for about half of New Rockhome Hall's population. But, only Flint has been accused."

"Under His Eminence Graystone, New Rockhome is going to become like Stonehaven and the Hall of the T'sa'wa," said Taylok. "This is horrible."

"We haven't quite fallen to the level of those halls," said Ganaga. "The village is still relatively safe and we don't discard our human misfits or sacrifice them to the Mohk'wa. I'll take you to the place I mentioned. Neither my family nor Lithica should know where that is until this settles down. His Eminence has jurisdiction over Eldar Temple and its grounds, but the council still controls the village and the hall entrance. His Eminence's warriors will not attempt to arrest you while you are in the village, but for your protection, you should not go near the temple."

"Mohk'wa's couldn't drag me there."

"I have to leave," chimed Lithica. "My aunt and uncle will be worried."

"Thanks for your help," said Taylok, earnestly. "I don't know what I would have done without you."

"I didn't really do anything, but glad I could help. Hope everything works out for you."

"I'll survive."

Lithica walked away, unhurriedly. The echo of her steps on the stone path lasted until Ganaga touched Taylok's arm.

"Are you ready?" he asked.

"Yes," she replied. "Thanks for your hospitality, Cobalta."

"Any time," Cobalta answered as she went to the back to bring the children inside.

Taylok walked alongside Ganaga as he led her down a well-traveled pathway to the village.

"Do you know if Flint and Shalea are safe?" she asked in a confidential tone.

"The entrance guard said they passed his station before word went out to detain them. He said they went toward Banestone Hall. A warrior party from Eldar Temple followed them about three turns later and they haven't returned as yet. I doubt they can catch Flint and Shalea before they reach Banestone Hall and the warriors won't be allowed to enter without breaking a long standing treaty."

"Shalea's leg still gave her pain from the snakebite. She will be slower than usual."

"Steel headed up the warriors and I suspect they will be slower than most parties while chasing Flint and Shalea."

"Do you think the council guard will let me out of the entrance, if I go there?"

"They will not. The council ordered its warriors to assist the temple warriors in bringing 'justice' to the hall. I fear it will be His Eminence's 'justice.'"

"It seems to me that Graystone has executed the perfect coup. His snakes almost murder the Shotai and Graystone steps into the Shotai's shoes. Then, he gets rid of enemies, like Flint, by falsely accusing him of the attack. Next he removes everyone he doesn't like from Eldar Temple by applying a rent fee or accusing them of crimes they didn't commit."

"Be careful to whom you make that accusation, Taylok. There are many villagers who supported Graystone before, and continue to support him. You don't need to fetch an accusation of 'treasonous talk' from the villagers."

"Is the man you're taking me to stay with one of Graystone's supporters?"

"I honestly don't know. I doubt that he is, but you should find out for yourself."

Chapter 11 - Halite

"You said this man imports ulok from other halls?"

"Yes. He brings in some of the rare edible varieties as well as medicinal ones. Based on my dealings with him, he seems an honest merchant."

"Does he have a family?"

"He has a Fireseasoned mate but no children. He hires two or three people to help in his business. I thought you could be one of those."

"You think he might have a job for someone like me? I am blind."

"Yes, I do. I mentioned your condition to him before and it didn't seem to perturb him. He was more concerned about your attitude and willingness to work."

"I haven't worked much before. I've been going to school."

"He's aware of that, Taylok. He's also aware of what you did at age three in the sling trials."

"He has a good memory."

"He's not the only one who remembers that. You were incredible. I'd bet that half the village knows who you are and what you did. You're famous for that feat of athleticism."

"Being famous has its drawbacks, doesn't it? Makes it hard to hide."

"You've changed a bit since then. You're a lot prettier."

"Right. You can say that since I can't see my reflection."

"Think I'd lie to you?"

"About that? Maybe."

"I'm a doctor."

"And I'm blind."

"And a tease."

"I try to have fun," countered Taylok. "It's hard being blind, though. I have to depend on voice inflections instead of facial expressions to understand someone's feelings. The old Shotai taught me that."

"True. One should not be too quick to dismiss voice inflections.

115

A lot of people are good at hiding their feelings behind a facial mask. It's harder disguising your tone and words. Wait. This is it."

"We're here?"

"Yes. Follow me inside. I'll introduce you."

"Ganaga," said a man's voice. "Good isa. Come in."

Somewhere in her dim past, Taylok thought she remembered hearing a younger version of that voice before, but she couldn't place it. Somehow, it did not seem a pleasant memory. She decided it could not be one of the warriors who took her and her mother to the Hall of the T'sa'wa. Those voices were etched into her memory so deeply they would never be lost. No, the voice came from somewhere else.

"Good isa, Halite. This is the girl about whom we spoke. Say hello to Taylok."

"Good isa, Taylok. Please sit and have a drink with me. You too, Ganaga."

In the Nehwisna vernacular, "having a drink," usually meant some kind of ulok broth, but sometimes the concoction had been fermented into an alcoholic beverage. Friends offered her a "drink," on three different occasions but never an alcoholic one. She remembered a strong coppery odor from those few drinks. She had found it distasteful from the first and, although trying it twice again to make sure whether she liked it, attempted to avoid the liquid thereafter. When Halite pressed a cup into her hand, she lingered for a moment before tasting. She sniffed the warm broth and it smelled sweet, neither metallic nor alcoholic. She took a sip. It tasted rich and slightly tangy.

"It's from suillus stems," announced Taylok. "Delicious. I never tasted it before."

The immediate quiet gave Taylok the impression that Halite and Ganaga had exchanged "looks" for some reason.

"Most impressive," said Halite. "And you knew this, how?"

"Taste and smell," said Taylok. "Our teachers rubbed our tongues and noses into these things."

"Amazing. I can use you, Taylok," Halite offered. "My business depends upon accuracy in sorting fine ulok from ulok'neh and less desirable ulok varieties. Would you be interested in working for me as a sorter?"

"Maybe. What does it pay?"

"Taylok . . ." began Ganaga, wearily.

"No, Ganaga," interrupted Halite. "That's a fair question. Taylok, I'll pay you two shells plus a room with a bed and all the food you need every seven isas. You will work at least three isas in seven."

"Does that include fish?"

"Once every seven isas."

"Make it three good shells and it's a deal."

"Why should I pay you three shells when all my other people work for two?"

"You won't have to furnish me with light baskets. Those aren't cheap."

Both Halite and Ganaga laughed.

"You drive a hard bargain, Taylok. All right, three shells"

"Three good shells."

"Three good shells. Done. How old did you say she is, Ganaga?"

"She's seven rings, going on thirty."

"She reminds me of the council lawmaker."

"Hey. I'm blind, but I can still hear."

"No offense intended," said Halite. "The council lawmaker is a brilliant man."

"I have to go," laughed Ganaga. "You have your hands full, Halite. Good luck. Goodbye, Taylok. Don't hesitate to contact me if you need anything. Okay?"

"Thanks for your help Ganaga. I'll be fine."

The medicine man departed and Halite came to Taylok.

"Take my hand, Taylok, and I'll escort you to your room. Along the way, I'll introduce you to your workmates. Okay?"

"Okay. When do you want me to start work?"

Halite's hand felt smooth and youthful to Taylok's touch. She still had the feeling that she had heard his voice before, but it was in the dim past and she couldn't put a face or place to the vaguely familiar sound.

"We'll talk about that next isa, after the sleep period."

"I may be too excited to sleep."

"Not too excited to rest, though, are you?"

"How soft is the bed?"

A young woman approached them. Although, without touching her, Taylok could tell little of her features she could determine that the woman stood just slightly taller than her from the sound of her breathing.

"Oh," said Halite. "This is my Fireseasoned mate, Ruby. Ruby, this is Taylok."

"Hi, Taylok. Welcome to our . . . say, aren't you the girl who scored the perfect round at the trials a few rings ago?"

"I did pretty well, until the warriors captured my mother and me."

"Oh, I'm sorry, Taylok. I didn't intend to bring up a sad memory. Will you be eating with us this isa?"

"I haven't started to work, yet."

Halite said, "In my haste to get you set up in your room, I forgot the late meal. Ruby will let us know when it's ready. I still want you to meet Pumice and Garnet."

"I knew a Pumice from school."

"Maybe it's the same girl. She's a bit older than you. I haven't mentioned your name to her."

"I haven't been around Pumice in a couple of rings. She could have forgotten . . ."

"Taylok," cried a familiar voice. "Taylok. It's me, Pumice."

Pumice rushed to Taylok and hugged her.

"It's good to hear your voice, Pumice," said Taylok, hugging her in return. "How are you?"

"Good, good," declared Pumice; although Taylok thought her tone left something unsaid. "What about you?"

"Well, aside from the fact that I just got thrown out of Eldar Temple and lost my friends, Shalea and Flint, I'm good."

"I heard that Shalea killed twenty sacred snakes."

"Rumors always get it wrong. Twenty snakes? Did you ever see Shalea use her sling?"

"Yes. I never thought she'd be able to kill snakes with it, though. She must have really improved."

"Not that much."

"What . . ."

"I'll tell you later."

"Garnet," called Halite. "Come here a moment. I want you to meet someone."

Taylok heard the tread of shoes coming toward them.

"This is Taylok. Taylok meet Garnet."

"Well, well," said an unfamiliar male voice. "If it isn't the sling girl. I'm Garnet."

The voice location placed him at a hand taller than Taylok. She thought he might be reaching out to her and offered her hand. He did not take it.

"Sorry," he said. "I've been up to my elbows in the slime pot. You wouldn't want to touch my hand at this moment."

"Slime pot? Halite, you didn't tell me about any slime pot."

"What," Halite replied, "and miss all this fun? In truth, Garnet's the only one who digs around in that pot. You'll have a chance to get your hands dirty in other ways, though. Some of the ulok varieties are slimy enough when they're fresh, as you know."

"The meal's ready," announced Ruby.

The late isa meal consisted of three varieties of ulok, each prepared differently, a hot cup of suillus ulok stem broth and some bite sized fish nibbles. After the meal, Halite led Taylok to her room on the upper level.

"This will be your room, Taylok," Halite announced. "The doors have no locks, but there is little need since only the five of us are allowed in this hallway. The door closes for privacy and you should tap before entering any other room. Ruby and my room is here, your room is there and Pumice's is on the other side of your room. Garnet's space is adjacent to Pumice's. You have a window in your room, though I realize you won't be able to see out. It does allow the air to circulate. The courtesy room is at the end of the hallway. Tap before entering. You may wash your hands in the basin in your room, using the water pot located right of the bed. Should you need it, another basin is located in the work area. I don't like getting the rare ulok stained with dirt from anyone's fingers. Understood?"

"Understood."

"When do you expect to get the rest of your belongings?" asked Halite.

"I don't know. They're in Eldar Temple and I can't go back

there without risking arrest."

"Perhaps, I can get one of our delivery people to pick them up."

"I'd just as soon His Eminence didn't learn where I am. If they know the delivery people that work for you, they might figure it out."

"You are an exceptional young lady, Taylok. How did you figure that out?"

"Survival instinct, I guess."

"Maybe we can get Ganaga to pick them up. No one need know where he delivers them."

"I don't want to make any trouble for Ganaga."

"Okay. We'll find a way. If worse comes to worse, you can purchase a new shift at the market for four or five shells. Sleep well. Next isa will be a busy one for you."

* * * * *

During the next three rings, Taylok worked steadily for Halite and by her tenth birthring had saved forty shells. In the process, she became extremely adept at recognizing ulok and ulok'neh varieties by odor alone. Rarely did she need to resort to the spore test, saving her many turns of meticulous preparation, which most other people required to identify unique species.

She spent her income on clothes, slings and worked stones; i.e. stones that are shaped by rolling in the sandy riverbed and used for accuracy in sling throwing. The new, longer slings had been necessary because as she grew taller, the old ones became too short for best results. She practiced religiously four out of seven isas. Until lately, Pumice had joined her and often both Pumice and Garnet, only fair with the sling, came along. Taylok had lost none of her sling skill and as long as she could properly visualize her target, always hit it. They practiced at the remote stalagmite field downriver from the village, away from Eldar Temple and its warriors. His Eminence's patrols rarely came that far downriver since no cultivated ulok fields grew nearby. Taylok knew the path so well that she could run to the field alone without fear of hitting, or falling into, anything along the way.

When practicing alone, she occasionally made a side trip to the

Shaman's home to visit with the slowly recovering Shotai. His spirits had revived, but his age worked against him and the healing process took longer than Ganaga had anticipated. The Shaman worked his own remedies to assist the healing, but still the Shotai remained in poor condition. On this particular isa she found Ganaga, who arrived ahead of her, sitting on a low bench near the Shotai's bed.

"Peace and tranquility, Taylok," said the Shotai. "I haven't seen you in a ring."

"Peace and tranquility, Shotai. I come to see you more often than that," said Taylok.

"Perhaps you do. It's always good to see you. How have you been? Still working for Halite?"

"Yes. I did have a serious misadventure three isas ago. I went to the bathing area in the village and then accidentally took someone else's coat and wore it when I walked back. Everyone I passed started laughing and I finally asked someone why she was laughing. She said the coat was the brightest yellow she had ever seen. I got all embarrassed so I took it off, not remembering that I didn't have anything on underneath. Luckily, I found two headbands I could put around myself until I got back home. Being blind is really bad, sometimes."

Ganaga, the Shaman and the Shotai laughed.

"Not as bad as almost dying from a snakebite, I trust," said the Shotai, still laughing.

"When do you think you will be able to start being the Shotai again?"

"We were just discussing that. My memory is returning and my body is almost ready to carry me back to my post in the temple. Maybe the next quarter ring will bring my return."

"I hope so. His Eminence is wrecking the economy. Get well soon, Shotai. Good isa."

Increase in the cost of merchandise stunned Taylok each ring. His Eminence had imposed taxes on almost everything and, since Eldar Temple controlled the ulok fields, raised the price of ulok to almost triple what it had been. Poor people in the village starved as the fields of natural ulok had been cut off to the public by continual patrols of His Eminence's warriors. He also increased the size of his warrior guard to three hundred men, equaling that of the council. A tax on imports hit Halite's business directly and made Taylok fear for her job.

Four councilmen mysteriously died in separate "accidents" that included two snake related deaths. Unrest grew among the village populace. Posters appeared on village buildings and stalagmites offering a thirty-crystal reward for the capture of Flint, dead or alive. The reward for Shalea had been raised to five hundred shells and for Taylok three hundred shells. Lesser amounts were offered for twenty-six others who owed Eldar Temple, according to His Eminence, as little as ten shells. The crystal to shell rate soared to fifty shells per crystal.

Through it all, Taylok worked steadily, always with a thought as to how she could improve herself and her work, while maintaining a very low profile in the village. A bothersome fact crept into the process, however, when she discovered that halulok, a variety of hallucinogenic mushroom that had been banned from the hall two rings earlier because of related deaths, had begun to appear regularly in shipments, usually hidden beneath some of the rare edible varieties. Halite told her to place the illegal and dangerous caps in a clay jar. He promised to destroy the contraband quickly. Soon, however, illegal halulok in the shipments increased to a point that Taylok could not ignore it and the clay jar had become a large vat.

"What's going on, Halite?" Taylok asked. "Almost half this shipment contains banned halulok."

"Oh, Ganaga uses the fungus in the preparation of certain medicines," he replied. "It brings a good price in this market and gives us a strong profit."

"So it's legal for Ganaga to use?"

"Yes. Well, you shouldn't mention it to anyone."

His tone suddenly changed to a menacing whisper.

"If you can no longer handle this sorting job and keep quiet about our imports, I will find a replacement for you. Do you understand?"

Taylok recoiled from Halite's threatening words as though avoiding a striking snake.

"Yes," she mumbled.

Taylok couldn't believe the change that came over Halite when she brought up the halulok increase. Did Ganaga really use the substance to make medicine? Did Halite plan to become, or had he already become, a dealer in an illegal hallucinogen? Didn't that make her a part of a criminal group? Not that it mattered too much on that score since His Eminence already deemed her a criminal, but this was more than she could stomach as it made her an actual criminal. She had to make a decision about the job, about Halite and Ganaga. She also needed to learn whether Pumice, Garnet and Ruby were involved. Halite's Fireseasoned mate had to know. Taylok's nice, safe environment quite suddenly began unraveling.

Taylok's dreams became troubled as well. Her mother came to her frequently and Flint usually appeared as well. Her mother, frail and haggard looking, wore flimsy, tattered clothing that fluttered in the slightest breeze. She had one thing to say; the beginning of the last words she ever spoke to her daughter.

"Be strong, Taylok. I love you."

But there, in her breast, glittering in the bright light of the Sun God's face, stood Xantopec's knife, bloodied with her mother's life. Windsong didn't seem to notice, but Taylok wanted to remove it and return the mother that she now needed so desperately. Usually in the dream, Taylok could hardly move as her feet mired in mud. Once, however, she found a stone and stuffed it into her sling. She whirled it and aimed at Xantopec. The missile struck the Crystal Master in the forehead, between his crystal eyes, but dissolved into soft mud that ran down his nose. Xantopec laughed at her.

Flint stood in the vague crowd with His Eminence Graystone, waiting for the right moment to rescue her. His Eminence looked askance at Flint and Taylok realized the evil man plotted Flint's demise even then. Taylok never saw Shalea in the dream but felt that she lingered nearby.

Taylok startled herself awake from the dream when she heard muffled sounds. Halite and Ruby often made similar noises late in the sleep period, but these sounds came from the opposite room. She arose from bed, stepped into the hall, and found Pumice's door. She listened for a moment and unmistakable voices of passion reached her through the door.

Taylok had never been prudish but it startled her to realize that Pumice had found someone, someone intimate, that Taylok didn't know about. She backed away from the door as if it had burned her, embarrassed for Pumice and Garnet. Surely, it had to be Garnet with Pumice. They probably had become Fireseasoned without telling anyone. It must be Garnet with her because Halite, the only other male in the home, had Fireseasoned with Ruby, hadn't he? And Ruby and Halite slept in the room next to Taylok opposite Pumice didn't they? A gnawing feeling of doubt crept into her stomach and for a moment she touched the hopelessness deep within her blindness.

"Taylok?" hissed the voice of Garnet from his door down the hall. "What are you doing out here?"

Taylok walked toward the sound of Garnet's voice. She did not speak until close enough to whisper.

"I heard noises."

"Go back to bed," said Garnet. " It's none of your business."

"Is Halite . . .?"

"That is none of your business. Go back to your bed."

"Garnet, sometimes I think you are a coward. I'm pretty sure of it at the moment."

"I need my job, Taylok, so I turn my head. You should do the same. My family would starve if I couldn't help them. At least, I'm not on any wanted posters."

"What does that mean, Garnet?"

"It means that someone could walk off with a lot of shells just by turning you in to His Eminence's warriors."

"I guess you turn your head to the halulok sales as well?"

"Halulok? What halulok? I never see any halulok."

"I thought as much. That even sounds like a lie. You must be in pretty deep."

"What? No. No. I mean, I never see any of that junk. All I ever see is ulok. If we're selling halulok, the entire business is jeopardized."

"This whole thing is getting 'way too complicated."

"Shh! Come inside. He's leaving."

Garnet pulled Taylok inside his room, closed the door and covered her mouth with his hand when she started to object. Garnet slept without a shirt and Taylok's hands pushed against his firm stomach muscles as she resisted.

"Be quiet," he whispered. "He'll be gone in a moment and you can go back to your room. You can't see him but he could see you."

Taylok heard Pumice's door close softly and the tread of someone stealthily moving away. The sounds faded quickly. Garnet opened his door a crack, still holding Taylok.

"Okay, he's gone."

He closed the door again, however, and took Taylok by the arm.

"Are you sure about the halulok?" he whispered, fiercely.

"Yes," Taylok replied, "and Halite was furious with me for bringing it up. He threatened to fire me. If you do anything about it, be careful."

"Thanks for letting me know. I still can't believe it."

Garnet opened his door and released Taylok's arm, quietly closing the door behind her. Taylok walked silently toward her room, but as she passed Pumice's door, she heard her friend sobbing. Why would Pumice be entertaining Halite if she didn't want to. All she would have to do would be loud enough for Ruby to hear. No. The thought slammed Taylok like a blow. Ruby knew. She had to know. It was loud enough to awaken Taylok from a sound sleep and Ruby's room was just one door further away. She'd have to be under the influence of some . . . halulok. It all seemed to fit in Taylok's mind . . . until someone stepped into the hallway from Halite and Ruby's room.

"Taylok?" said Ruby's voice. "Are you all right? I heard you walking around out here and thought you might be ill."

"No, I'm okay, thanks."

"Okay. I've been restless all sleep period and Halite's snoring kept me awake. I guess there'll be times like that."

"Yes. Sorry to disturb you. Good isa."

"Good isa."

Taylok couldn't wrap her mind around the information. Unless Ruby had just told the most outlandish lie ever concocted at a moment's notice, then it wasn't Halite in Pumice's room. Come to think of it, she had heard Halite's snoring, herself, so if not Halite and not Garnet, then, who? And to whom could she talk about it?

Certainly not Pumice, yet she might be the only one who knew the identity of the visitor for sure. Taylok found her bed and lay on it as the questions assailed her. She did not close her eyes for the remainder of the sleep period.

Next isa brought a regularly scheduled off for the crew. Taylok tapped on Pumice's door.

"What?" came the terse reply.

"It's me, Taylok," she answered.

"What do you want?" Pumice's voice softened.

"Wondered if you wanted to go to the field and practice slings with me?"

A slight hesitation followed.

"No," Pumice finally answered. "Maybe next time."

"Okay."

Taylok moved down the hall to Garnet's room. She tapped on his door, but he did not answer. Taylok availed herself of the empty courtesy room, and then stopped by her room to gather a sling and full bag of stones. She departed without hearing Halite or Ruby and set out for the stalagmite field, alone.

Chapter 12 - Citrinon

She had made the solitary trek several times before, so it presented no unknowns to her. She listened more carefully when alone, but heard nothing that aroused her cautionary instincts. Only when she reached the edge of the stalagmite field, did she sense a change. She heard faint sounds of difficult breathing from deep in the field.

"Hello," she called. "Who's there?"

No one answered, but the ragged breathing continued. Taylok made her way closer to the source, mentally visualizing, then physically sidestepping the myriad stalagmites. When she arrived within a few steps of the sounds, she called out again.

"Can you hear me?" Taylok asked.

"Who . . . help me," said a strained voice, its owner obviously in distress.

"I'm here," said Taylok. "I'm blind but I will try to help you if I can."

The man laughed and then fell into a coughing spasm. With each cough, he groaned in pain.

"Sorry," he croaked, when he regained his voice. "But, I'm also blind. His Eminence's warriors blinded me, beat me and left me for dead. Are you Taylok?"

"How did you . . .?"

"Playa often spoke of Taylok, the blind girl in her class and I saw you at the sling trials many rings ago. I'm Citrinon, Playa's father."

A coughing spasm hit him again and Taylok smelled blood.

"I remember Playa. We talked a lot. Can you make it back to Ganaga's place? I think you need more help than I can give you."

"How can we find it? We're both blind."

"I know my way around."

"There are several very dangerous domepits in this area. That's why I couldn't risk moving."

"I know where they're located. Can you walk?"

"My left leg is broken, I think. If you can support me on that

127

side, I can hobble along on my right foot. I may have to rest often, though; because I'm certain that I suffered several broken ribs when they kept hitting me in the chest. Breathing hurts."

Taylok remembered something Playa had said about her father. He liked halulok. She wondered if that had anything to do with his being here in this condition.

"Do you know Ganaga?" Taylok asked.

"Of course. Everyone knows Ganaga."

He began coughing again. When he stopped coughing, he spoke in a raspy whisper.

"You wouldn't have any halulok with you, would you?" he asked, and then answered his own question. "No, of course not."

Taylok helped Citrinon to his feet . . . more precisely his right foot . . . and let him lean on her shoulder as they walked the difficult zigzag path out of the stalagmite field.

"Please stop for a moment," Citrinon croaked before they had cleared the field. "I can't go further without a rest."

Taylok eased Citrinon to the ground and helped him lean him against a large stalagmite. New sounds had entered the picture, anyway. At least three rattlers lay ahead and to the right of them, sheltered by a pair of stalagmites. Snakes seldom foraged this far from the canyon, so Taylok became extra wary.

"There are a few snakes ahead," she said. "I'll knock them off before we try to pass. I can't use my sling while I'm holding you up."

"Snakes?" croaked Citrinon. "What are they doing this far from the canyon? Maybe His Eminence left me a present in case the beating didn't finish me off."

He coughed again.

"I'm more concerned that His Eminence's warriors came this far downriver."

"I had forgotten that you are on a wanted poster," said Citrinon. "Never mind that. Be careful."

"You don't happen to have any snake serum with you, do you?" scoffed Taylok. "No, of course you don't."

He chuckled at the sarcasm, starting another coughing and groaning spate.

Sling in hand, Taylok carefully walked around the continuing sounds of the snakes until she located an open path to the rattlers. When Taylok came into view of the snakes, they sounded angry, hissing and buzzing distinct warning rattles.

One snake set out toward her while the other two slithered behind different stalagmites. A quick throw finished the attacking snake, but the other two hid well and Taylok circled to relocate their sounds. The game became more interesting as Taylok had to dodge between the all but silent stalagmites, without running into one of them, and at the same time keep the changing location of the two snakes fixed in her mind. With the snakes separated, Taylok neared panic. Whether intentional, which would presume an unnatural intelligence for the snakes, or accidental, equally dangerous but less disturbing, the poisonous creatures had arrived at the most threatening and difficult locations with which Taylok ever had to deal. One lay in front of her, shielded by two stalagmites while the other coiled behind her, also keeping various stalagmites between them.

Then, she heard the sounds of both snakes as they began slithering and advancing toward her. If she could see, the scene would be only slightly less terrifying because the dense population of stalagmites acted as shields for the rattlers. Her blindness made the situation worse, of course. It coalesced into a maze within a puzzle and two death-dealing venom mongers against one, albeit very talented, sling bearer. Only once before in Taylok's life had a pleasing outcome seemed more in doubt than this one. When Xantopec held her captive and prepared to sacrifice her to the Sun God, things were worse, but not much.

As the snakes closed in, Taylok readied her sling with a stone. She would have to be faster than she had ever been or die. An idea flashed across her mind as a virtual scene flickered into view behind her closed eyes. The snake behind her had gained a half pace that translated to a single heartbeat over the one in front, given their joint speed. In addition, the one behind her would have to reach out from behind a stalagmite to strike, exposing itself momentarily. There would be too little time to replace the sling stone in the brief interval between strikes of the two snakes, so it would be necessary to temporarily delay one while she attended to the other. Taylok readied her sling for the imminent attempt.

Citrinon's ragged cough distracted her for an instant but she forced herself to concentrate, relocating the approaching snakes just as they came within striking distance.

Taylok whirled the sling rapidly without releasing its stone as she continued to grasp both ends of the weapon's strings. When the first snake appeared and coiled beside the stalagmite behind her, she backed a step toward it. As it released from its coil to strike, Taylok timed the strap, holding the fast moving rock, to slam into the snake's underside. Her motion continued and tossed the serpent high into the air. Taylok wheeled and, since the sling had lost little momentum, released the stone almost into the mouth of the second rattler as it stretched into a terrifying strike, venom spewing from its fangs.

She reloaded the sling, without checking the condition of the downed snake, whirled it while listening intently for the airborne reptile to hit the ground. A thump registered far too close to her, easily within the rattler's striking range. The viper must have been thrown almost straight up into the air based on where it had fallen. The thought flickered through her mind that she should consider herself lucky it had not landed on her head. The buzzing sound precisely identified its location for Taylok but after her stone released from the sling, the rattle continued, sporadically buzzing sharply. Taylok reloaded, but it proved unnecessary, as the snake's rattle had merely been sounding as its muscles quivered in death throes. Taylok turned and made a stance to finish off the other serpent if it had survived the stone she had administered, but it gave no signs of life. Soon, continuing silence indicated that she had succeeded in fending off the reptiles.

"Taylok," cried Citrinon. "Are you okay?"

"Yes," she answered. "I'll be there in a moment."

Taylok dropped her stone back into the bag. She gingerly felt along the ulok'neh fiber sling to make sure no fangs had been imbedded there. Then, she drew her knife and stooped to remove the snakeheads for burial. In a way, this part was more dangerous for a blind Taylok than the original live attacks as the snakes remained dangerous, even in death. She considered leaving them intact, but in the end performed the ritual and protective removal. By the time she had completed the decapitation and encasement, sweat trickled down her cheeks but she arose and made her way back to Citrinon.

She planned to help Citrinon reach the healer's home and while treating him, question Ganaga regarding the halulok problem at work and the puzzling actions of Pumice. Actually, she decided, she would be relieved if Ganaga knew nothing of either. But, Ganaga had told her to contact him if she needed anything and she had not requested a favor before.

The trip back to Ganaga's home tortured both Citrinon and Taylok. Citrinon took frequent rests, coughing and groaning constantly. Taylok tried to comfort the man, but he had been so severely beaten that she could really do nothing to ease his pain. A short distance from the healer's home, Citrinon collapsed on the side of the path.

"I can go no further," he rasped.

"We're almost there," Taylok said. "I'll go get Ganaga to help us. Wait here."

"Believe me, I'm not going anywhere," Citrinon whispered, convulsing with another coughing spell.

Alone, Taylok covered the remaining distance in a very short time. She rapped on the door of the healer. Amazingly, Ganaga answered the door.

"Taylok. What are you doing here?" he said.

"I found a seriously injured man in the stalagmite fields. His name is Citrinon and he has been beaten something awful, broken leg, coughing up blood."

"I know Citrinon. Where is he now?"

"About two hundred steps that way," Taylok pointed. "I was bringing him to you. I can't do anything for him."

"Cobalta," Ganaga called. "I'm going with Taylok to help a patient. We'll be back in a few moments."

Ganaga took a sack of instruments from somewhere inside and joined Taylok in front of the house. Taylok could hardly wait to question the healer about the halulok she had found at work and Pumice's unusual behavior. She tackled the halulok issue first.

"Ganaga, do you use much halulok in a professional way," she began, as they walked briskly toward the location where she had left Citrinon.

131

He didn't answer immediately and Taylok felt he was looking at her.

"I wondered," she continued, "because we have been receiving quite a lot in recent shipments."

"Halulok has been banned," said Ganaga. "It is useful in certain painkillers, however, and council approves import of small amounts for that purpose. Are you finding too much in the shipments?"

"It seems to me there is far too much for the purpose you indicated. Sometimes half our shipment is halulok."

"Some are addicted to the substance and willing to pay large amounts to secure a steady source. It surprises me, though, that Halite would be involved in that illegal business. It is particularly lamentable because regular use can result in death and often the user loses all desire to conduct a useful life."

"That may be what happened to Citrinon. Someone beat him mercilessly."

"And you think he is a user of halulok?"

"His daughter, Playa, said he was, four rings ago."

"You have a good memory, Taylok. I've been meaning to ask you, how do you find your way around? It must be difficult without someone to guide you. Is your sight returning?"

"No. But I have very good hearing and the old Shotai taught me to use sounds to replace my vision. I admit that it gets scary sometimes, though."

"Yes, I would think it could get very scary. Ah, here is Citrinon. Citrinon. Can you hear me?"

"Is that you, Ganaga? I can't see." Citrinon coughed.

After a brief examination of the injured man, Ganaga said, "I need to move you to a place where I can treat you more effectively, Citrinon. I'll find a couple of men from the village to carry you. Taylok can stay with you while I get help."

Ganaga departed, leaving Taylok alone with Citrinon.

"Are you holding up okay?" asked Taylok.

"I think I'm dying, Taylok," said Citrinon. He coughed for several moments. "I need you to do something for me."

"What?"

"Give this to Playa."

He handed Taylok a bag.

"This is the last possession I have in all Rockworld."

"What is it?" asked Taylok.

"It's a crystal. Please get it to Playa."

The bag felt as though it had been woven from hair and the crystal seemed only moderate in size.

"Where is she?" Taylok asked.

"In the temple."

"I can't go to Eldar Temple. I'm wanted there, remember?"

"Find a way, Taylok. Above all else, I want Playa to have this crystal. Promise me. It's important."

"I can't promise that, Citrinon. What you're asking could get me thrown into His Eminence's prison. Give it to Ganaga. He can go in and out of Eldar Temple freely."

"I may not make it until Ganaga returns. Make sure Playa gets it."

He thrust the bag into Taylok's hand, coughed once and, mercifully, lost consciousness. She felt his throat for a pulse but found none. Taylok listened for sounds of Ganaga's return, but it seemed like a turn before she heard his steps approaching.

"Taylok," cried Ganaga, "how is he doing?"

"He's not responsive and I can't find a pulse," she replied, stepping back from Citrinon.

Ganaga moved between Taylok and Citrinon. The people who had come with Ganaga moved farther away.

"Is he dead?" asked a youthful voice.

"I'm not certain, T'Sander. Let's get him to my healing room. You and Whiterock get into the carry position."

"I don't want to carry a dead man," said Whiterock.

"No one is safer to carry," said Ganaga. "But, I'm not certain that he is dead. He is severely injured, however, and we should get him to the healing room at once."

"Ganaga, Citrinon gave me . . ." Taylok began.

"Not now, Taylok. We must get Citrinon to the healing room."

Taylok dropped the bag into her pouch. She walked alongside Ganaga as T'Sander and Whiterock carried the critically injured man toward Ganaga's home. When they reach Ganaga's place he took a side door and brought them inside. He immediately began work on Citrinon doing things that Taylok could not recognize from the sounds.

"Is that all you need from us?" said Whiterock. "I should be going."

"Yes, yes," replied Ganaga. "Here is a shell each for your trouble."

"Thanks," said T'Sander, who sounded to be near Taylok's age.

"Carrying a dead man should be worth at least two shells," complained Whiterock.

"Citrinon is not dead, yet," said Ganaga. "But he is very close. Get out, all of you."

Taylok departed with the two men. When they were outside, Whiterock left them.

"You're Taylok, aren't you?" asked T'Sander.

"Yes. Don't tell me you saw me at the sling trials all those rings ago."

"Sling trials? No. A friend of mine, Lithica, said that she knew a girl named Taylok who had been blinded at the age of three. I assumed you might be her from Lithica's description."

"Oh. I remember Lithica."

"Can I help you get home? Wherever that is?"

"No, thanks. Don't need help. Wait. Can you get into Eldar Temple okay?"

"Sure. Want me to take you there?"

"No. I'm actually wanted by His Eminence's warriors. I need to get this crystal to a young lady named Playa who lives there."

"A crystal? Why?"

"Her father, Citrinon, wanted her to have it."

"Let me see it."

"It's in this bag."

T'Sander took the bag from Taylok.

"It's a nice looking fused crystal pair; ruby and pyrite. Mine is the pyrite."

"The pyrite crystal is your stone?"

"That's what the crystal lady told me. I never held a fine one before. It feels good."

"Can you make it spark?"

"Don't know for sure. Want me to try it?"

"Um, better not. I couldn't see it, anyway. Besides, we're too close to the village. It could be dangerous."

"Yes, you're right. I'm probably extremely good with crystal sparks."

His disingenuous tone made her laugh and he joined her.

"Are you going back home?" he asked, after the laughter subsided.

"I'm not sure I have a home."

"Why not?"

"It's just that everything went wrong at the same time."

"Yes. I know what you mean. Things can pile up when you least expect it. Your mother?"

"I wish. No. She's been dead for a long time. I live with Halite's group. I work there, too."

"All right," congratulated T'Sander. "You must be rich."

"Hardly. Halite's mate, Ruby, does feed us pretty well, though."

They had walked almost to Halite's home and shop when T'Sander said goodbye and trotted off into the village, taking the crystal and promising to deliver it to Playa. Taylok stopped outside her home and thought about the people inside, wondering if things would change drastically with the episode last isa. She felt that she might not be able to live there any longer and wondered where she would go if she left Halite.

She found a low bench nearby and sat down, tired and feeling sorry for herself. As she considered moving, Taylok felt a wave of regret and depression over losing her vision. She always tried to keep an upbeat attitude but sometimes reality dropped her like a stone into the pits of depression. Losing her vision had been bad but losing her mother at the same time had been almost more than she could bear. Time had helped her recover from the loss of her mother, but the sightlessness hampered every move she made. Ganaga helped her find the job with Halite and with it a place to live with food and a bed. Maybe he could help her again although she hated to ask the healer. She would have to explain a situation that she really didn't understand. Ganaga had said that at some point he might be able to bring her vision back with the right crystals. The prospect, however faint, of restoring her vision had kept hope alive and preserved her sanity through the most fearsome times. Why did her world always become so complicated? Why couldn't she just accept the bad things that came along and move past them?

"Because, I'm not made that way," she said aloud.

"You're not made what way?" said a man's voice.

Taylok jumped, because her thoughts had all turned inward and the man had come fairly close without her notice. A familiar ring to the voice brought a flood of fond memories.

"Tektitus," said Taylok. "Is that you?"

"How do . . . Taylok?" said the temple guard. "What are you doing here?"

"I live here, now. What are you doing here?"

"I came to see Halite. Do you know if he's in?"

"No, sorry, I don't know. I just returned from the stalagmite field."

Tektitus approached and whispered to Taylok.

"I have news of our friends, Flint and Shalea."

"Tell me," demanded Taylok.

"Yes, I will, but not here. Let's go to one of the ulok shops with a table. We can sit and catch up on the rumors from Banestone Hall."

"I don't have any shells with me," confessed Taylok.

"I'll pay," laughed Tektitus. "Or did you think I was going to charge you for the information?"

"No," replied Taylok. "I meant that I couldn't pay for the ulok. I left my shells in my room. My luck has been so rotten, lately, I guess I expected the worst. I went to practice my sling earlier and found a man half beaten to death. Then, when I tried to take him to Ganaga's, we ran into several snakes at the edge of the stalagmite field. They almost bit me before I stoned them. When I finally got him near Ganaga's, Citrinon collapsed and made me take a stone he had found for his daughter, Playa. If I had known I would run into you, I wouldn't have given it to a village boy to take to Playa but asked you to take it instead."

"That's quite a story, Taylok. Citrinon? We heard he was missing last isa and Playa left the temple to find him. I don't know where she went."

"Well, she needs to go to Ganaga's. Last I heard, Citrinon might not make it."

"That bad?"

"Yes. He told me that temple warriors had beaten him and left him for dead."

"Temple warriors? I heard nothing of this. That's disgraceful."

"How do you find working for His Eminence?"

"I'm surprised that I kept my position, frankly. I never see His Eminence, but the stories that come out of Eldar Temple are frightening."

"What kind of stories?"

"I'd be embarrassed to tell you."

"Well, it can't be any worse than what I learned about Halite's business and my friend, Pumice."

"Halite's business? Is he into something besides fine ulok imports?"

"From what I've learned, I'd say yes."

"What's this hall coming to? Here. This is a good shop and there are empty tables in the dining room. Let's sit."

The room held eight tables. Four of the tables contained ten or twelve seated customers in the moderately sized dining room. Taylok could hear low conversations from the occupied tables.

A man approached their table.

"Peace and tranquility," said the voice of the proprietor. "How may I serve you this isa?"

"Peace and tranquility," responded Tektitus. "I haven't heard that for several rings. How are you, Bentonite?"

"Things could be better, Tektitus. And you?"

"Surviving. Oh, this young lady is a friend of mine

"Peace and tranquility," said Bentonite. "Your face seems vaguely familiar. Have we met before?"

"Not that I recall," said Taylok.

"I thought I had seen you at Halite's and I heard that one of his girl's . . . never mind. What can I get for the two of you?"

"Wait a moment, Bentonite," said Tektitus. "What are you saying about Halite?"

"Nothing. Nothing. I spoke out of turn."

"Hm. I don't get into the village often enough. Very well. We'll take two of the sweet flavored ulok drinks. You like those, don't you?" He touched Taylok's arm.

"Of course," said Taylok. "But, they're pretty expensive aren't they?"

"I'm buying, remember? Er, how much are they, Bentonite?"

"Two drinks are six shells."

"Six shells?" Tektitus' voice rose. "Why, that's . . . that's . . . expensive," he finished, weakly.

"Told you," Taylok laughed.

"Why so high, Bentonite?" Tektitus inquired.

"Ask His Eminence," the proprietor replied. "The cost of New Rockhome Hall ulok has tripled in the past two rings. Some of the fine imported ulok is cheaper than the ordinary, locally grown food. Makes me wish I had a bigger garden."

"I remember when you could buy two drinks for one shell," Tektitus remarked.

"Do you want the drinks or no?"

"Yes. They'd better be good, though."

"My drinks are the best."

Bentonite disappeared into another room, reappearing moments later with two large mugs filled with a thick reddish liquid. He placed them on the table and left without saying more.

"The village is changing more rapidly than I feared," Tektitus remarked.

"Tell me news of Flint and Shalea," implored Taylok, whispering. "I've heard nothing about them since they left the hall."

"Ah, yes. Shalea became Fireseasoned to a Banestone man; I forget his name. She had a baby last ring, a boy, if I remember correctly. She and her family are said to be doing well. They have a comfortable Banestone Hall home.

"Flint grew a beard, changed his name, joined Banestone's warriors and rose to the rank of Chief Scout."

"Changed his name? What does he call himself, now?"

"The man who told me, made me swear to keep it secret because Flint is wanted both in this hall and the Hall of the T'sa'wa. With his change in appearance and new name, he can roam the tunnels freely. He has even been to this hall, briefly, not long ago."

"Flint in this hall?"

"Well, not by that name, of course. I didn't recognize him when he first appeared at the temple door. When he told me his real name, I was astonished."

"I'm mad he didn't try to see me."

"He couldn't. That would have given him away for sure. I can tell you that he has changed so completely that you would not recognize him."

"Well, maybe Halite would have recognized him."

"I doubt it. I'm surprised you would work for Halite, given your background with him."

"My background with Halite? His voice sounded familiar to me when we first met, but I couldn't place him."

"He's the youth who heckled you at the trials when you were three. You probably don't even remember the incident. I had to forcefully take him out of the area you were working."

"I do remember. He said like, 'You'll never hit this one,' or something, when I started to throw on number four. I knew I had heard his voice before."

"You didn't remember him?"

"No. I couldn't place his voice. Maybe, if I could have seen his face . . ."

"Well, he grew up and changed into a decent man and became quite the entrepreneur." Tektitus lowered his voice so that no one except Taylok could hear. "I have arranged for a shipment of exotic ulok to be used for a party His Eminence is giving to announce the new High Council."

"What is that?" Taylok whispered.

"I think the position is new, at least I never heard of it before."

"Then, why now?"

"The Village Council forced him into naming a new temple voice because His Eminence trampled the rights of the village citizens. It came to either that or battle the village warriors and His Eminence wisely chose the former."

"Your mention of the council reminds me, has anyone ever been arrested for the deaths of those four councilmen?"

"No. As far as I know, those are still considered accidents. I know that some citizens think otherwise, though."

"What do you think?"

"I think that I should only voice the official ruling of accidental deaths," said Tektitus, noncommittally.

A commotion on the main stoneway caused both Taylok and Tektitus to turn in that direction. Tektitus arose and went to the door.

"Sounds like a lot of people," said Taylok.

"Yes. It's a team of village warriors," said Tektitus, from the doorway. "They're taking four people to the council room. Stones! One of them is Halite. And I think I see his Fireseasoned mate, Ruby. I remember the faces of the other two, but don't recall the names. They're a young man and woman."

"Is it Pumice and Garnet?"

"Yes. That's their names. How could you tell?"

"Because they work for Halite like I do."

"What will you do?"

"I'll have to wait and see what happens to them. My money and clothes are in my room at Halite's place."

"Wait here. I'll see if I can find out what's happening to them. I know some of the councilmen and warriors. I'll be back soon."

Taylok sat in the dining room with her mug and listened as she sipped the sweet drink.

"Where has Tektitus gone?" said Bentonite from across the room. "What is the commotion up the stoneway?"

"He's gone to find out," said Taylok. "He told me to wait for him here. Is it okay?"

"Yes. The drinks are not paid for as yet."

"Tektitus said he would pay. I have no shells with me."

"You may wait. Someone will have to pay for the drinks."

Chapter 13 - The Familiar Stranger

Bentonite busied himself with other customers. The customers who were there when Taylok and Tektitus arrived were eating their mid-isa meal when another person entered. Bentonite seated the individual as soon as he arrived. Taylok heard the clang of a large metal piece striking the table and the jangle of metal wristbands. She did not deliberately try to listen, but the proximity and the man's clear, cold voice made it impossible not to hear.

"Peace and tranquility," said Bentonite. "What can I serve you, this isa?"

"I would like your finest platter of ulok," said the man.

"Yes, of course," said Bentonite. "We serve a mix that will delight you and it is only twenty shells, twenty three shells with a drink."

"I'll have that, with the drink," said the man.

"Excellent choice," said Bentonite.

"I have to tell you," said the man, "that in Stonehaven Hall, this meal would cost fifty shells, minimum."

"Ah, you come from Stonehaven? We get very few customers from there."

"Actually, I am from the Hall of the Tadi'wa but I frequent Stonehaven Hall. Our halls and New Rockhome Hall seem at odds most of the time over the misfits. I have been summoned here partly to remedy that issue. I trust there will be no problem."

"Of course not. I am most happy to serve you."

"Good. I plan to see His Eminence later this isa."

"Ah, you are of the Tadi'wa?"

"Yes. I am His Excellence, Pebblic."

"I am Bentonite. I will prepare your meal immediately."

Taylok almost dropped her mug. Her mother had seldom spoken it but Taylok remembered. Pebblic was her father's name.

"Before you go," said His Excellence Pebblic, "I noticed signs on several of your stalagmites offering rewards for a man named Flint, a woman named Shalea and a girl named Taylok."

"I believe that is true, Excellence."

"Do you happen to know the whereabouts of any of these miscreants?"

"Oh, no, Excellence. I would most assuredly have told the authorities if I had such intelligence. There is a handsome reward for information about them."

"Yes. Well, no matter."

Taylok heard Bentonite scurry into the other room and soon reappear with wonderful smelling food.

"This is the best meal that money can buy, Excellence," bragged Bentonite. "And, here is your drink."

Taylok heard the scrape of utensils on the plate.

"This is fairly good ulok, Bentonite," said Pebblic. "I may return often, for I am going to discuss the position of High Council with His Eminence. I may be moving to Eldar Temple in New Rockhome Hall."

If Bentonite answered, Taylok never heard because she reeled from the effects of Pebblic's revelation. He might attempt to have her sacrificed again if he should, indeed, be her father. The one thing in her favor; he didn't know what she looked like. However, many villagers recognized her from a moment of success long ago and she had gone to school with a few of the girls in the temple. Pebblic probably knew she was blind, though, and that would be hard to hide. Even getting out of this place presented Taylok with problems. If she faltered or made a misstep, her blindness would stand out like rotten ulok. She forced herself to sit and patiently wait for Tektitus' return. She tried to keep her back to Pebblic and felt greatly relieved when he finished his meal and departed. Bentonite came to her table.

"What has happened to Tektitus?" he demanded. "He must pay for the drinks."

"He should be back soon. He only went to find out what the disturbance was about."

"I dislike people who leave without paying. The law is clear on that subject."

"I have some shells in my room."

"Oh, no. You are not leaving until your drinks are paid. If you try to deceive me, it will not work. I've seen every trick anyone ever tried to pull."

"I would not . . ."

Tektitus returned at that moment.

"That was interesting," said Tektitus. "Halite and the people arrested in that group are being charged with importing halulok to sell on the illegal market. The warriors say Halite leads a ring with three or four more individuals involved. The girl, Pumice, is also being charged with prostitution in addition to the halulok charge. The warriors say they have several witnesses who will testify against her."

"Are they being held for trial?" asked Taylok.

"Yes," answered Tektitus. "The warriors told me they sent two of their group, on the advice of Pumice, to the stalagmite field to find you. They're also searching for the couriers."

"I never trusted that Halite," said Bentonite. "He has a criminal look."

"Indeed," said Tektitus. "Here are your six shells, Bentonite."

"Come again, Tektitus, and you, too, friend of Tektitus."

Tektitus placed his arm firmly around Taylok's shoulder and walked her briskly to the door. When they were outside, he spoke.

"There are few citizens on the stoneway, probably because of the warrior activity. We need to get you somewhere you will be safe for a few isas. Is there someone you trust?"

"Lithica brought me to the village," said Taylok, "but she lives with her aunt and uncle and I don't even know where. Also there's Ganaga and his family, but I think they would be put in jeopardy if I stayed with them. I'm afraid there's no one. Don't worry, Tektitus, I can hide in the stalagmite field. Few ever visit so it should be safe for a few isas after those warriors discover I'm not there any longer."

"What would you do, sleep on the ground?"

"It would help if I could get some food and my stuff from Halite's place."

"No good. You would be arrested if you tried to go there."

"Maybe Ganaga would lend me some ulok and a pallet for a few isas."

"A good plan."

"By the way, Tektitus, a man who called himself 'His Excellence Pebblic' came to Bentonite's eating place less than a turn ago and told Bentonite he was going to see His Eminence to discuss the High Council position in Eldar Temple."

"I wish I had seen him."

"So do I. That name, Pebblic, is the same as my father, who tried to have me sacrificed once before and succeeded in having my mother sacrificed. He's also the reason I'm blind."

"Are you sure this man is your father and not some other Pebblic?"

"No. That's the infuriating part. The name is the same, but it could be a common name in Stonehaven Hall, couldn't it? I've never seen my father or heard him speak."

"Maybe I can find out for you, Taylok. Do you know how he was dressed?"

"All in black? No, seriously, I haven't a clue."

"What? Oh, I see."

"Right, I don't. Bentonite could tell you. Wait. I just remembered that he had a large pendant hanging on a necklace and several metal bracelets. I heard those."

"I'll go back and ask Bentonite. Wait for me here."

Taylok leaned against the wall of Bentonite's place as she waited for Tektitus. He returned, shortly.

"Pebblic should be easy to identify from what you and Bentonite told me," Tektitus said. "Now. Would you like me to walk with you to Ganaga's?"

"Weren't you going to Halite's to pick up an order of ulok?"

"Yes, but he's in jail."

"I could put your order together for you if you would get me in and out without me being arrested."

"Perhaps, if you go as my assistant, we could avoid the warriors. I know some of them as well so they might not ask too many questions."

"I'm willing to try."

"I'm beginning to see why Flint held you in such high regard, Taylok. You're fearless."

"Then, why do my teeth chatter when I think about going past those warriors?"

"Even better, you go where you fear to go. The village warriors hold some respect for me and many of them knew Flint. He had been well liked among the warrior guard. I think they will look the other way as we enter Halite's establishment. Are you ready?"

"I'm ready. We can't wait here forever."

Tektitus walked alongside Taylok as they made their way up the main stoneway. Before they arrived at their destination, Tektitus spoke to two warriors who stood guarding the jail entrance.

"Who's your friend, Tektitus?" asked one.

"My assistant," said Tektitus, smoothly. "We are going to Halite's shop to retrieve His Eminence's order. Will one of you go with us?"

"We must stay on guard, here. I think it's okay for you to go inside Halite's shop, though. All the illegal halulok has been removed. Do you think your 'assistant' can find your order?"

"Oh, yes. We'll have no trouble."

"Then, good isa, Tektitus."

"Thanks and good isa," grunted Tektitus, as he and Taylok walked past the warriors.

Taylok did not speak until they were beyond the hearing of the warriors.

"Glad they didn't recognize me," she said.

"Oh, they recognized you," Tektitus laughed. "Both men were at the trials when you broke all the records. You have changed, but you are still recognizable."

"Then, why . . .?"

"Why didn't they arrest you? One is a friend of mine and Flint trained the other. Both admire you for overcoming your handicap, not to mention your unique expertise with the sling. You are in no danger of arrest from those two or several others in the guard."

Taylok walked a little taller. She had friends in important places. They reached Halite's shop in short order. Two warriors were posted at the shop entrance.

"What is your business here?" demanded one of the warriors.

"We are on a mission for His Eminence," said Tektitus. "He purchased two large baskets of fine ulok from Halite for a special meal. I trust the baskets are ready?"

"I know nothing of such baskets," replied the warrior. "I suppose, since His Eminence has already paid for them, you can retrieve the ulok baskets if you can find them. I'll help you search."

"Greatly appreciated," said Tektitus, in a good-humored tone. "My assistant has been trained to evaluate ulok species and quality. She will check the baskets for proper content."

"She may have to do more than that," said the warrior. "Our men went over the merchandise thoroughly to remove any halulok and I fear they may have scattered any baskets arranged to sell."

"That shouldn't be a problem for my assistant. She can reassemble the baskets if you'll give us a little time."

"Very well. Shall we go inside?"

Taylok located four baskets prepared for sale. None contained halulok, but the warriors had dumped them out, ostensibly, to make sure. As Tektitus and the warrior looked on, Taylok expertly separated the common varieties of ulok from the finer ones and filled a basket, pretending to look through the piles of ulok while actually feeling and smelling.

"You're very adept at discerning the better ulok," said the warrior, watching Taylok work rapidly with the fungus.

"I learned under the Shotai," said Taylok, pretending to glance toward the warrior.

"Very well. You can finish here without me, Tektitus. We're waiting for a blind girl who worked here."

"Oh," said Tektitus. "What did she do?"

"All I know is that she might be part of an illegal ring selling halulok."

"We'll be out of here in a short time."

The warrior departed and Taylok raced up the narrow hallway to her room with Tektitus alongside.

"Here are my shells," said Taylok, lifting the basket covered by clothing.

She folded her bedding pad and placed it in the basket with her shells and clothes.

"This is it," she exclaimed. "Let's go."

"Won't you have a hard time carrying all this to the stalagmite field?"

"Maybe I can get the shells exchanged for a couple of crystals."

"That's a good idea. A trader is located nearby. I'll carry your basket and you carry the ulok. Okay?"

They made it to the trader and Tektitus handled the exchange for Taylok. He received two crystals with four shells remaining.

"This crystal is very high quality," Tektitus remarked, handing the stone to Taylok. "This one is good quality, but smaller and therefore of less value. The shells will buy a drink. Be careful, Taylok, for there are thieves on the lookout for someone like you. They might believe they can take your possessions. They're mostly in the village, but some ply their nefarious activities on the stoneways. Not only that, but there are rumors that a large band of Xantopec's warriors have invaded Banestone Hall. Thus far they have not challenged New Rockhome Hall, but I fear that war is approaching. You should not be out alone if it comes."

He pressed the second stone and the shells into Taylok's hand.

"I never ran into any thieves on the path to the stalagmite field," said Taylok.

"Maybe you never carried anything worth stealing before."

"I'll keep my money hidden. Thanks for your help, Tektitus."

"Glad to be of service. Thank you for helping me with the ulok basket. Be careful, Taylok. I must repeat, it is not safe for you to be alone."

Chapter 14 - Flint

Banestone Hall bustled with activity. Many warriors camped by Ohana for the sleep period. There were far too many to be a defensive force.

Flint walked the perimeter of the encampment, recognizing that these warriors were not from Banestone Hall. Many wore the trappings of Xantopec, high priest of the Sun God, marking them from the Hall of the T'sa'wa. The incursion into Banestone Hall had been unexpected and although there had been no resistance, the villagers were visibly upset, lining their village limits with Banestone warriors. Seven of these warriors stopped and questioned him before allowing Flint to enter to the village. He trudged to the council house where he spoke to two more warriors before entering. Inside, he faced three guards, barring his way to the council chamber.

"Who are you and what is your business here?" demanded the senior guard.

"I am Diamond," said Flint. "The council is expecting me."

The guard consulted his tablet.

"Yes, Diamond. You may enter."

Inside the council room twelve council members and two warriors turned to welcome Flint with stony faces. Among the council members sat Warrior Chief Lithic, Flint/Diamond's superior officer. Next to the Warrior Chief sat his minion, Sericite, with whom Flint/Diamond had become all too familiar, as Sericite opposed him at every opportunity.

"Please be seated, Diamond," said Leana. "We have discussed your assignment and agree that, difficult as it may be, the spy mission is needed to gain enough information to save our citizens from death at the hands of Xantopec's warriors who camp on the outskirts of our village."

He had known Leana for several rings as New Rockhome Hall business brought him to Banestone Hall on several occasions. Leana looked to be about thirty rings in age and Flint considered her a strikingly handsome woman. Her height seemed average and her platinum hair fell straight and shining to her shoulders. Her eyes were large and inquisitive, with pale blue irises. The clothes she chose hid a rather intriguing figure, which only now and again made itself noticeable through her movements. She wore no facial enhancements such as the red clay paint some of the bolder women used on their lips and cheeks. Leana had never succumbed to the allure of repeated requests for Fireseasoning and remained childless. Her hands exhibited an active gardening hobby, which many knew to be enhancement of ulok'neh strains for improved lighting.

Leana held the position of Speaker Chief in the council and had a reputation for decisive action. No one considered her warlike but she directed the council to certain scientific and practical endeavors that could be seen as defensive. The men of the council had been unwilling to assign the simpler and better known name of Council Chief to a woman, although that is precisely the position she occupied.

Since the infringement of warriors of the T'sa'wa, there had been considerable anxiety in the village and the council. The angst became more apparent as Flint sat to receive his assignment. The council bickered on many occasions, but the high tension created by the incursion brought them together. Leana spoke directly to Flint/Diamond, but the council members continually nodded solemn agreement.

She said, "Your scouting mission is twofold; first, determine if Xantopec's warriors have made an incursion, similar to our own, into New Rockhome Hall and second; discover who the temple warriors will support if there is conflict. We must gain information on New Rockhome Hall's position with regard to Xantopec's bellicose actions. Since His Eminence Graystone has taken control of Eldar Temple and brought in Pebblic, we can no longer trust him to side with Banestone Hall. His Eminence Graystone refuses to meet with us to discuss this question and we must assume the worst until we have direct information."

"Have you attempted to contact the village council? Someone like Driggett Ventaya might have a sympathetic ear." suggested Flint/Diamond.

"Of course," answered Leana. "Unfortunately, Eldar Temple

149

warriors now outnumber the village guard by more than three hundred. The village would be overwhelmed if His Eminence wished it so. The village council is with us, but powerless. We feel this war is coming and are not in a position to stop or survive it."

Warrior Chief Lithic stared at the floor as Leana spoke. As Flint/Diamond's superior, he should have given the orders, not Leana. Flint's brow sagged as Lithic's eyes refused to meet his.

Leana continued, "This mission demands two strong men who excel at diplomacy, can fight and know the territory to which they are being sent. Two serve better than one for if one falls victim to foul play, the mission may still be completed. Chief Lithic has chosen Sericite to accompany you."

Sericite's presence became suddenly clear. Still, he remained the one man in Banestone Hall's tribe that Flint would not have chosen. Sericite had been a continual stumbling block in Flint's quest to improve his rank with the warriors. Sericite carried the mantle of Lithic's favor and seemed bent at every turn to impede or destroy Flint/Diamond. Flint had come to realize that Lithic encouraged Sericite to defeat him, possibly out of fear that Diamond might be considered Lithic's replacement if the Warrior Chief fell to disfavor in the council. Often, rising in the ranks too quickly rendered political enemies.

"Is Sericite acquainted with New Rockhome Hall?" asked Flint.

"I defer to Warrior Chief Lithic for that answer," responded Leana.

Sericite stared at the table. Lithic raised his head but did not look at anyone and still refused to lock eyes with Flint. He crossed his arms defiantly before speaking yet his voice seemed equivocal and lacking sincerity.

"Sericite went to New Rockhome Hall two rings ago," Chief Lithic said, his eyes blinking rapidly. "He assures me that he knows the territory well and the political landscape equally."

Flint shrugged at the lie. Sericite declared less than a ring before that he had never been to New Rockhome Hall nor would he ever go to that, 'Dome-pit of the world.' Sericite ended his sentences like he had asked a question, dangling his final word in a most aggravating manner.

"When do you wish us to leave?" asked Flint/Diamond,

resignedly.

"As soon as feasible," said Leana, "this isa if possible."

Sericite spoke, "I do not believe Diamond is the right man for this assignment. He is too close to some of the New Rockhome citizens."

Sericite's habit of raising the pitch of each ending word made Flint/Diamond grind his teeth.

Chief Lithic nodded his head.

"You are out of line, Warrior Sericite," spat Leana. "Diamond is the council's choice for the mission. You will accompany him because Chief Lithic recommends you. If you do not wish to go with Diamond on this mission, there are numerous others who, in my opinion, better qualify for the journey."

Abashed, Sericite looked to Chief Lithic, but the Warrior Chief sat stolidly examining his feet. Sericite glanced at Flint/Diamond, then at Leana.

"My apology, Speaker Chief. I spoke out of turn," he said, making two questions out of the speech.

"Then, let there be an end to this conversation and a beginning of action," declared Leana, pounding her fist on the table.

Flint/Diamond stayed ready for a quick departure, as it seemed in his nature to be prepared for new adventure or adversity. It struck him that this assignment contained both. He had made several friends in Banestone village, but the men would understand that work took him away while the women would argue that his compensation lacked sufficiently that he should reconsider. Both were right, but in the end, the adventure won out. He would mention his imminent absence to Sapphirus, his Fireseasoned mate and close female companion, and Banic, whom he trusted. Sapphirus would let Shalea know he would be gone for a while. The rest might wonder at his absence, but by the time they figured it out, he would be back.

He wondered at Sericite's real role in this endeavor. Flint did not believe for a moment that Sericite had been chosen because he fit the assignment, so what did his part entail? It would be easy to believe that Sericite had orders to kill Diamond once they were outside the Banestone Hall purview. Flint did not fear Sericite in a fair fight, but knew that the man would seek some advantage before acting. He would have to sleep lightly.

Flint/Diamond arrived at the exit as the wheel reached the marking for a new isa. Most of the Village would be asleep. He waited half a turn for Sericite and finally the man appeared, carrying a bundle.

"Ready?" Flint asked.

"Yes," replied Sericite, yawning, making a question even though he only said one word.

Flint resisted the urge to yawn and instead took a deep breath.

"Did you tell Sapphirus you would be gone for a while?" asked Sericite.

"Yes. She seemed distraught over the news," Flint/Diamond laughed.

"I'm sure," grinned Sericite, mischievously. "She probably has another in her bed already."

"No doubt," said Flint/Diamond, "Although it will be harder since she's staying with her mother while I'm gone."

"They all say that."

"Stop doing that."

"Doing what?"

"That. Everything you say sounds like a question."

"That's just the way I talk. Get over it."

Flint/Diamond shrugged.

"I don't have time for this. Why did Chief Lithic assign you to this trip?"

"Why not? It's his prerogative, isn't it?"

"Not to lie to the council. That's a death wish. You told me that you had never been to New Rockhome Hall. So did you lie to Lithic or me? Or, did Lithic lie to the council?"

"Yes, Lithic lied to the council," admitted Sericite. "Not that the information will do you any good."

"Do me any good? Why would I think that? I challenged him before he spoke but he lied anyway. The council knows where you have been . . . and where you haven't. Don't think they will accept his lie without confirmation. It would not surprise me if Lithic was gone when we return . . . if we return."

"What's that supposed to mean, Diamond? Is that a threat?"

"I only state the obvious, Sericite. This is a dangerous mission

152

and our chances of success are minimal as are our chances of survival. We are entering a hostile territory where you have never been and are charged with gathering sensitive information. Spies are thrown into Snake Canyon."

"And this Snake Canyon is a dangerous place?"

"Large stones and boulders offer the snakes excellent hiding places. Just walking through the area is a death warrant. If you are a good swimmer, you can escape to the far banks of Ohana, but I'm not even sure what awaits on that side of the river."

"Swim? No one said anything about swimming," said Sericite, a deep frown furrowing his brow.

"Are you a poor swimmer, Sericite? Better not get caught, then."

The men fell silent as they moved quickly through the main tunnel. They stopped twice to rest and eat, and then returned to the lengthy trek. When they arrived at the New Rockhome entrance tunnel, three warrior guards stopped them.

"What is your business in New Rockhome Hall?" asked one of the guards.

"We came to see the Mystical Grotto," said Flint/Diamond.

"You and a thousand others," laughed the guard. "Very well, you must pay thirty shells each to visit the Mystical Grotto viewing site."

"Thirty shells? That's robbery. You collect that here?" asked Sericite. "But, will someone else be trying to collect inside?"

"Yes, we collect here and no, no one else will try to collect," said the guard, handing both men a paper with "Mystical Grotto Admission" written on it.

Flint/Diamond and Sericite paid the guard and continued through to the hall where several more warriors were stationed. They examined the papers and waved the two men onto the path to the village. Flint noticed four warriors that he knew well, but none indicated that they recognized him. They probably would not have detained him in any event.

Tired, Flint sought a place to stay during the sleep turns. They found rooms at Fairstone Inn near the center of the village. Sericite grumbled about the price of the rooms, but Flint knew they were cheaper than in Banestone Hall. Flint chose a room with a solid lock on the door. He didn't want Sericite making a sneak attempt on his life while he slept.

They ate in the dining area of the Fairstone and had a good quality meal of fish and ulok. Flint didn't know any of the people who served their meal, but asked a few questions, anyway.

"This is excellent food," Flint said to their waitress.

"We serve only the best at Fairstone," she responded.

"I'll bet you get a lot of temple people in here to eat, right?"

"We get a few," she answered.

Seeming nervous, her eyes darted from Flint to Sericite.

"Does His Eminence ever eat here?" asked Flint.

"I saw him in here only once."

"How about the Shotai?"

"I haven't seen him in two rings."

"Clayra," came the call from the kitchen. "We have other guests."

"I have to go," she said.

Suiting action to her words, Clayra left their table to serve others.

"What was that about?" asked Sericite.

"I happen to know that His Eminence eats here at least one isa in five. He always bragged about his accomplishments to whoever would listen."

"How will that help us?"

"Someone here knows His Eminence's plans. If we can get them to talk, we can at least get the street version."

"You're insane. No one will talk to us here. If they did, we couldn't trust their words."

"You'd prefer to just sit here looking at the ulok? Ulok doesn't talk, Sericite."

"It talks a little inside my stomach."

Flint/Diamond smiled in spite of himself. Sericite almost laughed out loud at his own joke. Flint circulated through the room, trying unsuccessfully, to get information. Sericite also moved through the room. At one table, Flint heard a part of Sericite's question.

" . . . Called Flame?"

The negative response brought a frown to Sericite's face. Flint heard nothing more of the conversations.

After the sleep period, Flint found that Sericite had risen earlier and gone. Flint decided to find the Shotai. He traveled to the Shaman's home and found it in disarray with several warriors working inside. He did not recognize any of the men.

"What happened?" Flint asked a warrior who seemed in charge.

The warrior looked Flint over carefully and took him aside before answering.

"Assassins attacked and killed the Shaman last isa," the warrior finally replied.

"The Shaman dead? What about the Shotai? He stayed here not too long ago."

"The Shotai lives but has been injured in the attack. A blind girl saved him. Who are you and what is your interest in this?"

"I am Diamond from Banestone Hall," said Flint. "I am an old friend of the Shotai. Can you tell me where they have taken him?"

"Diamond? You name is unknown to me, yet your face is somehow familiar."

"What is your name?" asked Flint.

"I am Cobalt. Yes, I will think of where I have seen you before. Have you always worn the beard?"

"No. I'm sure you have a very good memory, Cobalt. Again, I ask if you can tell me where they took the Shotai?"

"They took him to Eldar Temple to attend his wounds."

"The temple? Someone there tried to kill the Shotai in the Ring of the Water God."

"That was a man called Flint, who is wanted and no longer resides in New Rockhome Hall."

"Flint did not attempt to harm the Shotai. Someone with a particularly good knowledge of snakes did it. Someone who is still inside Eldar Temple."

Cobalt stared grimly at Flint. When he spoke, the words were carefully articulated.

"Tell me how you think you know this, Diamond."

Cobalt's hand rested on the hilt of his sword, menacingly.

"When you mentioned the blind girl, it stirred memories of that time. I never believed the man called Flint attacked the Shotai. He had nothing to gain and everything to lose. Did the blind girl attend

155

the Shotai to the temple?"

"The offer was made, but she refused. I believe her to be Taylok, the girl wanted by His Eminence and the High Council."

"But, you didn't take her into custody?"

A slow smile crossed Cobalt's face.

"You ask a lot of questions for a foreigner, Diamond," Cobalt emphasized the name as if making an inference.

"Do you question my identity, Cobalt? Then, I take my leave."

Cobalt took Flint by the arm in a steel grip.

"Before you go, I will favor you with one more bit of information, although you have not requested it. The blind girl departed in the direction of the stalagmite field. She is young, but fully capable of defending herself against enemies. I believe, however, that she could use a friend. You may or may not be interested, but in case you are, give her my regards. She is an uncommonly brave and selfless girl."

Flint stared at the man, incredulous at his intuition. Cobalt had reached the conclusion that he was Flint and deliberately given him needed information. Honor and fairness survived in New Rockhome Hall despite His Eminence's hold over Eldar Temple.

"You are a man of honor," said Flint, softly. "Thank you."

Cobalt nodded curtly, released Flint's arm and turned to rejoin his warriors. Flint walked rapidly toward the stalagmite field, images of Taylok crowding his thoughts. He tried to fathom how much she might have changed in the three rings since he had seen her. Surely, she would remember him.

Chapter 15 - Flint's Return

Taylok's left shoulder hurt from the stone bruise. She fretted over how she had misjudged the speed and angle of the missile. Had the rock been higher and to the right . . . if the Shotai hadn't pushed the man as he released the stone . . . Taylok shuddered, involuntarily.

Her involvement had been purely fortuitous. She visited the Shaman's home to see the Shotai and maybe borrow a couple of ulok caps from him, if he had them to spare. Shouting alerted her to the dangerous situation developing and she ran toward them, her sling out and ready.

"Run away, Taylok," cried the Shotai, gasping for breath. "These men are murderers."

Taylok's acute hearing discerned four men in close quarters. The bigger man had to be the Shotai. A stone fairly leapt into her sling cradle and the first of three sped toward its target. Only two struck their mark. The third man had somehow anticipated the shot and moved behind the Shotai and away from the path of the third stone. The stone he returned possessed a huge curve, which she did not anticipate properly, and struck Taylok on the left shoulder. Recovering, she got a fourth stone away and smacked the man on the rear as he bent over to avoid her throw. He cried out and sprawled on the sandy surface. The Shotai sat on him. Taylok ran to the men.

"Are you okay, Shotai?" she called.

"I will be all right, Taylok, but the Shaman is badly hurt," the Shotai said.

"Where is he?" Taylok asked.

"Inside. These men attacked us there."

"Is this all of them?"

"Yes. They must have thought we would die quietly and quickly for they only sent three men. They would have succeeded, too, if not for you. I'll tie this one up if you will bring me some rope from inside the house. There is a sufficient length just right of the door. These other two seem to be out for a while."

"What will you do with them?"

"Turn them over to the warrior guard. They should be making rounds in less than a quarter turn. Maybe I can get some information out of this one before the warriors arrive. I doubt His Eminence will bother to try them, as I believe he sent them. Still, they may suffer his pronouncement since they have failed, at least, in part."

Taylok found the Shaman's door and entered. A strong scent of blood assailed her inside the room but she heard nothing. She called out for the Shaman but he did not answer. Taylok located the short rope by feel and again listened for sign of the Shaman's breathing or heartbeat. Hearing none, she departed and gave the rope to the Shotai, fearful that the Shaman had died. The Shotai trussed the attacker, went inside to check on the Shaman and returned.

"The Shaman is dead, which makes you three murderers," the Shotai barked, addressing the tied man. "Who sent you?"

Taylok did not think the attacker would answer and expectedly, the man did not respond. Taylok heard the Shotai move slightly, and although she could not tell exactly what the Shotai had done, the man on the ground cried out in pain.

"Who sent you?" the Shotai repeated. "Was it His Eminence?"

"No," the man chirped through clenched teeth. "No."

"Then, who?"

The Shotai made another move with similar result to the first.

"High Council," sobbed the man, almost in tears.

Taylok turned unseeing eyes toward the attacker.

"I have heard the voice of the one called High Council," she said.

"You?" said the Shotai. "When was this?"

"Maybe a quarter-ring ago. Before he became High Council. He's named Pebblic. He could be my father."

"I hope not," said the Shotai. "The man is ruthless."

"Sounds like him. My father had my mother sacrificed and would have got me sacrificed, too, if not for you, Flint and His Eminence."

"We will know for sure when the isa of truth arrives. No man such as that should be allowed to remain in any hall. And His

Eminence has also taken to evil ways. The temple is fraught with foul deeds. I must return as the Shotai or Eldar Temple will be destroyed."

"Please," groaned the attacker, "I have given what you asked. Take away the pain."

The Shotai arose and the attacker sighed with relief. Taylok heard warriors approaching and readied her sling.

"No need, Taylok," said the Shotai, touching Taylok's arm. "These are the regulars, making rounds."

"Shotai," called one, "what happened? Who are these men?"

"Assassins," said the Shotai. "The Shaman is dead by their hands."

"You're wounded. And so is the young lady. We'll take you to the healer."

"I don't want to go to Eldar Temple," said Taylok.

"But, your wound looks painful."

"If she doesn't want to go, it's all right, Cobalt," said the Shotai.

"Very well. But, it appears to be a deep bruise and her shoulder could be broken. You must go, Shotai. You're bleeding heavily and your wounds could be fatal if not attended. We will bind your most serious cuts here, and then a few of our warriors will escort you and also take these three to prison to await their execution."

Taylok departed as the warriors searched the Shaman's house. Now, she felt more alone than ever with the Shaman dead and the Shotai gone from the home by the river. She sat, dejected, on a flat stone carved by the river from a sandstone bed. It occurred to her that she had not been able to borrow any ulok from the Shotai and hunger descended upon her with a vengeful, gnawing sensation in her stomach.

"Taylok?"

The voice was so close that she jumped and had her sling ready before she hit the ground.

"Don't throw it, I come in peace," the voice called, laughing, familiar.

"Flint?" she cried, running toward the sound of his voice.

She found herself wrapped in his strong arms and her heart overflowed with joy until her own overzealous hug jammed her left shoulder into his ribs and she cried out in pain.

"Taylok, are you okay?" asked Flint.

"I got hit with a stone," she replied, rubbing her shoulder. "Nothing serious."

"What are you doing out here all alone?"

"Everyone where I lived and worked has been arrested and the house is being watched by warriors."

"What did they do to get arrested?"

"I think they were selling halulok."

"That's illegal here?" asked Flint.

"A recent edict by Eldar Temple."

"Can you go into the village?"

"I suppose. The village warriors don't seem too interested in arresting me. Question is, can you go into the village?"

"Feel my chin."

"Oh. Whiskers. When did . . .?"

"A disguise."

"I wish I could see it," she said, laughing, feeling the silky growth.

"It's not that much to look at, but it gets me past most of the warriors. I'm known as Diamond in Banestone Hall."

"Diamond. Couldn't you come up with something more fitting?"

"You don't like it?"

"I don't know," giggling. "Maybe it will grow on me."

He drew her to him and gently hugged her again. He saw a teardrop race down her cheek.

"It's been far too long since I saw you," he said, still holding her.

"How is Shalea?" she asked, happy for the first time in ages to be in the warmth of his fatherly embrace.

"She's a mother with a one-ring old son named Whirl. Her mate, Claymaker, is a pottery designer. She's living a normal, healthy life."

"I envy her."

"You could have lived with my Fireseasoned mate, Sapphirus, and me in Banestone if you had been able to leave New Rockhome. I always thought of you as my daughter and I regret not being able to get you out of here sooner. This time, when I

160

leave, you're coming with me . . . if you still want to. Do you?"

"I didn't know that you had joined with anyone in Fireseasoning, Flint. That makes me happy."

She didn't look happy.

"You didn't answer my question."

"I never liked living by myself; too many problems. I'll come with you if we can get out of this hall together and you really want me."

"Taylok, you are like a daughter to me and I'll always love you. Of course I want you with me."

"How will Sapphirus feel about you bringing home a blind teen?"

"I told her all about you and how much you mean to me. I believe she will love you like I do."

"I have a couple of things to pick up back in the stalagmite field. Want to come with me?"

"Sure. By the way, when did you eat last? Are you hungry? I have some ulok and dried fish with me."

"Incredible. Flint, you're the best. I'm starving. I had gone to see the Shotai to borrow some ulok when I ran into that fight."

Flint handed Taylok several ulok caps and two pieces of dried fish, which she hastily began devouring.

"Aren't the fields by the river still yielding?"

"Only when the warriors aren't looking," she said, swallowing. "They're very strict and they check the fields often."

"Those fields are volunteer ulok," said Flint, "and have always been free to anyone who was hungry."

"Not any more. The temple claimed and cultivated them. Now they harvest and sell them at a high price."

"I can imagine. I'm surprised the villagers didn't revolt over that one."

"They probably would have except when the village council started making waves, they began to die off mysteriously, one by one. Everyone knew Eldar Temple was behind the deaths but couldn't prove it."

"Did Driggett Ventaya survive?"

"I haven't heard of anything happening to him. I saw him once but don't really know him. Ganaga says Driggett's the toughest of the council members and probably the smartest. I think His Eminence is also smart enough to leave Driggett alone, but I'm not sure. There are rumors that Driggett is trying to form an alliance with Stonehaven Hall to avoid a war."

"Stonehaven? Why wouldn't he make a Banestone Hall alliance, first?"

"Don't ask me. I'm not a politico and don't want to be. Maybe Ganaga could tell you."

"Mind if we go by Ganaga's house on the way to the village?"

"We could, but I'm pretty sure he's at the palace tending to the Shotai's wounds at the moment."

"You know, for a blind recluse, you are full of information."

"Not really. I talk to the Shotai and Ganaga fairly often and Tektitus now and again. Anyway, don't you have to be older than eleven to be a recluse?"

Flint laughed and dropped the subject. When they reached the location in the stalagmite field where Taylok had been sleeping, Flint looked at her belongings.

"Is this it?" he asked, seriously.

"I travel light," she said, a little ashamed that she could hold all her things in two hands. "I was going to enter the sling contest next ring. If I won, I'd have a lot more stuff."

"Why didn't Ganaga take you in? Surely he had room."

"I didn't ask. I am wanted, you know. There's a price on my head, I'm told."

"I saw the posters. It seems that you, Shalea and I are bad to the stem. His Eminence hasn't changed much from when I left."

"Yes, he has. He brought in an evil High Council named Pebblic. The temple has gotten much worse."

"Pebblic? Where did he come from?"

"Stonehaven by way of the Hall of the Tadi'wa."

"Sand! Is he your father?"

"Probably. I can't find out for sure."

"Maybe Tektitus can find out," reasoned Flint.

"No. He tried when Pebblic first showed up. Everything we know about Pebblic fits for him to be my father, but nothing ties him directly to mother or me. Someone in the Hall of the Tadi'wa knows for sure. That's where my father got mother and me convicted."

"Yes, and I heard that your father had risen in the temple of the Tadi'wa. How did this Pebblic get to be High Council to His Eminence?"

"I don't know the details. I heard Pebblic talking to the owner of a food service place. He said he had been 'His Excellence' while in service to the Priests of the Tadi'wa. I think His Eminence hired Pebblic to gain favor with the Tadi'wa Priests and to keep the Shotai from returning too soon."

"I can't imagine a Tadi'wa Priest taking a position with an Eldar Temple pretender. Something is very wrong with that picture."

"What do you mean?"

"The disdain held by the Tadi'wa Priests for lower Rockworld halls is legendary. They throw their misfits away to us without the blink of an eye . . . at least those they don't sacrifice to the Mohk'wa. No self-respecting Tadi'wa Priest would even think about accepting a position in New Rockhome Hall unless he was in trouble."

"So, how can I find out?"

"Do you really want to know?"

"Of course I do . . . I think. Why did you ask that?"

"Think about it. Just assume, for a moment, that he is your father. What will you do with the information?"

"Why, I will . . . I will . . . hit him with my sling."

"Gaining what?"

"Revenge for having me blinded and mother killed."

"You're already wanted. If you killed Pebblic in cold blood, Eldar Temple would have no choice but to turn the hall inside out to find you and try you for murdering one of their priests. The sentence would be death in Snake Canyon. Is revenge that important to you?"

Taylok cocked her head to one side as she thought about Flint's words.

"So, you don't think I should do anything about Pebblic even if he killed my mother and had me blinded?"

"Oh, no. I didn't say that. If he is your father, he is guilty of some pretty awful deeds and, if capable of those crimes, he probably committed others. Maybe those are the reason he came here. I think we can find out, but it will require a trip to The Temple of the Tadi'wa."

"Wait, that's where they condemned mother and me for leaving my father."

"I understand if you're afraid to go. I can go by myself."

"Okay, let me ask you this; what will you do with the information, if you get it?"

"If he is your father and therefore guilty of crimes that are punishable here, we can get the Shotai to try him and pass sentence. That way, you don't have to kill your own father, but you still get him punished for what he did."

"You think the Shotai will be back in power? There's a good chance His Eminence and the High Council will try to kill him, again. I don't think the Shotai has much chance, going up against those two. They're power hungry."

"You may be right. We have to protect the Shotai, first, and then get the information on Pebblic."

"Okay, now that's a plan," Taylok said.

"First, let's drop your things off at the inn where I have a room." Said Flint. "Then, we can go to the temple and find the Shotai. I have one more complication; a man who came here with me last isa and a report I have to complete."

"That's two complications."

"They're both part of the same complication."

"My head hurts."

"I'll fill you in on the way back to the village."

As they neared the village outskirts, Flint saw a runner hustling up the mainway.

"Let's go into the village," Flint said. "I want to hear what the runner says. They usually have important news from the other halls."

"Okay. Lead the way."

She took Flint's hand as they hurried into the village. They had not gone far when someone called out.

"Taylok! Where have you been?"

"Halite," Taylok responded. "I thought you were in prison. Oh, this is um . . . Diamond. Diamond, Halite."

"Good isa," said Halite. "And this is Garnet."

"Hi," said Garnet.

"Garnet," exclaimed Taylok. "Good to hear your voice."

"Good isa," replied Diamond/Flint. "We were going to hear the runner's news. Join us."

"Yes, we will," Halite answered.

"Where are Ruby and Pumice?" Taylok asked.

"Set free and back at work," said Halite.

"The village warriors decided they didn't have the right to detain us after their witnesses recanted," added Garnet.

"All of them?"

"All of them," said Garnet. "When they heard that the Shotai might return to Eldar Temple, everything changed for the better."

They reached the center of the village, where the runner stood on an elevated podium.

"Citizens of New Rockhome village," began the runner, "greetings from the other halls. A great event has occurred. The Fronds'wa (Giant God) visits Rockworld. He is a mighty warrior who killed the Mohk'wa, a feat never before accomplished, and brought one of its cruel claws to Stonehaven Hall as proof of the kill."

The audience, about two hundred men and women, gasped in unison.

The runner continued, "A Councilman from New Rockhome Hall, one from Stonehaven Hall and a young woman condemned to die and chained to the Deathstone, accompanied the Fronds'wa from the Hall of the Mohk'wa. The Fronds'wa promised to help us and stop the sacrifices. The people can talk of nothing else."

"Is He coming here?" someone asked.

"I don't know," answered the runner.

"What reactions are the Priests of the Tadi'wa expressing?"

"Fear, I think. But there are rumors of warfare from the Crystal Dreamer of the Tadi'wa."

"Why warfare if the Fronds'wa is here to help us?"

"The priests seem fearful that their power will be reduced or taken from them."

Taylok tugged at Flint's arm. "What will this do to our plan?"

"Nothing. We still have to keep the Shotai safe. These events

165

may have no effect on this hall, except that a New Rockhome Councilman is part of them."

"Where have you been, Taylok?" whispered Garnet. "We missed you."

"I've been living in the stalagmite field," she whispered back.

"Alone?"

"Yes."

Garnet took her hand and squeezed it, gently.

"You are really a brave girl, Taylok."

Her heart beat faster and she could think of nothing to say. Flint released her other hand.

"If you two want to stroll around for a while," offered Flint/Diamond, "I have to take Taylok's things to a place they can be stored. Taylok, meet me on Eldar Temple path, just outside the village, in one turn. Okay?'

"Okay, Fl . . . Diamond. I'll be there," she stammered.

"I must get back to my business," said Halite, a smile in his voice. "Will you be returning to work, Taylok?"

"No," she said. "Diamond and I have some work to do."

"Be careful if you go to Eldar Temple. The warriors say major chaos is imminent."

Both Flint and Halite walked off into the noisy, crowded mainway, leaving Garnet and Taylok alone in the midst of the excited throng.

"I can't hear myself think," shouted Garnet. "Let's get out of here."

He led her toward the temple side of the village but turned off the mainway onto a lengthy, curving path where they found an ulok'neh garden.

"I have a couple of ulok caps," said Garnet. "I know you can't see the garden, so let me tell you about it while we eat."

He handed Taylok a large cap of ulok.

"The cover is a thin, smooth, carved, circular sandstone slab supported by five columns, one of which is in the middle. Two of the columns are natural, but three hand carved. The diameter of the ceiling slab is about twenty steps and I think it must be almost white in color. The ulok'neh light makes it look pale green, though. The ceiling is high but the grains reflect light well.

166

"Eight thin, flat shadow stones, about the width of my head, are hung from the ceiling by strong cords. The shadow stones are each carved into a different shape and hung flat and low enough to touch if you reach. There are narrow paths that let you walk almost beneath the hanging, shaped stones. When the stones are slowly turned, they make fantastic moving shadows on the ceiling. I wish you could see them."

"I almost can with your description. How did you find it?"

"My family used to come here when I was in school. Mother always loved this place."

"You must have liked it, too."

"I did," admitted Garnet. "That's why I brought you here, although you can't get the maximum appreciation for it. I was thinking about what happened the sleep turn before everything went bad. I keep remembering how you felt in my arms. I didn't want you to leave."

Taylok turned toward Garnet and tilted her face to his. He kissed her and she kissed him back. When they parted, she couldn't believe the feelings that rushed through her.

"I knew it would be like this," she whispered.

"So did I," he replied, gently touching her lips with his fingers.

A distant keeper tolled the end/beginning of a turn.

"I have to go," she said, sadly. "Diamond is waiting for me."

Garnet kissed her again, unwilling to release her easily.

"Come back to me when you can, and don't forget," he said. "Come on, I'll walk you to the mainway."

"I told Diamond that I would go back with him to Banestone Hall."

"You're not going to Fireseason with him, are you?"

"No. He's going to adopt me as his daughter. He already has a woman he's Fireseasoned with. I'll be living with them."

"Guess it's better than the stalagmite field. But, you could come back to Halite's place. Then, I'd get to see you."

"I'll talk to Diamond. I've known him since forever."

When they reached the mainway, Taylok heard Flint/Diamond talking to someone with an unfamiliar voice. It sounded like a Banestone Hall dialect and the man talked with a distinct 'up speak,' finishing every sentence like a question.

"He won't last long with those two out to kill him," the man said.

"My friends and I will do what we can to restore him to his rightful position," said Flint/Diamond. "Here they are, now."

"I'll take my leave. Get word to me when you finish your task," said the unknown man with the strange manner of speech who walked away as Taylok and Garnet came near.

"Am I late?" asked Taylok as she moved toward Flint/Diamond, exaggerating the 'up speak.'

"You just did that to annoy me, didn't you?" said Flint.

"Oh?" Taylok said, smiling.

"Just stop it. You timed it perfectly," said Flint. "Your things are in room seven at the Fairstone Inn. Hi Garnet."

"Good isa," said Garnet.

"Who was that?" Taylok asked.

"He's Sericite from Banestone Hall. He came here with me, but I don't trust him. We're trying to determine whether New Rockhome Hall will side with Xantopec in case of war. It's rumored that Xantopec is here with an entourage to talk with His Eminence and the High Council."

"Xantopec won't get my help," said Taylok.

"I'll see you two later," said Garnet. "Don't forget, Taylok."

"I won't. Bye, Garnet."

"Be careful, Garnet," said Flint. "Something is about to break and it could be dangerous."

"Thanks for the advice, Diamond. Take care of Taylok."

"Are you joking? She'll probably be taking care of me."

Flint and Taylok found the first body after traveling less than a quarter turn. The young warrior had been slashed and beaten to death very recently as his body still felt warm. Flint looked around for the assailant.

"I can't see anyone, Taylok," he said in a hushed voice. "There are plenty of hiding places, though. Do you hear anything out of the ordinary?"

"No," she admitted, after a brief pause to listen. "Only the usual stuff. Maybe the killer left the area. Did your friend mention that he had seen a body?"

"No, and Sericite came this way. He couldn't have missed it if the body was here when he passed by and he would have told me."

"Unless, he contributed to it being here."

"That's a possibility. He's reputed to be a good swordsman. This warrior put up a fight, though, because his sword is lying next to his hand and there is blood on the blade. Sericite didn't seem to be wounded, so we should be on guard for robbers along here."

"Do you see a blood trail leading away from the body?"

"No. There's plenty of blood around, but it looks as though it all came from this warrior."

They traveled another half turn when they found more bodies littering the side of the mainway. Three warriors had apparently put up a struggle before succumbing to a superior force.

"Taylok," said Flint, "it's too dangerous for you to go with me. It seems the war has already begun. I'll take you back to the village. At least, you'll find some shelter . . . and Garnet's there."

Taylok wanted to go back and see Garnet again, but felt her place was with Flint at the moment. Still, the words came with difficulty.

"I won't go back, Flint. I'm with you. I like Garnet in a different way, but you're family and I'm not running out on you. If it comes to a battle, I can take care of myself."

"I never doubted that for a moment, Taylok. But do you have any other reason to expose yourself to the violence at Eldar Temple than to be with me? If I survive, I'll come for you in the village. If I don't . . . you'll be safe and near Garnet."

"I'm willing to fight to the death with you, Flint."

"I know you are." He hugged her fiercely. "That part worries me, Taylok. This is beginning to shape up like a suicide mission. And you're too young to be risking it all. I thought we could go and stay with the Shotai until he was safe, but I think Eldar Temple will see a bloodbath this isa. It's a lot more dangerous than I first thought."

"You still need someone to watch your back, Flint. And, that's me. Who would you rather have, me or Sericite?"

"I'd rather have you with me than anyone. But right now, I'd rather have you safe."

"If you take me back, I'll just follow behind you to the temple. You can't keep me away. Save us some steps."

"Taylok, you are one tough ulok. Okay, come on. Just try hard to stay alive."

"Flint. Someone's coming up behind us . . . fast."

"I see him. It's Sericite. What's that maniac doing following us into this melee?"

Chapter 16 - Sericite's Mission

"Diamond, Diamond," called Sericite from a distance. "We have to get out of here. The fighting has begun in the village. And I saw dead warriors along the mainway as I came here. We can do nothing to help the people of New Rockhome Hall."

In spite of his fear, or perhaps because of it, his 'up speak' was pronounced.

"Calm down, Sericite," said Flint/Diamond. "You should go back to Banestone Hall. Taylok and I will go to see if we can help the Shotai."

"I can't get back through the village," lamented Sericite, moving close to Flint/Diamond.

"There is a route that bypasses the village and leads to the hall entrance," said Flint/Diamond You should take that."

"Yes, yes," said Sericite. "How do I find it?"

He fidgeted and placed his hand on his sword hilt.

"It's not well marked. Just pick your way, keeping the village on your left and walk toward the largest stalagmite," Flint pointed. "It's near the entrance. And watch for snakes."

Sericite grimaced, and then smiled a feral grin as he worked his way behind Flint/Diamond.

"First, I must do what I was sent here to do," growled Sericite, desperately.

He drew his sword with the quickness of a striking snake and swung viciously at Flint/Diamond's back. But Flint, mistrusting Sericite, anticipated the move, crouched to avoid the swing and jumped away, drawing his own sword.

"Taylok. Stay well behind me. This fool is full of treachery."

Sericite swung his sword again, this time clanging into Flint's weapon, and deflecting above Flint's head. Taylok could hear the activity, but the location sounds, usually heard from the light wind, were obscured by the fighting noises. She knew that Flint could handle himself, but she didn't know how good a swordsman Sericite might be. The sounds became a jumble of clangs and grunts interspersed with gasps and groans. When the two men emerged from a close quarters, spinning entanglement, Taylok could not distinguish Flint from Sericite. She backed away toward the edge of the mainway.

"Ahh," cried the voice of Sericite and then silence prevailed as one of the men crumpled to the ground. Taylok held her sling loosely as the standing man walked toward her.

"Diamond?" she said, tenuously.

"Not this isa," said Sericite in his strange 'up speak' voice. "Your friend Flint - oh, yes, I know his true name - follows the fate of your friend in the village."

"Garnet?"

"Was that his name? He's dead by my sword, like the warriors along the mainway. When I saw that he didn't go with you, I waited for him. And to find him unarmed made things very easy for me. At least, he died like a man and didn't whine."

Sericite's speech became slurred as Taylok readied her stone in the sling.

"You won't need the stone, Taylok," said the calm voice of Flint from behind Sericite. "Sericite is dead and just doesn't know it, yet."

"Flint?" she said.

"I'm okay," he answered, standing.

As Flint spoke, She heard Sericite slump to his knees.

"Sericite," said Flint, "if you didn't have that annoying way of talking, I might have let you live to go back and tell Leana what you learned."

"What happened?" gurgled Sericite, unable to rise.

"My sword found your jugular," said Flint. "Otherwise, the blow to my head could have proved fatal as you'd had the strength to follow through. Now, it seems you'll be just another dead body along the mainway."

"Help me," pleaded Sericite.

Taylok smelled fresh blood, which must have been gushing down Sericite's neck from the wound that Flint had inflicted, and heard the dying man's labored breathing.

"The time that I might have helped you is past," said Flint. "Your intent is resolved but you will die with it. I still might have helped you if you hadn't threatened to kill Taylok . . . but, I doubt it."

Sericite fell forward and Taylok stepped back when the traitorous Banestoneite collapsed with a clatter as the sword fell from his failing hand.

Chapter 17 - The Sunstone Globe

"Flint?"

"I'm here," he replied, grunting as he pulled Sericite's body off the mainway.

He walked toward Taylok and briefly stood beside her.

"Do you think he told the truth about killing Garnet?" she asked.

"I don't know, Taylok . . . maybe. He had the time after we left. We know for certain that someone killed the warriors along the mainway. Sericite had nothing to gain by lying about them or Garnet . . . and Sericite was dying."

"He didn't even know Garnet's name," whispered Taylok.

"Men like Sericite don't think like we do. They trust no one and hold no mere friendship bonds as relevant. Their cause is foremost and everything else, unimportant."

"Isn't it always good against evil? You know, Xantopec and his followers are evil, right? Sericite was evil because he killed indiscriminately."

"I think they're both evil, because they sacrifice human lives to get what they want. Xantopec's acolytes must think the Crystal Master is doing the Sun God's will, though, and Sericite accepted his Chief Warrior's orders. It isn't always simple to see another man's point of view and we all think our viewpoint is the right one or we wouldn't hold it."

"I don't think you should kill anyone unless they're trying to kill you," Taylok stated.

"I agree. But, I also think you should protect those who can't protect themselves."

Taylok asked, "Is the Shotai good?"

"I think he's better than His Eminence or High Council Pebblic," replied Flint. "No one is all good or all bad. Every person is a product of many different spheres of influence and individuals react differently to each influence, whether good or bad."

"But, some people favor His Eminence, right?"

"His Eminence isn't all bad, although he has a strong desire to attain power and will do anything to win. But, he did come with me and rescue you, didn't he?"

"After you forced him to do it."

Flint laughed and said, "Let's go."

"Don't ever let anything happen to you, Flint."

"Don't worry, Taylok. Everyone knows that Flint is a rock. Right?"

Taylok laughed in spite of the dire situation.

"Did you feel that?" she asked, suddenly.

"That feeling of heat? I thought it was just me. Let's get to the temple."

They encountered no more carnage, but Flint cried out as they neared their destination.

"What's happening, Flint?" Taylok asked, unsheathing her sling.

"I have to check this out," he said. "A bright flash just came from Eldar Temple, I felt another warm pulse and there's no guard on entrance duty. Stay here, Taylok. I'll be back as soon as I can."

"Wait. I'll go with you."

Flint didn't answer and Taylok found herself standing alone at the temple entrance.

She quickly located the door and stepped inside.

"Flint?" she called.

No answer.

"Anyone?"

Only the echo of her voice filled the hallway. A short distance inside, Taylok tripped and fell, with a clatter of stones, over a body lying on the cool marble floor. She felt along the limp figure until she reached the neck, where she located a pulse. It thumped very slowly and faintly, but the man lived. She examined his face. It felt very warm and smooth. It wasn't Flint.

Taylok arose and cautiously trilled to get echoes. She discerned bodies strewn up and down the hallway. Taylok felt another wave of heat course through her body and she cringed in anticipation of something worse, which did not come. She could hold her own in a fair fight, but this might prove deadly and she didn't know what she was fighting.

"Flint! Flint! Answer me, Flint," her plea chorused down the hallway.

She received no answer as she made her way along the corridor. Taylok poked her head into several rooms along the way, but found them all the same. Fallen bodies littered the main floor rooms. The only good part being that the ones she checked still had a heartbeat.

The terrible waves of heat that rhythmically coursed through her body continued and, as she neared the geode room, worsened. She could find no respite from the pounding, intense pulses. Her face flushed and her body trembled as she approached the geode room door. She felt weak, near fainting and with the bodies lying around she gave herself little chance to survive.

Chanting sounds flowed from the geode room and bare feet slapped the floor in rhythm that seemed to correspond with the waves of heat. Taylok removed the sling from her shoulder and felt her stone sack. Three stones. Her fall, far back near the entrance, had spilled most of her stones onto the hallway. Taylok did not think she could make it back to retrieve them. Three would have to be enough.

She stepped through the doorway. Taylok heard four people moving rhythmically around a separate single individual. The central figure grasped a long staff with both hands. Atop the staff rested a head-sized, globe-shaped stone that emitted the heat pulses. Taylok recognized the shape from the sounds of chanting and dancers feet, echoing from the surface of a hard floor, bouncing off the globe. She couldn't understand why the people inside the geode room weren't rendered unconscious by the pulses.

"A female intruder stands at the entrance," said a man's voice that made her cringe.

The memory of that voice had etched a permanent scar on her brain. It was the Crystal Master, Xantopec. The evil priest stood at the center of the circle formed by the priestesses, holding the staff and globe.

"How is she still standing?" said the shrill voice of one of the dancers, alerted to Taylok's presence.

"She's blind, Priestess Osar," said Xantopec.

"But . . ."

"If your eyes weren't covered, you would be unconscious like the others outside this room. She must be killed. Release the snakes. Remove your eye covers, Osar, and move quickly," said Xantopec. "We will not reactivate the sunstone until you return. Release the snakes close enough to her that they will kill quickly."

Priestess Osar broke from the circle around Xantopec, momentarily interrupting the rhythm. She moved toward, what Taylok assumed to be, a basket alive with the sounds of buzzing snakes. Taylok couldn't tell how many writhed within the basket because of the echoes and large number, but it hardly mattered since only three stones remained in her pouch. If the princess released the snakes, Taylok would have no choice but to run away or use her limited arsenal to divert snakes, leaving nothing to launch at the sunstone.

Taylok acted quickly. Her first stone cut the heated air and struck Osar on the temple just as she reached the snake basket. The priestess dropped noisily to the floor, groaned and then fell silent.

Taylok desperately wanted to eliminate Xantopec, but knew she must first destroy the sunstone globe they were using to paralyze Eldar Temple defenders. Taylok had learned about sunstone from the Shotai's teachings. The Shotai had not mentioned that the stone possessed the capability to generate heat or light, however, as that combination seemed to be the cause of the paralysis effect.

She remembered that sunstone had a weakness. It contained many inclusions of red copper in tiny, thin sheets. She vividly recalled accidentally fracturing a school sample by striking it along one edge. If she could do the same thing to the globe held by Xantopec . . . however, with only two stones remaining, destroying the sunstone seemed a distant hope, yet represented her fading chance to save the people of Eldar Temple.

"Priestess Karma," screamed Xantopec. "Osar is injured, perhaps dead. Remove your eye protectors and rid us of the girl. If she survives, our efforts will be spoiled."

Another priestess departed the ring and ran directly at Taylok with one arm raised as though holding a knife. The blind girl had no choice but to waste a stone on the fast approaching danger. Taylok's missile struck the hapless woman directly between her eyes. Priestess Karma's legs turned limp and she dropped instantly to the floor, writhing in pain and screaming. The knife she had been holding skittered noisily across the floor.

Taylok ran a hand inside her weapon sack. One stone remained. It seemed too light, too uneven to be a decent projectile. How could it have all come down to this? Taylok felt the weight of the hall on her inexperienced shoulders. But, she had to save Flint and the others, didn't she? She readied herself once again, adrenaline coursing through her veins.

"Augh!" cried Xantopec. "The girl is a blind sorceress! Ready the snakes, Whisper. Mudra, stop the girl. Do your work quickly and let us complete our destruction of the temple warriors. We must not allow a lone, sightless girl to ruin our plans. Warriors of the Sun God will be here within a turn to finish off those unconscious temple protectors. Our force is limited so the enemy must remain unconscious for the plan to succeed. If we don't begin the chant once more, Eldar Temple warriors will reawaken far too soon."

A third priestess withdrew from the circle and lunged toward the snake basket while the fourth priestess raced toward Taylok. This left the sunstone unguarded except by Xantopec himself.

Taylok made a diving roll to her right, stood upright, swung her sling in a forceful arc and loosed her final rock at the sunstone, held high above the head of Xantopec. The enraged Crystal Master tried desperately to move the sunstone globe aside to avoid Taylok's missile, but the excessive weight of the globe and speed with which Taylok delivered the throw thwarted his maneuver. The projectile unerringly struck the sunstone. The blow caused the large globe to vibrate so hard that Taylok felt the floor shake where she stood. But, before she could determine whether the sunstone had fractured, or been damaged at all, Priestess Mudra fell upon her and brought her to the floor.

The ensuing fight tested the blind teen's ability to defend herself against a sighted, capable enemy. She pushed Mudra's forehead away as the priestess clawed and tried to hold on to Taylok's legs. Mudra scratched and bit and struck Taylok with her fist as the women rolled around the floor. Taylok kicked and swung her fists at her protagonist, giving as well as she got. Taylok pushed Mudra away, arose and faced the bigger woman. Remembering the priestesses were barefooted, Taylok brought her own right foot down hard onto Mudra's left foot. The priestess screamed and fell to the floor.

"Get out of the way, Mudra," cried Priestess Whisper. "I have the snakes."

From the sound of the priestess' voice, Taylok could tell that she stood very near and held the basket to her left side. Taylok chanced a wild idea and grabbed for the basket. She located the lid, removed it and tilted the writhing, angrily buzzing contents back toward the screaming priestess. Whisper released the basket and ran from the snakes, as did Taylok. Taylok thought the snakes had dropped very near the prone figure of Priestess Karma but she couldn't be certain any longer.

A deep, raspy, vibrating gong shook the room as the thin staff holding the globe broke and the globe dropped to the marble floor and bounced. A loud cracking sound followed when the sunstone struck the floor a second time, causing everyone to pause. Taylok used the lull to make a dive for the door while avoiding the snakes.

"Aieee," she heard Xantopec scream. "Broken. Broken. The image of the god is defiled. Mudra and Whisper, you must kill the defiler and then help Osar. We must abandon our quest in New Rockhome Hall this isa and warn our warriors. Priestess Karma lies dead and snakes cover her body. She will, no doubt, be removed to Mordane Pit. I will attend to Osar."

The Crystal Master's voice faded as Taylok ran hard, falling twice over the slowly rousing bodies of temple warriors. One grabbed her by the arm before she could rise.

"Who're you?" he said, his voice barely comprehensible.

"I'm the Shotai," she said in a deep falsetto, which no one would have normally accepted as the Shotai's voice.

"Oh, shorry, Sotai," the drowsy warrior slurred, releasing her.

His eyes flew open and he bolted upright.

"Wait a thump. You're not the Sotai . . . um . . . Shotai."

But, Taylok raced away with two women chasing her.

"Stop," the warrior said, rising, but with no authority in his voice. "Wha's going on?"

The priestesses did not answer, pushed the warrior aside, and careened after Taylok, who had fallen again. The women were quick to take advantage of Taylok's spill and Mudra held the blind girl as Whisper approached.

"Now, you die, defiler," said the chilling voice of Whisper.

She raised her hand, in which Taylok guessed there must be a knife. Taylok tried to wrest her arms away from Priestess Mudra, but the woman possessed great strength and held firm. Taylok kicked out to deter Whisper, but the priestess evaded the blow and continued to approach.

"Stop," said the warrior, much closer.

"Get away from me," screamed Whisper.

A blur of sounds greeted Taylok. She heard the clank of metal against metal as the warrior's sword met Whisper's knife. The material of the warrior's mantle made a ripping sound as Whisper tried to cut him. Then, Whisper cried out in pain as the warrior struck her with his sword handle. Mudra released her grip, cursed and stumbled backwards when Taylok stomped her bare, left foot again. Both priestesses whirled away from the fight and returned the way they had come to rejoin Xantopec. The warrior did not pursue them but turned to Taylok.

"So," he said, "You are very thin to be the Shotai. Who are you?"

"I'm Taylok," she said, knowing the chance she took. "Thanks for your help. Those two are priestesses of the Sun God, helping Xantopec knock everyone out with a sunstone globe. They would have killed me if you hadn't been here."

"Xantopec?" mused the warrior. "I heard that the Crystal Master visited the hall. So, he is responsible for my bruised elbow."

"I heard him say that warriors of the Sun God were on their way here to kill the temple defenders while they were unconscious. Everyone should be waking up now, though, so you can be ready for his attempt to take over."

"And just how did you come by all this information?"

"I . . . uh . . . fought the Crystal Master and those Sun God priestesses and heard them talking."

"Why weren't you knocked out like the rest of us?"

"Xantopec said it was because I'm blind. It took the combination of light and heat to make everyone else unconscious."

"Taylok, you said? Isn't that one of the names on all those

posters?"

"It's a very common name."

"Really? I never heard it before I saw it on the poster."

"Your voice sounds familiar. Are you sure we don't know each other?"

"You've never been to my house. I'm sure of that."

"Do you know a man called Diamond?"

"I've heard the name."

"Have you seen him?"

"You don't remember me, do you?"

"Your voice sounds . . ."

"We met once in the geode room. You were hiding beneath the great geode from His Eminence's Warriors."

"That was you? You're Steel?"

"So you remembered."

"Of course. You saved my life then and now you just saved me again."

"I know, I know," he said, feigning arrogance, still slightly groggy. "New Rockhome Hall is not a big place. Listen, I have to go and inform Chief Iron that Xantopec's warriors may be on their way to the hall. Wait for me here, if you can, and I'll help you find . . . um . . . Diamond. The hallway is becoming chaotic, though, so if you have to leave, I'll be at the front entrance in a half-turn."

"G'bye, Steel."

"Later, Taylok."

The activity and noise developing in the hallway quickly drowned out Steel's departure. She sensed, rather than heard, the two men who approached her. Too late, she felt their hands grip her arms.

"So, you're Taylok," said one.

"No," she lied. "I'm Whitewave."

"Too bad, Taylok, I heard you tell Steel who you are. We aren't going to hurt you, if you behave. We just want to turn you in for the reward. Isn't that right, Ran?"

"Right, Fell."

"What reward?" she asked, innocently. "They removed the reward when Xantopec came here last isa. His Eminence is afraid I might tell who helped me escape from the Crystal Master when I was going to be sacrificed to the T'sa'wa seven rings ago."

"You have a brave imagination, blind one," said Fell. "You are not dealing with new recruits, however. His Eminence fears no one, including the Crystal Master."

"Are you saying that His Eminence is so stupid that he isn't afraid of the Crystal Master's power?"

"His Eminence does not allow Xantopec to bring warriors with him into New Rockhome Hall; only four priestesses."

"One of whom lies dead in the geode room. Why do you think you were unconscious just a moment ago?"

"I . . . I don't know . . . nor care."

"Wait!" said Ran. "I do care. So, what made us unconscious?"

"The Crystal Master and his four priestesses activated a sunstone globe to knock out everyone in the temple except me," said Taylok.

"Right. I remember seeing a flash of light just before I woke up on the floor."

"It didn't make me unconscious because I'm blind," she continued. "So, I attacked Xantopec and the priestesses in the geode room. I used my sling to break the sunstone globe and knock down two of the priestesses."

"You? How did you break this sunstone globe if you couldn't see it?"

"I can sense where things are with my hearing. And I'm pretty good with the sling."

"I don't believe you," said Fell.

"Want me to demonstrate?"

"It's too crowded in here," offered Ran.

"Take me out of Eldar Temple and I'll show you."

"Why would we do that?" scoffed Fell.

"Because you don't believe me? You can also go to the geode room and see the broken globe and a dead priestess. I'm telling the truth."

"So," said Fell, "you're a heroine and saved us from unconsciousness. You're still worth eighty shells."

"I saved you from the Crystal Master's warriors who were on their way to kill everyone in the temple."

"Can you believe the audacity of this one, Ran? Trying to make us believe she saved us from some fantastic plot to overthrow the temple?"

"Something did knock everyone out," said Ran. "Her story has a ring of truth."

"I say we take her to His Eminence," said Fell, "collect the reward, and let His Eminence figure out whether she's telling the truth."

"It works for me," said Ran.

"That doesn't work for me," said the voice of Flint. "This girl is my Fireseasoned mate and I will kill you both if I must to get her back."

"Your . . . what?" began Fell. "She's too young to be Fireseasoned to an old . . . Urk!"

"You should rethink your words," said Flint.

Taylok heard the raspy sound of Ran's sword being drawn.

"Stop," cried Ran. "That's my sword."

"Let her go," said Flint.

The hands fell away from Taylok's arms.

"Who are you to be interfering with temple warriors on official business?" grated Fell.

"Someone you don't want to tangle with, warrior. Both of you be on your way before I change my mind and carve some new scars."

"Silver will hear about this," grumbled Fell.

"Are you crazy? You're going to tell Silver that we let one man . . ." Ran's voice trailed off into the cacophonous hallway.

Flint's strong arms grasped Taylok in a hug.

"I was afraid you had been hurt," said Flint. "Where have you been? Were you knocked out like the rest of the temple?"

"Your Fireseasoned mate?" laughed Taylok, not answering his questions immediately. "Is that the best you could come up with?"

"Hey, I've been unconscious," he smiled. "It was the first thing that came to my mind."

Taylok retold her story to Flint, who stood awestruck.

"Unbelievable!" Flint opined. "No, no. I believe you, Taylok. I just meant the story is fantastic. You saved the whole temple, me included, against Xantopec and four priestesses of the sun? And you destroyed their sunstone globe that had caused the unconsciousness? You are incredible."

"I was lucky, Flint. I fell when I first entered the temple and lost all but three of my stones for the sling. I couldn't find you because of all the bodies lying on the hallway floor and when I got to the geode room, I didn't know if the sling could even damage, much less destroy, the sunstone globe. I lucked out there. And when the priestesses caught me in the hallway, I thought I was a goner. I got lucky again because Steel saved me. And just now, I lucked out once more when you saved me from Ran and Fell."

She stopped and laughed.

"Ran and Fell, get it?" she laughed, again, before she continued. "They were an odd pair anyway. I almost had them talked out of turning me in for the reward."

"Taylok," said the voice of Steel, "are you all right? Is this your friend Diamond?"

"Yes, it is," answered Taylok. "Diamond, this is Steel."

"Steel, is it?" said 'Diamond.' "I've heard much of your deeds."

"You son of a river worm," laughed Steel. "It's good to see you . . . um . . . 'Diamond.'"

Flint said, "Steel and I have been friends since before you were born, Taylok."

"Well, how would I have known?" Taylok answered, petulantly.

"Where are you bound?" asked Flint.

"To the front," said Steel. "Taylok informed us that Xantopec's warriors might be on their way to cut us down. Or, they may try to steal the treasure on level four since Taylok foiled their attempt to catch us unaware."

"What treasure?" asked Taylok. "The Shotai warned us against going into the fourth level room, but he didn't mention a treasure."

"It's a standing joke with the warriors," Steel laughed. "A guard team is always posted and no one enters level four, not His Eminence Graystone or His Excellence Pebblic. Rumors say that if you got past the guards, death awaits inside the room."

"I've been as far as the door," Flint reminisced. "Fifteen rings ago I retrieved a staurolite crystal for the Shotai at the room entrance. The Shotai warned me about going further than the door, and the room is so dark that I didn't even seriously consider going inside."

"Do you think there's a treasure?" asked Taylok.

"I doubt it. If there is, it's well guarded," said Flint. "The Shotai called it the 'Spirit of Evil,' and not even he will go inside. People have died, trying to find out what's inside the room. At least, they went in and never came out. The Shotai told me that the ancients once made a practice of throwing their enemies into it."

Flint stopped for a moment before continuing, leaving Taylok with a terrifying picture of ancients casting people into the evil darkness of the room and some monstrous beast devouring them one by one.

"I personally know of three people who disappeared there in recent times," Flint continued. "One acolyte slipped past the guards and went in. I heard a hollow scream and then nothing. The other two, which I witnessed, were guards. One of them drifted over and ran inside, probably a suicide. A second guard ran after the first, trying to save him, I think. Both vanished and the chief guard raced to the entrance and barred the door to keep others from following. There were probably many more disappearances that I don't know about since the room is so old. "

"Someone must know what it is," commented Steel. "Who put it there?"

"The temple builders," said Flint. "The Shotai says it's been almost a thousand rings since someone stored whatever is inside in that room."

"Then, it can't be alive," said Taylok.

"If it's alive, it's really old," laughed Steel. "Why don't they just destroy the room?"

"There are records showing that about one hundred rings ago, someone tried that," admitted Flint. "The workers, who were supposed to tear the walls down, died one by one as they toiled to break stones in the wall. The Shaman said it was their hearts. After three of them died, though, the rest quit. No one else has ventured to repeat the effort since then. The Shotai thinks there could have been other earlier attempts, but they were never recorded, and therefore, lost in antiquity. Anyway, suffice it to say that up to now, no one has figured out how to rid Eldar Temple of the terror."

"What's your best guess that it is?" asked Taylok.

"I think it's a gateway," said Flint.

"A gateway to . . . where?"

"I don't know, maybe Mordane Pit. It may be a crystal that's powerful enough to transport people to another place. Otherwise, it just seems impossible that people could go inside and simply disappear. No foul stench, which usually accompanies the dead, or anything else comes out."

"If it's a gateway, it must be one way," reckoned Taylok. "There doesn't seem to be any way back."

"Maybe it's a gateway to the Hall of the Mohk'wa," said Steel. "Wouldn't that be a shock?"

"Steel," said Flint, "enough about the room. We came to the temple to see the Shotai. Do you know where he is?"

"I believe he's in the room across from the geode chamber."

"Why don't you come with us to see him?"

"I don't want to give the chief any more reason to suspect me of helping the Shotai. I do what I can from inside the warrior ranks."

"Thanks for your help, Steel," said Taylok.

She hugged the warrior.

"Stay out of trouble, Taylok," said Steel, departing. "Nice to meet you, Diamond. See you around sometime."

The sound of Steel's sturdy walk faded into the voices of people reorienting after the near disaster. Taylok held onto Flint's arm as they navigated the hall filled with confused people. Someone stopped them after a short distance.

"Taylok, it's Playa," said the young woman's voice. "I just heard about my father. He died a few turns ago."

"He was badly injured, Playa," said Taylok. "Ganaga tried to help him. Did you get the crystal he wanted you to have?"

"Yes. T'Sander brought it to me this isa." She placed the crystal in Taylok's hand. "Thank you for helping my father."

"No," said Taylok. "He wanted you to have this. It was important to him."

"The stone is a good one and I know that you have trouble activating your crystal. Maybe this one will work for you. It's the only way I have of thanking you for helping."

"I don't really need any thanks, Playa. Anyone would have done the same."

"Not anyone," said Playa, her voice fading into the crowd as she hurried away.

When they reached the geode chamber, Flint stopped and said, "The room is half full of warriors. Let's step back. They're bringing out a priestess, now."

"Make way for the dead," yelled a warrior.

Flint paused and then resumed, "There are more warriors carrying dead snakes. And here come two with halves of the broken sunstone globe. We can go, now."

As Flint prepared to open the door to the room across the hall, a warrior, who had been standing in the hall, watching the proceedings in the geode chamber, called out.

"Stop. You can't go in there."

"It's okay, Stonic," said Flint. "We are friends of the Shotai."

"Do I know you?" responded Stonic.

"Yes. But, it's been a while since we spoke."

The warrior walked across the hall and peered into Flint's eyes.

"Flint," he said in hushed tones. "What are you doing back here? You're still wanted, although none of us, who knew you, believe you did it."

"That's why I wear the beard," said Flint. "We've come a long way to see the Shotai."

"I'll have to escort you in," said Stonic. "His Eminence still insists you are the one who tried to kill the Shotai."

"The Shotai knows that I did not."

"Rumors spread that the Shotai's life is still in danger."

"Did they get any information from the men who tried to kill the Shotai?"

"They mysteriously disappeared from a locked cell before they could be interrogated."

"Convenient for someone."

"Follow me inside. If the Shotai says it's okay, you can stay. I think that Ganaga is still with him as well."

The warrior tapped on the closed door and opened it.

"Shotai," said Stonic, "someone is here to see you."

"Yes, yes," answered the Shotai. "Bring them in. Flint, Taylok, peace and tranquility."

"Peace and tranquility," answered Flint and Taylok in unison.

"So good to see you again, Flint," said the Shotai. "And Taylok is always welcome in my home. Flint, did you know that this young woman saved my life?"

"She always seems to be there when needed," said Flint, turning to the man sitting across from the Shotai. "Peace and tranquility, Ganaga."

"Peace and tranquility, Flint, Taylok," answered Ganaga. "Always a pleasure."

Flint and the Shotai repaired to an alcove to talk while Taylok stayed with Ganaga.

"Playa told me that Citrinon died," she said.

"Yes. I couldn't save him," replied Ganaga. "His injuries were too severe. I told her just half a turn ago, before we fell unconscious."

"She gave me the crystal that her father had given her."

"Doesn't surprise me. Playa is generous in her honor. May I see the stone?"

"Of course."

Taylok handed the crystal to Ganaga.

"Interesting crystal," Ganaga commented. He held the stone for Taylok to feel. "The facets on this end are so smooth they seem polished, but they aren't. It is a deep red in color, a beautiful stone, indeed. The other end is an ordinary pyrite crystal."

"What kind of crystal is the red one?"

"I'm a doctor, not a gemologist, but I think it's gemstone quality cuprite. A ruby."

"That's a copper mineral, isn't it?"

"Yes it is. It's a magnificent stone, worthy of a try for you to sing it."

"Me? I couldn't even get my own tourmaline crystal to respond like most students do. I have a lousy record when it comes to singing crystals."

"This one could be different. This end could be prime, except for the fusing with pyrite."

"Could it be used to help me see again?"

"Let's take a look at your eyes."

Ganaga wrapped his large hands around Taylok's head and gently lifted her eyelids with his thumbs.

"Hmm . . . uh huh, hmm," he opined.

"What does that mean, uh huh, hmm?"

"In my opinion, another ring is needed for your eyes to be ready for the crystal treatment. You have improved but are not quite there, yet. When you are, this ruby could be a vital part."

"I've waited eight rings. What's another ring?"

"If you aren't going to try singing it, I suggest that you entrust the ruby to the Shotai for safekeeping. You lead such an active life that you could lose it and I don't know where another might be found with these properties."

"That's a good idea, Ganaga. I don't have a place to keep it, anyway."

Taylok could hear parts of the conversation between Flint and the Shotai. She tried not to listen, but couldn't avoid hearing some of it.

"We could stay in those rooms and protect you until you move back to your quarters," said Flint.

"I can handle His Eminence," responded the Shotai.

"The Shaman died in the last attack. Are you certain you would have survived if Taylok hadn't arrived when she did?"

"That's true, I'm not sure. Her help proved timely and welcome."

"His Eminence has consorted with High Council, now, Shotai. The pair could be . . ."

His voice was lost as a stone chair scraped noisily on the floor. Quickly, thereafter, a pair of footsteps padded softly toward her and she heard Flint's voice.

"Taylok. We'll be staying in the Shotai's guest rooms for a few isas until the threat to his life is eliminated or reduced to a manageable level."

"Now, Flint," said the Shotai, "I don't want Taylok to be exposed to another fight like the one she stepped into at the Shaman's lodge."

"We are here to prevent another assault like that one, Shotai," responded Flint. "I will gladly take the brunt of any attack that develops. Taylok can back me up, though."

"Make certain no harm comes to her."

"I can take care of myself, Shotai," chimed Taylok.

"This one is very capable of protecting herself," agreed Ganaga.

"Yes, yes," agreed the Shotai, "but unforeseen events often bring unexpected results."

"I must be going," said Ganaga. "Cobalta might give me an unexpected result if I haven't returned by the time she foresees."

They laughed at Ganaga's twist of the Shotai's old adage.

Ganaga departed and Taylok persuaded the Shotai to hold the stone given to her by Playa. The Shotai also checked Taylok's eyes and agreed with Ganaga that her eyes were not ready for the crystal treatment as yet.

The temple remained in confusion after, what had become known as, the sunstone episode. Warriors spoke of it in bitter tones and anger escalated in the ranks. The temple warriors wanted to attack Xantopec to retaliate for his attempted coup but knew that the Crystal Master's fighters outnumbered them ten to one. Frustration thus grew among the warriors. Fights broke out among them and neither His Eminence nor the High Council made appearances to try and quell the situation. The temple warriors began deserting to join the village warriors.

Chapter 18 - A Cruel Deception

On the fourth isa following the 'sunstone episode' Flint roused Taylok from a sound sleep.

"Taylok," he whispered, "Steel just warned that an attack on the Shotai is imminent. Get ready for a little action."

Taylok arose and dressed in the heavy clothing that Flint had purchased for her protection. It would not protect her from a sword blow to the head or shoulders, but might deflect a body hit. She checked the carrying pouch for stones, a habit she conducted each isa. Twenty-two missiles lay ready for quick access. She mechanically tested the strong ulok'neh fabric of the two slings she bore with her since they began the security watch. Her weapons seemed ready.

They ushered the Shotai into a room with an escape door, which locked from the inside, in case Flint and Taylok proved unsuccessful in diverting an attack. Then, they waited until a knock brought them to attention. Tektitus stood at the door. His dark look told them that something had happened.

"What's wrong, Tektitus?" asked Flint.

"His Eminence has been killed," said Tektitus. "A sword in the back ended his life."

"His Eminence, dead?" said Flint. "We thought that the Shotai was the target."

"Perhaps he still is a target," said Tektitus. "The High Council has barricaded himself in his quarters with a handful of warriors. I will stay with you until the threat is over."

"Who can be trying to take over?" asked Taylok. "Do you think Xantopec has returned?"

"Xantopec only had a few priestesses with him," said Tektitus. "It's true that all but one escaped, but our temple warriors met the Sun God's invaders at the entrance to the hall. They are no longer a threat."

"Then, who?" asked Flint.

"I think Chief Iron has become entangled with High Council and they plan to take over Eldar Temple."

"Chief Iron?" questioned Flint. "He controls the Eldar Temple warriors. If he wanted to take over, he would simply do it. Why would he hide his actions? Or include High Council in a plan that he must conduct with his own men?"

"Tektitus," called the Shotai, venturing from his locked room. "Peace and tranquility. Where have you been? I haven't seen you since I arrived."

"I was rendered unconscious like the rest," said Tektitus, walking toward the Shotai. "Since then, I performed my duties at front entrance."

"Wait, Tektitus. Stop, I warn you," barked Flint.

Tektitus stopped and slowly turned toward Flint. Taylok could only guess that his face was a mask of anguish.

"What's wrong, Flint?" he asked, his tone cool and even.

"For one thing, your sword sheath is dripping blood, my friend. Who have you fought?"

Taylok heard Tektitus' sword sheath creak softly as he obviously looked at it.

"So it is," said Tektitus.

"My friend," said the Shotai, now alerted, "are you here to assassinate me?"

"Of course not, Shotai."

His tone carried the sound of a lie.

"Then," interjected Flint, "step toward me and away from the Shotai."

"How could you think such a thing, Flint?"

"We were alerted, not a turn hence, that someone would make an attempt on the Shotai's life. You are the last I would have suspected, Tektitus, yet you are here, carrying blood on your sword. Lay your weapon at my feet so that my trust may be restored."

Tektitus did not move for a moment and then he slowly withdrew his sword from its sheath. Taylok placed a stone into her sling pocket and swung it gently.

"Please, Tektitus," she said. "Do what Flint asked. I always believed in you almost as much as Flint. Don't betray that trust."

"Ah, yes, Taylok," grated Tektitus. "This is not your fight. Stay out of it. I have no wish to harm you."

"Yet," said Flint, "you would kill the Shotai, who has been nothing but your friend, teacher and mentor since you came to the temple."

"The Shotai has remained my chief," said Tektitus. "I am still a lowly temple guard, not even well placed in the temple warriors. High Council promises me much."

"So High Council Pebblic is behind all this," said the Shotai.

"You would return to your position and previous ways," said Tektitus. "I need more."

"Removing the Shotai would not help you as much as you think," said Flint. "Besides me, you would still have Chief Iron and his men to consider. They would not allow High Council Pebblic to become the new Shotai. And the village council would never allow an unknown element to take over the temple. They have too much to lose."

"Tektitus," said Taylok, "I think that Pebblic is my father and the man who had my mother's heart cut out by Xantopec. He also had me blinded. Maybe you could stomach him as Shotai, but I could not."

"What you are doing," said Flint, "is irreversible. I will not allow you to be successful. The Shotai is the best leader this temple ever had."

"Then, why did you attempt to kill him?" rasped Tektitus.

"Flint never tried to harm me," interjected the Shotai.

Tektitus shot back, "I saw him running from the temple just after you were bitten by the snakes. If Flint didn't do it, why did he run?"

"He was coming to get Shalea and me," fretted Taylok. "We had been waiting for him to give us a sling lesson and he came to tell us about the Shotai and bring us back to the temple. He took us straight to the Shotai's room when we arrived."

"Is that true, Shotai?" asked Tektitus, his sword tip dropping.

"I was delirious by then. What I know is that Ganaga showed up very quickly and told me later that Flint had sent for him. I never considered Flint a suspect then, and still do not."

"I would never harm nor allow harm to come to the Shotai," said Flint. "The malicious lie of my guilt was spread by His Eminence. Or by you, Tektitus."

"I may have told someone what I had seen, but I told only the truth."

"Didn't you ever stop to think that I might have had a logical reason to be running? I had sent for Ganaga. The girls were waiting for me at the practice grounds. I would have been remiss to leave them there alone. I didn't know if the Shotai would survive and the girls were vulnerable in an exposed area. And, while this explains my running from the temple, why have you not placed your sword at my feet?"

"My way is set with High Council," said Tektitus. "If I must kill you also, then so be it."

"Tektitus, no," shouted the Shotai.

But, the knowledge of Flint's innocence came too late to change the warrior guard's mind. He charged Flint with his sword, extending a flurry of thrusts and jabs. Flint nimbly rejected the sudden assault but had not mounted a counter attack. Taylok swung her sling rapidly, but held the stone in check; still hoping the encounter would come to a peaceful conclusion.

"Why don't you fight back?" screamed Tektitus, sword high, backing away.

"I do not find it easy to fight one I listed as my friend," said Flint. "I never considered crossing swords with you until this moment. I'm still willing to allow you to serve prison time rather than die here."

"Never. I'd sooner be cast into . . ."

He stopped as though struck by a thought and Taylok heard his footsteps running for the door, Flint hot on his heels. Taylok followed at a slower pace.

"Get to the safe room, Shotai," shouted Flint over his shoulder. "We'll return as soon as possible after we settle with Tektitus. Let no one enter until we return."

Tektitus charged up the stairway at the end of the hall dodging warriors and citizens milling around the area. Flint and Taylok followed, but Taylok could not keep up as it became harder and harder for her to navigate through the crowd. She quickly learned to follow the agitation revealed in loud, angry voices that Tektitus and Flint left in their wake.

When Taylok reached second level, she found the hallway less crowded, thus the trail more difficult to follow. She succeeded only after she heard a man screaming oaths at Tektitus on the stairway to third floor. Then, it occurred to her that Tektitus headed toward the fourth floor room of death. Surely, he didn't intend to go into . . . the thought stopped her on the stairway between second and third floor.

Taylok had rarely explored third floor, thus could not anticipate the obstacles as well as on the other floors. And she had never been to the fourth floor. She only hesitated for a moment on the stairway between second and third level and, knowing the stair locations, hurried directly to the fourth floor stairway. She heard talking from above.

"Don't do this, Tektitus," soothed the voice of Flint. "You have a lot of life remaining."

"What are they doing?" said a voice Taylok didn't recognize.

"You should have stopped them," said another unknown voice.

"It's Tektitus, you idiot. Why should we have stopped him?" wondered a third voice.

"No one is to blame," said a fourth voice. "We have not been sufficiently alert since the 'sunstone episode.' Anyone could have wandered into the room in the past four isas and we wouldn't have stopped them. But, now we need to keep everyone from going inside."

They must be the guards charged with the security of the fourth floor room, Taylok thought as she continued up the stairs.

"Halt!" said the fourth voice almost in Taylok's face. "You can't go any further."

"Stay where you are, Taylok," said Flint from somewhere above her. "Tektitus is standing in the doorway to the room."

The fourth level grew deathly quiet as everyone sensed Tektitus was about to commit the unthinkable. Taylok listened to room sounds during the brief conversation lull. She discerned the hollow sound of an opening to the fourth level room and a solid image of Tektitus and Flint standing near it. On the wall by the door Taylok detected a simple, circular pattern, similar to one that she had found before on first level. Flint had told her that what she sensed was a relief of the T'sa'wa, no doubt a carved portrait of the Sun God. The guard interrupted her thought.

195

"Flint?" said the guard. "Stones! Is that you?"

"It's me, Boron. How did you know?"

"Your voice," said Boron. "That and Taylok being here. Tektitus isn't going inside the room, is he?"

"I don't know. He said he killed His Eminence and was going to try and kill the Shotai. Then, he ran all the way up here."

"Sorry we weren't ready to stop him. We don't get too many suicide attempts here."

"Tektitus," said Flint, "you can still get out of this."

"I promised High Council."

"Forget High Council. He's trying to get you to do his dirty work. You're better than that."

"I once thought myself better, Flint, but not now. I killed His Eminence."

"Are you even sure that he's dead?"

"My sword found his heart. He is dead."

"I'm trying to help you here, Tektitus."

"There is no help for me, Flint. Better the unknown than the certain loss of freedom. Goodbye, my friend."

"Tektitus, don't . . ."

The situation demanded action and Taylok sprang into the fray. A stone from her sling slammed into the side of Tektitus' helm causing the man's knees to buckle. Flint ran to Tektitus' side and pulled him away from the door of the menacing room. Boron and two other warriors bolted up the stairs and helped carry Tektitus' unconscious form down to third level.

"You okay, Taylok?" asked Flint.

"Yes. I'm okay. Why was Tektitus so bent on self destruction?"

"There are actions that can't be changed or taken back. He's in that situation. He killed a man and is going to have to pay for it. Chief Iron or the Shotai will judge him and his clean record may or may not help lighten his sentence. In a way, though, I wouldn't have been too unhappy for him if he had gone into the room."

"Did I mess up?"

"Oh, no, Taylok. You did what was needed. Tektitus will live and maybe, someday, he'll thank you. Now, we have to go back to protect the Shotai. High Council Pebblic will probably try again to kill him when he learns that Tektitus failed."

Steel met them at the Shotai's door.

"Word has it that you two captured Tektitus," said Steel.

"It didn't exactly go like that," replied Flint. "Suffice to say that Tektitus is alive and going to face judgment."

"Since His Eminence is gone, I can help you protect the Shotai against High Council, if he is still aggressive enough to try and take over the temple."

"Glad to have you, Steel. Let's go inside and tell the Shotai what happened."

"What do you want me to do, Flint?" asked Taylok.

"Whatever you want, Taylok. You did a great job up there so you earned it. And now, since His Eminence is dead, we have no price on our heads. We're free to do anything within legal boundaries."

"Yes. I should have thanked Tektitus instead of knocking him out."

"It seems he did us a favor, all right," reminisced Flint. "Too bad it required a major offense and High Council didn't protect him. Tektitus was a good man until all this. Steel and I are going to talk with the Shotai. Want to come along?"

"No, thanks. I think I'll try to find some of my friends from school. I'll be back in a couple of turns."

"I doubt you'll find any of your friends this isa," said Steel. "The temple remains unsettled since His Eminence' killing and several dead warriors have been found along the mainway to the village, so people are hesitant to travel to the temple. I'm not even sure it's safe to walk around the temple until we figure out who is responsible for those deaths along the stoneway. Tektitus didn't kill all those people."

Taylok considered telling Steel of the events leading up to this juncture, but decided that Flint would decide for himself whether or not to tell.

"I want to visit my first room in the temple," she said. "It isn't far and I believe I can still find it without any help. I'll be back by the time you finish filling in the Shotai."

"Stay safe, Taylok," said Flint. "We'll see you back here."

CHAPTER 19 - JADE AND THE GLYPH STONE

Taylok made her way cautiously toward the second floor stairway. A high level of activity continued in the hallway and Taylok had to use every decibel of her acute hearing to avoid collisions with distracted people. According to open talk, most of the warriors had departed the temple to stop a possible invasion from outside but acolytes and curiosity seekers still mired the stairs and hallways.

Taylok found the entrance to the second level room and started to go inside when she remembered that someone else probably lived there, now. She tapped on the door and waited until it opened.

"Hi," said a woman. "What can I do for you?"

"I used to live here and thought, if you didn't mind, that I'd like to visit it again."

"Taylok, isn't it?" said the vaguely familiar woman's voice.

Taylok stopped. "Do I know you?"

"I'm Jade," said the woman. "I transcribe history scrolls. I have written your name on occasion in the past, and, yes, we met long ago in the Shotai's school when you were very young. I taught language."

"You recognized me from that long ago?"

"No. But, your description is vivid in the scrolls," laughed Jade. "You were unmistakable to me."

"Uh . . . Nice to hear your voice again."

Taylok and Jade made a brief tour of the room and terrace. Taylok felt comfortable in the old surroundings.

"It was good to visit with you, Taylok," said Jade. "I have to go, though. I have an appointment."

"Thanks for letting me walk around the room."

"I enjoyed your company. You know, I'm going to examine an old rock face that one of the acolytes found embedded in the temple building stones. He says it contains some glyphs that appear to be letters, but he can't read them. He thought it might be

198

ancient script. Like to come along?"

"Sounds more exciting than going back down stairs. Okay, sure. Where is the stone?"

"He says it's on third level."

The crowded conditions did not ameliorate until they reached the stairway to the third level.

"It's scary isn't it?" said Jade, as they climbed the stairs.

"What's scary?"

"All this; everyone going unconscious for a turn, the killing of His Eminence, the attack on the Shotai, the unusual crowds. Seems as though the world is going crazy."

"Yes," said Taylok, "it's definitely crazy."

They reached third level and Jade walked a short distance.

"This is where my friend asked me to meet him." She said. "We must be early."

"Maybe you could start looking at the stone while we wait."

"I don't know exactly where it is. He said it's pretty well hidden. Guess that's why no one else has discovered it for a while."

They waited for almost half a turn and the acolyte had not appeared. The third level seldom seemed crowded and this was no exception.

"This is odd," said Jade. "My friend is usually very punctual."

"Who is your friend?"

"His name is Flame. Do you know him?"

"No. The name is not familiar. I mean, the name is familiar, of course, flame. But, I'm not familiar with a person who has that name."

"I get what you're saying. Let's walk over to the alcove beyond the fourth level stairway. That area is dark and it could be where the glyphs are located."

Lighting inside the temple, generally considered excellent, nevertheless, contained pockets of total darkness that no one had bothered to illuminate. Numerous narrow windows, constructed to give the feel of openness, allowed very little outside light into the upper levels due to the wall angles and height above the soil where the phosphorescent ulok'neh grew.

"Wait a tic," said Taylok. "I hear something on the floor in that

199

area."

"You hear something? Snake?" said Jade, anxiously.

"No. Bigger. But it doesn't seem to be alive."

"Let me get a light basket," said Jade. "I can't see a thing."

Jade required only a short time to assemble a light basket, and she returned, breathless.

"Okay, now," she began, but immediately started screaming.

Her scream caused Taylok to jump backwards. Two young guards from fourth level came running down the stairs with swords drawn.

"What's wrong?" said a youthful male voice.

"It's my friend, Flame. He's lying on the floor," answered Jade.

Taylok became highly alert and listened carefully as the warrior bent over the form.

"He's dead," pronounced the warrior. "There's a knife in his back. What in the name of Ohana is happening to us?"

"His name is Flame," Jade offered. "He said he found a stone with glyphs on it."

"Glyphs?" said the warrior.

"You know, symbols carved in stone."

"Oh. That doesn't seem reason enough for someone to kill him," said the warrior.

"Didn't you warriors hear or see anything?" asked Taylok. "This had to happen here, didn't it?"

A moment of silence transpired where, Taylok assumed, the men exchanged glances and shrugs. One of them finally answered.

"There was a slight commotion down here almost a turn ago. It subsided quickly, however and when we came downstairs to look, we saw no one and dismissed it as a non event."

"What do you mean by 'a slight commotion?'" asked Jade.

"Sounds of a brief scuffle and a man's grunt. We had just taken our shift and were making noise, ourselves. When we looked around we found no blood or anyone who seemed out of place. We thought it had been just a couple of people pushing each other, or something. Unfortunately, we didn't check the alcove thoroughly since it's always dark and we had no light basket. Besides, our job is to prevent people from getting up to fourth level, not to police third level."

"Whose job is it to police third level?" asked Jade.

"Well, the warriors who normally police this level are with the party looking to engage Xantopec's warriors outside the temple."

"You'd think they'd be back by now. It's been four isas. Everything is a little out of kilter," agreed the second warrior.

"So, what do we do now?" asked Taylok.

Another moment of silence followed while the men looked at each other. Taylok could imagine the discomfort expressed by the two men although neither spoke.

"Who is in charge of your detail?" asked Taylok.

"Grain," said the first warrior.

"Shade," said the second almost simultaneously.

"I thought you were in charge," said Shade.

"No, it's you," said Grain.

"Okay," said Shade. "Warrior Grain, go down and find one of the warriors left to police the floors."

"What?"

"You heard me. If I'm in charge, you have to follow my orders."

"Damn," cursed Grain. "Stepped right into that one didn't I?"

A gruff, angry voice drifted to them from the stairs above.

"If you two don't begin acting like warriors, you'll be back in training next isa."

Grain raced down the stairs without a word and Shade mumbled an apology. Grain appeared a half turn later accompanied by another warrior.

"The new guy is older," whispered Jade to Taylok. "He looks like he's been asleep for three isas."

"Grain claims there is a dead man here," said the warrior to Shade. "Show me."

Shade took the light basket that Jade had constructed and approached the body.

"It's here, Warrior Stoner."

The older man turned Flame's body and examined the knife. Taylok lost track of the proceedings when Grain and Shade stepped between her and the opening to the alcove. Jade stood beside her.

"I'm sorry, Taylok," she said. "I never thought anything like this could happen or I wouldn't have invited you to come with me."

"You couldn't have anticipated this, Jade. Who might have killed him?"

"I don't know, but maybe the glyph stone will give us some clues . . . if we can find it."

"He told you it was on third level, right?"

"Yes, but he didn't offer any details about where on this level. He planned to show it to me."

"One thing we know is that it has to be hidden from view. At least, no one has reported finding it before, have they?"

"I never heard of it before Flame told me. Of course, it could be some unimportant bit of history or something one of the builders did on a whim."

"Where is Flame's room?"

"Room three-fifty-seven."

"That's no help. Did he work with anyone or have a partner?"

"No."

"Did he keep a diary or take scroll notes like we did in school?"

"Not that I . . . wait, I think he did make some scroll notes. Let's go down to his room and see if we can find them."

"Just a moment," said Shade. "You two aren't going anywhere until we unravel this killing."

"Let me see your hands," said Stoner.

Taylok held her hands out for the warrior to examine.

"You're both clean," he announced. "You can go."

"We'll be back," said Jade. "If we find anything, we'll tell you."

"You're going to let them go and search this guy's room?" questioned Shade. "What if there are clues to his murder?"

"I said, 'if we find anything, we'll tell you,'" said Jade. "What more do you want?"

"Go," said Stoner. "Go with them if you're worried, Shade."

"That might not be a bad idea," replied Shade. "If the girls didn't do this, there's a murderer still in the temple. Could be in Flame's room. Tell Boron where I've gone, Grain."

Taylok heard Shade's footsteps trailing after them as they walked the curving corridor to Flame's room.

"Which did you say is Flame's room?" asked Taylok.

"Room three-fifty-seven. It's just around this curve."

"Don't go inside until Shade checks it out. Okay?"

"Okay by me. I'm not anxious. Things are really weird."

"Did I hear you say room three-fifty-seven?" asked Shade.

"Yes," replied Jade.

"I'll look in before you go," the warrior said.

Shade passed them in the wide hallway and walked into Flame's room with sword drawn.

"Oh, sorry sir," Taylok heard Shade say. "I didn't realize you were . . . unggh."

Taylok heard the frightening sounds of a body collapsing to the floor and a sword clattering as it dropped from a lifeless hand. Then, she heard a metallic tinkle that she couldn't quite identify.

"Run," shouted Jade. "Something's wrong."

Taylok needed no encouragement. She raced beside Jade until they reached fourth level stairway.

"Help," shouted Jade.

"What's wrong?" called Grain as he descended the stairs two at a time.

"It's Shade," said Taylok. "Someone attacked him in Flame's room. It's room three-fifty-seven."

Warrior Stoner shuffled after Grain as the young warrior raced to the room with his sword drawn. Taylok and Jade cautiously retraced their steps, behind the warriors, toward Flame's room. Taylok heard a few people milling in the hallway, but they stood quietly, curious about the activity.

"There's no one here except Shade," said Grain. "He's dead with a knife in his chest."

"How could someone have done this and gotten away without anyone seeing him?" said Stoner. "I'm going to check those girls hands again."

He looked carefully at Taylok's hands and then went to Jade.

"We didn't do it,' said Taylok. "I heard Warrior Shade say, 'Oh, sorry sir,' and then he groaned when he was stabbed."

"The odd thing," said Stoner, "is that Shade had his weapon drawn but never used it, even though he faced his attacker. He must have recognized his killer and never suspected the danger he was in. You, Jade. Did you see anything that might help identify the killer?"

"No, nothing," said Jade, miserably. "We stayed back when the warrior went inside and then ran to get you when we heard the attack."

"How many people would Warrior Shade call sir?'" asked Taylok.

"Too many for it to be a clue," said Grain. "But it must have been one of the warriors or temple upper rank or . . . no, he even called the acolytes, sir."

"Taylok?" Flint's voice carried from the stairway to second level.

"Flint," she replied, glad to hear his voice. "Over here."

Flint approached them walking swiftly.

"What happened to you, Taylok?" he said. "I thought you were just going to look at your old room."

"I ran into Jade and we went to meet Flame, who found an old glyph stone, and Flame was dead and we came to his room and now Shade is dead."

"Who? What?"

"Flint?" said Jade. "I didn't recognize you with the beard."

"Hi, Jade. Nice to see you. It's been a while."

"You're Flint?" asked Stoner. "Let me see your hands."

"My hands? What's going on here?"

"It's like Taylok said," Grain chirped. "A fourth floor warrior and an acolyte have been killed."

"I'll handle this," growled Stoner. "You have some dried blood on your hands, Flint."

"It couldn't be him, then," offered Grain, "Shade hasn't been dead long enough for his blood to dry."

"Well, it could be that Flint killed Flame, then," said Stoner. "Is that your knife in the sheath? Did you kill Flame with it?"

"Come on, Stoner," said Grain. "The knife that killed Flame is still in his back."

"Oh, yes, so it is," said Stoner. "All this has me a little rattled."

Footsteps alerted Taylok that someone else had arrived.

"What's going on, Flint?" asked Steel.

"A pair of murders," Flint answered. "One is a warrior who was guarding fourth level.

"Steel," said Stoner, "I'm glad you're here. I'm confused. I'll fill you in as best I can."

Steel, Stoner and Grain walked into room three fifty-seven where Stoner and Grain proceeded to tell Steel about the murders as they searched the room.

"You have to help us, Flint," said Taylok. "Jade thinks there's a note scroll inside Flame's room that could shed some light on the murders . . . at least Flame's."

"The same person probably killed them both," added Jade.

"You said something earlier about an old stone," said Flint. "What does that have to do with all this?"

"Maybe nothing," replied Jade. "Flame was going to show me the stone because he couldn't decipher the glyphs carved on it. Trouble is, he didn't tell me exactly where it's located."

"And you think the scroll holds the reason for his murder?"

"Maybe," said Jade. "We won't know until we look at it."

"I'll ask Steel if they found a scroll."

He entered Flame's room. A few moments later, Flint returned.

"Steel says they didn't find a scroll, but they found some writing sheets, if you're interested."

"I'll take a look at them," said Jade. "That's strange, though, because there should have been a scroll. Can we go inside, Flint?"

"I think they're through examining it."

Jade and Taylok walked into the room and Taylok surprised herself by the wind sounds she could identify. The three men walking around and the body of Shade were easiest, but she discerned a bed with a table beside it and several articles on the table. She located two overturned chairs and a pot with either ulok or ulok'neh growing in it. One of the chairs had a thicker back than the other.

"These are just class notes," said Jade, after looking at the writing sheets.

"Maybe the killer took the scroll," said Taylok.

"I think Shade interrupted him before he found what he was looking for."

"Is there anything unusual about the room beside the fact that it's messed up?"

"Flame was pretty messy himself, so, no."

Grain and Stoner carried Shade's body out the door and Steel followed them. Flint entered while the two girls searched the room.

"Find anything?" he asked.

"No, it's a dead end," replied Jade. "The sheets are school notes, some of them written three or four rings ago."

"Jade," said Taylok, "let's take a look at the back of this chair."

She carefully righted the chair and ran her hands over the thick back.

"It's just a chair," said Jade.

"Wait," said Flint. "I see what Taylok is talking about. That back looks odd when you compare it with the other."

"The fiber pad does look thicker," said Jade. "If I . . ."

She pulled the back and the fiber lifted away, revealing a scroll.

"You're a genius, Taylok," said Jade. "This is the scroll."

"Read it, Jade," said Taylok. "What does it say?"

"Okay, this first part is from several isas ago, about fourth level room and . . . here it is. Flame writes, 'found the glyph stone two isas ago and tried to decipher it. He told Jade,' me,' about it when he discovered that he couldn't read the glyphs,' and notes here that, 'he also told . . . His Eminence Graystone.'"

"That one is truly a dead end," said Flint. "Tektitus killed His Eminence less than four turns ago."

"Who would His Eminence have told?" wondered Taylok.

Flint opined, "We may never know for certain, but, I'd bet on his next in command, High Council Pebblic. Tektitus claimed that High Council convinced him to kill His Eminence Graystone and the Shotai."

"How can we find out if His Eminence told Pebblic?" asked Taylok.

"It would take a confession by Pebblic or a séance," observed Flint, jokingly.

"I think that Flame never told anyone the exact location of the stone script," said Jade. "If the site isn't on this scroll, we may not be able to find it."

"Read it, then," said Taylok.

"Okay, okay. Let's see, 'he told His Eminence about the find and then made a tracing of the first letters.' Here they are. Oh, this is ancient script. I'll have to check it, but I'd guess it's older than seven hundred rings. It could be as old as the temple itself."

"I didn't think they had writing back then," said Flint.

"The Nehwisna developed an alphabet three thousand rings ago in Stonehaven Hall and the Hall of the Tadi'wa. It just didn't seem important to anyone but the priests until a few hundred rings ago. Few people learned it and even fewer started to write back then. But, some records remain that were written by priests of the Tadi'wa almost twenty-five hundred rings ago. These trace the history . . ."

"We get the idea, Jade," said Taylok. "Tell us what the tracing says."

"I have no idea," replied Jade. "I'll have to take it back and go over it with my books. Wait . . . I do recognize one symbol. Key. This is the key to something. I'm going to my room and see if I can decipher this first part."

"You shouldn't be alone until we solve these murders,' said Flint. "How about if Taylok and I go with you?"

"What about the rest of the scroll?" asked Taylok. "Does it have the location of the glyphs on it?"

"Sorry," said Jade, "I got absorbed in the translation. Let's see, yes, it's here. The stone is . . . 'Under the fourth floor stairway.' Under the fourth floor stairway? We were standing right next to it all that time?"

"Who looks under a stairway?" asked Taylok.

"Let's check it out, now," said Jade, hurrying toward the door with Taylok close behind.

"Taylok, Jade," said Flint, "remember that there's still a killer loose who has taken two lives already and it might have something to do with the stone and the glyphs. I'll escort you to those stairs, but I need to return to the Shotai and check on him. I shouldn't be gone long. The fourth floor guards can help protect you until I get back."

"We'll be fine," said Taylok. "I have plenty of stones for my sling."

"When did you sleep last?"

"I can't remember for sure. It hasn't been too long."

"Didn't you get knocked out like the rest of us?" asked Jade.

"She was the only person in the temple, aside from Xantopec

and his priestesses, who didn't get knocked out. But, that was four isas ago. I think she's slept a couple of turns since then."

"You'd better get some sleep, then, Taylok," said Jade.

"I'm too excited to sleep until we find the glyph stone. I can sleep in your room while you translate."

"Stay alert," said Flint. "Your lives may depend on it."

Flint walked with the girls to the dark stairwell and Jade looked beneath it. Taylok felt along the walls while Flint talked to the warriors guarding fourth level. He soon returned to the girls.

"Warrior Boron said they would watch after you," said Flint. "Just call out to them if you need help. I'll be back in less than a half turn."

With that, Flint hurried down the stairs, leaving Jade and Taylok alone on third level beneath fourth level stairway.

"It's a time like this when I miss my vision most," lamented Taylok, still feeling the walls.

"This area is too dark to see, anyway," consoled Jade. "I need to get another light basket."

"Check the alcove where we found Flame," said Taylok. "I think that light basket you made earlier may still be there."

"Good idea, Taylok. I'll be back in a moment."

"Hang on. I'll go with you. We shouldn't separate while Flint is gone."

"Not necessary. I'll only be gone for a moment. If the light basket is in the alcove, it will be easy to find. Right now, I can't even see you and I know that you're only a couple of steps away. It's really dark under here."

"Okay. I'll keep feeling along the walls, then. The light won't help me, anyway."

Taylok heard Jade walk leisurely toward the alcove. She had only been gone a short time, when Taylok heard numerous footsteps hurriedly walking toward them. Taylok wanted to warn Jade, but realized there were five or six people in the approaching group and they were already at the stairway.

"Warrior Boron," said a vaguely familiar voice. "My men will patrol third level for a few turns."

"Yes, sir," answered the voice from the fourth floor. "May we be of help?"

"No. Do your job and keep everyone away from fourth level."

Taylok heard a tinkle of metal. She tried desperately to recall where she had heard that voice before. When the realization came to her, she made a sharp, inadvertent intake of breath.

"Did you hear something?" said High Council Pebblic.

"Someone coughed," said a warrior. "Probably one of the men upstairs."

"Hm. Get some light baskets up here. Search this floor thoroughly. When you find her, bring her to me."

"Yes, sir."

Taylok backed deeper into the darkness beneath the stairway as the High Council and two warriors walked back as they had come, the metallic tinkle accompanying them. One of the remaining warriors walked toward Taylok with his sword drawn. She dropped silently to her knees as she heard him slashing the darkness near her, coming closer with each swing of his weapon. She crawled away just in time to avoid a vicious slash. Then, he stopped, abruptly.

"There's nothing here," he said, cheerily.

"There are several more dark areas, Fell. Go and get some light baskets."

Fell. She remembered him. She wondered if Ran was with this group, too. She touched the base stone next to her shoulder. It felt rough, but not like unpolished stone. Taylok ran her hands along the long stone. The glyphs.

The warriors walked up the hallway in a group, probably searching for material to make light baskets. After they had passed the curve in the hall, Taylok raced from the stairwell and ran toward the alcove. She heard Jade, cowering in a corner.

"Jade," she shouted, hoarsely. "We have to get out of here."

"Are they gone?" Jade whispered.

"Yes. But, we have to hurry. They're coming back with light baskets. And I think they're looking for you."

"Why?"

"High Council Pebblic said, 'If you find her, bring her to me.' Probably wants you to translate, or make you give him the scroll."

"Did he call me by name?"

"No. I just assumed . . ."

"Okay, let's go."

"Did you find the light basket?"

"Yes. I have it here."

"How did you keep them from seeing you?"

"I put the basket under my tunic and hid in the corner of the alcove."

"Smart thinking, Jade."

"I wasn't born last isa. But, when I heard them coming I was afraid they'd find you under the stairs."

"If they had had a light basket, they would have. We're lucky. Oh, by the way, I found the glyphs. They're 'way back under the stairs on the wall base slab."

"What? You found the glyphs? I have to see them."

"Not now, you don't. Those warriors will be back any moment. Let's get out of here. We can come back later."

"Okay, okay. You're right. Those glyphs have been there for almost a thousand rings. They should last one more isa. Let's go back to my room."

As the pair started down stairs to second level, they heard the warriors returning. When they reached second level, Jade stopped.

"Wait," she said. "High Council knows my room is on second level. Wouldn't he set a scout there if he were trying to find me? Why would he look for me on third level?"

"He probably looked in your room first and . . ."

"But, how would he even know that I'm involved?"

Both pondered that question as they walked around the second floor hallway.

"It's the glyphs," said Taylok. "You're the only one in the temple who can readily translate them. Flame couldn't do it and the only other translators are priests in the Hall of the Tadi'wa. You're it, Jade."

"Not true, Taylok. The Shotai can translate them. He taught me how to do it."

"High Council might have a difficult time convincing the Shotai to translate something like that for High Council's personal use. I doubt Flint would even let High Council Pebblic in to see the Shotai, unless the Shotai insisted on it."

"This is giving me a headache."

"Let's go down to first level and see if we can find Flint."

"You love Flint, don't you?"

"What? Of course I love Flint. I've known him all my life."

"I mean you love him a lot don't you?"

"Well . . . sure, I do. But not in the way you seem to be thinking. Flint is the best friend I ever had. He rescued me from certain death . . . I don't know how many times. Flint is the one person I could always depend on since my mother died. He's the father that I never had in my life."

"I see," said Jade, pensively.

She turned and walked the other direction.

"Wait," said Taylok. "You're heading back toward your room."

"I have to get my books. I can't do any translations without them."

"Can't you get them later? If High council finds you, he may put you in prison if you don't help him."

"You're being overly dramatic, Taylok. High Council wouldn't do anything like that."

"If High council is who I think he is, he has done much worse, believe me."

"Who do you think he is?"

"All I know is that he has the same name and comes from the same hall as my mother's Fireseasoned mate of eleven rings ago. And if he is my father, he had my mother put to death by sacrifice and had Xantopec blind me with the T'sa'wa. He would have had me sacrificed as well, but Flint saved me."

"Do you know for sure that he's your father?"

"No, I don't know for sure. But, if he is, he's evil. I'm going to stay as far away from him as I can."

"Okay, wait for me, there. That alcove is dark. Wait inside while I get my books."

Taylok reluctantly went into the alcove and sat on the floor.

"I'm only going to wait a short time, then I'm going downstairs," Taylok called.

"I won't be gone long," assured Jade.

Taylok remembered the alcove from the rings she lived in the room Jade now occupied. It seemed different with her blindness, but still more familiar than the upper levels. She hummed to herself and tried to think positively about High Council. Maybe he wasn't her father. She hadn't given that option much chance. Maybe he was a good person with a bad name. Maybe . . . sounds of people moving down the corridor interrupted her thoughts. Six people, warriors by the sounds they made, trotted at double time toward Jade's room. Taylok backed deeper into the alcove. Jade could hardly avoid being captured with such a force hunting her.

The warrior party stopped at Jade's door and knocked, loudly. This was hardly the normal method of warriors hunting for a person. Taylok had thought they would crash right in and capture Jade.

Then, in another surprise to Taylok, Jade answered the knock.

"Are you Jade?" asked one of the warriors.

"Yes," Taylok heard. "I'm Jade."

"We are looking for a friend of yours . . ."

The hallway became noisy and Taylok missed the end of the conversation. But, it had to be Taylok they were after. Maybe her father had decided to finish what he had started when he had decreed the death of her and her mother. Taylok trembled in the dark alcove as she waited. It seemed that she had been hiding there forever and Taylok resolved to leave even if it meant running into the warriors.

But, before she could leave, Jade's voice whispered, "Taylok?"

"Yes," Taylok answered, resignedly. "I'm still here."

"Good. Let's go down and see if we can find Flint."

"What?"

"I have the most important books. Let's find Flint."

"Wait," said Taylok. "What were the warriors doing at your door?"

"They were looking for Playa. Not me . . . or you."

"Playa? What do they want with Playa?"

"I don't know for sure, but they hinted something about a stone. Maybe they were talking about the glyph stone, but I don't think so."

"Uh oh," breathed Taylok.

"What's wrong?"

"Nothing," Taylok answered, lightly. "I hope Playa is in the village, not the temple."

"Yes. Nothing is usually too good when you have warriors looking for you."

Jade and Taylok walked downstairs to the Shotai's room. Flint met them at the door.

"Come in, you two," he said. "I was just about to go up and find you."

"Jade," said the Shotai, walking across the room, "How good to see you again. Peace and tranquility. And, to you, Taylok."

Taylok smiled and waved at the sound of his voice.

"Peace and tranquility, Shotai," said Jade. "How are you?"

"I'm healing, my child. But fit enough to help you decipher the glyph stone."

"It's on level three," said Jade. "I have a fragment, though, on a tracing."

"Good, good. Let's look."

Taylok listened as Jade opened the scroll.

"Oh, my," said the Shotai. "This is ancient."

"Can you translate it?" asked Jade.

"Oh, yes, of course. But, the fragment doesn't tell us much. It says, 'The key to the Toptli . . .' and that's as far as it gets."

"What's the Toptli?" asked Jade.

"It could mean 'secret,' or 'box.' It depends on the next words."

"But, what is it?" pressed Jade.

"We won't know until we see more of the glyph. Sorry to disappoint you, Jade, but that's all you have, here. We can check the books, but I think we have found our end point without more data."

"Ah," came Steel's voice from the door. "We have a quorum, I see."

"Anything new on the murders?" asked Flint.

"We learned that there was more to Flame than just serving as an acolyte. He received a visitor from the Hall of the Tadi'wa about five isas ago. We know this because a next room neighbor saw the man enter Flame's room and asked Flame about it. Flame told him, and asked him to keep it secret. Said the man was a relative from Tadi'wa Hall. But, Flame's relatives are all in the New Rockhome Hall village. They say they have no relatives in other halls."

"Ah, intrigue," said Flint, with a smile in his voice.

"It's a starting point," said Steel, defensively. "We need to find the man who visited Flame if the lead is going anywhere."

"Let me see," said Flint, "you don't know what he looks like or where he might have gone or if he had anything to do with the murders. Is that it?"

"Like I said, Flint, it's a starting point."

"It just seems . . . wait. Did you say the neighbor saw the man?"

"Yes."

"Is the neighbor willing to look at a body," asked Flint. "I have an idea."

"A body? You think the man who visited Flame is dead, too?"

"Maybe it's the same man. I killed him in self-defense, four isas ago, before the sunstone episode, on the pathway to the village. He's from Banestone Hall, however, not Tadi'wa Hall.."

"Flame may have lied about where the man came from. You think you killed our witness?"

"I don't know for sure that he is your witness. It was a man I knew from Banestone Hall who attacked Taylok and me as we neared the temple. He left me no choice but to kill him."

"Where is the body?"

"I saw them bring it in last isa with several others who had been killed along the pathway. The bodies are in the dead room. We need to hurry. They go to Mordane Pit, next isa."

"I'll get the neighbor. If it's the man he saw visiting Flame, we can stop searching. I'll expect you to fill us in on who he was."

"Of course," said Flint.

Steel hurried out of the room.

"You think Sericite is the one who visited Flame?" asked Taylok, yawning.

"I think it's a good possibility," said Flint. "I know that Sericite had a hidden agenda when he came here. I originally thought it was just to kill me, but now . . ."

Steel arrived shortly with an older man.

"Come with us, Flint. You'll need to show us which body you thought might be the one."

"Certainly. Keep the door locked, Shotai. Don't let anyone in except us."

"Yes, yes," said the Shotai, flipping the pages of one of Jade's books.

Taylok excused herself and went to the room that the Shotai had arranged for her. She fell asleep almost immediately. When she awoke, Taylok had no idea how long she had slept, but felt refreshed. Strangely, she detected no one in the big room.

"Shotai? Jade?" she called into her darkness.

No response. Where had they gone? She walked to the exit and opened the door. She assumed it to be the sleep turns since the hall carried only light foot traffic. Taylok singled out the stationary figure across from the room.

"Stonic?"

"No, I'm Blade," said the man. "Stonic is on break."

"Did you see the Shotai leave this room with a young woman?"

"No," replied Blade. "You are the first to come or go since I began watch."

"How long have you been on watch?"

"About a quarter turn. Stonic should return shortly if you want to talk to him."

"Thanks, but I think I'll go upstairs and look for them. If you should see the Shotai soon will you tell him I'm looking for him on second and third level?"

"Yes. And I'll tell Stonic when he returns. You're Taylok, right?"

"Right. Thanks."

Taylok walked alertly through the lightly inhabited hallway toward second level stairs. She heard voices along the way, but recognized none. When she reached the stairs, she clung to the handrail and made her way to second level. She paused long enough at Jade's door to ascertain that the translator wasn't inside. They must be on third level, working on the translation of the glyph stone. She found third level stairs. Taylok detected no one on the stairs or in second level hallway. Even being the sleep turns, this seemed extraordinary. It felt too quiet and too empty.

Taylok wondered if her senses were deceiving her and there really were people around. She stood very still, held her breath and listened intently. No breathing, no heartbeats - except her own - no footsteps could be heard. The soundlessness worried Taylok because it never happened to her before. Some kind of human utterance, tap, thump, ring or echo always resonated in the temple. Taylok could think of no exception.

Then, it hit her. It had to be a dream. She relaxed and smiled. Yet, it didn't seem quite right. Usually in dreams, she could see. This dream found her as blind as in real life. She backed away from third level stairs and retreated to the dark alcove where she sat and tried to understand her situation. Even in dreams, Taylok usually found people. Often, when she slept alone in the stalagmite forest, she dreamed of people. She had never been afraid to be alone, yet humans, friends or enemies, dead or alive, had forever occupied her dreams, until now.

A familiar, thin, reedy voice broke the silence and Taylok knew that it was a dream. The Shaman died many isas ago.

"Taylok, girl of dreams, your gifts will save you," said the Shaman's voice.

"Save me from what?" she asked.

"Choose the right."

"Choose the right what?" she screamed.

"It's all right," said another voice. Confusion, then recognition coursed through her.

She heard the Shotai's voice. Taylok jerked awake when a hand gently touched her shoulder.

"Shotai?"

"Yes, Taylok. Don't be alarmed. You were dreaming."

"The Shaman came to me in my dream, Shotai."

"I see him sometimes in my own dreams, Taylok. He was a true friend to us."

"He told me, 'Your gifts will save you.' And then he said, 'Choose the right.'"

"Profound advice, Taylok. Use your gifts to the best of your ability and choose the right path to walk."

"What are my gifts?"

"You have many gifts; your acute hearing, your uncanny ability with the sling, your fabulous mind, your swift feet . . ."

"Those are gifts?"

"Of course."

"Oh. I thought he meant something like the sling that Flint gave me or the stone that Playa gave me."

"Dreams are curious things, Taylok. Sometime straightforward, they often seem to contain several meanings when told to others. You are probably best served to interpret your own dream. After all, your thoughts produced it."

"It does seem to help when you get someone else's input, though."

"Happy to oblige."

"How long have I been asleep?"

"Only a few turns. How do you feel?"

"Better. Have you found anything new on the scroll?"

"No. And we're still waiting for Flint and Steel to return."

As if on spoken cue, a knock came from the door.

"Shotai. It's Flint and Steel," said Flint's voice.

The men came inside.

"Our witness identified Sericite as the man who visited Flame," said Steel.

"Now, we have to figure out what it means," added Flint.

"Maybe this all goes back to the original builders," said the Shotai. "In a more youthful time, the halls worked together and built things. Songs contained history and the priests of the Tadi'wa spent much time teaching those songs to acolytes. Perhaps someone remembered a song that related to the room on level four. Flame found the glyph stone shortly after Sericite's visit."

"But, how does High Council Pebblic fit into all this?" asked Taylok.

"The Tadi'wa priest structure placed High Council Pebblic highly," said Steel. "Maybe he rediscovered something of level four from those ancient songs."

"Perhaps, he is more than one step ahead of us," said the Shotai. "He may have already interpreted the glyph stone and now seeks the key to the room."

"Let's catch up," said Jade. "We know where the glyph stone is located."

"And we may already have the key," added Taylok.

"Why does the room need a key? The door is open," recalled the Shotai.

"I have a feeling that the key is important," Taylok responded.

"Maybe the glyph will enlighten us," said the Shotai. "My interest is now piqued, and that hasn't happened for a while."

Flint and Steel expressed doubts as to the safety of the temple's upper levels for him, but the Shotai dismissed their fears and departed with Jade and Taylok for fourth floor stairway. Flint and Steel followed, jaws set firmly, daring anyone to rouse their concern.

When they reached third level, Taylok led the way to the area beneath the fourth floor stairs where she had discovered the glyph stone. Jade held the light basket while the Shotai translated the glyph.

"This first part is the glyph that Flame traced," said the Shotai, running his hands over the carved letters. He read, "Key to the secret box is eye of T'sa'wa. Absent its turn, Mordane Pit; with it, riches of paradise - Glyphsong."

"So, there is a treasure," said Steel.

"Don't be too sure," said the Shotai. "These phrases often have more than one meaning. We don't know to what the 'riches of paradise' refers. It could mean treasure, but it might have a metaphoric meaning like 'the afterlife.' I, for one, prefer to wait a while for the afterlife. On the other hand, if there actually was a treasure, it could have been taken by others many rings ago."

"Maybe, Shotai," offered Flint, "it means that there is a treasure of some sort for someone with the key."

"But, who is willing to risk the alternative?"

"I still don't understand the glyph," said Taylok. "What is the eye of T'sa'wa and what is its turn?"

"In the early rings of the temple," said the Shotai, "many stone circles were carved to represent the T'sa'wa. Some of the carvings placed a crystal, centered in the circle or somewhere on the sphere, depicting an eye to illustrate that the T'sa'wa watched over us. Since the time when we recognized that other creations helped protect us, some of the idols were destroyed or stored away. One such crystal once rested in the large geode carving on level one."

"I remember that one," said Flint. "What happened to it?"

"Stolen by vandals, I believe, in the ring of the Water God while I was stricken," replied the Shotai.

"Could the stone that I gave you to hold for me be that one?"

asked Taylok. "Citrinon acted very curiously about it."

"It is possible," said the Shotai. "I would have to see if it fit the indention to be certain. Even if it is the missing stone, there is no guarantee that it is the eye mentioned in the glyph."

"What about the turn?" asked Taylok.

"I presume it means that something must be turned to bring the correct action."

"'Turn' could mean several things, couldn't it?"

"Yes. Many words are similar and could have had the same derivation. But 'turn' could mean a span of time, a twist, or next in line."

"I'm not sure," said Flint, "why we are going to this trouble for an unknown quantity such as the mysterious room. It has gone undisturbed for hundreds of rings."

"You said it, Flint," laughed Taylok. "It's the mystery room. We don't know if it's valuable or not. And if it is valuable, how valuable is it?"

"I hope the mystery isn't its only value. We should be trying to get the Shotai restored to temple head instead of chasing a possible answer to that sinister room."

"There have been two murders, that we know about, related to the glyphs and the glyphs are related to the room."

"Yes, but you are only assuming that the glyphs explain the room's secret."

"Did anyone ever stop to think that using the key might be disastrous?" asked Steel. "What if it's a monstrous weapon? It could kill us all."

"The room itself seems to be the disaster," said Jade. "We have no record of anyone who went inside, ever coming out. We presume they're dead, but maybe they aren't."

"Yes, but why the sudden interest in it? Is it just the new information provided by the glyph? Or have I missed something?" Steel asked.

Taylok reacted first. In the midst of their fervent conversation, Taylok heard the sounds of steel against steel, sword against sword. She held her hand up and everyone stopped the conversation and looked at her.

"I hear fighting," she blurted.

"Can you tell where it is?" Steel inquired.

"Not exactly. Maybe first level. It's getting louder, though."

"We need to get the Shotai to safety," said Flint, urgently.

He moved to the Shotai's side and escorted him to second level as Steel and the rest of the party followed. When the sounds grew loud enough for all to hear, Steel raced to stand with Flint and the Shotai.

"What do you think, Flint?" said Steel. "Is it Xantopec?"

"Maybe," Flint replied, "but I wouldn't bet against a temple revolt with His Eminence dead and the Shotai still recovering. High Council seems to make dangerous moves."

By the time they reached first level, the sounds were cacophonous yet they had seen no one engaged in combat. At the Shotai's door, Stonic stood with sword at the ready, looking in both directions up and down the hallway for the combatants.

"Shotai," he called, opening the door. "Hurry inside."

Flint went in first, followed by the Shotai and then Steel and the girls.

"Come inside, Stonic," said the Shotai. "The door is sturdy and when locked, not likely to be penetrated."

"I'll go to the battle," said Flint. "We need to know with whom we're fighting."

"I'll go with you," said Steel. "Two swords . . ."

"Agreed," interrupted Flint as they dashed toward sounds of the fray. "Taylok, Stonic, defend the Shotai until we return."

The Shotai smiled and placed his arm about Taylok's shoulder.

"It is good to have young blood on your side," the Shotai said, seriously.

Taylok smiled broadly.

"The door is locked securely," announced Stonic.

Jade approached Taylok and touched her on the arm.

"I'm afraid," she said, "but I know how good you are with your sling."

"Can you fight if you have to?" Taylok asked.

"Not so much, as I have no weapon," said Jade. "Best I can do is recite history and bore someone to death."

Tension-laced laughter echoed in the room.

"We can probably defend the door for a brief time," voiced

Stonic, after the laughter subsided. "And someone must be here to admit Flint and Steel when they return."

The Shotai walked to a wall of the room and pushed a hidden panel aside, revealing a large case.

"Oh," said Jade, "it's an arsenal of swords and knives. There are even a couple of slings."

"My emergency weapons," said the Shotai, lifting a sword from its holder.

Jade took a sword and swished the air with the narrow blade.

"I'll go down defending us, if I must," she avowed.

Taylok had not removed the sling from her shoulder but walked unerringly to the weapons and found another sling. She removed it from the holder and cradled a stone from her pouch, swinging it gently, getting the feel of the straps and length.

"Something wrong with your sling?" asked Jade.

"No," responded Taylok, somberly. "I just wanted a spare in case mine breaks and your history recital leaves any warriors standing."

Jade laughed nervously and then spoke seriously.

"You knew I was joking, didn't you?" she said.

"Of course," laughed Taylok as she cinched the new sling around her middle like a belt. She turned quickly toward the door and said, "It's too late for more jokes, though, someone's at the door."

Immediately following Taylok's alert, someone banged solidly on the door and tension rose inside the room.

"Who's there?" shouted Stonic.

"Open the door, Stonic," registered Steel's voice. "Flint's been injured."

Stonic raced to the door and opened it.

"What's happening?" Taylok asked Jade.

"Stonic and the Shotai are helping Steel with Flint. Flint has a bleeding wound on his chest. It looks serious."

"What did you run into, Steel?" asked the Shotai. "Have we been invaded by Xantopec?"

"Worse," replied Steel. "Pebblic has formed a large group of rebels and they're trying to take over the temple."

"How many did you see?"

"At least thirty, maybe more. Pebblic selected well. They are all strong fighters. His Eminence's warriors, now loyal to you, Shotai, are holding them in check thus far. When we arrived, they had broken through the defense. Flint and I fought back five of Pebblic's warriors. Flint killed one before three of them acted in a tandem rush attack I had never seen before. Flint didn't have a chance against them, good as he is. He's lucky to be alive and that won't be for long if we don't stop the bleeding."

"Girls," said the Shotai, "you must leave the temple. You are unseasoned as fighters and the men Steel describes are well trained. It would be unfair to ask you to face them. Go now and save yourselves."

"Okay," replied Jade, standing.

"I can help Flint," demurred Taylok. "I don't have to fight, Shotai. I can doctor."

"His wounds are severe, Taylok," said Steel. "He needs professional mending."

"Then, I can run and get Ganaga," said Taylok.

"That would be most helpful," said the Shotai. "Wait, Taylok. You should take the gift from Playa in case Pebblic's warriors overtake this room."

He removed the crystal from a niche and placed it in Taylok's hand. She dropped it into her stone pouch. Taylok and Jade allowed the Shotai to usher them into a hidden passageway that led to a well-disguised door at the base of the temple.

"There is no one in sight," said Jade, scurrying into the garden that helped hide the secret door. Taylok followed, listening for less visible landmarks to help guide them and making certain she could find the door again. She dropped back for a moment and scooped out a hole, deposited the crystal and covered it with dirt.

"What are you doing?" said Jade in a loud whisper. "We have to go."

Taylok hurried toward Jade's voice as sounds of fighting echoed from the temple.

"There's the main stoneway to the village," said Jade. "We'll make better time when we're on it."

Taylok listened to Jade's footsteps, following closely as she dared. To a casual observer they were two girls running toward the village without a care.

Two merchants, unaware of the fighting in the temple and announcing their wares, called to them as they passed.

"Fine ulok for only a shell," said one.

"Get the best ulok here," voiced another.

"There's a civil disturbance in Eldar Temple," said Jade, not slowing her pace.

"What? Wait," said one of the merchants.

But, Taylok and Jade did not stop. When they reached the heart of the village, Taylok led the way to Ganaga's abode.

"Ganaga," Taylok shouted. "Flint's been hurt. He needs your help."

Ganaga opened the door.

"Taylok. Jade. What's this about Flint? Where is he?" Ganaga asked.

"He's in the Shotai's suite at the temple. He's cut badly on the chest. We need you to treat him and stop the bleeding."

"I'll get my kit."

"I'm not going back with you," said Jade. "I can't do anything for Flint and the Shotai told us to stay away from the temple."

Taylok nodded.

"Thanks for your help, Jade," Taylok said.

Jade walked away as Ganaga returned with his kit.

"You don't have to go back with me," he said. "I know where the Shotai's rooms are located."

"There's fighting on the main level and you may not be able to reach the Shotai's suite through the hallways."

"How, then?"

"I can show you a secret passage."

"Lead on, Taylok."

When they reached the garden Taylok unerringly led Ganaga to the hidden door, and pressed a stone in the temple wall. The door opened slowly.

"Incredible, Taylok, that you could find this. I still can't see the stone that you pushed. I'll leave you here. You can find your way back to the village, can't you?"

"Yes."

"Ask Cobalta to prepare the guest room for you."

"Thank you, Ganaga. Save Flint."
"I'll do my best."

Chapter 20 - Captured

Taylok walked a short distance down the path to the village before she remembered that earlier she left the paired crystal in the garden. She started back to retrieve it when she picked up the sound of warriors nearby, their clanking swords being a defining clue. Taylok stopped, hoping that the warriors were either friendly or uninterested in her. Unluckily, that was not the case.

"Well, well," said an all too familiar voice. "If it isn't the blind girl, Taylok."

"You know her?" said another voice.

"I would have collected three hundred shells for her, Whiteknife, if some men hadn't interfered."

"You never had your hands on anything worth three hundred shells, Fell," said Whiteknife.

"Ask Ran. He was with me."

"Okay. If she's worth three hundred shells, let's take her in and collect."

"She is no longer worth anything," said Fell. "His Eminence would have paid, but since he was assassinated she's worth nothing . . . less than nothing."

Taylok loosened her sling, but she counted nine warriors in the party. If they came after her, she would have no choice but to surrender or die.

"She may still be worth something," said another voice that Taylok remembered . . . Ran. "The girl, Playa, said she gave a paired crystal to Taylok. High Council Pebblic wants it."

Rough hands grabbed Taylok's arms and held firm.

"Want to just hand it over?" said Whiteknife, "or do we have to search you for it?"

"I don't have a crystal, just my sling stones," said Taylok. "You can search if you don't believe me."

"Well, now, searching you might be fun at that," said Whiteknife, "if you weren't such a young, skinny thing. Hand me your stone pouch."

Taylok complied and listened as Whiteknife dumped the stones on the ground. She heard Ran and Whiteknife rummaging through the pebbles.

"There's no crystal here, Ran," said Whiteknife. "You sure about the information?"

"I heard Playa say she gave the stone to Taylok. High Council Pebblic tortured the girl for four turns and she never wavered from that story. Playa didn't have the crystal. We searched her room, stripped her bare and encouraged her to be forthcoming with whips and crystal sparks. By the time we finished, Playa had told us the truth as she knew it."

"So, Taylok," said Whiteknife, "tell us where the stone is hidden."

"I gave it to the Shotai for safekeeping. It's not worth anything, anyway, just an ordinary paired crystal."

"That's the one Pebblic's looking for," said Ran, softly. "If Taylok is telling the truth, it may be hard to get."

"Search her," said Whiteknife, "and be thorough. If it's not on her, she's probably telling the truth."

Three of the warriors participated in the search, some of the hands and fingers becoming extremely intimate with her as the men laughed, raucously. Taylok fought back tears long before they finished and they continued to search long after they knew she hid nothing.

"She's been a sharp stone underfoot," said Fell, after the brutal search concluded. "I say we dispose of her."

"I agree," said Ran.

"What, you just want to finish her right here?" said Whiteknife. "No. I don't think so . . . too close to Eldar Temple for me. Anybody looking out could see you. Silver, for instance."

"Here is as good as anywhere," argued Ran.

"Maybe not," said Fell. "I don't want Silver to find out we killed a young girl. I think we should take her to the view of Mystical Grotto atop Megalith Rise and turn her loose. It will be fun to watch her scratch around up there until she falls over the edge. I always wanted to blindfold someone, tie his hands behind him and watch him try to make it down that path. We won't even have to blindfold this one. And no one will be the wiser as to her death."

"Harsh," said Ran. "I like it."

"We don't have time for such rash foolishness," said Whiteknife. "If you want to do that, you're on your own. You have two turns left on your skirmish break. If you're late returning, I will personally deliver your punishment. We still have work to do on the battlefield. Just finish what you must and return to duty within two turns."

"Anyone else want to come along?" said Fell.

Taylok breathed a hidden sigh of relief when no one else volunteered to, " . . . make the hike to Megalith Rise to watch the blind girl fall to her death." Taylok began to have some hope of escape. She thought of making an attempt to retrieve the crystal, which lay close by, but decided any ploy she might use could be too risky. If she survived this excursion with Fell and Ran, she would come back for the crystal. Ironically, she had not even told Jade where she hid the gemstone, so if she died, it would be lost until some garden worker stumbled across it or accidentally buried it in which case it might be lost forever.

Neither warrior had noticed Taylok's second sling, concealed in the guise of a belt, holding up her shorts. During the search they had run their hands beneath it to make sure nothing was hidden there, but they had not recognized its potential dual purpose and thus had not removed it. Taylok kept her hands away to avoid drawing attention to the weapon.

"Can I have my pouch back?" she asked.

"You won't need it," said Fell. "Where you're going, you'll need a very tall pile of ulok to break your fall."

The men laughed cruelly.

"We'd better get going," said Ran. "It's a long way to the view site."

The men each took one of Taylok's arms and walked rapidly toward the highest point in New Rockhome Hall. The mission almost ended before it began when they reached the base of the trail of steep ascent. Two village warriors blocked the way.

"You need passes to go up the trail to Mystical Grotto view site," said one.

"We're temple warriors," said Fell. "This waif is being punished by High Council Pebblic himself."

"Looks like she's already been punished," noted the second warrior.

"You still need passes," insisted the first warrior.

"How much?" asked Ran, resignedly.

After a brief negotiation and payment, the village warriors allowed Fell and Ran, dragging Taylok, access to the steep path. Taylok used every trick she knew to slow their progress; stumbling against one of them when the men were most vulnerable to falling; sliding down and making them come back to retrieve her; screaming for help although her screams were lost in the waterfall noise. But, she could not match the physical strength of the two warriors and they warned that they would kill her where she stood if she didn't cooperate. They convinced her of their sincerity by occasional nicks with the points of their swords.

The trip took almost half a turn and both men perspired freely before they reached the view site. When they arrived, a glance at the time-telling water wheel created new urgency.

"We have to hurry, Ran," said Fell. "Whiteknife will kill us both if we're not back in time and it's getting late."

"I know. Let's turn her loose near the edge of the view site. It's really wet and slick there so it shouldn't take long for her to fall and going back will be faster for us. It's downhill and we won't have her to deal with."

"Let's just push her over the side."

"No. No. I want to watch her fall by herself."

They pushed Taylok forward and she stumbled over a slightly raised stone, falling painfully on her stomach. The disquieting roar of the waterfall interfered with Taylok's hearing to the extent that she had to concentrate, as she had never done before, to grasp her surroundings. The warriors would not allow her time to complete her auditory "view" so she could only partially visualize the parameters of the view site. Fortunately, the cliff edges were easiest because the waterfall sounds helped identify those. Fell and Ran had removed the ropes that normally warned people to stay well back from the precipice, leaving nothing to help Taylok except her senses.

"Get up, stupid bat," said Fell. "Here let me help you."

He shoved his sword between her legs and under her body, as

she lay sprawled awkwardly on the view site floor. Fell then raised her slender hips with the broad blade, using it like a spatula lifting a pancake, bruising her while the sword-tip bit into her stomach. She screamed as the men laughed.

The scream had been only part due to pain and part to make the men believe that the pain had been greater than it had. She lurched forward and away from the sharp sword, dangerously close to the precipice edge. Taylok understood that the stone she tripped over was too big and heavy to make a good sling missile and, even if she had the strength to whirl it, insufficient to stop both the warriors. She needed at least two good sling sized stones before making a move. She stood and walked sideways on the slippery floor, deliberately venturing close to the precipice so that the men wouldn't become discouraged and throw her over before she could mount a defense. As she stumbled along, she tried to find sling stones but located none large enough. The crowds that usually visited the viewpoint kept the ground mostly clear of stones. Taylok remembered that warriors, who looked after such things when she could see, did not allow anyone to throw stones over the edge into the canyon. Still, they could not watch all the time and Taylok remembered throwing a pebble over the edge on one occasion.

In her mind, Taylok labored hard to picture the platform where they stood. Although it had been many rings since seeing the site, she remembered most of the hazards and some of the rocky formations that formed the wall at the safe edge of the view site. She stumbled toward a remembered conglomerate exposure, which had previously contained some throwing size pebbles imbedded in the matrix. Somehow, if the bed remained intact, she would have to dig at least two of them out and eliminate Fell and Ran before they could use their swords in earnest on her or catch her and throw her over the precipice. The closer she came to the outcrop, the more futile it seemed.

"What's she doing?" she heard Ran's voice grate over the waterfall sound. "She's going the wrong direction. This is taking too long."

Panic.

"We're going to have to push her over the edge," said Fell. "She

229

could fool around several turns if we let her. She's getting too far away, as well."

Greater panic. Have to act, now. She ran her hands along the rough conglomerate outcrop. She found three sling size stones and the matrix felt soft enough . . .

"Why is she taking her belt off?" laughed Ran. "Does she think she'll strip her clothes off and make us . . . Wa, that's not a belt . . . it's a sling."

Taylok heard Ran pull his sword from its scabbard at the same time Fell drew his own. She heard the footsteps as they raced toward her. She dug her hand into the pebbly conglomerate outcrop and dislodged a stone.

If the area had not been so slick, the warriors would have reached Taylok before she accomplished her task. The warrior's panic-stricken rush to stop Taylok cost them time when they lost traction on the wet surface. As it occurred, Ran pulled slightly ahead of Fell in their wild dash to reach her and Taylok rewarded him with the first stone, squarely in the middle of his forehead. The impact of her fist-sized missile striking Ran's head created a sickening thud and crunch. Ran's head jerked back and blood sprayed from his nose, spattering both Fell and Taylok. His legs no longer held him upright and his sword slashed out one final time, involuntarily, narrowly missing Fell's head. Fell jerked aside, stumbling as he avoided being slashed by Ran's sword.

"You blind witch," he screamed, rising with mounting anger.

Taylok's second stone blasted Fell directly in the mouth. Blood and teeth drenched both Fell and Taylok as she located a fourth stone. Fell continued to scream and reel from the initial strike. Taylok sensed that he could no longer see as he hesitated and then began weaving with erratic motion, swinging his sword maniacally. Fell staggered backwards when Taylok's next stone careened off his jaw.

Fell dropped to his knees for a moment, stunned, arose and continued to wobble around and slash at Taylok, but now she had become the invisible demon who plagued him.

Taylok listened and carefully located the canyon edge. She walked silently and carefully to within a hands length of the deadly edge before she turned and spoke.

"How do you like it, being blind, Fell?" she yelled, scornfully. "I'm so sorry that you can't see yourself now, since you wanted to see someone blind run around the view site. Do be careful. It's slick here."

Fell stumbled over Ran's body in his blind search for Taylok. He reached a hand out to touch Ran's face and then felt for his carotid artery.

"Dead," spat the warrior, with deep fear making his voice tremble.

Anger steadily replaced his fear and Taylok heard Fell stand, crazily swishing the sword in his hand.

"I'll kill you if it's the last thing I do, you daughter of a whore," he babbled.

She considered using her last stone to end Fell's ranting, but realized that the previous blows had already driven him to a state of utter confusion. All he needed was a little push. Or tug.

"You want me? Come and get me," she screamed, and then stepped quietly and carefully away from the precipice.

Fell's sword sliced the air furiously as he wobbled blindly toward the area where he had heard Taylok's voice. Taylok listened as Fell angrily assaulted the air where she had been. Her throat tightened when she heard his footsteps nearing the canyon edge, listened, with relief and something approaching glee, as the deadly warrior stepped into the nothingness of the deep canyon.

"Die," screamed the crazed warrior, "you filthy piece of . . . Oops. Nooo. Yaaiiieeee."

The sound of Fell's scream continued for several heartbeats before it blended into the noisy music of the waterfall. Taylok sat on the floor of the view site, her feelings mixed; wishing she could see the magnificent view, hating the men and situation that brought her here. She tied her sling back around her waist and began to wonder about getting down Megalith Rise trail, remembering the difficult climb and steep steps involved. Mercifully, she heard the gravelly crunch of someone coming up the trail.

"What's going on up here?" said the warrior who had taken the shells from Ran at the foot of the rise.

"I don't know," said Taylok. "I'm blind."

"No doubt, no doubt," said the warrior. "Hm. Where's the other warrior who was with you?"

"He went over the edge."

"Over the edge, you say? How did that happen?"

"I'd say it was suicide."

"Suicide? What was his name?"

"Fell."

"What about this other warrior?"

"His name is Ran."

She heard him bending over Ran's prone body.

"Huh. Ran's dead," the warrior said, without emotion. "Looks like a stone hit him squarely in the center of the forehead; a quick death."

"Maybe it was suicide, too," Taylok offered.

"You think Ran hit himself in the head with a stone to commit suicide? Oh, I think that might be reaching."

"Might have been done by Fell if they had, like, quarreled or anything."

"There's a lot of blood and some broken teeth lying around here beside Ran. Not his teeth, either. He still has most of his. And you have blood splattered all over you. How do you explain that?"

"I must have been standing too close when the fighting started. I didn't see anything. I told you, I'm blind."

The warrior's chuckle let her know that he didn't believe her denial.

"I also see loose stones lying here that have quite a bit of blood on them. I believe four of them were pried out of that conglomerate bed and you have bloody, ragged fingernails that look like you've been digging. Did you know that it's illegal to take stones from this area and throw them? Don't suppose you know anything about that, either?"

"Those stones could have been dug out some time ago, couldn't they?"

"What about the blood on them and on you and your fingernails?"

"I almost fell over the edge on the way up here. I scraped my knee, too."

"What's your name, young lady?"

"Taylok."

"Where do you live?"

"Uh, the village."

"The village is a big place."

"I'm currently staying at Ganaga's house."

"I have to report this, you know. It's all very suspicious."

"Fell and Ran were trying to kill me."

"Now, we're getting somewhere."

"They came after me and I did what I had to do."

"Are you saying that you took out both these warriors? Blind or not, that's an incredible feat for a young woman who is . . . what, thirteen rings old?"

"Eleven."

"Unbelievable. Yet, I do believe you and I'm not just a little terrified that you could have done it."

"That would seem unbelievable in a report, warrior. Would your chief believe you? It isn't plausible that I could have done this, is it? I really am blind and I don't even have a weapon."

The warrior laughed.

"I suppose your belt has been around your middle all this time?"

"My belt?"

"Please. Do I have to remove it to prove that it's a sling? There's blood on it, too."

"No," sighed Taylok, resignedly. "It's a sling."

The warrior remained silent for a few moments.

At last, he said, "Come on, then. I'll help you down the trail. Wouldn't want a helpless, blind, eleven-ring-old girl to go traipsing around Megalith Rise trail and get hurt. I believe your story that they were trying to kill you, by the way, although I can't imagine why. And, I'll write a believable piece of fiction for my report, which will exonerate you from culpability in their deaths. Then, you'll go home and stay out of trouble. Understand?"

"Yes. What's your name, warrior?"

"I am called Rock by my friends."

"Can I call you Rock?"

"I would not have told you, otherwise."

Contrary to Ran's prediction, the trip down the mountain took longer than the trip up. Rock carefully led Taylok through the most treacherous declines, advising her to climb downward with her face to the hillside as a safety precaution. Even with the extra care, Taylok slipped twice and might have been dashed on rocks far below if not for Rock's strength and positioning himself below her. Taylok needed a lengthy rest, after the long climb down, before she departed for the village. The warriors gave her food and water and allowed her to recline on a pad of ulok'neh fiber they usually reserved for their own rest periods.

"What happened up there, Rock?' asked the second warrior.

"My report will show that two warriors, Fell and Ran, reached the summit with their charge, Taylok, and quarreled," said Rock. "They showered each other with stones, one of which struck Ran in the forehead, killing him. Fell became so distraught that he committed suicide by jumping off the cliff. The girl, Taylok, is blind and had no pertinent information to add."

"What about the body on the summit?"

"Ran's body? We'll send for bearers to retrieve it and close the trail until it is done."

"A worthy conclusion, Rock. Good work."

Taylok never learned the name of the second warrior.

Chapter 21 - A Lonely Path

After resting, Taylok made her way to the temple, being careful to listen from a distance before slipping into the garden. She still heard sounds of fighting inside the temple, but detected no one outside. She wondered if Flint survived his wounds, but felt confident that Ganaga would do his best to heal her closest friend. She found her pouch exactly where Whiteknife had discarded it after he dumped the contents. The empty pouch had been trampled a bit by the warriors, but remained in usable condition. The stones still lay as the warriors scattered them and Taylok refilled her pouch quickly.

After her ordeal with the murderous Fell and Ran, Taylok's thoughts had, understandably, become somewhat muddled and confused. She knew the approximate location where she had buried the paired crystal, but her first search turned up nothing, not unusual, as blindness limited perfect recall on many occasions. The more she searched, however, the more uncertain she became as to where she had hidden the stone. She retraced her steps from the hidden door and replayed the scene where she paused and quickly scooped out the soft dirt and deposited the paired crystals. She had covered it with dirt and patted it lightly to disguise the location. Now, her fingers, already sore from digging sling stones out of the conglomerate matrix on the summit, had become very sore and painful as she clawed through the softer, but still abrasive, earth of the garden. After digging for half a turn, the realization, which had gnawed at her instinct for the last quarter turn, waded into her acceptance with rare certainty. So much for her fear that if something happened to her, the strange, paired stone might be lost forever.

Someone had already found and removed it.

Taylok sat in the garden as disconsolate as if her very life depended on the vanished paired crystal. She cried, sobbing like she hadn't done since her mother died, pouring out all the pent up emotions of the past few events.

She didn't know how long she lay in the garden weeping, but

Taylok suddenly noticed that sounds of fighting in the temple had ceased. With the back of her hands she wiped moisture from her unseeing eyes and listened carefully for any new sounds escaping the temple. After a brief time she perceived a deep, solemn chant originating outside the front entrance. The sonorous litany continued for almost two turns, with the voices increasing in number until the air became electrified, echoing and reverberating the essential, primitive, plaintive call that awakened the living in the entire hall.

Taylok finally realized that the warriors had declared a truce to clear the temple of dead. The people trudging from the entrance trod heavily toward Mordane Pit, carrying warriors who had fallen in battle. The line of death bearers reached from the temple to the extremely remote Mordane Pit, an awesome distance. Taylok had never before heard the chant of the dead sung by so many voices. Death bearers usually moved during the sleep period and then the dirge came from only one or two carriers.

Now and again the cry of a mate, mother or sister of the fallen warrior punctuated the chant. The mournful tones and heavy sorrow that permeated the music brought fresh tears to Taylok's eyes.

The procession continued for more than two turns, but at last the final unit departed for Mordane Pit. Taylok remembered that the acolytes would be busily cleaning the hallways and rooms in which fighting had occurred. She wondered whether the battle would resume quickly or if a rest period had been agreed. She hadn't long to wait as warriors on both sides, angry over the loss of friends and comrades in arms, began quarreling again. The clang of swords spelled a beginning of renewed conflict.

Raking the dirt half-heartedly with her fingers for a final time, Taylok arose, still empty handed and saddened, and commenced the long walk to the village.

She remembered that Flint had left her spare clothing at Fairmont Inn and made her way to that establishment. A clerk helped her find the room and informed Taylok pointedly that the inn had bathing facilities. She located her things after a brief search.

Taylok sat on the edge of a cushioned stone chair and went

through her meager belongings. She had a pair of soft fabric shorts, a couple of top covers, an extra pair of shoes and some underwear. That constituted her total clothing supply as the garments she wore had blood spattered or smeared over almost every finger width. In addition to the clothing, Taylok found a mica comb, two monetary crystals, worth fifty or sixty shells each, ten shells, a few crumbs of top grade ulok and a spare sling.

Taylok found the bathing room empty. She took a towel and her clean clothes and stepped into the accommodation. As she undressed, she remembered the sling/belt around her waist and, after washing the blood from it in a sink, placed it with her clean things, along with a couple of stones, beside the bath.

The water felt warm and comfortable as she eased into the bath. She soaked her body in the warm water, feeling some of the tension drain away. She used a soapy pumice bar to scrub the blood from her hair and face. Then she relaxed. The soothing water almost lulled her to sleep.

Someone rapped on the door while she luxuriated in the water and she shouted, "Occupied."

She heard the door open briefly and an unfamiliar male voice say, "Sorry," before quickly closing it.

Taylok thought that she no longer cared about someone seeing her naked. The body search by the temple warriors had been much worse and she now had her sling and a couple of stones. But, after the unwanted visitor closed the door, Taylok discovered herself standing in the middle of the pool, sling in hand and a stone in the pocket. She smiled as she replaced the weapon next to her clothing by the side of the bathing pool and confidently resumed her bath. When finished, she toweled dry, combed her stringy hair and donned the clean clothes, feeling almost normal again. She returned to the room and lay down to sleep for just a short time on the comfortable bed.

Nine turns later, Taylok awoke and hurriedly assembled her things, left the inn and walked to Ganaga's home. She tapped on the door and Cobalta answered.

"Taylok!" Cobalta exclaimed. "How wonderful you look. Come inside."

"How are you, Cobalta?" said Taylok.

"Okay, I guess. Have you seen my mate?"

"Not since we arrived at the temple together last isa."

"I'm worried about him. Word from the temple is that High Council has taken over third level. The Shotai holds first and second levels."

"Are they still fighting?"

"Sporadically," said Cobalta. "Many have been killed."

"I hate to bother you, but Ganaga said to ask if you would prepare the guest room for me. Do you mind if I stay with you for a while? I can help around the house."

Cobalta hugged Taylok briefly in response.

"Of course, I don't mind," she said. "Take my hand and come with me."

Cobalta's children spied Taylok and yelled and screamed in welcome.

Several isas passed and no word came from Ganaga. Cobalta became frantic with worry and Taylok did all she could to relieve the burden of household duties. Although she cooked fairly well, the pantries ran low and the children complained of hunger. Cobalta would not go to the village for fear of missing Ganaga so Taylok took her own crystals and bought ulok and fish. She had been gone no longer than a turn, but when she returned, Cobalta and the children were gone, leaving no message. The main room lay in disarray, with a chair knocked over and some of Ganaga's papers scattered about. Taylok cooked a meal and waited, but Cobalta and the children did not return. She ate alone and tried to rest through the sleep period, but next isa Cobalta still had not returned.

Taylok packed her belongings and the food she had bought in a sack and walked back to Fairmont Inn. The clerk smiled pleasantly, but did not have much information.

"Sorry, Taylok. I have not seen Ganaga or any of his household for several isas," said the clerk. "A few of our visitors occasionally journey to the temple, however. Maybe they know something. I'll be happy to introduce you to them."

After speaking to three of the men, including one whose voice sounded like the man who had intruded on her bath, she learned that rumor placed Ganaga as prisoner of High Council warriors.

None of the men had seen or heard news of Cobalta and her children.

Without much to go on, Taylok toyed with the idea of returning to the stalagmite field, but after thinking it over, decided Eldar Temple gave her the best chance. At least, she could learn of Flint's condition and perhaps discover what had happened to Cobalta and her children. She feared another encounter with Pebblic's warriors, but knew it might happen regardless of what she did. Before she departed, she talked again to the clerk.

"I'm going back to the temple," she said. "Can I leave some of my things in the room Diamond rented?"

"Yes," said the clerk. "He reserved the room for another twelve isas. After that, a new rental must be paid, if you wish to stay longer."

"I understand," Taylok nodded.

"I dislike seeing a young woman walk the mainway alone," said the clerk. "There is another woman staying here who might be willing to accompany you to Eldar Temple. Her name is Jade. Have you met her?"

"Yes, I know her, but I doubt she would go back to Eldar Temple. Jade and I were told to stay away from the temple by the Shotai."

"Then, why are you going back?"

"Most of my friends are there. Maybe I can help them."

"But, you're blind," he reminded her, unnecessarily. "You could be more trouble than help for them. Do you know what I mean?"

"I can handle myself," she said, curtly.

"Taylok?" said a familiar voice.

"Jade? Is that you?"

"Yes. I thought you had gone back to Eldar Temple with Ganaga."

"I did, but things haven't gone exactly right since then. I'm going back to the temple now."

"Why? Aren't they still fighting there?" asked Jade.

"Rumors say it's died down to sporadic skirmishes. I haven't heard from Flint or Ganaga since I left the healer at the secret entrance to the Shotai's room. I lost the crystal, too."

"No, you didn't. When you failed to return, I went back and got the crystal. I saw you hide it when we left Eldar. It's in my room."

For an unknown reason, a great weight lifted from Taylok.

"Oh, that's good. I was afraid that High Council Pebblic might have taken it."

"Have you heard that Pebblic had Playa killed?" Jade asked, on the verge of tears.

"Killed? No. I heard warriors talking about Pebblic torturing Playa. Are you sure that she's dead?"

"I don't think the warriors would lie about that," responded Jade. "They seemed upset that Pebblic let the torture go that far."

"He sounds desperate to get that crystal," said Taylok.

"The crystal? You mean the one I have in my room? Is that why he had her tortured and killed?"

"That's what I heard one warrior say. Unfortunately for Playa, she couldn't tell Pebblic where the crystal was located because she didn't know."

"Now, I'm really feeling uncomfortable having that stone in my room."

"We need to take it to Eldar Temple because that's where it can be used."

"What do you mean?"

"I think it's the key to fourth level," said Taylok. "We could solve the mystery of that room if we knew how to use the key."

"Okay, fooling around that fourth level room is very dangerous. Whatever we did, eventually we would have to go inside, knowing that no one has ever come back out. That scares the explorer right out of me, along with some other stuff."

"Come on, Jade. You got me into this. See it through with me."

"Wait a breath. All I got you into was reading a glyph with me."

"That . . . and two murders . . . one right in front of our noses."

"Well, you can't blame me for those. I'm the victim here . . . just like you."

"I guess you're right," Taylok agreed, at length. "Let me have the crystal back and I'll try it on my own."

"You can't go into Eldar Temple on your own," argued Jade. "The fighting is still going on. At least wait until that stops. You could step right into the middle of that revolt and get yourself killed . . . or worse."

"I already did worse, Jade. Some warriors captured me and searched me for the crystal. That was terrifying. Then, two of them took me to the top of Megalith Rise and tried to make me fall over the precipice."

"How did you escape that?"

"I got lucky. See this belt?"

"So?"

"It's a sling. I found a couple of rocks in the conglomerate beds, took off my sling and got rid of the creepy warriors. One of them went over the precipice."

"You took out a pair of warriors by yourself?" Jade asked, incredulously.

"It was desperation, believe me. I don't think I ever told you that Flint gave me my first sling and taught me how to use it. He saved my life several times since, when he wasn't even around. He's one reason that I need to go back to Eldar Temple. I have to find out what happened to him."

"Are you going to use the secret entrance to the Shotai's suite?"

"That's the quickest and easiest way in."

"Okay. I'll go with you to the Shotai's place, but I'm not going to fourth level. That's crazy. It's a suicide wish."

"Fair enough. Get the crystal and let's get started."

"Wait! Tell me again why I'm leaving my nice, quiet room in the village to go to Eldar Temple where all the fighting is taking place?"

Jade kept asking the question, in jest, all the way to Eldar Temple. When Jade proclaimed that she could see the structure, Taylok stopped.

"Can you see anyone outside, Jade?"

"Noooo," Jade assessed, drawing out the negation as she scanned the temple base.

"Nobody near the garden?"

"No. Can you locate the door opener when we get there?"

"I did it before. Let's find out."

They ran toward the temple, hurried through the garden and Taylok went straight to the hidden pressure pad stone, and pressed. The door swung open with minimum sound and they scurried inside, closing the secret entry behind them. Jade led the way as they walked through the short tunnel to the Shotai's suite of rooms.

"This door opens into the Shotai's study room," said Jade. "Try not to startle anybody or else we might be attacked."

She opened the door and stepped inside.

"Hello," she shouted. "It's Jade and Taylok."

Silence greeted them and Taylok automatically loosened her sling and dropped a stone into the pocket. A quick search of the suite turned up no one. Jade peeked out the regular entry door into the hallway, but, again, found no one.

"They must have moved to another suite," said Jade.

"Where are the warriors?" asked Taylok. "The hall should be full of them."

"Don't know," ventured Jade. "Can you hear anything?"

Taylok listened carefully at the hallway door.

"The only thing I hear is your breathing," said Taylok, seriously. "This is really weird. I should be able to hear the warriors on this level, at least. The suite seems empty."

"Let's go down to the Shotai's original rooms," suggested Jade. "They might have moved there, now that His Eminence is gone."

They entered the hall and had only gone a short distance when a whispering voice, coming from inside the geode room, stopped them.

"You. You there, Taylok, stop or I'll kill you."

Taylok armed herself with the sling and kept walking. She knew the voice. It was Whiteknife.

"Stop," he cried, hoarsely.

"What do you want, Whiteknife?" shouted Taylok.

"You know this guy?" asked Jade.

"He captured and searched me just outside the garden. Then, he let Fell and Ran take me to Megalith Rise."

"Wait," cried Whiteknife, conciliatorily. "Just tell me what happened to my men. Did the village warriors arrest them?"

"I don't think so," said Taylok, shifting position as she detected movement inside the geode room. "If you set foot out of that room, I'll send you to the same place as Fell and Ran."

"What's that supposed to mean?" countered Whiteknife, moving toward the door.

"Look out, Taylok," said Jade, "he has a sword and a sling."

"Lay down your weapons, Whiteknife," said Taylok. "I won't warn you again."

"Warn me? Warn me? Warn this!" he said, moving to use his sling.

Taylok's stone found Whiteknife's right eye precisely as the warrior released his missile. The strike twisted Whiteknife sufficiently that his projectile pulled wide of Taylok and Jade and smashed high on the wall of the hallway behind them. Whiteknife grunted once and slumped to the floor in the doorway of the geode room. His sword clanged as it bounced oddly on the hard stone floor.

Taylok detected movement behind Whiteknife and reloaded her sling.

"Wait, don't," said the vaguely familiar voice. "I surrender."

"Who are you?" demanded Taylok.

"I'm Mudrock," he said. "I was part of Whiteknife's party."

"Where are the rest?"

"Dead, I guess. All of them, except Fell and Ran, in the fighting on level two. Only Whiteknife and I escaped with our lives. We were hiding in the geode room until Whiteknife saw you walk by and shouted at you."

"I remember your voice," said Taylok. "You were with the party that searched me."

"No, no. I joined them long after that," he said, miserably.

"Of course you did. Then, why do I remember your voice?"

"He has a sling in his hand, Taylok," interjected Jade.

"Okay, I was with them when they searched you, but I didn't participate in the search. I wanted them to stop."

"I don't remember hearing your objection. And where were you when those two idiots, Fell and Ran, forced me to go with them to Megalith Rise? I didn't hear you raise a fuss over that, either."

"I've made a lot of mistakes. I'm sorry."

The warrior made a move toward the door as he swung his sling.

"You're about to make another one with that sling, Mudrock," warned Taylok.

"You're blind. You can't see me. You can't tell what I'm

doing."

"Wrong," said Taylok, grunting as she released a rock from her sling.

The high-speed missile struck Mudrock on the knee and the crack of his kneecap being crushed echoed down the hallway. He screamed as he fell and the sling skittered across the hallway holding its unfired missile as it parted from his limp fingers.

"Don't leave me here," Mudrock cried, between clenched teeth. "I can't walk. The Shotai's warriors will kill me."

"No they won't," laughed Taylok. "All you have to do is convince them that you killed Whiteknife. They'll probably throw you a big party . . . unless Pebblic's warriors find you first, in which case you'll have to convince them that you didn't kill Whiteknife. That slope will be as slippery as Megalith Rise."

"Taylok," said Jade, as they walked away, "I'm beginning to see how you survive. The warriors are so vain about their own fighting skill that they always underestimate yours."

"Being blind helps to put them off guard."

"It also helps to be as fast and accurate as you are."

Taylok laughed.

"That's just practice."

Chapter 22 - Return From The Dead

High Council Pebblic sat quietly, far in the back of the geode room, gazing at his warrior, Mudrock, who writhed on the threshold floor, moaning in pain. Behind Pebblic, tightly gagged and arms bound, lay Ganaga. Next to High council, a new sword loosely fitted into the scabbard hanging by his side, stood Garnet.

"She is an awesome adversary," admitted Pebblic. "Who'd have thought that my blind daughter would . . . could be a stumbling block to our taking over Eldar Temple?"

"I know," agreed Garnet. "I worked with her for almost three rings. If not for Halite and then Flint, I might have taken her virginity. She proved much harder to manipulate than Pumice."

Pebblic glanced briefly at Garnet with a mixture of amusement and disgust.

"Seeing the condition of my two best fighters," he said, "I think that you, Garnet, are the logical choice to take her life, instead. It appears that she is too skilled with the sling to be taken by a frontal attack."

"There was a time when I could have done that easily," said Garnet. "Sericite told her that I'm dead. She might receive a shock when I return alive, but I doubt I can just walk in and kill her with my sword. She's too quick and self-preserving for that. If I could just get that sling away from her . . ."

"Yes. A romantic interlude might disarm her. Cobalta confirmed, under the threat of harm to her children, that Sericite planted the seeds of your death. It is unfortunate that Flint proved the better swordsman. My plan was to have Sericite plant the lie in Taylok's mind and then kill Flint. Taylok would have been left alone and friendless and might have given up the stone easily, without need for her blood. Now, her death would please me, for she helps protect the Shotai."

"How do you wish me to proceed?" asked Garnet.

"First, there must be a joyous reunion between you," said Pebblic. "Ganaga will be forced to bring you back to life for her, in a manner of speaking."

"The healer allies himself with the girl. You can't trust Ganaga," said Garnet, glancing at the bound and gagged healer.

"Yes, I can," said Pebblic, confidently. "Now that I have his family, Ganaga will do exactly as I command."

Ganaga turned his head away from Pebblic and Garnet, a dark frown on his face.

"Taylok believes that you are dead," said Pebblic to Garnet. "Our best chance to convince her differently is to alter the story but slightly and present you, alive, with fitting injuries that might have been administered by Sericite's sword. That, and Ganaga swearing he healed you, might be enough."

Garnet's face registered surprise as High Council Pebblic drew his sword.

* * * * *

Jade tapped lightly on the entrance to the rooms that the Shotai had occupied three rings before, while Taylok lingered a few steps away, her stone-loaded sling swinging nonchalantly, but ready for action if needed.

"Identify yourself," called the familiar voice of Steel.

"It's Jade and Taylok," replied Jade.

The door opened slightly and then widened. Jade rushed inside, closely followed by Taylok.

"Why have you returned?" asked Steel, mildly. "You were safe in the village."

"It's my fault," said Taylok. "I had to know if you were all still alive. Jade tried to talk me out of it."

"Peace and tranquility," said the Shotai, joining them.

"Neither of which can be found here," said Flint's voice, echoing from an adjoining room.

The Shotai laughed. "I'm afraid Flint is correct. Still, it is worth striving for and conveys my wishes."

Stonic had been asleep on a padded stone bench near one wall of the room. He raised his head, greeted the girls and then returned to sleep.

Taylok found her way to the door from which Flint's voice had echoed. She pushed her head inside.

"You must be getting better, cracking jokes," she said. "How do you feel?"

"Terrible," he laughed. "My arm aches and my chest is so sore that it hurts to breathe."

"You don't have to be here, you know. You could have gone back to Banestone Hall."

"And miss your exasperating company? How could I stay away?"

"Can I come in?"

"No. I'm naked."

"That's okay. I'm blind . . . and you're not naked, anyway."

"No, I'm not," he laughed again. "Come over here and give me a hug. But, how could you tell?"

"You would have been scrambling to get your clothes on, for one. For two, the Shotai wouldn't let you lie there naked, anyway."

Taylok located Flint and hugged him gently as he returned her hug while sitting, fully clothed, on the side of his bed. She touched his face and felt a tear running down his cheek.

"Oh, sorry. Did I hit a tender spot?" she asked, backing away.

"Taylok, there'll always be a tender spot in my heart for you. And no, you didn't hurt me."

"I think that I've figured out the fourth level puzzle," she said, changing the subject.

"Be careful with anything you do regarding the fourth level room," his tone became serious. "I think, beside the obvious ones, there are some well-hidden dangers."

"I think the key I have will get us past the dangers."

"Us?"

"Jade and me. If I can talk her into it."

"Why do you want to go there? People who have gone there in the past have not ever returned. You have no idea what the room does or if there is any benefit if you survive."

"The ancients built that room for some purpose."

"Yes. But maybe it was to get rid of their enemies."

"They had Mordane pit for that. No, they used very special crystals in the construction and set it up to be controlled by another crystal. This one."

"Taylok, you don't know if that crystal controls the room. And even if it does, you don't know how to use it."

"I'll figure it out if Jade and I can spend a little time up there."

"The warriors won't let you close enough to do that."

"Have you been up there recently?" she asked, coyly.

"No, why?"

"The third level is held by Pebblic's warriors. I'm betting that no one is watching fourth level, now."

"And you'll get past third level, how?"

"Who's going to pay any attention to a blind girl and her friend?"

A commotion in the main room interrupted their conversation. Flint arose and limped to the door of his little room.

"It's Ganaga with someone else," Flint said. "We thought he had been captured by High Council warriors. Let's go and see him."

Flint and Taylok walked into the main room. Ganaga stood talking to the Shotai with a wounded man standing beside him.

"Garnet," said Flint, in a shocked tone. "We thought you had been killed."

"I almost died," replied Garnet. "Ganaga saved me. Hello, Taylok."

"Garnet?" said Taylok. "How badly are you hurt?"

"I can still get around," said Garnet. "My shoulder is in pretty bad shape, though. It's good to see you."

"Good to hear your voice, back from Mordane Pit," said Taylok, facetiously. "Sericite told us he had killed you."

"He probably thought he had. If not for Ganaga, I would be dead."

Taylok approached Garnet and put out a hand to touch him and he took her hand in his. He smelled of fresh blood and Taylok wondered why, since his injuries from Sericite had occurred several isas earlier.

"Ganaga," Taylok said, turning from Garnet, her hand still in his grasp, "how are you?"

"I'm alive," he responded, crisply.

"Were you hurt during your capture?"

"Tied up, but not seriously injured."

"Have you seen Cobalta and your children?" Taylok asked. "I

went to stay with them and they disappeared from the house while I was out buying food. I feared they might have been captured by High Council warriors."

"I . . . uh . . . perhaps Cobalta visited her mother when I failed to return home."

"Her mother?" said the Shotai.

"Yes. She often goes there," Ganaga answered, smoothly.

"I see," said the Shotai. "May I offer you both lodging until you are ready to return home?"

"Thank you," said Ganaga, wearily, "but I must take Garnet to the second level treatment room."

"Nonsense," said the Shotai. "You'll stay here."

"Shotai, we really must go," said Garnet.

"That's a nice sword, Garnet," remarked Flint.

"Thanks. I found it on the way to the temple. It feels like a good one."

"Can I see it?"

"Uh, I guess," said Garnet, not moving to withdraw it from its scabbard.

"I won't break it," laughed Flint.

"No. It's just a warrior giving up his sword . . ."

"Oh. You're a warrior, now?" interjected Steel.

"Well . . ."

"What party are you with?" asked Flint.

"I'm . . . not actually with a party."

"A warrior without a party is like a fish in an ulok field," said the Shotai. "Neither survives too long."

"I'll join a party on second level," responded Garnet, hastily.

"I may know of a party you can join," ventured Steel. "How long before you'll be ready for fighting duty?"

Garnet still held Taylok's hand as he unsteadily backed away. His other hand rested on the hilt of his sword. Jade stood near Stonic who, now, barred the door.

"What's wrong, Garnet?" demanded Taylok, twisting her hand, trying unsuccessfully to release his grip.

"I . . . I'm not feeling well," he said.

"Let go of me," Taylok insisted. "I'll help you to lie down."

Glancing rapidly around the room, Garnet reluctantly released

Taylok's hand.

"I'll be all right soon," he said. "I'm sorry for the misunderstanding."

"Oh, I don't believe there has been a misunderstanding," remarked the Shotai.

"I'll trouble you for your sword, now," said Steel.

"Wait," said Ganaga, softly. "If harm comes to Garnet, my family dies."

"Where are they being held?" asked Flint.

"I don't know," said Ganaga, hoarsely. "I think they are on third level, but I never saw the children. They brought Cobalta so I could see her while I was bound on third level. But, I saw Pebblic on first level just a few moments ago in the geode room."

Taylok turned toward Ganaga. She said, "A couple of Pebblic's warriors tried to attack Jade and me from that room just before we came here. We left them in bad shape."

"That was the bright spot of my isa," smiled Ganaga. "Whiteknife is dead and Mudrock has a shattered kneecap."

"You'd better shut up, you fool," said Garnet. "When I tell Pebblic what you have done, he will kill Cobalta while you watch."

"Oh, you'll be very lucky to escape this room with your own life," said the Shotai. "Perhaps the only way you may survive is to tell us exactly where Ganaga's family is being held."

"Why would I do that?" cried Garnet.

"The Shotai has ways of making people confess their scurrilous secrets," said Steel. "And so do I."

Taylok heard the rasp of Steel's sword being drawn and Garnet's sword slid quickly from his scabbard.

"Wait a blink, Steel," said Flint. "We agreed that I'd get the next easy one, since I got hurt last time."

"No," replied Steel, "we agreed that you'd get the next easy one only after you healed. You don't even have your sword with you."

Taylok detected mirth in their voices.

"Okay," intoned Flint. "I'll tell you what. You spar around with him and nick him a few times, but don't kill him until I get back with my sword."

"Well, I guess that's all right," agreed Steel. "You'd better be quick, though. I hate traitors."

Taylok heard the swords clang together and one weapon clattered to the floor.

"Pick up your sword, Garnet," said Steel. "I do not make it a practice to kill unarmed warriors. I would make an exception in your case, but we have to wait for Flint."

"Stop, Please," sobbed Garnet in a fearful and pain-filled voice that Taylok had not heard before. "I'll tell you what you want. Just let me live."

"What are you doing here with Ganaga?"

"I'm running from Pebblic."

"That's a lie," said Ganaga. "He came here to kill Taylok and get the keystone to fourth level for Pebblic."

Flint emerged from his room with a sword in his hand.

"He came to do what?" Flint roared. "I'll cut his scrawny little head off. There's no brain in it, anyway."

"No, let me," said Taylok, swinging her sling, forcefully. "I'm the one he was going to kill."

"No, please," sobbed Garnet. "I know where Cobalta and Ganaga's children are being held."

"Tell us," said Ganaga levelly.

"They are in Flame's old room on third level."

"What do you think?" said Steel.

"That's probably what he believes to be true," said the Shotai.

"I agree," said Flint. "Garnet, you are a traitor to both sides. I swear I would kill you if you weren't such a wimp. Let's lock him in one of the holding cells, Stonic."

"My pleasure," said Stonic.

Stonic departed with the whimpering Garnet.

"How did you guys know that Garnet lied?" asked Taylok.

"It was your conversation with Ganaga," said the Shotai.

"When he said that Cobalta might have visited her mother, we knew something was wrong," said Steel.

"Cobalta's mother has been dead for ten rings," recalled the Shotai. "Everybody, except Garnet and you, apparently, knew that."

"Pretty smart, Ganaga," Taylok offered.

"I wasn't born last ring."

"We have to get to third level and rescue Cobalta, now," said Flint.

"We must do it before Pebblic discovers Garnet's failure," said Steel.

"Wait," said the Shotai. "Do any of you know where Flame's room is located?"

"I do," said Taylok and Jade together.

"We all know," said Flint. "We were there after Flame was killed. I'll lead the way."

"You're not going," said Steel. "You can hardly walk."

"Well, you can't go by yourself and I don't think the Shotai should go to third level."

"I can pick up a rescue party on second level," suggested Steel. "There are plenty of idle warriors up there right now."

"Hold it," said Taylok. "Jade and I know the place and the room inside and out. Warrior guards around the door could be troublesome, but we can take care of those, if there aren't too many."

"Me?" objected Jade. "I would be of no use whatsoever in a fight. I'd just be extra weight in a party to rescue anyone."

"Actually, you wouldn't," said Taylok. "We'll need help with the children, getting them off third level and out of the temple."

"I can certainly handle a few children," agreed Jade.

"Don't think that you're going after them without me," interjected Ganaga. "You'll need Cobalta's cooperation and you'll get it easier with me along."

"So you guys are planning this rescue without me?" complained Flint.

"Someone needs to protect the Shotai during this raid," said Steel. "Do you think you're up to that?"

"Of course I am."

"Have you guys wondered," began Taylok, "if maybe High Council planned all this, including Garnet's meltdown?"

"Garnet told the truth," said Steel.

"I think he did, too. But, consider this. If High Council believed Garnet would collapse under pressure and reveal Ganaga's family's location, what would he have planned? What would you plan if you set this up?"

"Me?" said Steel, "I would either ambush the party sent to rescue Cobalta or attack the Shotai once the rescue party left this room. Or maybe both."

"By the tail of the bat," said Ganaga. "I think Taylok's onto something."

"How do we protect against both, though?" asked Flint. "If we leave the Shotai here with a minimum guard, Pebblic could come after him."

"Jade, Ganaga and I can go," said Taylok. "If they ambush us at Flame's room, they'll only get a couple of girls and the healer. The healer won't be any good to you until he gets his family back and Jade and I aren't going to be warriors, anyway."

"How old are you, Taylok?" asked Steel.

"I'm . . ."

"She's eleven going on forty," said Flint, dryly.

"Okay. I can see it's possible," said Steel. "How do we defend against it without sacrificing Ganaga, Jade and Taylok?"

"When he returns, send Stonic for twenty warriors from second level," said Flint. "Bring ten of them here to help Stonic and me guard the Shotai. Steel, you take Ganaga, Jade and Taylok to third level, but have those other ten warriors back you up in case of an ambush. If it's an ambush, they may have moved Ganaga's family, anyway, so you can let the warriors carry the fight while you come back here. In that case, we'll have to decide what the next step will be. If you find Ganaga's family, they may be well guarded and an open attack could put them in danger of being killed by their captors. If you should get them out, take them to second level and order our warriors to block pursuit while you evacuate them from the temple."

"Do you think they moved my family?" asked Ganaga.

"I think it's possible that Pebblic gave Garnet false information," said Flint. "We have to check out Flame's old room just to be sure."

"Please remember," said the Shotai, "that the Mohk'wa sleeps lightest when first you enter his lair."

"We'll be cautious, Shotai," said Steel.

"Also remember," added Flint, "that you must expect the unexpected. Raids like this never turn out exactly the way you plan because your enemy has a plan, too."

Stonic returned shortly and the Shotai sent him immediately to enlist warriors from second level. Eager to begin, the search team met Stonic and the warriors in the hallway outside the Shotai's rooms. In a few moments Steel's party found themselves on the stairway leading to third level. Steel, Ganaga, Jade and Taylok stood with shoulders touching as they mounted the stairs.

"We could run into hostiles at any time," whispered Steel. "If it happens, Jade and Taylok will fall back and alert the warriors behind us. And then, you two get back to the Shotai's quarters. Clear?"

"Clear," answered Jade and Taylok, in a whisper.

The top of the stairway waited for them, ominously dark.

"I don't hear anyone," whispered Taylok.

"This smells like a trap," said Jade. "It's too easy."

"How much light can you see?" asked Taylok.

"They removed all the light baskets. It's black as pitch."

"Then, I should be leading," said Taylok. "I know the way and light doesn't matter to me. If we run into a trap, I'll know it before any of the rest of you."

Steel stopped.

"Okay. I hadn't considered this darkness angle. Come here, Taylok. Lead us to Flame's room. You're the best point we could have here."

Taylok listened carefully to make sure that no one occupied the hall. Everything went well as they approached Flame's old room down the long curving hallway. Taylok pushed open the door, already ajar, slowly and quietly.

She heard a child's voice begin a sound, only to be muffled. She pulled back to whisper to Steel.

"Is there light in the room?"

"No, I can't even see you or tell where the room is located," he whispered.

Taylok turned to the door, made a high-pitched rapid sound and listened for echoes. The children might hear the sound, but the men would not. Luckily, someone had removed the furniture from the room, making Taylok's assessment easier.

She counted eleven people, six of whom unquestionably held

swords or knives. Three of the eleven returned very tight echoes . . . Cobalta's youngest children. Two were larger and did not seem to hold weapons. Those had to be Cobalta and her oldest. The other six were warriors, waiting to ambush Taylok and her party, or possibly worse, kill the hostages.

Aside from the humanity, she discovered four lumps of material lying on the floor. Clothing? Maybe. But, why the little clumps?

Good news; darkness wouldn't allow the hostiles to see Taylok and her party so she had a huge advantage. She ran her fingers across the pouch hanging by her side holding loose stones. Full. A plan formed in her mind. This could work, but it had to be done quickly before the enemy warriors suspected anything.

Taylok's heart hammered in her chest and her "vision" of the room became hazy. Her plan required a perfect image of the room and its occupants. Anything less could be disastrous for Cobalta and the kids. Taylok took a deep breath and thought of the sling course that she had mastered at age three. Her vision had been perfect, then, though. She tried hard to relax before making the first throw.

And then, it happened. Just as the stories of the blind boy, Beach, who claimed to be able to envision an entire scene, Taylok suddenly "saw" the room full of people. It seemed as clear in her mind as if they were in a brightly lighted ulok'neh garden. Now, she had to rapidly prioritize her targets.

Several of the shots would be easy. Three warriors stood behind the younger children, using them as shields. The children's size left the warriors holding them easy targets for Taylok's sling. A man stood alone near the door beside one of the clumps of cloth. He lingered, unshielded, brandishing his sword excitedly, the only simple shot.

The two warriors holding Cobalta and her oldest would be more difficult as they stood directly behind the women. The necessary trajectory resembled that on course number four of the sling trials; a strong curving stone would be needed and success depended on the targets as well as their hostages remaining still. Moving targets complicated the shots but Taylok had no control over that factor.

And then, it occurred to her that the cloth stacks must cover light baskets. The hostiles would certainly need light to finish their ambush. It made sense.

Taylok's plan began to simplify in her mind; take out the man by the door first, the two hard shots next and then the three men holding the smaller children. If she could get it all done before they uncovered any of the light baskets, it might work. She couldn't take the time and risk to stop and tell Steel the plan. He probably wouldn't like it anyway.

She "stared" hard at the man standing near the door with sword in hand. The image came clear. He had clinking chains around his neck. Pebblic? She couldn't make out the detail of his facial features, but that didn't matter - she'd never seen Pebblic's face before, anyway. It unnerved her to think the man might be her father, standing there, waiting to kill her and her friends. And, it seemed to Taylok an ultimate irony that the reason for her dominant position was the blinding that this very man had ordered. She "watched" him lift his sword back into strike position, preparing to kill the first person to enter the room. Her anger mounted.

Taylok swung the sling with force.

The first shot hit its mark with a resounding thump and the man by the door - maybe her father, maybe not - fell without a sound escaping his lips. His sword fell across the covered light basket and hardly made a noise. The chains around his neck, however, rattled.

"Did you hear something?" whispered one of the men across the room.

"Yes . . . you. Shut up," whispered another.

Although the process played out in an incredibly brief time, Taylok's mind went through layout, stone arc and movement of target, simultaneously. She even compared it to course four on the sling trials. Thus, the stone that flew from Taylok's sling curved sharply to the left and Cobalta cooperated unintentionally by leaning out of its path.

"What if it's Tay . . . lunhh?" whispered the voice of the warrior behind Cobalta, cut off mid sentence.

Almost before that stone struck its target, another strongly curving missile left Taylok's sling. The warrior using Cobalta's oldest as a shield actually leaned into the oncoming stone as he sought to figure out the sounds he heard.

"What is . . . gurk?" rasped the man as Taylok's stone found its mark on the forehead of the third captor.

The warrior fell heavily and made considerable noise as his sword and metal scabbard hit the marble floor. The three men holding the younger children panicked.

"We're under attack," shouted the fourth man. "Kill the host . . . aggg."

"Another complication," she thought. "This one is acute. Now, I also have to be aware of any warrior readying his sword or knife to harm the children."

"Uncover the light bas . . . koooot," croaked the fifth warrior falling heavily to the floor.

The final warrior dived toward one of the covered light baskets before Taylok could release another stone, leaving his human shield behind. But Taylok had anticipated the movement and held back, preparing to deal the final warrior a disabling blow.

"Taylok," shouted Steel, rushing into the room and hitting her accidentally, causing her last shot to dribble harmlessly to the floor. "What's happening?"

"That's the last one," Taylok cried.

"Ah, light," said Steel.

He sprinted across the room and disarmed the last standing warrior without having to draw blood. Ganaga's family uncovered the remaining light baskets, which cheered everyone except Taylok, whose sound/mind picture quickly faded into her darkness. It did not, however, remove the smile from her face. Ganaga muffled his shout for joy as he rushed to Cobalta's side. The children gathered around their parents, crying and babbling happily. Jade hurried into the room.

"We should get out of here," urged Jade. "There are other hostile warriors on this level and they could capture you again."

The children and Cobalta scurried out the door as a friendly second level warrior from their party appeared.

"Do you need us for anything?" he asked Steel.

"Yes. We need to check the downed warriors to see whether they are alive or dead. Take the live ones to holding cells," Steel ordered. "Deploy some of your best fighters to cover our move back to first level."

"Yes, sir," answered the warrior.

"Steel," said Taylok, bending over the man nearest the door. "I think this one may be Pebblic."

"Pebblic? If it is, Taylok, you may have just ended the war. Let me look at him."

Steel bent over the prone man.

"This is Pebblic, all right," said Steel. "And, there's a weak pulse. Ganaga, will you examine him?"

"Maybe I shouldn't," said the healer. "He's caused me and my family so much pain that I am tempted to cut his throat."

"He should be tried before the village council and the Shotai," said Steel. "New Rockhome Hall is still a land of law. I have no doubt that he will be cast into Mordane Pit when the evidence of his evil is proved."

"Very well. I'll look at him," muttered Ganaga. "But, I confess that I hope Taylok's stone did too much damage to repair."

"Taylok," said Steel, "brave as you were, you endangered Cobalta and her children. They could have been killed and so could you."

"Sorry I couldn't warn you first, Steel. It all seemed so well set up for me to take them out while the light baskets were covered that I couldn't hesitate. And, it did work."

"There is no question, it did work."

Steel came to her and put his hands on her shoulders.

"Flint always said you were special. I never realized how special until this moment. You may grow up to be the princess of Eldar Temple. Now, let's get out of here."

"Wait a blink," laughed Taylok. "Eldar Temple has no princess."

"Well . . . not yet."

Chapter 23 - The Accounting

Second to third level stairway remained crowded as Taylok and Steel made their way to first level. Men poured into third level from second level as the hostile warriors, including Pebblic, who had tried to ambush Steel's party were placed in holding cells. Pebblic did not regain consciousness for several isas and when he did, he could not speak.

Faced with the prospect of continuing the fight without their leader, Pebblic's warriors capitulated and threw down their weapons. The villagers, happy to have an end to the fighting and the Shotai back in charge of the temple, threw a large party that had the streets full of people.

Taylok's name came up in many conversations, but most people did not believe that she could have done the deeds Steel ascribed to her. The average New Rockhome citizen believed that Steel had saved Eldar Temple from Pebblic and his warriors and that the heroic warrior had manufactured the story about Taylok just because he had no desire to bask in glory. But some of the ultra conservative citizenry gave it a much darker spin.

"Did you hear what Taylok did?"

"Yes. It was a miracle."

"I think the child is a . . . a witch. How else could she have done that?"

"A witch? She's lived among us all her life."

"Think about it. Remember what she did at the sling trials? Perfect scores. Remember how she saved herself from Xantopec? You know how she can tell the difference between ulok varieties even though she's blind? And, now, this feat that no normal human could do."

"Stones. Maybe she is a witch."

"She has all the indications."

Taylok could understand the villagers and everyone else having a difficult time believing that she could have done what she did. Her age and blindness were ample reasons to discredit her deeds and, because of the darkness, no one had actually seen her do it.

They had just seen the results. Steel was the only one who would know deep in his heart that she had accomplished the impossible in that room. And he proclaimed to all who would listen that Taylok had made the victory theirs.

But, even Flint questioned that she had done it.

"You're telling me that you single-handedly took out six warriors holding hostages?" he asked Taylok. "I know how good you are with the sling, but that's over the top."

"Flint," Taylok replied, "it was awesome. The entire blacked-out room appeared to me like in a dream. I could 'see' everyone inside the room and had to make a couple of shots that would have made you proud."

"You mean that you 'saw' something like the Shotai's story of Beach, or did you actually see it?"

"It was like the Shotai's story of Beach," said Taylok, excitedly. "I couldn't believe my good luck that it happened when it did. I had to save them, Flint. I never did anything that felt more right." She moved her arm to indicate the Shotai's room. "What happened down here while we were gone?"

"Only a few hostiles came after the Shotai . . . eight or nine," replied Flint "I could have taken them by myself, but I never got to draw my sword. The warriors from second level had the hostiles surrounded and made them surrender before I got into action."

"It's good how few lives were lost," quipped Taylok.

"I still don't know how you managed to figure all that out," Flint said. "If we hadn't been prepared, Pebblic would be in charge of Eldar Temple, now."

"He is my father. Maybe we just think alike."

"Maybe so. By the way, did Ganaga look at your eyes?"

"No. Why?"

"If you were able to see, even for an instant, your eyes might be healing."

He turned away from her. "Ganaga," he called. "Could you come over here for a moment?"

Ganaga hurried to them.

"What is it?" he said.

"Would you check Taylok's eyes? She said that she 'saw' a vision of that third level room with all the people inside."

Ganaga bent over Taylok and gently examined her eyes.

"This young lady saved my family from a horrible fate," Ganaga murmured, earnestly, as he examined Taylok's eyes."

At last, he grunted, "No. Nothing has changed."

"Couldn't you treat her eyes, anyway?" asked Flint.

"My fear remains as before," said Ganaga. "If treatment is administered too early, it could render her blindness permanent. There will come a time, Taylok. I beg you, be patient."

"What caused her to be able to 'see' that room?"

"I think it involves hysterical phenomenon that incredibly amplified her already acute hearing and focused her trained ability to identify and translate sounds to images. The Shotai might come close to replicating it, but you or I could never do it like she does, in darkness. We have neither her incredible, innate hearing ability nor the learned characteristics of the wind sounds."

"The only part of that I understood was the part where you said, 'you or I could never do it.'"

Ganaga laughed.

"Okay. Put another way, Taylok had a surge of adrenaline, energy, if you prefer, that focused her mind and ability on the scene, enough so that she could distinguish and locate people and things separately in the darkness."

"It felt awesome," said Taylok.

"Can you do it again?" Flint asked.

"I can always tell where some things are located around me," replied Taylok. "But I never could just call up an image like the one I had in that room. That was a first . . . and maybe a last."

"I think you may be right," said Ganaga. "Events like the one in which you were involved are, fortunately, rare."

* * * * *

The celebrations lasted for ten isas in the village and in Eldar Temple. At the conclusion, trials began for the prisoners. Pebblic's came first.

The trial took place in the village council hall, a large, roomy structure. Grulok, a council member, acted as prosecutor. Council

Chief Redrock led the panel of judges. Ganaga and Cobalta testified against Pebblic, but the children were spared from the proceedings. Steel also testified, but when he began to extol Taylok's heroic effort in the room on level three, the advisor for Pebblic, a knowledgeable man named Abo, objected with a lengthy speech.

Abo said, "This is not a forum for making a heroine of an eleven-ring-old who has been credited with a highly improbable effort. This trial concerns a man subjected to tremendous agony over the past few isas and whose mind is forever changed by the vicious attack on level three of Eldar Temple. Pebblic prepared to surrender to Steel, when he came into the room, and turn over the Ganaga family, who a few errant warriors had held by accident during the conflict. The attack disabled Pebblic and his men and thwarted his peaceful plan to hand over Ganaga's family. Nevertheless, the Ganaga family remained unhurt."

"That is an interesting testimonial twist on reality," said Steel. "If your speech is a cross examination to which I may respond, I call it a lie. In the first place, the room was totally dark and silent when we arrived, so there had never been any intent to surrender or to hand over hostages. Pebblic's warriors were well armed with swords and knives and each held a hostage, all women and children, ready to deliver a fatal blow. They had light baskets hidden beneath cloth covers, ready to ambush any who walked, unaware, into the room. Pebblic stood at the door holding a sword to slash whoever entered first. If not for Taylok's ability to envision the room in darkness, Pebblic would have killed her."

"Only because she is convicted of desertion along with her mother, Windsong, who was executed, properly, by Xantopec. Besides, what you ascribe to Taylok cannot be done," screamed Abo.

Pebblic sat, his head bandaged, looking straight ahead, seemingly unaware of the proceedings. He reacted only slightly when Abo raised his voice.

"You are testifying to unproved items," said Grulok.

"I told you, Abo," growled Redrock, "you may not testify. Ask questions or sit down."

"It can be and was done by Taylok," said Steel, ignoring

262

Redrock and answering Abo's taunt.

"I insist that the witness, Ganaga, be brought back to the witness stall," said the Advisor.

"You declined to interview him when he testified earlier," said Redrock.

"He knows the truth about Taylok," said Abo.

Ganaga took the stall and Steel retired to a chair.

"Healer Ganaga," said the Advisor. "Is the girl, Taylok, blind? Please answer yes or no."

"Yes, but . . ."

"That's all, healer."

"Another question for this witness," said prosecutor Grulok.

"Granted," said Redrock.

"Healer," said Grulok, "you testified that the girl Taylok is blind. Does she possess special abilities as a result of her blindness?"

"Indeed, she does," said Ganaga.

"I object," said Abo.

"You brought it up, Advisor," said Redrock.

"Could you tell us what those abilities are, healer Ganaga?" continued Grulok.

"Taylok has the ability to discern objects through the use of sound echoes. In other words, she can 'see' almost as well in total darkness as we see in the light. And, she can image people as well as objects."

"That's impossible," shouted Abo.

"No," said Ganaga, "it's not impossible and Taylok has almost perfected the ability."

"Call the girl, Taylok, to the stall," said Abo.

"I am not finished with Ganaga," shouted Grulok, and then spoke softly to Ganaga. "You described her ability, healer, but you failed to tell us how her blindness led her to these abilities."

"The Shotai would be a better teller of this information, since he taught Taylok how to use the sounds."

"The Shotai cannot testify, since he will also judge the High Council."

"Pity. Very well," sighed Ganaga. "The Shotai taught Taylok to utilize sounds that the wind makes as it passes by an object or person. These are sounds so subtle that few can discern them. Taylok's blindness heightened her hearing ability to the point that she routinely makes these partial discretions from the sounds emitted by the wind. That is the simple explanation without delving into the unknowable details of how her brain's recognition of the sounds allows her to 'visualize' a subject."

"Rubble," said Abo. "That would imply that anyone with good hearing could accomplish this, so called, feat, in total darkness. No one can do that. Not Taylok or anyone else."

"I object," said Grulok. "This is testimony."

"Are you testifying, Advisor?" said Redrock. "Are you offering expert testimony? Keep your comments to the facts at hand and do not testify."

"My apologies, Redrock," said Abo. "Are you finished with Ganaga, Grulok?"

"Yes."

"Then, I ask the council to bring Taylok to the stall."

Taylok had been sitting with Flint in the large audience that filled the capacious room. Flint led her to the stall and helped her to the seat.

"Now," began Abo, " . . . you may be seated, Flint. Now, Taylok we have heard some interesting and might I say, impossible stories of your ability. Do you think any of the stories could be true?"

"Which stories?"

"The ridiculous story that you, standing at the door of room three-fifty-seven on level three of Eldar Temple, struck six warriors with stones from your sling."

"No, that's not what happened."

"I knew it. What really happened?"

"I hit Pebblic first because he was standing near the door with a sword in his hand. Then, I only struck four of the warriors who were holding Cobalta and her children. Steel ran into me in the dark and I missed the last one."

"Er . . . you're saying you struck five of those warriors while you were standing in the dark and never hit any of the hostages . . . I mean, guests?"

"Well, Steel said it was dark. I couldn't tell. I'm blind."

"What you are describing is physically impossible, young lady. No matter how good you are with this ability to envision a scene, you could not successfully select and hit just the warriors. You could not do that even if you could see."

"Is a question in there somewhere, Abo?" said Grulok.

"Abo," growled Redrock," you will treat this young woman with due respect. And I remind you once more that you are not allowed to give testimony."

"I am merely serving my client with the best I can offer since he is unable to communicate with me."

"Try questioning the facts, instead."

"Yes, indeed. Facts. Isn't it a fact, Taylok, that Pebblic is your father and that you are a witch?"

A gasp came from the audience.

"I don't know," Taylok replied. "I don't think that I am a witch and no one ever told me that Pebblic is my father. But, his name is the same one that my mother said was my father's name. I was already blind when Pebblic entered New Rockhome Hall, so I never saw him. Not that it would have made any difference since I hadn't seen him before I was blinded, either."

"What is the difference, Abo?" said Redrock. "What does all this have to do with the crimes of Pebblic?"

"First, if Taylok is a witch, she should be on trial instead of my client."

"Taylok did not indulge in sedition as has your client."

"A witch could have made my client act as he did, including the kidnapping of Cobalta and her children."

"So you admit that your client did these things?" interjected Grulok.

"I . . . I make no such admission. I charge that Taylok caused, by witchcraft, my client to do the things that he did."

"That sounds like an admission to me," said Grulok.

"And to me," said Redrock.

"You're twisting my words," screamed Abo.

"Taylok is my daughter, " rasped Pebblic, his face without mien.

The courtroom became suddenly quiet. Everyone focused, with shocked expressions, on the accused man.

"Taylok is my daughter," Pebblic repeated.

"This changes everything," screamed Abo. "Taylok has retaliated against my client for his part in her conviction of a heinous crime in Stonehaven Hall."

"Indeed it does change everything," said Redrock. "Taylok has been convicted in Stonehaven of breaking the law and her death punishment has not been carried out in full as can be proved by the fact that she is sitting without visible support and apparently breathing on her own. Therefore, all her testimony shall be stricken from the record and she may not testify in this or any other trial until and unless she is cleared of all charges."

"What?" screamed Abo. "This is totally unfair to my client."

"I leave the final word, regarding Taylok, to the Shotai. If she is a witch, as Abo claims, then the Shotai will add a suitable punishment to be carried out after that already decreed by Stonehaven Hall. Flint, please assist the young lady down from the stall and back to her seat. Have you another witness to call, Advisor Abo?"

Abo shook with rage while his client, High Council Pebblic, suddenly collapsed in his chair. Abo rushed to Pebblic's side and felt for a pulse.

"There's no pulse," Abo cried.

"Call for Ganaga," said Redrock.

"I'm here, Council Chief," said Ganaga who had been sitting in the room since completing his testimony.

"Please check out the accused, healer. He appears to have fainted or died."

Ganaga ambled slowly to the chair in which Pebblic sprawled. He casually felt for a pulse.

"Pebblic has no pulse," Ganaga said. "I pronounce him dead."

"Take the body to Mordane Pit and discard it," said Redrock. "This trial is done. The gods have spoken."

"I object," squeaked Abo.

* * * * *

"They're taking him out, now," said Flint. "Are you all right?"

"Yes. It's sort of strange," replied Taylok, "I hardly feel

anything. You know, I never knew him or saw him and the closest we ever were to each other was when he stood in that doorway with his sword, waiting to kill me. Somehow, that doesn't qualify him for father of the ring. It doesn't qualify him for father at all."

"The real pity is that he never knew you . . . never knew what he missed. He might have been a different man if he had."

"I doubt it. Look what he had Xantopec do to mother and me without even knowing me. Anyone who could do that had an evil heart. I do wonder if he came to New Rockhome Hall to find me or just to take over Eldar Temple."

"I don't think he expected to find you like he did," laughed Flint.

"Have they tried Tektitus, yet?" Taylok asked.

"No. I think they'll leave Tektitus' fate up to the Shotai. He'll probably be more lenient than he should, considering that Tektitus killed His Eminence and would have killed the Shotai if he could."

"Will you have to testify against him?"

"I doubt it. I didn't witness Tektitus kill His Eminence Graystone and that is the crime for which he will be tried."

"You did hear him confess to killing His Eminence, though. So did I."

"So did the Shotai. No, I think I will be able to return to Banestone Hall right away."

"What about Garnet?" asked Taylok.

"I fear that he will suffer Pebblic's fate of death. The council decreed that Pebblic is guilty by reason of the gods having punished him. That means everyone who supported Pebblic falls under the same decree and could be treated the same.

"Taylok, let's go to Banestone Hall," finished Flint.

"Not yet, Flint. We're going to solve the mystery room on level four."

"You keep saying we are going to do this."

"Jade and I will do it, then."

"I thought you were going back with me."

"No. I thought about it. You have your life back in Banestone Hall and you don't need me. You'll have a bunch of children and I'll just be in the way. What would I do there, anyway?"

"What will you do here? Where will you live?"

"I think that Jade and I might room together in Eldar Temple. Or I can go back to Halite's place. I haven't decided, yet."

"Are you sure that I can't talk you into going back with me? I'm really going to miss you, Taylok."

"You'll get so involved in Banestone Hall and raising your family that you'll forget me in a few isas. I know how you throw yourself into your work. Think of me once in a while, Flint."

"Every isa. I'll never forget you, Taylok."

He hugged Taylok, bringing tears to both their eyes.

Flint departed New Rockhome Hall the following isa with a huge party of citizens and warriors congregated to see him off. Limping slightly and waving goodbye, he disappeared into the tunnel leading to Banestone Hall.

Later, she would hear that Flint had risen to warrior chief in Banestone Hall and had a family of three sons and a daughter with his Fireseasoned Mate, Sapphirus. Taylok wondered if he would teach his daughter to use the sling. Sometimes, tears came to her eyes when she thought about Flint or Shalea or her mother and the old times, but mostly, she remained stoic about the losses.

Chapter 24 - Fourth Level

When Jade invited Taylok to live with her in Eldar Temple, Taylok quickly accepted.

"Oh, good," said Jade. "I hoped we could labor on the fourth level puzzle together."

"I appreciate the chance to work with you," agreed Taylok. "And, since I once lived in these rooms, I feel right at home here."

Before they could start their project to solve level four, the Shotai called a meeting of the remaining senior officials of Eldar Temple and sent two acolytes to summon Taylok and Jade. They waited outside a large room as the Shotai pronounced the sentence of Tektitus. Taylok's extraordinary hearing allowed her to hear the brief oration by the Shotai.

"Tektitus, you have entered a plea of guilty to the charge of assassinating His Eminence Graystone. Your sentence shall be twenty rings in prison.

"Bring in Taylok and Jade, now."

The acolytes ushered both girls into the large room and announced their names to those already seated.

"Peace and tranquility, Taylok, Jade," said the Shotai from an elevated position in the room. "Please join me here."

"Peace and tranquility," answered Taylok, tentatively.

"Peace and tranquility," said Jade, questioningly.

Taylok walked toward the Shotai's voice with Jade's guiding hand helping her. Strong hands helped to seat Taylok on a high stool and she recognized, from his voice, that Steel sat next to her.

"Taylok," began the Shotai, "you have been accused of being a witch. Did you know that?"

"I heard some people say that," said Taylok, "but, I didn't believe them."

"Good. This hearing is to put that notion to the test. There are many from the village and many Eldarfiles here as witnesses and judges. Steel will be your council should you need one. I will first lay some ground rules. It has come to my attention, in reading the ancient laws and decrees, that the only person who can unerringly recognize a witch is another witch. Since we have no register of witches, it will be necessary for someone to prove to this administrative panel that he or she is a witch so that a clear identification of other witches may be conducted. Do we have anyone who wishes to make that admission?"

A buzz of talk and protests ensued from the crowded room, but no one came forward.

"So," continued the Shotai, "we have no admission by anyone that he or she is a witch. Pity. Does anyone wish to make a formal accusation of witchcraft against Taylok?"

Again the audience made loud protestations, but no one dared make the accusation. It had become obvious that to accuse someone of being a witch would unhappily cast the shade of witchcraft upon the accuser. The Shotai had carefully crafted the catch.

"No?" said the Shotai. "The only other test administered by the ancients to identify a witch is the poisoned water test. Three cups of water sit on the table in front of me. One of them contains a poisonous substance made from the most deadly ulok'neh fungus in our world. So, Taylok, will you approach the table?"

Taylok gulped, anxiously, arose and walked, with Jade's assistance, to the table.

"I wish for you to only smell the liquid within the three cups," said the Shotai. "Do not touch the cup or drink. The ancients declared that a witch would be unable to detect the deadly fungus. Our new shaman, Ladida, has prepared the samples."

The audience tittered and the shaman, sitting beside the Shotai, looked surprised.

"My name is Laida," he reminded.

"Of course," smiled the Shotai as the audience laughed.

Jade held the first cup beneath Taylok's nose.

"This is not deadly," said Taylok, after sniffing the liquid.

The second cup came to Taylok's nose. She smelled the mixture.

"This is a deadly mix," she declared. "It has booted amanita and . . ."

"Shaman," interrupted the Shotai, "is she correct?"

Shaman Laida nodded vigorously, and said, "She is correct."

"Then, it is decreed that Taylok is absolved of the charge of being a witch. Now, to another matter that still hangs over your head, Taylok; the conviction of leaving your father while still in the womb and coming from Tadi'wa Hall to New Rockhome Hall. Is that charge correct?"

Taylok thought for a moment.

"I did not leave of my own free will," said Taylok.

"And who forced you to leave?"

"My mother carried me with her."

"And where is your mother, now?"

"She was sacrificed by Xantopec eight rings ago."

"So we can not question her?"

"No."

"Where were you born, Taylok?"

"In New Rockhome Hall."

"New Rockhome Hall? Are you sure?"

"Yes."

"Is there someone who can verify that?"

"Yes. Chalka witnessed my birth in New Rockhome Hall."

"Yet, your sentence was passed in The Hall of the Tadi'wa?"

"Yes."

"Very well. I hereby decree that the sentence rendered by the priests of the Tadi'wa, and in that hall, is without validity since you are a citizen of New Rockhome Hall and not the Hall of the Tadi'wa. Taylok is absolved of any wrongdoing and is herein exonerated and her conviction overturned and stricken from the records. Does that cover everything, Steel?"

"It does, Shotai."

"Taylok, you are a free woman and may live in Eldar Temple for as long as you wish. Peace and tranquility. Go, now, and please, stay out of trouble."

"Peace and tranquility, Shotai. And, thank you."

Jade held Taylok's arm as they walked out of the meeting room.

"Now we can solve the fourth level mystery," said Taylok, loud enough that everyone in the room heard.

"They're shaking their heads, no, Taylok," whispered Jade.

"Okay," whispered Taylok, "we'll wait an isa or two."

* * * * *

Six isas later found the two girls at the entrance to the room on level four. Previously, each acquaintance who had seen them out on their own inevitably locked them in conversation and prevented them from reaching fourth level. This isa had been different. Everyone seemed to be in a hurry and did not wish to bother with Taylok and Jade. Access to fourth level had also been easier than expected. No warriors guarded the stairway or the level four room.

"We made it," said Jade. "There's even a light basket lying beside the door."

"Won't do me any good," countered Taylok, in good humor. "But, it might help you to find the other information."

"What other information?"

"The glyphs we found under the stairs didn't give any real help for operating this room. There have to be some other instructions, somewhere."

"Rational," said Jade, "but where should we look?"

"I don't know. Describe the door and the wall to me."

"Not much to tell," said Jade. "The door is really kind of ordinary. It's about two men high and has a nice arch at the top. The bricks forming the doorframe stick out from the wall about half as far as my little finger is long. It's ornately carved, but there are no glyphs.

"The wall has a relief sculpture of the T'sa'wa about three steps left of the door. Its diameter is my height. The bottom is knee high off the floor and the top is almost as high as I can reach. The raised middle sticks out a hands-length from the wall. There are some characters carved around the edges, but I've looked at those before and they seem meaningless. There are other dots and an eye in the center but most of it looks ornamental. The mud used to cement the sculpture in place is ageing and you can see a thin crack that runs all the way around the edge of the circle.

"Don't bother asking me to describe fourth level room. I can't see inside it at all. Even when I place the light basket at the opening, I can't see the floor inside. It's as if you would drop off into nothingness if you stepped in."

"What's below this room in the rest of the temple?" Taylok

asked.

"It's walled off on this level. On third level, I don't know. I guess we could check it out."

"Walk me over to the relief sculpture."

"Okay. I looked before, though, and didn't find anything."

Taylok meticulously felt around the beautifully carved stone. She placed her ear against it and listened.

"What are you doing?" asked Jade.

"Listening. I thought I heard a voice."

"It was probably one of the warriors on third level."

"Probably."

"What did the voice say?"

"I couldn't understand any words."

"Like I said, it was probably one of the warriors on level three and it came through muffled so you couldn't understand it."

"It only happened when I ran my fingers over part of the sculpture. Like this."

Both girls heard a muffled voice and laughed at the sound.

"What did it say?" asked Jade, still laughing.

"Rubble obble," said Taylok, and the girls laughed harder.

They lost it for a moment and could not suppress laughter. When they finally regained a modicum of control, Jade spoke, soberly.

"Do it again."

Tickle box overturned, they laughed as if Jade had told a joke.

"This isn't funny," said Taylok, and they again collapsed in uncontrollable laughter.

Soon, they recovered.

"Seriously," said Jade, "do it again."

Taylok dutifully complied but her face contorted in an unsuppressed smile.

"That still sounds like a muffled voice," she said.

"Let me see that part you're rubbing," suggested Jade.

She examined the carving carefully.

"You know," Jade said, "these little raised bumps could be crystals. They're worn down, almost to the level of the smooth part of the carving. Someone used these extensively in the past."

"Whoever used them probably knew how to run their fingers

over them. Can you see any particular direction of wear?"

"They seem smooth, except for the top one. It looks a little more worn on the low side."

"What does that mean? Did they start there or end there?" Taylok asked.

"No clue," said Jade. "But, there are only two directions to try. Which way did you go the first time?"

"Bottom to top."

"Okay. Try top to bottom."

Taylok reached high and felt for the crystal buttons. She swiped her finger over the knobby surface. The voice sounded clearer.

"Better," said Taylok. "What did it say?"

"Elbow elbur."

Jade's pronunciation brought immediate laughter from both girls.

"No, seriously," laughed Taylok.

"That's what it sounded like to me," replied Jade. But in a moment, she offered, "Wait, maybe it's ancient dialect."

"What does 'Elbow elbur' mean in ancient?"

"Nothing that I know," said Jade.

More laughter.

"I know what this is," said Taylok.

"You do? What? Please tell me."

"It's frustrating, that's what it is."

At that moment, the large disk of the sculpture moved. It sank a short distance into the wall with a scraping sound, revealing a flat panel along the bottom. Both girls sobered at the event, losing all desire to laugh.

"Okay, this is new," sputtered Jade. "There's a circular onyx dial, the size of my hand, with a square hole in the middle. It's inset into the lowermost brick framing the T'sa'wa carving. The dial looks free, like it should turn."

Taylok ran her hand over the onyx plate. She tried to turn it, but found it impossible to grip the flat, polished stone. She couldn't move it in either direction.

"Maybe it's broken," she said.

"Maybe," mused Jade. "But, maybe it needs the stone that Playa gave you. The pyrite cube on the end of that crystal might fit into this slot."

"Good idea. Let's try it."

"Check this out," said Jade, walking to the opening. "There are four faint grooves, evenly spaced, on the stone around the onyx. There is also a different character at the end of each of the marks. If Flint is right, and the room is a gateway to other places, this may determine where it takes you."

"Don't mention his name. It makes me want to cry," Taylok sniffed. But a moment later she said, "Are there any marks or grooves on the onyx plate?"

"No. It's perfectly smooth."

"Then, how will we tell at which groove the plate is pointing?"

"Good question."

"Do you think any of the four are places we'd want to go?" asked Taylok.

"I think the ancients used some really powerful crystals to set this up. Why would they go to all that expense and not include a few good places to go?"

"I wish we knew why they set this up at all. Maybe if we go to one of the other places, we can get some idea as to why they did it," Taylok remarked.

"I think the one it's set on now is Mordane Pit," said Jade, bitterly. "That's why the people we know about, who went into the room, never came back."

"We definitely need to change that setting and remember which one it is. I'm not ready for Mordane Pit. Why would they even have the pit on this thing?"

"Body removal, is my guess, or refuse disposal," offered Jade.

"Pretty classy for a garbage disposal."

"It might have been handy for enemy removal, though."

"Then, they should have put it on level one."

"Give me the stone and we'll try it," said Jade, touching Taylok on the arm.

Taylok reached into the bag hanging around her waist and retrieved the paired crystal. She handed it to her friend.

"I'm trying it in the slot," grunted Jade. "Uh oh. It doesn't fit. Wait, I'll turn it another way. No, not that way, either. Last chance. There. It fits that way, Taylok. And look at this. The ruby crystal makes a pointer with the way it's shaped on one side. It doesn't really show until you get the stone into its proper position in the slot. At the moment, it's pointed toward the topmost groove."

"I thought the pyrite crystal was a perfect cube."

"Apparently it's off just enough to make it fit only one way."

"Can you turn the onyx now?"

"I'll try. Ung! Turn, damn you. Uff! It won't turn."

"Let me try it."

"Okay, Hold here."

"Got it. Unh." She tried the other direction. "Augh! No. Doesn't budge for me either."

"Maybe it's rusted, it's been so long since used."

"Onyx doesn't rust."

"No, but it's connected to something. Maybe it's rusted iron."

"Or, maybe we're missing something."

"You mean like a big, strong man?" Jade's innuendo did not go unnoticed.

"Noooo," Taylok made a rolling exasperated sound. "More like another key that lets the onyx turn when the crystal is in the slot. Like the first key that opened the T'sa'wa carving."

"Beautiful. If there is a third key, they sure built a lot of failsafe into this thing. And where is that other key?"

"It might be on the carving, like the first one."

"I'll say one thing for you, Taylok, you are persistent."

"Do you have somewhere to go?"

Jade laughed; a deep guffaw that vibrated through fourth level.

She said, "Oh, you're cruel. Get out of my way so I can look at the carving."

Taylok stood aside as her friend retrieved the light basket and began to reexamine the sculpture. While Jade inspected, she talked, making a startling revelation.

"Last isa, Steel asked me to join him in Fireseasoning," Jade said, casually.

"He did? What did you tell him?" Taylok tried to hold her emotions down.

"I'm thinking about it. I think I'll accept."

Taylok wilted, but immediately straightened. She didn't want Jade to see her fear. It seemed that her best friends were making new lives for themselves, which didn't include her.

But, she said, "Good for you, Jade. He seems like a great guy."

"That's what I thought."

"Are you going to move in with him?"

"No. He'll move in with us. His quarters are pretty tight down with the warriors. You can stay with us if you want."

"Right," said Taylok, unenthusiastically.

Following a long period of silence, Jade backed away from the sculpture.

She said, "I've checked out every dot and mark on this thing and can't even raise another sound when I run my finger across them. We just hit the proverbial stone wall."

Taylok walked to the sculpture.

"Maybe we're not thinking big enough," Taylok said.

"What do you mean?"

"Maybe the entire disk turns."

"We tried that."

"No. I mean the entire disk of the T'sa'wa."

"The whole sculpture?"

"Got any better ideas?"

"Not at the moment. Okay, let's give it a try."

Taylok took one side and Jade the other.

"I'll push up from here," Taylok offered. "You pull down from your position. Ready?"

"Ready."

With a little effort, the disk turned smoothly. When they released it, however, the sculpture slowly returned to its original position.

"Well, that didn't do any good," remarked Taylok.

"Don't be too sure," said Jade. "The ruby tip is pointing at a different groove than before."

"All right," Taylok gushed. "We did it, Jade. We solved the puzzle."

"I think you may be right, Taylok. And, now comes the really scary part."

"You're right. We have to go into the room. I'm excited about it, but I'm scared, like you."

She sounded more frightened than excited.

"Let's give this some thought before we do it," Jade advised.

"Yes . . . Maybe we should take some provisions with us; like water and ulok, at least, in case there's nothing to eat," proposed Taylok.

"And a light basket."

"And plenty of stones for our slings, in case there are snakes."

"What if there's a Mohk'wa?"

"Then we won't have to worry about water and ulok," laughed Taylok.

They raced downstairs to assemble their gear and were almost finished when a tap at the door startled them.

"Who is it?" called Jade.

"It is the Shotai," said the voice.

Hesitantly, Jade opened the door. The Shotai stood before her, smiling.

"Peace and tranquility," he said.

"Peace and tranquility," said Jade, slowly. "Shotai. It's good to see you. Please come inside. What have we done to deserve this honor?"

The Shotai didn't answer immediately. Instead, he looked around the room and his eyes came to rest on the assortment of gear laid out on the floor.

"Taking a trip?" he asked.

"We . . . we're . . . maybe, Shotai."

"So, you have found the long lost secret to level four?" he asked.

A long pause ensued, followed by a knowing smile from Taylok.

"We think so, Shotai," she chimed. "We found the onyx and put the crystal into it, then turned the carving . . ."

"Slowly, Taylok," said the Shotai, gesturing with his hands. "My old mind does not work as quickly as it used to."

Taylok and Jade described the process that they had discovered. The Shotai nodded his head.

"Your description fits that which I have heard," he said.

"How did you know what we did, Shotai?" asked Jade.

"Perhaps," he replied, "you did not notice how the acolytes and the warriors allowed you access to level four. I decided it was better to encourage your experiment than to continue frustrating your desire. Actually, I did not think you could solve the ancient riddle as many have tried and failed. At any rate, we had people watching you at all times and would have interfered if you had tried to enter the room."

"You can credit Taylok, Shotai," said Jade. "She is the most persistent person I ever knew."

"I appreciate your generosity," said Taylok, "but, Jade is the brains behind the discovery."

"I give you both credit for a brilliant solve," said the Shotai. "Now, however, we come to a different phase of the experiment. It is dangerous, even foolhardy, to walk into that room without additional safeguards."

"What do you mean, Shotai?" asked Taylok.

"You . . . we . . . still do not know what happens to someone who steps into that room. Perhaps it transports the person to another part of the universe, or it might disintegrate them. Or both. Nothing instructs or prepares us for that last step."

"Can't we figure it out, Shotai?" asked Taylok.

"We know very little about it; the room is probably powered by crystals and we know of no one who returned to New Rockhome Hall after entering."

"But, the settings . . ." began Taylok.

"Yes, you changed the setting on the onyx. But to the best of our knowledge, crystals produce a spark when sung and the intensity of the spark depends upon the singer and the stone being sung. If there is a way to transport a human body to another location using crystals, it is a use that has been lost. It is far beyond our current knowledge."

"But crystals can also heal, can't they?" asked Taylok.

"True enough," said the Shotai. "There are a few types of injury that can be healed by crystal power. But, this . . . we are talking a form of transport, which we have never seen . . . if that is what the room does. That knowledge, as well as the expertise to build it, has been lost to us over the past thousand rings."

"But, we'll never know, until someone goes in and comes back to tell about it."

"I cannot allow you to risk your lives and that is most assuredly what you would be doing."

"I would do it," said Taylok. "My mother and father are dead, Flint and Shalea are in Banestone Hall, I don't want to go back to Ganaga's or Halite's and Jade is going to Fireseason with Steel. I have nowhere to go, I'm not doing anybody any good right now . . . and I'm blind. This would be the most exciting thing I ever did."

Jade added, "I believe in what we've discovered about the room, Shotai. I think we have reset the dial so we wouldn't go to Mordane Pit. I don't know where we would go, but if it isn't the pit, there's a good chance we would live to return. Maybe there's even a treasure waiting for us at this setting."

"Or a different kind of death," lamented the Shotai.

"I'm willing to bet this one is not something that will kill," Taylok said.

"Taylok, that bet is for your life, against something unknown . . . or maybe nothing," argued the Shotai. "Both of you underestimate your worth to Eldar Temple and New Rockhome Hall."

"It's more than that, Shotai," said Taylok. "I want my life to mean something. Oh, sure, I've done a couple of things that will get a footnote in the New Rockhome Hall history books, but I'd like to do something really significant . . . like you do, Shotai."

"You are a charmer, Taylok. But, I know what you're doing and I'm still not going to give my blessing to you risking your life in that level four room. What if you found yourself somewhere that ulok would not grow?"

"I'd have to eat gravel gravy."

Jade snickered but the Shotai sighed.

"Be serious, Taylok. Lack of food or water would be as deadly as Mordane Pit . . . just not as quick."

"I'd take enough food and water to last ten isas. I can get back from almost anywhere in ten isas."

"And how do you know that what you take in with you will travel with you?"

"These are things we need the experiment to discover, aren't they?" Taylok insisted.

"Taylok, you are only eleven. That's far too young to be exploring and risking your life. You need more practical experience to qualify for this experiment."

"Shotai, Xantopec's warriors captured me, blinded and would have sacrificed me to the T'sa'wa by the age of three if you, His Eminence and Flint hadn't saved me. When you come that close to death and survive, it doesn't seem so bad to take a little risk."

"We don't know if the room ever worked properly," the Shotai raised his voice. "The ancients didn't leave enough information on it and we know that they tried to destroy it, at least once, and failed. They could have had lofty ambitions for the room and never attained them."

"But, Shotai, we need to know if changing the setting makes a difference, don't we?" asked Jade.

"If I can't talk you out of this, I want to make sure you are properly outfitted and supported for a dangerous journey," said the Shotai. "Is this your travel gear?"

"We were just assembling it," answered Jade.

"I want you to take these two crystals with you. They are fine singing crystals."

"Shotai, neither of us have good crystal singing voices," said Taylok.

"That doesn't matter. Do you realize that only one person in a thousand can sing a crystal to any significant spark, such as those used on the battlefield?" queried the Shotai. "And only one person in three generations has a voice that can be trained to become a crystal master. Fewer than that could do what Taylok does with her auditory perception and sling skills. No one alive this isa can achieve the maximum result from his or her crystal, including the crystal masters. Yet, even I can start a fire with a crystal spark. And so can you. I will teach you how."

"Why would we need a fire?" asked Jade.

"Believe it or not, some parts of our world are colder than New Rockhome Hall, just as some do not have ulok'neh or ulok."

"I wouldn't miss the ulok'neh," quipped Taylok.

"No, but Jade would. Without phosphorescent ulok'neh or the lighted waters, the world is as dark for Jade as you normally view it, Taylok. And, Jade is not equipped to cope with that darkness as you are."

The girls were silent for a moment.

"We'll have to go together, then," said Taylok. "That way, it won't matter if there is no light. I can keep us safe in the dark, even if there are many pits and snakes around us. And Jade can catalog all the things that she hears and sees."

"Very well," said the Shotai. "Let's gather some lignite and I will show you how to start a fire with your crystals. I further insist on bringing together a team of specialists to help you reach your goals without losing your lives."

"What are they going to do, tie a rope around us?" Jade asked, facetiously.

"Excellent suggestion, Jade," responded the Shotai, seriously.

"What? But, that was just a joke."

"Think what it would mean if you were still tied to the rope when you reached the place the room took you. We might even be able to pull you back to the room. We need to accumulate all the data possible from this undertaking."

"Oooh!" said Taylok, her face lined with feigned fear. "Don't say undertaking."

Not amused, the Shotai raised his voice, again.

"You two must take this seriously. If you do not, I will replace the guard on level four."

"Not fair, Shotai," laughed Taylok. "We'll be good. Really."

The next four isas found a group of six scientists, four men and two women, sitting in Jade's room, going over a lengthy list of goods to be taken with the explorers. Taylok and Jade watched the proceedings, trying to follow the arguments of the scientists. Suddenly, Jade stood.

"We won't be able to carry all this," she complained. "We'll need three strong men to lift it."

"Our idea," said Ignus, a village scientist, "is to push these goods into the room ahead of you. The room should move the food, drink and phosphorescent ulok'neh to the same place that it takes you, wherever that is. But first, we will put a highly flammable mixture of dried ulok'neh and lignite, into the room. We'll have someone watching Mordane Pit to see if a flare occurs when and if the room moves the lignite. If there is, we'll know that it's still unsafe for you to go."

"Wait," said Taylok. "You're going to put some highly

flammable stuff into the room just before we go in? We'll land right on top of it if it doesn't go into Mordane Pit."

"The mixture won't be on fire, Taylok," laughed Ignus, "unless it falls into Mordane Pit. But you can use it to start a fire if you need one. This procedure is a precaution to make sure that you aren't being sent to the pit."

Jade took Taylok's arm.

"It's okay, Taylok," she said. "It may give us a soft place to land."

"No, we'll land on the food, drink and ulok'neh, which is going in right ahead of us."

The meeting continued, the scientists taking little further notice of Taylok and Jade. The stack of goods to be sent ahead of them continued to mount.

"Let's go check out level four," whispered Taylok to Jade. "I don't like where this is going."

"I don't either," whispered Jade. "But there's nothing we can do. The Shotai appointed these people to oversee the journey."

Aloud, Taylok said to the scientists, "You guys don't need us for anything right now, do you?"

"Not at the moment," said Ignus, looking up from his list. "Where are you going?"

"Out for a walk," said Taylok.

"Why are you taking your sling?"

"I don't go anywhere without my sling. Snakes, you know."

"Yes, yes. Hurry back."

Laughing nervously, the two women struck out for the stairs to level three. Taylok fell silent as they climbed.

"What do you have in mind, Taylok?" asked Jade. "I know this is not just for a walk."

"Oh, nothing," Taylok replied. "I want to make sure the settings stayed where we left them."

"Who would have moved them?"

"What if the room resets itself after a while. That may be why it took everyone to Mordane Pit. That could be the default position, while the other settings remain fixed only a short time."

"Oh. You could be right. It certainly wouldn't hurt to check it out."

They continued to climb and eventually reached fourth level. Two warriors stood guarding the door.

"Taylok, Jade," called one of the warriors. "What brings you to up here, now?"

"We want to check the onyx setting again," said Jade.

"The onyx setting? No one has changed that since you reset it."

"Taylok thinks that the room may reset itself after a while. We just want to make sure."

The warriors hesitated and conferred briefly.

"No problem," said the warrior. "We'll help you check it."

"Thanks," said Taylok.

Jade and Taylok walked to the wall sculpture and Taylok ran her fingers over the buttons. The sculpture groaned as it sank into the wall, revealing the onyx dial.

It had reset to the original position, pointing inward toward the sculpture.

"You were right. I don't know how you thought of it, Taylok," said Jade. "We would have gone straight into Mordane Pit if you hadn't reconsidered the problem."

"We need to reset again," said Taylok. "Will you guys help us?"

"We'd be honored," said the guard. "What can we do?"

"You stand on this side of the sculpture and you on the other side. We need to rotate it a quarter turn to the right. Okay?"

"Okay."

Taylok and Jade stood back from the raised sculpture as the warriors worked to rotate it. Taylok could hear the large depiction of the sun slowly turn. She took Jade's hand and inched toward the door to room four.

"Stay with me," she whispered. Aloud, she said, "Did the onyx move?"

"Yes, it did," said the warrior.

"Thanks for your help," said Taylok.

Pulling Jade with her, Taylok plunged through the doorway of the forbidden room on level four.

For an instant, Taylok heard the warriors cry out, "No. Stop. Wait" . . . and then, no sound penetrated.

The first sensation that struck Taylok strongly resembled falling. Like in a bad dream, the floor dissolved beneath them and

Taylok sensed that only the pit of her stomach remained high on level four. She then endured a surge of intense heat for an instant, turning to freezing cold. Jade screamed as they plunged through the bottomless void and their fall accelerated. Taylok struggled with all her might to hold onto Jade's hand. Jade stopped screaming, but her hand went limp. Taylok hoped that her friend had only fainted. And then, they began to drift more slowly, still downward. When Taylok's feet hit a hard surface, her knees buckled and she dropped to the ground. Jade also collapsed when they encountered the firm surface. Taylok felt Jade's neck. She found a good, strong pulse.

Taylok assessed the minor injuries she acquired in the fall and only one elbow felt really tender. No doubt, she would be bruised in a couple of other spots, but she lived and so did Jade. They had made it to . . . somewhere.

Taylok loosened her sling when she heard the distant buzz of rattlesnakes to her right. Snakes didn't bother her as long as they kept their distance. She heard a steady, roaring sound from the other direction . . . probably a waterfall. Taylok trilled briefly and listened to the echoes.

She counted several columns of stone; a few stalagmites and stalactites; one fairly long, thin wall of stone with some windows or openings; four pits within thirty steps of their location; and . . . she paused her assessment as the snakes moved toward them. Taylok readied her sling and picked out a stone to use in it. Then, she resumed her appraisal. She located dozens of rounded, seemingly hollow stones and an abundance of thin, spiny, curved columns . . . Taylok shuddered. These were human bones. The Shotai had warned them that there might be another kind of death.

The next sounds that she heard were human voices, faint at first then louder as they approached. Separated from the girls by the thin wall, the people talking obviously walked behind an abundance of windows or open columns because the voices sounded clear. Taylok almost called out to the party, but caution made her wait. When she heard the conversation, she was glad she waited.

"I hate these crawls," grunted the first man's voice.

"Yes, me too," said another.

"Let's dump the body here and be done with it."

"Maybe you want to face the Crystal Master when the Stonehavenite walks out, but not me," voiced the second man. "No. We have to deposit the body deep into the crawl. We don't want this one to ever make it out."

Taylok's face blanched with the implications.

"It'll be another isa or two before awakening," said the first man. "The snakes are bound to kill . . ."

A third voice shrilly interrupted, " . . . Snake."

"Got it," a fourth voice declared, followed by the sound of a sling whirring and three stones striking flesh and rock, arousing a jangle of rattles.

"Why don't we make the kill and leave?" the first man persisted.

"Where have you been, Bedrock? The High Priest doesn't want that new god to have something else to get angry over."

"Okay. So, you're saying that if death is by natural causes . . ."

"Now you have it. No one can blame us if death comes from natural causes."

"Snake," cried the shrill voice.

"I'm on it," growled a fifth voice.

Whir, thump; whir, thump; whir, thump; the sling stones sounded.

This procedure repeated several times as the voices receded into the distance. Taylok counted five separate voices. Two of them carried the victim they were leaving to die. The snakes she had heard earlier seemed to be moving in the direction of the men, more importantly, away from Taylok and Jade.

Jade awoke with a scream on her lips. Taylok hurriedly covered her friend's mouth with her hand to stifle the sound.

"It's okay, Jade. We made it," Taylok assured.

"G . . . r . . . nd . . . uf . . . um . . .mf."

"What? Oh, sorry. Now, what did you say?"

Taylok took her hand away from Jade's mouth.

"I said, 'Get your hand off my mouth.'"

"Okay, but keep it down. We're not alone."

"Where are we?'"

"I don't know. We'll have to explore it when the men leave."

286

"Why don't we get them to help us find our way out?"

"There's more to it. They're kidnappers and are going to leave someone to die in a crawl."

"That's awful. What should we do?" Jade's voice trembled.

"There are five men including two Snakers . . . too many for us to fight. We have to avoid them."

"I'm for that."

"There is a waterfall in that direction," Taylok pointed to the sounds.

"Yes. I hear it."

"The crawl is in the other direction."

"How can you tell that?"

"That's the way the kidnappers were headed."

"Let's go toward the waterfall."

"That's what I thought. But, we could wait until the men return and follow them out of this place at a safe distance."

"I like the waterfall idea best," Jade intoned.

"Okay."

"Taylok, that was the dumbest thing you ever did."

"What?"

"Dragging me into the level four room without any of the stuff we wanted to take."

"It was getting out of hand, Jade. Those scientists were going to load us down with all kind of stuff we didn't need and push it in ahead of us. If that dried ulok'neh and lignite mix had gone in before we did, it would have caught fire when it hit that hot place in the transfer. You did feel that, didn't you?"

"Oh, did I ever. I thought, for a moment, we were going to be burned alive in Mordane Pit. I was really glad when we arrived at the cold spot. Sorry I screamed. I couldn't help it."

"Anyway, if the mix had been here and on fire, we would have landed right in the middle of it and burned up."

"Well, the mix might not have caught fire. It happened very quickly."

"Feel the hem of our tunics."

"Wow. Scorched. Both of them."

"And they're fairly fire retardant."

"It was definitely hot."

"My hair smells kind of singed, too."

"Yes. So does mine. We should have had some water with us."

"I still think that lignite mix would have been a mistake."

"I think you're right."

"Is this area lighted?" Taylok asked.

"There are a few bright ulok'neh clumps in the area ahead and I can see more light toward the waterfall. I can't tell much about the other side of that wall. It looks pretty dark from here."

"Are you up to walking?"

"Yes. I'd like to get out of here and back to New Rockhome Hall."

"Eldar Temple will be mad at us," confided Taylok.

"Because we jumped ahead on level four?"

"Yes. You can tell them it was my fault . . . which it was."

"I didn't pull back. I think I knew what you were going to do. I wouldn't have had the nerve to do it myself," Jade revealed.

"We have to tell them about the hot and cold phases the transition takes you through. It should make a difference how you prepare."

"We have to find our way back, first."

"We'll be able to do that when we find out where we are," laughed Taylok.

"What if it's one of those, 'You can't get there from here,' places?"

"That's fiction. There's no place that you can't get back from."

"Maybe. But, it would be hard to get back from Mordane Pit."

Taylok helped Jade to her feet and they walked toward the sound of the waterfall. Taylok kept thinking about the party of men and what they were up to. Happy that she and Jade hadn't been discovered, she didn't believe that they would have walked away unscathed from the encounter.

"What does the place look like?" Taylok asked.

"There are lots of speleothems. I see a couple of acid pits on the right and six . . . seven stalactites. Several crystals are imbedded in the matrices of the limestone bed of the roof and floor. I can see lots of quartz crystals and a few blue stones . . . probably some copper deposits here and there. I count four stalagmites, one of which almost touch's the roof and another that connects with one of the stalactites. Ahead, I can see lots of stalactites and a few more stalagmites. There are travertine soda straws hanging down at a big opening and some inside as well. And the place is full of bright ulok'neh. Beautiful, really."

"Wait a blink. You just described Mystical Grotto."

"You're right," agreed Jade. "I never saw it from this side. But, if it is Mystical Grotto, how are we going to get back into New Rockhome Hall? It's a long drop from the grotto to the canyon floor."

"Can you see beyond the opening? Can you see Megalith Rise?"

"Not yet," answered Jade. "We'll be in the grotto soon and then I should be able to see it."

"Do you see an opening on the left? I think I heard a sound like a void space in the left wall."

"No, I . . . wait, there is an opening here. Let me . . . this tunnel looks man-made."

"This is our way back to New Rockhome Hall. Let's check out Mystical Grotto before we go into the tunnel. We should bring something back to prove we were here."

"Good idea. What do you think we should take back with us?"

"It should be something that will be missed when you look at it from the other side."

"We don't want to mess up the grotto."

"No. Just change it enough so that everyone will know we were here."

"Okay, we're here. Find anything we can chang . . . uh . . . ha, ha."

"What's wrong?"

"Nothing. Our little problem just solved itself. I know that you can't see them, but a group of people are standing on the view site of Megalith Rise . . . and waving frantically at us."

"Perfect."

The girls waved to the spectators across the canyon as though it was an every isa occurrence.

"I'm going to take a travertine icicle back with us," declared Jade.

"Good idea," said Taylok. "Not too many of those growing in

New Rockhome Hall."

Taylok heard the snap of the straw-like icicle being taken from its mooring. Jade then collected a light basket from the prolific ulok'neh of the grotto. The two explorers waved to the crowd once more then retreated to the passage they had found. Just as they entered, Taylok heard voices of the kidnappers.

"I'm telling you," said one, "I heard something like a scream over here when we came this way. I don't want to leave any loose ends."

"Well, hurry up," said another. "I want to get out of here."

The voices of the men faded as Jade led the way into the corridor using the light basket to avoid snakes or pitfalls. The downward slope of the passage made for rapid and less tiresome walking, but the tunnel extended much further than the girls had imagined. Taylok could not fathom where the shaft would lead them, but it didn't matter as long as they escaped the murderous men.

Several landings had been employed where the girls could stop and rest but there were some very steep steps as well. Handholds had been carved at some of the most difficult drops to assist anyone making the descent. Taylok tried to mentally catalog the most treacherous places, but there were too many and the passage far too long.

"I see light ahead," said Jade after they had been descending for several turns. "We're coming to a grotto . . . on the wrong side of the river."

"Can you see the village or Eldar Temple?"

"Not yet. But it is New Rockhome Hall. I see the stalagmite field just across Ohana."

"Are you a good swimmer?"

"Not great, but I think I can make it across the river here."

"Can you do it carrying the travertine icicle?"

"I'd rather not try it," lamented Jade. "Oh, no. A crowd is gathering across the river. They've seen us."

"I hear them yelling."

"One of them just dived into the river. He's swimming this way and he has a rope or something tied to his waist."

"The Shotai isn't in the crowd, is he?"

"I don't see him . . . but there's Steel. STEEL," she yelled. "Yes, he sees us."

The man swam the river with ease and soon joined them on the sandy shore.

"Welcome back. I'm Trouter," he said.

"Hi, thanks. What's the rope for?" asked Jade.

"It's to pull you across. We didn't know whether or not you could swim the river."

"We can," said Taylok, "but we have a couple of things with which we need help. Think you can get this travertine icicle across without breaking it?"

Trouter said, "It looks fragile but, I'll do my best. People atop Megalith Rise said they saw you in Mystical Grotto a few turns ago. Made a big uproar about it. That's why everyone turned out. They wanted to see if it could be true. Is this icicle from the grotto?"

"Yes," said Jade.

"You know that the Shotai is upset with you, Taylok," said Trouter. "The fourth level guards reported how you tricked them and went into the forbidden room, dragging Jade along. Some of the villagers think you are a hero, though, and would throw a welcome back party for you."

"What do you think, Trouter?" asked Taylok.

"I think it took a lot of guts to go into that room at all. But, the warriors of Eldar Temple are going to arrest you as soon as you return."

"Why? We made it back and nobody got hurt. We have valuable information about how the room operates."

"Maybe so, but Garnet escaped during the uproar and hasn't been found, yet. The warriors claim that Garnet went with you, although the guards on duty deny it. Regardless, the temple warriors blame you and the fourth level fiasco for his escape."

"As opposed to blaming themselves for leaving him unguarded."

"Precisely. Half of the Hall is with you, though."

"So . . .?"

"So, if I were you, Taylok, I would stay away from Eldar Temple for a while . . . at least until Garnet is found."

"Suits me. I can live in the stalagmite field until then."

"Wouldn't Garnet look for you there?" said Jade.

"Why should he? The men that he worked for in the temple are dead, so he has no reason to be after me, now."

"He seemed pretty upset with you when he came to the Shotai's room. He wanted to kill you."

"That was for the crystal that controls the level four room. I don't have it anymore."

"Think he knows that?"

"The pullers are ready on the other side," interrupted Trouter. "Who wants to go first?"

"You go, Jade," said Taylok. "I'm in no hurry to be arrested."

"That group across Ohana won't arrest you," said Trouter. "They want to throw you a party to celebrate your safe return."

"Including Steel?" asked Taylok.

"Steel just wants to get Jade back."

"All the more reason that she should go first. So, how do you get the rope back?"

"I'll swim over and bring it back," laughed Trouter.

"No need for that," offered Taylok. "I can swim the river. I've done it before."

"Are you certain? I wouldn't want anything to happen to you now, after you survived the level four room. How can you tell where you are going once you get in the river?"

"Easy. Just feel the current and go across it."

"I guess."

He walked to the water's edge where Jade had just entered.

"Hold onto the knot in the rope, Jade. That's it. Good. Good. Well, that's okay."

"She's drifting downriver, isn't she?"

"How could you tell?"

"If you don't swim against it, you'll drift with the current. But, you already knew that."

"True. But, I didn't know that you knew it."

"How are you going to get the icicle across without breaking it?" Taylok asked.

"I'll swim on my back and hold the icicle above the water. Shouldn't be a hard swim."

"The icicle is pretty long. Are you sure you can make it across one-handed?"

"Easy as picking ulok. I float very well."

"You go ahead. I'll watch you."

Trouter laughed.

"Sorry, Taylok. In the first place, you can't see, so you couldn't watch me, and I can't let you get away with that, this time. You go first and I'll watch. That way, if you get into trouble, I can come to help you . . . and, I can make sure that you arrive at the other side."

"What if I want to stay over here?"

"Taylok, you have a lot of friends and well-wishers waiting on the other side. Maybe you don't feel that you owe them anything, but they came here to see you and Jade and we shouldn't disappoint them. This place needs some happy events after all the fighting for control of the temple."

"Okay. I'll go. One more good feast won't ruin me."

Taylok waded into the river and quickly swam toward the other shore. She felt a degree of exhilaration in the water that she hadn't felt since leaving Mystical Grotto. When she arrived at the far bank, ready hands waited to lift her and offer drying cloth. Jade found her quickly.

"You swim beautifully, Taylok," Jade said. "Trouter looks a little awkward bringing the icicle back."

"He's a nice guy. Good swimmer, too."

"Hi, Taylok."

"Steel?"

"Yes. It's me. Sorry about the bad news from the temple. The Shotai isn't all that mad at you, but the warriors are concerned that you helped Garnet escape."

"I never saw Garnet after they took him to his cell. How could they have gotten the idea that I helped him escape?"

"It's the timing, I guess," Steel said. "The warriors are currently searching the temple, room by room, to find him."

"I hope they get him," Jade said. "I still think that he is a danger to Taylok."

"Welcome back Taylok and Jade," said a voice that Taylok didn't recognize. "We have a celebration being set up in the village for you two heroes. It's the first time the room on level four has been successfully utilized in more than five hundred rings. It's a miracle that you survived."

The crowd swept Taylok and Jade into the village where the villagers had hurriedly arranged the feast and festivities in the heart of the town. Everyone wanted to touch the heroes and for a time, Taylok's heart filled with happiness. The party lasted more than five turns and the villagers danced and sang until everyone became weary. One by one, or in pairs, they paid their respects to the two brave women and departed to their homes. Halite and Ruby were among the last to leave.

"So good to see you, Taylok," said Halite. "I knew you'd make something of yourself."

"We miss you," said Ruby.

"Have you filled the positions that Garnet and I left?" asked Taylok.

"Oh, yes," replied Halite. "After that little incident with the warriors, business picked up again and we hired three people to take your places and help Pumice. Things are going well for her, too. Come around and see us sometime."

"Sure," said Taylok.

Ganaga and his family stopped by to wish Taylok well, to thank her for saving them, again, and then left for home. After everyone else had gone, Steel and Jade, arm in arm, walked to Taylok's side.

"Well, Taylok, we did it," said Jade. "They placed the travertine icicle on a stone base in front of the meeting hall with the carved inscription, 'Icicle From mystical Grotto.' The Shotai wants to debrief me on the workings of the fourth level room. This has been the best isa of my life."

"Be sure to tell the Shotai that the lignite idea would have burned us alive."

"You two are the greatest," Steel interjected. "Where are you going, now, Taylok?"

"I'm going to camp out in the stalagmite field," Taylok replied.

"You could come stay with us," offered Jade, but her voiced lacked sincerity.

"Thanks," said Taylok, "but I'd be in the way. Besides, the temple warriors will arrest me if I go back there, now."

"Come and see us after the ruckus dies down, then," said Steel.

"We'll look for you soon."

Jade and Steel walked toward the temple and Taylok stood alone. She waited for a while, listening to the wind drift through the empty mainway, and then turned and walked toward the stalagmite field.

"Being a hero isn't so great," she mumbled to herself.

Chapter 25 - Garnet

After stumbling twice on irregularities in the path, Taylok braced herself and paid more attention to the sounds of the environment. As she approached the stalagmite field she felt an emptiness that she had seldom known. But, a sound ahead, and to her right, made her stop and move her sling into readiness.

"Who's there?" she called.

"Don't throw a stone at me," said the voice of Garnet.

"Keep your distance, Garnet," said Taylok. "What are you doing here?"

Garnet said, "I escaped from Eldar Temple last isa, when you and Jade went into the fourth level room. You guys created chaos among the warriors, and it gave me the opportunity to get away. They were going to execute me in a couple of isas."

"You're a traitor, Garnet. And, you were going to kill me for that crystal."

"I've made some mistakes."

"That is one gross understatement. And if you try to come any closer, it'll be your last mistake."

"Okay, okay. I'll keep my distance. Anyway, I need to get out of the hall. Would you be willing to help me?"

"Help you? How?"

"Show me how to use the fourth level room," Garnet cried.

"Not a chance. I can't go back to Eldar Temple at the moment. And I would think that you'd be walking in the other direction as well, now that you've escaped."

"I'm not safe anywhere in New Rockhome Hall and they've doubled the warriors guarding the hall exit. Level four is my only hope of staying alive."

"Maybe not. Can you swim?"

"Swim? No. I never learned. Why?"

"It doesn't matter, then. There's another way out. It's just on the other side of Ohana."

"It might as well be in the Hall of the Mohk'wa for all the good it'll do me."

"Look," said Taylok. "I don't want you to be executed, even if you did try to kill me. I'll tell you how to use the room, but don't expect me to go there with you."

"Thanks, Taylok. My life is all that I have left."

"What happened to that family you were supporting?"

"My parents moved to Stonehaven Hall five rings ago. It's just me, now."

"You're a liar, then, as well as a traitor and would-be assassin. But, why did you lie about having a family? It couldn't help you any."

"Halite was a little more generous with my pay when he thought I supported a family."

"Garnet, you are one of the worst people that I ever met."

"I made mistakes."

"Let's not go through that again."

"So tell me how to use the fourth level room . . . please."

"Okay. There is a relief sculpture of the T'sa'wa on the wall next to the door. You have to run your fingers down the buttons on the left side of the sculpture. That causes the sculpture to recede into the wall, revealing an onyx dial. If the crystal is still in the onyx dial, then turn the sculpture a quarter turn to the right. This moves the onyx dial a quarter turn to the right. You can go into the room, then, and it will take you to a place behind Mystical Grotto. Take some food and water with you . . . and a sling. There are snakes. That's all there is to it."

"That's too much to learn. And what if the crystal is not in the onyx dial?"

"Then, you're screwed. I don't have it, any more. I left it in the onyx dial."

"I'll never remember all that, Taylok. It's too complicated. You have to come with me."

"Write it down, Garnet. I'm not going to the temple."

Garnet darted toward her, but with sling ready, Taylok spun a stone that tipped Garnet's ear. He stopped, holding his ear, and cried out in pain.

"Kill me then," he shouted. "I'm going to die anyway if you don't help me."

"I did help you," Taylok spoke softly. "Whatever you do, you'll be taking a chance. I think the level four room is unreliable, but at the setting I just gave you, the room took Jade and me across the river to Mystical Grotto. It gets hot, cold and then you're there. That's all I can tell you. If that doesn't work for you, jump into Ohana and try to make it across."

"Unreliable? Swim? You have to help me, Taylok."

"Give me one good reason why I should help you, Garnet. Just one."

"You . . . I . . . we . . . had some moments."

Taylok laughed. "That's the best you could come up with?"

"I never wanted to hurt you, Taylok," said Garnet. "I know what you think . . . that I was going to assassinate you for the crystal, but that was never my intent. I'm devious, not a killer. But, I had to convince your father that I would kill for the crystal, although I never killed anyone in my life. And I wasn't going to start with you. I wanted to get the crystal for him and I would have stolen it if I had the chance."

"So, I'm supposed to help you because you didn't kill me?"

"I did have a chance, when I was holding your hand."

"Maybe, but you knew if you tried that, Steel or Flint would have killed you instantly. You protected yourself."

"True. But, I was trapped anyway. I didn't have much to lose at that point."

"Garnet, I have to say that you aren't helping your case much, but I think you are being honest for the first time in a while."

"You know, speaking of honesty, ever since we kissed when you were leaving the village, I've wanted to kiss you again," Garnet pleaded.

"I'm not letting you get that close to me, again . . . ever."

"Okay. Just help me get out of the hall, then. I don't care how."

"There is only one way, since you can't swim and the Hall's main exit tunnel is swarming with warriors, and that's level four," said Taylok. "Although, I think that Eldar Temple all the way up to level four would also be full of warriors, looking for you . . . and me."

"I know a way to get to level four without using the main stairs or the lower levels. It's said to be a hard climb, but it isn't guarded."

"What makes you think there's another access to level four?"

"Tektitus told me. His cell was next to mine."

"He would be one of the few people who might know about something like that, all right. I'm intrigued, Garnet. But, not enough to risk going to the temple."

"We wouldn't have to go into the temple until we reach level four, according to Tektitus."

"There could still be guards on fourth level stairs. We'd never get the dial set before they caught us, much less get into the fourth level room."

"Tektitus said there's a peephole so you can see when the stairs are empty or if warriors are present. We could wait until they changed guards."

"The idea is so simple that it could work," said Taylok. "I still don't see why I should go with you, though."

"Because you've already done it and know how it works. I need you, Taylok."

"I don't know . . ."

"It seems to me that you're just going back to the stalagmite field. That area has to be the most boring place in Rockworld. Not to mention that the warriors would look for you there if they really wanted to hunt you down. They aren't stupid and you always go there when you're in trouble."

"Pumice is the only one who knows that besides you."

"Do you really think that?"

"Who else, then?"

"Flint found you, didn't he? Halite knows and so does Ruby. I'll bet Ganaga knows and so does Tektitus. And didn't you visit the Shotai while you were there? And I'll bet you told Jade and Steel where you were going? Right?"

"All right, all right. I get it. You're right."

"Go with me, then. You're no safer in the stalagmite field than at the temple. You won't have to hear my voice again after I leave the hall, but it wouldn't hurt for you to leave as well in view of your current circumstances."

"Okay, Garnet, I'll go with you to level four. I should have stayed across the river, though. My life would be less complicated."

Taylok directed Garnet to lead the way to Eldar Temple so she could keep track of him as they walked the back paths. She didn't want any surprises from the untrustworthy ex friend.

"Be careful," he directed, "there's a pit on the right side."

Taylok already knew of the pit's existence, but she felt somewhat mollified that Garnet called it to her attention. She heard Garnet stoop to pick up a large rock as they approached the temple.

"What do you need with that?" Taylok asked.

"I don't have a weapon," Garnet replied. "If someone attacks me with a sword or knife, I have to defend myself, don't I?"

It bothered Taylok that he now had a weapon, but she had no rebuttal to Garnet's reason. He was talking self-defense.

Garnet took half a turn to locate the path that Tektitus had revealed to him. It began near the secret exit to the old room occupied by the Shotai and struck out at a low angle to the ground. Cleverly concealed as ornamental stones, its existence must have been known by an extremely select few. It smoothly skirted windows and patios allowing the climber to pass within a few steps of someone standing on a patio below without being seen. Since the stones were ornamental, and the temple boasted many such features, the path could not be discerned unless the climber had knowledge of its origination point ahead of time. Narrow, the steps were carefully roughed along the upper surface so as to minimize slippage. Still, the distance one might fall grew with each step and for once, Taylok was glad that she couldn't see how high they had reached. She wondered if she could have found the stairway by herself, even knowing it to be there. As it happened, she had to listen carefully to Garnet's steps in order to make the ascent. Turning the corners of the temple became the most difficult maneuver, but eventually, Garnet announced in a whisper that they had arrived at fourth level.

"How do we get inside?" Taylok asked.

"Tektitus said that a handhold to the right of the peephole would open a door."

"Do you see the peephole?"

"Yes. It's here."

"Can you see any guards?"

"No. We're in luck. No one's around at the moment."

"Open the door."

Taylok heard a click and the soft scrape of stone on stone.

"This is it," whispered Garnet. "We're on level four."

"Do you see the T'sa'wa sculpture?"

"Yes. Give me your hand."

"I can locate it by myself."

"We have to hurry. Guards might return at any moment."

Taylok walked to the sculpture and ran her fingers down then up the crystal buttons.

"Nothing is happening," said Garnet.

"It's slow. Just wait. There. The sculpture is moving into the wall."

"Yes. I see the onyx dial you mentioned."

"Is the crystal in place?"

"Yes. What now?"

She felt the crystal and recognized that it had returned to its original position, pointing in toward the sculpture. That dial position would almost certainly be a death sentence for anyone entering room four, as it would dump them into Mordane Pit.

She said, "Get on that side of the sculpture and lift when I pull down from this side. Understand?"

"Got it."

He placed the stone that he had been carrying on the floor and grasped the large disk of the T'sa'wa. Together, they turned the sculpture a quarter turn. She felt the crystal again. It now pointed toward the right. That position had taken Jade and her to Mystical Grotto.

"Is that it?" he asked.

"Yes. I don't know how long it holds this position, though. You need to go through quickly."

"Yes. I have one thing to do first."

He picked up the stone and smashed it into the onyx dial and the crystal.

"What are you doing?" she screamed.

"Keeping anyone from following us," he roared.

He rushed to the door of the room, hesitated for a moment, and then bolted inside. His scream echoed in the confines of fourth level, and then abruptly stopped. A loud pop and explosive pressure knocked Taylok to the floor.

Taylok arose and felt the space where the pointer had been. Only slender shards and granular bits of the onyx dial remained. The ruby and pyrite crystal partially survived the stone attack. Ominously, the pointer had returned to its original upward mark. Taylok suspected that Garnet had been transported to Mordane Pit. Served him right.

On a whim, she turned the sculpture. It now turned easily but made a grinding sound. When she felt the crystal, it pointed straight down. The room made loud crackling noises. Something was definitely wrong.

"You," came the guard's shout from the stairway. "Stay where you are. Don't move."

Taylok pulled the crystal from its broken holder and bolted toward the doorway. She didn't know where the room might take her, but anywhere seemed better than here. Even Mordane Pit.

Taylok dashed into the level four room, expecting to immediately meet her doom or gain her freedom, but, curiously, nothing happened. She felt electrical currents swarming around her as though the crystals tried to energize, but failed to work properly.

A concentration of searing heat materialized beside her forcing Taylok to jump away from the center of the room, narrowly avoiding a deadly burn. The heat radiated from a lava-covered mass that smelled of burning flesh. Her heart pounded when she realized that Garnet's body lay burning inside. Somehow, when he destroyed the onyx mechanism, he had generated some very unexpected results. No screams registered with her, so she decided that he must have died quickly. Poor Garnet. He tried so hard to be important, and now he would be refuse, quickly forgotten. What remained of him would be taken back and dumped into Mordane Pit.

Her hearing determined four very large crystals positioned against the walls, evenly spaced around the center of the room. Only three discharged energy. The quiescent crystal stood to her right and she walked toward it. She touched the enormous stone and ran her fingers along one of the crystal facets.

She stopped when she heard, through the crackle of electrical discharge, voices coming from the door. It sounded like the guard who had yelled at her.

"I'm telling you, I saw her go inside."

"Well, that's it, isn't it? She's gone back to Mystical Grotto . . . or she's done for."

"How'd she get up here?"

"Beats me. She didn't pass by third level that I saw."

"Something's not right about the room."

"You're right. I never saw it sparkle like that."

"Look what she did to the onyx dial."

"Why would she do that? It's broken for sure, now."

"She was a peculiar one, all right. Guess the blindness was more than she could take."

"No way we're going to catch her now. I'm not going into that room and let it fly me around somewhere."

"Me either. Maybe it's a good thing she broke it. It scared the crap out of me."

"Yes. Me, too."

"We better report this to Silver."

"Shouldn't one of us stay on guard?"

"No need, now. Who'd go into fourth level room with it doing that?"

The voices faded and Taylok realized they had gone away. She resumed her check of the dormant crystal. Running her hand along the largest facet she felt a gaping crack. The crystal had suffered probable terminal damage. Taylok doubted that it could ever be made to work again.

Chapter 26 - Taking the Crawl

She examined her options; she could go out and surrender to the guards, not an inviting option; she could try to walk down the outside stairway, the way she and Garnet had come up, but that seemed a lot more dangerous than going up while following Garnet; or . . . she could walk down the temple stairs and hope no one recognized her. That was much safer and could work if she was lucky.

She walked briskly out of the room, got her bearings, and hesitated only for a moment before descending the stairs. No warriors waited on fourth level. She stepped onto third level stairway and heard voices below her.

"What are you doing up there?" said a voice that she could only presume was directed at her.

"The guards said someone went into the fourth level room," answered Taylok, smoothly. "I wanted to look at it."

"Well, get down here with the rest of the acolytes. We're going on an excursion up the Ohana bank."

Taylok feared that one of the acolytes might recognize her, but had little choice when someone took her arm and pulled her along with them as they hurried down the second level stairs.

More voices greeted them on second level and Taylok tried to shrink into a nothingness that no one would recognize. The person holding her arm persisted, though, and Taylok had little option than to be pulled along with the group of acolytes.

"We have one stop to make before we leave," said the voice of the leader.

Taylok had become confused about where they were, but from the sounds and smells, she recognized the Shotai's room when they filed into it.

"Peace and tranquility," said the stentorian voice of the Shotai. "It is always a pleasure to see a new group of acolytes. I recognize the faces of some of . . . y . . . you."

His voice sounded much closer, now.

"Some of you," he continued, "I know much better than others and a few of you, I have never before met. Regardless of how long or short a time we have been acquainted, I wish you nothing but the safest and happiest of times in Eldar Temple. Be kind and generous to your fellow man and woman."

He held Taylok's face between his large hands.

"Peace and tranquility," he finished, releasing Taylok.

Taylok knew that he would not be pleased when he learned that she had been seen entering the level four room only a turn before.

"Everybody out," said the leader.

The group filed out and exited Eldar Temple through the back doorway. Taylok heard warriors talking occasionally along the path, but without a war to fight, they were more interested in personal matters than searching for escaped prisoners.

The girl who had taken Taylok's arm earlier remained by her side.

"What are you going to do?" said the vaguely familiar, female voice.

"I don't know. I might leave the hall."

"I doubt they'll let you leave."

"Who are you?"

"I'm Gneissa. We met at school many rings ago."

"I remember you, Gneissa. You were always getting in trouble with the Shotai."

"I still do, but not as much as you. Do you need anything?"

"No. I'm packed for a long trip. It's just that I have nowhere to go."

"You should have seen the Shotai's face when he recognized you. He loves you like a daughter, you know."

"I know. He taught me almost everything I know . . . between him and Flint."

"Where is Flint?"

"Gone to Banestone Hall. He has a Fireseasoned Mate there. Shalea's there, too. Has kids, I hear."

"Funny how we lose touch with people we knew well but don't see anymore."

"If I get out of here, I'm going to try and see them, maybe."

"Yes. I say that about my friends who have gone, but I never do."

"You're probably right. I need to set out in a new direction. I just don't know how."

"They say that the first step in a new direction is the hardest."

"I believe it."

"If I can help you any way, get in touch with me at the temple. We're stopping up ahead at a beach on a bend in the river. We'll get a break and scatter for a while. It'll probably be a good place for you to get away from this group before someone else discovers who you are."

Taylok hugged Gneissa, thankful for the small world in which they lived. The acolytes milled around the beach and Taylok slipped off toward the stalagmite field. She located a path that she had used before and walked carefully onward, checking sounds as she went to make sure nothing had severely changed. A casual observer would never know her to be blind.

When she reached the edge of the stalagmite field, she sat down for a moment before entering. The sounds emanating from the field gave no indication of change. A melancholy feeling swept over her and she sighed. She missed her friends and mostly her mother.

"Same old, same old," she whispered to herself.

"I don't have to do this," she said aloud to the stalagmites. "I'm going back to Mystical Grotto. That's what I'll do. It's an adventure."

She walked to the river. Taylok knew that she could swim it. She had done it before, just not with all the gear she wanted to take. The food felt light enough, but the stones for her sling would weight her down. It made for a risky swim. She could leave the stones on this side and try to find similar ones on the other side. Surely she could find enough on the other side of Ohana to give her an ample supply for the sling. Being blind hindered her search, of course, but she could sound out some of the stones and feel for smaller ones. Better than drowning while trying to carry a sack of rocks across. Or, maybe not.

She dumped most of her sling rocks into a gravel bed, holding onto three nice, smooth ones in case snakes found her as she searched for replacements across the river.

Ohana sounded quiet and inviting, but she knew it could be treacherous with swirling eddies and strong undertows. The brief thought of lurking monsters, that mothers planted in their children's mind to keep them away from the river, flitted through her brain. Her blindness brought the monsters to life even though she knew in her heart that they didn't exist.

"It doesn't matter," she said, under her breath.

A loud splash, far out mid river, caused her to jump from the tension and the monsters chased through her thoughts.

"It was only a fish," the voice startled her as much as the splash.

"Yes," she said, calming, "I knew that it was a fish."

"I am Laida, the Shaman."

"I'm Taylok."

"Yes. I was at your trial."

"Oh, I remember. The Shotai accidentally called you Ladida."

"No accident. It was his humor seeping through."

"What brings you to the stalagmite field?"

"Perhaps, it is a strange young woman who doesn't yet know her destiny. I do hope that your plan is to swim to the other side, not just out to the bottom of the river."

"What? Oh, no. I'm not ready to die. I know where I'm going right now," said Taylok.

"The other side is always an intriguing destination."

"I'm not going just to the other side of Ohana. I'm going to Mystical Grotto."

"Surely, Mystical Grotto is the other side of something?"

"It is across the river."

"Ah, yes, Ohana. Did you know that the ancients called the river Oshan?"

"Oshan? No. No one told me that. What does it mean?"

"Oshan is the ancient's word for 'big water.' This is the largest body of water in New Rockhome Hall."

"Why did it get changed to Ohana?"

"Language is dynamic. Young people grow up thinking that they heard a word one way when their parents actually spoke it differently. Soon the word is corrupted and a new word enters the language. Ohana could be one of those words. But, I think it means 'little big water.'"

"Do you think everyone will call you Ladida some isa?"

He laughed.

"Possibly. But I will resist it."

"Am I making a mistake crossing Ohana to Mystical Grotto?" Taylok asked.

"There is danger involved, especially with your visual condition," reminded Laida, unnecessarily.

"There is danger involved if I take a walk," Taylok bristled.

"But, not as much when you are familiar with the area in which you walk."

Taylok relented.

"I guess you're right. But, unknown territory is exciting. It's boring to walk among the stalagmites every isa."

"And, you crave excitement?"

"Sure. Who doesn't?"

"What was the most exciting time of your life thus far?"

"When I could see, it was the sling contest," said Taylok. "After that, my rescue from Xantopec and then the rescue of Ganaga's family in the temple."

"So everything you found exciting stemmed from encounters with people."

"Well, I guess so."

"But, now, you are going into the unknown where there may be no people."

"I'll come back if it gets boring. I'm just doing what seems right at this time."

"It is seldom a mistake to follow your heart, Taylok. Does your heart tell you that you should go to Mystical Grotto?"

"My heart tells me that I need a big change in my life. My parents are gone; my friends have all found new lives that don't include me. So now, I'm alone. The other side of Mystical Grotto may have the answer that I'm searching for."

"Then, by all means, go. It is a rite of passage. By the way, Garnet's body will soon be found in the fourth level room, covered with scoria from Mordane Pit. You will no longer be on a wanted poster in New Rockhome Hall."

"Are you really here or am I having this conversation with myself?"

"How can I reply without giving away the answer?"

"What?"

"Did you know before I told you that Ohana came from the ancient word Oshan?"

"I . . . I don't remember for sure. I could have learned that from Jade."

"Reach out and touch my hand if you are unsure of my presence."

"I . . . I think I'd rather not know for sure."

He laughed.

"Then, I will watch you until you safely reach the other side."

"I would appreciate it."

"Peace and tranquility, Taylok. Farewell."

Taylok waded into the darkness of her blindness and felt the water climb to her waist. She pushed off the sandy bottom and swam toward the distant shore. Eyes closed to the splashing water, she concentrated on making long, smooth strokes and breathing regularly. When she felt the current take her sideways, she changed direction and swam at an angle into the water's push. She let her instincts guide her and in a short time, with her hand, touched the gravelly river bottom of the other side. She stood, then, and walked to the river's edge, enjoying the coolness that the evaporation afforded while stumbling over some throwing-sized, riparian stones. It occurred to her that she had found a perfect spot to refill her limited sling stones.

Before she did that, however, she turned and, with a flourish, waved to the distant bank where she thought the Shaman stood. She would never know whether he waved back.

She filled her sling pouch, ulok supply and water holder, and searched for the grotto that concealed the tunnel to Mystical Grotto. She knew the approximate location and when she heard wind blowing its' revealing melody past a declivity in the long cavern wall, she went inside without hesitation.

Finding the tunnel that led upward to Mystical Grotto proved a bit more difficult, but after patiently searching the back of the grotto, she found the opening. Trekking up the stairs tested her resolve because some of the steps were steep, others shallow; and uphill is always more physically tiring than down. She also fretted over the matter of knowing when she had arrived. Jade had led the way when they came down before and had warned her when there were flat places or steep steps. It goaded Taylok's mind to the limit to remember even the most difficult areas of the climb and she occasionally broke down and cried bitterly after narrowly avoiding a disastrous fall. She told herself that she would do better if she ever made the journey again.

A snake surprised her with a warning rattle as she climbed a steep segment of the stairs. The narrow passage did not allow Taylok enough space to avoid the reptile and she didn't know how much higher Mystical Grotto lay above her. Besides, if she continued, her face could be the logical target of the animal's strike. If it wasn't too far to the top, she might drive the poisonous fang-tooth upward and avoid killing it. She tossed a pebble toward the buzzing sound, but the warning continued. Unable to avoid the snake, she loaded her sling and delivered a rock toward the animal. The stone struck the scaly, soft body and the snake hissed in anger or fear but slithered up the stairway. Taylok made some headway. Unfortunately, the snake had nowhere else to hide so the reptile took another stand a dozen steps above its first encounter with Taylok, its rattle intensely warning the intruder to come no closer.

"I don't want to have to kill you," Taylok whispered to the snake, and then raised her voice. "Go away."

Curiously, her voice had an effect that her stone lacked; the snake crawled up the stairs and Taylok never heard it again.

Taylok took three or four steps before she realized she had reached the top. She listened for snakes, but heard none. The waterfall's roar seemed subdued at this location, but provided the loudest sound present. Taylok sent a few trills into the unexplored part of the hall. She received echoes that suggested a low ceiling with thick walls and numerous columns. Abundant open space between walls and columns made the area seem hospitable and potentially useful. Taylok wondered that the area had never been developed for human use. Then, she remembered that Jade had said it was dark.

She tensed as she recalled the men who had been here when she and Jade first encountered this part of Rockworld and then gasped when she remembered that they claimed to be carrying someone they had kidnapped. That had been three or four isas ago, however, so whoever had been taken here would have found their way back by now; or lie dead somewhere.

Taylok stumbled. She felt to discover what she had fallen over and identified human bones. Her heart sank as she remembered finding others in the area. She wondered what it was about this place that took so many lives. The furious buzz of a pair of rattlers reminded her as she backed away from the warning.

"Go away," she shouted into her darkness.

The echoes greeted her with their stern warning, "Go away, go away, go away."

"Okay, okay," Taylok smiled faintly, recognizing she talked only to herself.

The buzz of rattlers continued and Taylok took a deep breath before sending a stone into the coils of one of the snakes. She aimed the stone at the thick body instead of the head so as to not kill it. The thump of rock against flesh let her know that she had been successful. The buzzing ceased and she heard the rapidly receding, raspy swirl of reptile bodies against the stone floor.

"One for Taylok," she said aloud, smiling when the echo agreed.

Fearlessly, Taylok plunged ahead into the unknown space of the cavern. Her blindness prevented her from knowing whether the way was lighted by the, almost, ever-present ulok'neh, but that didn't matter to her. Light wouldn't have helped her, after all. Mainly, she needed to identify the dangers. Where were the pits, the path-blocking walls and speleothems, the bluffs or cliffs? Where did the snakes lie in wait? She had to rely on her hearing to tell her those answers but she had done that all her life. If she let herself think too much about it here, she would stop and return the way she had come.

The adventure's excitement won out. Taylok would brave the unknown, at least for a while, to avoid the boredom of New Rockhome Hall. The farther she walked, the lower the ceiling forced her to bend. Soon, she moved on hands and knees.

When a rattlesnake sounded its patent warning, Taylok moved quickly to fend off the reptile. The confining space did not help, but Taylok remembered endlessly practicing this kind of shot for the sling trials. Flint had said that she would probably never have to use the position outside the trials, but she was glad she had learned the trick. The snake must have been unhappy about it, however, as it hissed and sped away.

"And stay away," Taylok whispered.

The snake had been close enough that Taylok relocated her sling rock after only a moment of searching.

The sound of movement by something bigger than a snake made Taylok pause and consider retreat. It sounded much larger than a rattler and it traveled on, at least, four legs . . . or it could be crawling as she did, except it didn't sound like a person crawling. It sounded ungainly and raspy as if moving, somehow, but not crawling . . . maybe hurt.

Whatever it was, snakes chased it. Taylok could hear the rattles and occasional hisses of several snakes as they closed in on the beleaguered victim. The desultory movements of the tormented creature told Taylok that there wasn't much fight left. A fairly large reptile approached to within striking distance of the unknown target, and coiled in seeming preparation.

Chapter 27 - Valea

"Fronds'wa, where are you?" mumbled a frightened female voice, filled with languor and fatigue.

Now that Taylok knew the victim to be human, she didn't hesitate and her stone smashed with a resounding crump into the rattler.

"Are you okay?" Taylok asked as the wounded snake slithered noisily away.

Only soft moans escaped the lips of the female. Of course, if this were the person she had heard being carried into the crawl, she would have had nothing to eat or drink for, what, four isas? It must have required incredible stamina to withstand the snakes and the crawl for that long. Taylok lifted her water container and wet her own fingers. Then, she rubbed the victim's lips and let a little water run into the victim's mouth. She ran her fingers over the victim's face, female, to be sure, and pretty.

Taylok's thought process included, "Maybe this is the beautiful princess who holds my destiny. Okay, long shot, but possible."

Taylok wet the woman's lips again, and then again.

The parched lips parted and words began to reach Taylok's ears.

"Thank you for saving me from the viper," she said. "I can't see. I must have gone blind when I fought the yellow crystal. What is your name?"

"Taylok."

"What is this place?"

"You don't even know where you are?" Taylok grated.

"No. I was unconscious when my friends brought me here."

"Some friends," Taylok spat. "This is a place of instant death if you don't know your way around. Who are you and who are the so-called friends who left you here?"

"I am Valea Tanista from Stone . . ." the girl stopped, and then began again, "Fireseasoned to the Fronds'wa."

"You're Fireseasoned to a Giant God? Right," Taylok almost laughed at the ludicrous notion. "I'll play along. And, I am the Crystal Master of Lower Rockworld. Wait . . ."

313

Taylok's acute hearing picked up a snake crawling in their direction and getting much too close. She spun a stone, hitting the snake, diverting it easily.

Taylok had become slightly cramped by the low ceiling and couldn't deliver the stones from her sling with enough force to really harm the rattlers. Besides that, the girl would block Taylok's shot should a snake approach from behind her.

"We should get out of this crawl," Taylok said, "unless your Giant God is here and you want to stay."

Taylok knew that her voice conveyed ridicule, but she couldn't help it. Imagine, someone left alone in a dangerous crawl, telling a stranger that she was Fireseasoned to a Giant God. Laughable.

"I'm too sore and tired to move," said Valea.

"Then, stay if you want, Valea, Fireseasoned to a Giant God," said Taylok, "but I'm leaving. This is a dangerous place."

"Wait, Taylok. I'll go with you, if I can. Ouch! Ow!"

Taylok slowed and waited for Valea. She couldn't just leave her alone here. Valea couldn't stand upright in the crawl and Taylok even felt the depression of the limited vertical space. She heard splashing ahead, but the odor told her that acid fouled the liquid. When Valea headed toward the pool, Taylok stopped her.

"Don't drink here," Taylok said. "Take some of my water, but sip slowly. You need to go slow at first. Okay?"

Valea sipped the liquid and handed the container back to Taylok.

"This is the worst place I have ever been," said Valea.

"Better than being killed by a bunch of rattlers, though," said Taylok.

"Is there light here?" Valea asked.

"Light? How should I know," answered Taylok. "I was blinded by the Sun God at three rings."

"Blind? You? But, how did you find me? How did you hit the rattlesnakes with your rocks? How . . ."

Taylok laughed. "How did you know where the water was located?"

"I heard . . . but the snakes are much quieter."

"Not for someone who's been blind for eight rings. When I heard merchant Halsha yell, 'Get out of my ulok,' I didn't need to see him running after me. I heard his footsteps. I didn't know he called the warriors until I heard their feet on the stoneway."

Taylok didn't know why she embellished her story to Valea. Maybe it was because of the lie she believed that Valea had told about being Fireseasoned to a Giant God.

"Anyway," she continued the fabrication, "they chased me up here into the crawl but gave up when I went inside. They don't like it any better than you do. Most people who come here fall victim to the snakes."

That part had a ring of truth. She had felt lots of human bones on her way.

"Anyway, I always carry my sling and a few stones to discourage the snaggletooth's. Feel," Taylok finished, taking Valea's hand and guiding it to her sling.

Valea touched the sling, and then ran her hands over Taylok's face and head. Taylok patiently waited until Valea finished, recognizing that the other tried to get some idea as to how Taylok looked as the girls in the Shotai's class had done. The memory made her eyes moist with tears.

"Taylok," said Valea, "tell me what you meant when you said you were blinded by the Sun God."

"The Crystal Master forced me to look at the face of the Sun God as punishment for my mother breaking some kind of law. He killed my mother and would have killed me, but I got rescued."

"But, where did you see the face of the Sun God?" asked Valea. "Not in Rockworld?"

"In the Temple of the T'sa'wa, of course," Taylok answered, derisively. "Did you fall from a stalactite?"

"Careful, young man. I may not be able to see, but I am twice your size," rasped Valea.

"Young man? Ha! You didn't feel low enough. The Crystal Master would have killed me first if I'd been a boy."

Taylok hesitated and a wave of bitterness coursed over her.

"Maybe it would have been better if he had," she finished, quietly.

Later, as she quietly, acoustically scanned Valea's image, Taylok's thoughts took another turn. Wow! Valea is taller than most other Nehwisna. What if she is the Fireseasoned Mate of a

Giant God? Maybe meeting her is the destiny for which I'm meant. That runner, several isas ago, spoke about a Giant God and his mate who killed a Mohk'wa. It sounded ridiculous then, but it might have happened. He said that a man from New Rockhome Hall, Driggett Ventaya, had been involved, too. This whole thing is crazy, but maybe the Giant God will be everything that a Giant God should be and save me from Xantopec and the T'sa'wa and the Tadi'wa, too.

Valea is easy to talk to. She might even let me stay with her after we get out of here.

Maybe, just maybe, things are looking up.

THE PAUSE

Author's Note: Taylok's story resumes in Chapter 24, p. 230 of "The Cavern."

For those readers unable to locate a copy of "The Cavern," rest assured that Taylok continues in her own fashion, meeting the Giant God, Driggett Ventaya and many others who will greatly influence her life. She survives innumerable trials and maintains her heroic and adventuresome ways. The Giant God attempts to heal Taylok's blindness and Valea becomes a second mother to her.

Taylok's saga is intertwined throughout Allen Mabra's Cavern Trilogy, which include; "The Cavern," ISBN 0-595-19027-8, "Escape From The Cavern," ISBN 0-595-66850-X, and "Crys Delchant and the Stone of Life," ISBN 978-1-4260-4588-4.

ABOUT THE AUTHOR

Allen Mabra holds a bachelors degree with a double major in geology and biology from Texas Christian University. He worked for thirty plus years in the oil, gas and coal industry, traveling to almost every continent in the world. He began a writing career after he retired from the oil business in 1985. Allen and his wife, Joy, raised four children who have blessed them with ten grandchildren and ten (and counting) great-grandchildren. Allen and Joy currently live in Carlsbad, California.
"Taylok" is Allen Mabra's fifth novel.